The Inseparable Twins

Anatoly Pristavkin

THE INSEPARABLE TWINS

Translated from the Russian
by MICHAEL GLENNY

published by Pan Books

First published 1991 by Pan Books Ltd,
Cavaye Place, London SW10 9PG
9 8 7 6 5 4 3 2 1
© Anatoly Pristavkin 1987
Translation © Michael Glenny 1991
ISBN 0 330 30443 7

Phototypeset by Intype, London
Printed and bound in Great Britain by
Billings & Sons Ltd, Worcester

This book is sold subject to the condition that it shall not,
by way of trade or otherwise, be lent, re-sold, hired out,
or otherwise circulated without the publisher's prior consent
in any form of binding or cover other than that in which
it is published and without a similar condition including this
condition being imposed on the subsequent purchaser

One

The word arose of its own accord, just as a wind will suddenly get up from nowhere.

It arose and passed, rustling, around every nook and cranny in the orphanage: 'Caucasus! . . . The Caucasus!' Where had the word come from? No one could rightly explain it.

In any case, what a strange fancy, in the drab hinterland of Moscow's suburban fringe, to be talking about something called the Caucasus, which the orphanage brats only knew existed from their teachers' oral lessons (there were no textbooks) – or rather, knew *had* existed, in some distant, incomprehensible era, when the crazy black-bearded mountain warrior Hadji Murat had blazed away at his enemies; when the Imam Shamil, leader of the rebellious Muslim *murids*, had defended himself in a besieged fortress, and two Russian soldiers, Zhilin and Kostylin, had languished as his prisoners in a deep pit. And then there was Pechorin, Lermontov's 'superfluous man', who had also travelled the Caucasus.

Against a background of rugged, snow-capped mountains a rider in a long, black Caucasian cloak gallops and gallops – no, flies along – mounted on a wild, black horse. And beneath him, in jagged uneven script, is the name of the topmost peak of the Caucasus, and of the brand of cigarettes named after it: KAZBEK.

Glancing at the pretty army nurse who had come to inspect the dressing-station, a young, handsome, moustached lieutenant-colonel, his head bandaged, was emphasizing a point by tapping his fingernail on the cardboard lid of a packet of cigarettes; he was unaware of Kolka Kuzmin, the breathless little ragamuffin standing beside him, mouth open wide in amazement.

Thus Kolka had his first sight of Kazbek, when looking for a crust of bread to scrounge from wounded soldiers.

What did the Caucasus range – or a rumour about it – have to do with anything? Absolutely nothing.

And no one knew how that angular, glittering, ice-bound little word had arisen in such unlikely surroundings, amid the drab everyday of orphanage life – days of cold, days without firewood and days of perpetual hunger, where the children's lives revolved entirely around frost-bitten potatoes, potato-peelings and – the summit of their yearning – a crust of bread, so that they might survive just one more wartime day.

The dearest but unattainable wish of each of them was to penetrate, if only but once, into that holy of holies of the orphanage: the BREAD-CUTTING ROOM. We print this in capitals because in the children's eyes it stood infinitely higher and farther out of reach than Mount Kazbek.

And those who were granted access to that room, rather as God allows some people into heaven, were the utmost élite, the luckiest, indeed one could say the happiest people on earth.

The Kuzmin Twins were not among them, and the twins never imagined being allowed in there. For it was the fief of the delinquents, the young toughs who had escaped the clutches of the police and ruled the roost in the orphanage – indeed, in the whole village.

Their dream was to penetrate into the bread-cutting room – not as of right, like the élite – but to slip in like mice just for one second, one tiny moment; to catch but one waking glimpse of the greatest treasure on earth, in the shape of those crusty loaves piled high on the table, and to breathe in, not with lungs but with stomachs, to inhale the intoxicating, stupefying smell of bread . . .

That was all. No more . . . no question of gathering up any of the crumbs that inevitably fell off when the loaves were sliced: those were for the élite to scoop up and enjoy; they were theirs by right.

Pressing oneself, however hard, against the steel-clad doors of the bread-room was no substitute for the fantastic picture that formed itself in the minds of the Kuzmin brothers the smell of bread could not penetrate steel.

The idea of getting past those doors by legitimate means never occurred to them. That was something from the realm of abstract fantasy, and the brothers were realists; but that did not prevent them from having more concrete ambitions, and by the winter of 1944 those ambitious thoughts had brought Kolka and Sashka Kuzmin to the point where they were determined to get into the bread-room by any – but *any* – means.

In those particularly dreary months when there weren't even any frost-bitten potatoes to be found, to say nothing of a crust of bread, it was more than they could do to walk past that outhouse with its double steel doors – to walk past it and to know, almost to see, that behind those grey walls, those dirty, barred windows those lucky few were busily practising their sorcery with knives and weighing-scales; that they were crumbling, cutting and mauling the soft, moist loaves, tipping handfuls of the warm, slightly salty crumbs into their mouths and putting aside a few thick slices for their confederates.

Their mouths would fill with saliva. Their stomachs contracted. They felt dizzy. They wanted to howl, to shout and beat, beat, beat against that steel door to make them open it, to make them finally realize: we want some too! It didn't matter if afterwards they ended up in solitary, anywhere . . . that they would be punished, beaten up, even killed . . . if only, even from the doorway, the bread-cutters would show them the bread on that table, its top scored with knife-marks – bread piled in mountains as high as Kazbek . . . and the smell of it!

Then life would be worthwhile again. Then faith would be restored, for as long as that bread was lying there in heaps it meant that the world existed . . . Then one could bear it all in silence and carry on living, for the tiny daily ration, even with an extra sliver of bread sticking to it, did not still one's hunger; it only made it worse.

One day a stupid teacher had read aloud the passage from Tolstoy's *War and Peace* in which the ageing Kutuzov was listlessly eating a chicken, chewing a tough wing almost with revulsion . . . This scene struck the children as the purest fantasy. The things writers dreamed up! *He didn't like a chicken wing?* They would have done anything to get their hands on even the chewed bone of a wing. After that lesson the children's stomachs twisted themselves into even worse knots, and they lost faith in writers for ever: if their characters didn't like eating chicken, it meant that the callous writers themselves were stuffed to bursting.

Since the expulsion of Sych, the chief bully among the delinquents, many young criminals large and small had passed through the village of Tomilino and its orphanage, spending the winter there in relative safety and sheltered from the fatherly eye of the police.

One thing, though, remained unchanged: devouring everything, the strong left the weak to pick up the leavings or to dream of crumbs, and they enmeshed the orphanage small fry in the toils of slavery.

For a crust of bread, the children enslaved themselves to the bully-boys for a month or two months. The top crust, baked a little harder, blacker, thicker and tastier, cost two months' slavery. Normally it would only be the outer edging of a slice, but we are talking of a bread ration consisting of a tiny slice so thin that when laid flat on the table it looked like a small, translucent piece of brown paper. The bottom crust – paler, poorer and thinner – was worth one month's slavery. And everyone remembered that for a bottom crust little Vaska the Shrimp, at eleven, the same age as the Kuzmin Twins, had served as a slave for six months before his relative, a soldier, had come to take him away. He had given away all his rations and had eaten buds from the trees to survive.

When times were hard, the Kuzmin Twins, too, would sell themselves – but always as a pair.

If you could have merged the Kuzmin Twins into a single person, they would have had no equal in the Tomilino orphanage in age – or, perhaps, in strength. As things were, they well knew the advantages of sticking together.

It is easier to hump a load with four arms than with two; with four legs you can make a faster getaway and four eyes are sharper than two when it comes to spotting trouble. While two eyes are busy with a job, the other two keep look-out for both. They can watch out in case anybody tries to steal something, such as clothes, or to pull your mattress from under you while you're asleep and dreaming of life in the bread-room. Their motto was: How can you hope to get into the bread-room if you let people pinch your things?

There was no end to the dodges the Kuzmin Twins would get up to. If a stall-keeper, shall we say, caught one of them nicking something in the market and was about to drag him off to the lock-up, that brother would whimper and howl and beg for mercy, while the other one distracted the man's attention. As soon as he turned round to the second boy, the first lad was gone like greased lightning – and the other was away after him. Both brothers were as slippery and nimble as quicksilver, and once you let go there was no catching them.

Eyes to see, hands to grab, legs to run away . . .

But somewhere, in some witches' cauldron, all these exploits had to be cooked up in advance: you don't survive unless you've hatched a sound plan about what to pinch, where and how to do it.

The two heads of the Kuzmin Twins worked in different ways. Sashka was more the calm, quiet philosopher who thought up the original ideas; how these notions came into his head, he knew not. Kolka, resourceful, adroit and practical, would always work out with lightning speed how to turn these ideas into reality: how to make them pay, if you like, or – more precisely – how to use them to scrounge food.

Scratching the top of his ash-blond head, Sashka might, for instance, suggest flying to the moon, because there was lots and lots of grub there. Kolka would not respond with an instant 'no'; he would first give the moon project some thought, wondering which airship might fly them there, then he would say, 'But why? We can pinch something a lot nearer . . .'

There were also times when Sashka would look pensively at Kolka, who would pick up his brother's thought out of the ether, like a radio receiver – and instantly devise ways to put it into effect.

Sashka's head was worth its weight in gold – in fact it wasn't so much a head as a Palace of Soviets! The brothers had once seen this on a picture postcard. Any number of American skyscrapers could have fitted into it several times over. We are the tallest, we are the first in the world . . . ! But the Kuzmin Twins were first in something else: they were the first to think up a way of surviving the winter of 1944 without kicking the bucket.

When the Bolsheviks made the revolution in Petrograd, thought the twins, apart from capturing the post office, the telegraph office and the railway stations, they surely must have captured the bread-room too! The brothers were walking past the bread-room; it was not the first time, but it was especially unbearable that day. Those walks could be sheer agony.

'What wouldn't I give for something to eat . . . If only we could gnaw through that door! If only we could eat through the frozen earth under the doorway!' said Sashka aloud – and as he said it the thought dawned on him: why eat it if . . . if we . . . Yes, that's it! If we could *dig* through it and under the walls! Of course – dig through it!

He said nothing but only looked at Kolka, who picked up the signal in a moment, switched on his brain, assessed the idea and even devised several variants. He too said nothing aloud, but a predatory gleam came into his eyes. Anyone who has had the experience will confirm that there is no more inventive and single-minded human being than someone who is hungry, especially if he is an orphanage inmate, his brain sharpened by wartime privation.

Without saying a word (all around them were desperate people who might hear and pass on anything, and then it would be curtains for Sashka's stroke of genius), the brothers went straight to the nearest garden shed, which was about a hundred yards from the main orphanage buildings and twenty-odd yards away from the bread-room.

Inside the shed, the brothers looked around. They stared simultaneously at the farthest corner, where behind a heap of useless scrap-iron and broken bricks there had once been a hiding-place. In the days when firewood had been kept there, no one had known what the Kuzmin Twins knew: that Vaska's uncle Andrei, the soldier whose rifle had been stolen, had lain hidden there.

Sashka whispered, 'Isn't it a bit far?'

'Where is there that's any nearer?' Kolka asked in reply.

Both realized there was nowhere closer to their objective.

It would have been far simpler to smash the lock on the bread-room door – less work and less time were needed, and they might just have the strength for it. But people had already tried that way of breaking into the bread-room; the Kuzmin Twins were not the first to have had that bright idea. As a result, the director of the orphanage had had the bread-room's double doors fitted with half a ton of ironmongery and a huge padlock. Even a hand-grenade would have scarcely harmed them: if the whole contraption had been draped across the front of a tank, that tank would have been safe from all enemy shells.

After the unsuccessful attempt to break in, the window had been provided with bars so thick that no file or crowbar could possibly shift them; the job could only have been done with an oxyacetylene torch. Kolka had even considered using this method – he had spotted a container of calcium carbide lying around – but there was no way of getting it into position or of igniting it, and there were too many people about.

But underground, now – no one would see them there!

The other alternative – to give up the assault on the bread-room altogether – did not suit the Kuzmin Twins at all. Shops, markets and still less private houses were useless as a source of edibles at that time, although ideas about them positively swarmed in Sashka's head. The trouble was that Kolka could think of no ways to put them into practical effect.

The little local general store was guarded all night by an evil-tempered old watchman, who neither drank nor slept on the job; he did all that in the daytime. He was not so much a night-watchman as a dog in the manger. The neighbouring houses, of which there were plenty, were full of wartime refugees who not only had no food to spare – they were forever on the scrounge themselves.

The Kuzmin Twins had once had their eye on a little house which the older delinquents had burgled in the days when Sych had been at the orphanage. Admittedly they had not stolen much: some old clothes and a sewing-machine. For a long time the ruffian element had taken turns to use it, in that same garden shed, until its handle had broken off and the rest of it had been scattered piecemeal.

This time it was not a matter of a mere sewing-machine but the bread-room. Nor was it the weighing-scales or the weights which so furiously taxed the twins' brains – it was bread, and bread alone. Their watchword was: In these hard times all roads lead to the bread-room.

Indeed it was less of a bread-room than a fortress. But then we all know that there are no fortresses, or rather bread-rooms, that a hungry boy cannot take by storm.

In the depth of that winter, despairing of ever picking up anything to eat at the local railway station or the market, all the ragged inmates would cluster around the stoves, leaning against them with bottoms, backs or necks, trying to absorb a few degrees of heat to warm themselves by a fraction in rooms where the plaster on the walls had been scratched away down to the brickwork. It was then that the Kuzmin Twins set about putting their improbable plan into action. Its only chance of success lay in its very improbability.

From their distant hiding-place in that garden shed they began their work of excavation with the aid of a bent crowbar and a piece of plywood.

Grasping the crowbar (those four hands on the job!) they would lift it up and bring it down on the frozen soil with a dull thump. The first few inches were the worst. The earth was so hard, it rang like a bell.

They carried the spoil away on a piece of plywood to the far corner of the shed, until it had piled up into a large mound. They now took it in turns to attend school and to dig: on one day Kolka would pound away, the next day Sashka.

The one whose turn it was to go to class would attend two lessons as himself (Kuzmin? Which Kuzmin is it? Nikolai? And where's the other? Where's Alexander Kuzmin?) and would then impersonate his brother, giving the impression that both were present, if only one half at a time. Anyway, no one demanded one hundred per cent attendance of them; that would have been too much to expect.

The chief thing, though, was for neither of them to miss meal-times. If one of them had not turned up for lunch or supper, their portion would have been instantly devoured by the other young jackals, leaving not a scrap. The digger-twin would therefore stop work and join his brother in the assault on the dining-room.

No one ever asked whether it was Sashka or Kolka. They were a single unit – the Kuzmins – and if only one showed up, then it was just half of the unit. But they were rarely, indeed virtually never seen singly.

They walked around together, ate together and always went to bed at the same time in adjacent beds. and if they got beaten up, they would both get a walloping, starting with the one who happened to be the first to run into that particular spot of bother.

Two

The excavations were in full swing when the strange rumours about the Caucasus began circulating.

Spontaneously but insistently, the same story was repeated, now softly, now loudly, from end to end of the dormitory. The orphanage, it seemed, was to be uprooted from its familiar home and transported bag and baggage to the Caucasus.

The teachers, the crazy cook, the bewhiskered music mistress and the crippled director ('Crippled from having to think,' was whispered behind his back) – in short, inmates and staff alike were all to be moved. There was much gossip and the news was chewed over again and again like last year's potato peelings, but no one could imagine just how this horde of little savages could be transferred wholesale to some distant mountainous land.

The Kuzmin Twins paid little attention to the gossip and believed it even less. They had other things to think about: urgently, furiously, they were hacking away at their mine-shaft. Anyway, what was the point of all the chatter? Any fool knew that the authorities couldn't move a single orphanage child against his will – unless they planned to transport them in a cage, as Catherine the Great had done with the rebel Pugachov. The obstreperous little beggars would scatter at the first change of trains and catching them would be like scooping up water with a sieve. Even if any of them were persuaded to go, the Caucasus would suffer for it: they would strip the place of everything movable, eat every last morsel in sight, carry off Mount Kazbek stone by stone . . . in short, they would quickly turn the Caucasus into something like the Sahara desert.

Thus reasoned the Kuzmin Twins and went on digging. One of them would use the iron bar to hack at the earth, which was now so soft that it fell loose of its own accord, while the other would haul the spoil back to the surface in a rusty bucket. By the spring

13

they had hit the brick foundations of the building that housed the bread-cutting room.

One day the Kuzmin Twins were resting at the far end of their tunnel. The bricks, dark red with the blue tinge of clay fired in old-fashioned kilns, were proving hard to crack, and breaking off each little chip cost blood. Ramming the crowbar into the brickwork from a sideways-on position was extremely awkward, and the boys' hands were sprouting blisters. There was no room to turn round in the tunnel, earth kept on trickling down the backs of their necks and their eyes were smarting from the homemade oil-lamp – an inkwell stolen from the orphanage office. At the start, they had had a real wax candle, also stolen, but they had eaten it. Unable to bear the loud rumbling of their guts, they had looked at each other and at the little candle. It wasn't much but it was something; they had cut it in half and eaten it, leaving only the inedible wick.

Now a twist of cloth served as a wick. They had cut out a niche in the wall of the tunnel – Sashka's idea – and from it flickered a little blue flame, producing more soot than light.

Suddenly Sashka asked, 'What's this rumour about the Caucasus? Is it just rubbish?'

'Yes,' Kolka replied.

'Perhaps they'll *make* us go?' Since Kolka did not reply, Sashka asked again, 'Wouldn't you like to? To go, I mean?'

'Where to?' asked his brother.

'To the Caucasus!'

'What for?'

'Oh, I don't know . . . Might be interesting.'

'Where *I'm* interested in going is in there!' And Kolka gave the bricks a vicious punch. In there, a yard or two from his fist, no farther, was their longed-for goal – the bread-room. There, on a table criss-crossed with knife-marks and giving off the slightly sour smell of rye bread, lay the loaves: many, many loaves of a greyish-golden colour, each one more beautiful than the other. To slice off a crust would be happiness enough – you could suck it, chew it slowly, and then swallow it – but inside the crust there was the softer bread which you could scoop out and stuff into your mouth by the handful.

Never in their lives had the Kuzmin Twins held a whole loaf of bread in their hands. They had not even touched one, although they had, of course, watched from a distance in a shop as bread was weighed and sold against ration coupons. The thin saleswoman of indeterminate age would take the ration cards, coloured differently

14

according to the holder's status (manual worker; non-manual worker; dependant; child) and with a fleeting glance, her eye being as sensitive and accurate as a spirit-level, she would check the authentication and the stamp on the back bearing the number of the shop at which the holder was registered – although she probably knew all her registered customers by name – after which she would go 'snip, snip' with her scissors, sending two or perhaps three coupons falling into an open drawer. In that drawer lay thousands, perhaps a million, of those little coupons with values of 100, 200 or 250 grammes. But each coupon – or two, or three – only equalled a small proportion of a whole loaf, from which the saleswoman could carefully slice a small piece with a sharp knife. (Not that handling all that bread had done her much good – far from putting on weight, she had shrivelled!) And in all the times the brothers had watched this happening, they had never seen anyone go out of the shop with a whole, uncut loaf.

A whole loaf! Such riches scarcely bore thinking about. But what a paradise would open up if there were to be not just a single loaf, not two, not even three, but . . . ! Utter, absolute, blessed paradise! Who needs any old Caucasus? Especially when that paradise was right to hand, and the vague murmur of voices could already be heard through the brickwork.

Although the twins were blinded by soot from the lamp, dulled by falling earth, sweat and exertion, every one of those noises sounded to them like one word: 'Bread. Bread . . .'

At such times the brothers stopped digging. They were no fools; somebody might hear them. On their way from the orphanage buildings to the shed they would always make an extra detour and pass by the steel doors to make sure that the massive padlock was in place – although it could be seen from a mile away! Only then would they crawl into the tunnel to chip away at those damned foundations. They had built them well in the good old days, no doubt never suspecting that one day someone would swear at them for that solid workmanship.

Only when the Kuzmin Twins reached their goal, when the breadroom was revealed to their entranced eyes in the dim evening light – only then would they consider themselves truly in paradise. Then . . . but the brothers knew exactly what would happen then; their two heads had already planned it all.

They would eat one loaf – but only one – on the spot, to avoid making themselves sick from too much richness. They would take away two more loaves and hide them in a safe place. That was the limit: three loaves and no more. However strong the urge, they would not touch the rest, otherwise the infuriated bread-cutters would tear the place apart.

Three was the number of loaves which, according to Kolka's estimate, were regularly stolen every day.

Some of them went to the mad cook; although everyone knew he was crazy and had spent time in an asylum, he still ate like a normal person. While another portion was stolen by the bread-cutters for themselves and for the pack of jackals who hung around them, the biggest share of all was taken by the director himself, his family and his dogs. But the director didn't just feed his dogs: he was surrounded by any number of relatives and spongers, all of whom got their share of the food that was siphoned out of the orphanage in a steady stream. Some of the inmates also took part in this, and those who did got their share, too, in payment for the job.

The Kuzmin Twins had carefully calculated that no one would raise a fuss over the disappearance of just three loaves. The bread-cutters wouldn't suffer, but the others wouldn't get their shares for once, and that would be that. After all, nobody wanted the government inspectors to find out about it (they had to be fed too – and they had *very* big mouths) and so discover why there was so much pilfering, why the orphanage children weren't getting enough to eat and why the director's dogs were growing as big as bull-calves.

But Sashka only sighed as he looked where Kolka was pointing.

'No,' he said thoughtfully, 'I still think it's interesting. I'd like to see the mountains. I expect they're higher than the orphanage buildings, aren't they?'

'Well, so what?' Kolka retorted. He was very hungry. Mountains, however high, were irrelevant. He thought he could smell the aroma of fresh bread through the earth.

They fell silent for a while, until Sashka said, 'We learned a poem today.'

It had been his turn that day to sit through the classes for both of them. 'By Mikhail Lermontov. It's called "The Cliff".'

Sashka could not remember it all by heart, although the poem was short – not like Lermontov's long poem called 'The Song of Tsar Ivan Vasilievich, the Young Oprichnik and the Bold Merchant Kalashnikov'... phew! The title alone was half a mile long, not to mention the poem itself! Sashka could only remember a few lines from 'The Cliff':

> **One night a little golden cloud did rest**

Upon a lonely mountain's rugged brow . . .

'Is that about the Caucasus?' Kolka asked in a bored voice.

'Uh-huh. Cliffs, you see . . .'

'If they're as horrible as this . . .' said Kolka, giving the foundations another thump, 'you can keep your cliffs!'

'They're not mine!'

Sashka relapsed into thought.

He had long since stopped thinking about the poem. He never had been able to understand poems; anyway there wasn't much in them to understand. If you could read poems on a full stomach, then you might find some sense in them. The curly-haired choir-mistress caused them agonies of boredom by making them sing in the choir, and if they hadn't been threatened with no dinner as a punishment they would have left the choir long ago. Much good all those songs and poems did them . . . it didn't matter if you were singing or reading, you still thought of nothing but food.

'Well, what about it?' Kolka suddenly asked.

'What about what?' Sashka countered, mimicking him.

'What was it doing, that cliff of yours? Did it fall down or something?'

'I don't know,' Sashka replied in a silly voice.

'You don't know? What about the poem – doesn't it tell you?'

'The poem? Well, you see, that . . . cloud, it leaned against the cliff . . .'

'Like we're leaning against these foundations?'

'No, it stayed for a kip . . . then flew away again . . .'

Kolka gave a low whistle.

'Is *that* all?'

'That's all.'

'What rubbish they write! If it isn't about a chicken, it's a cloud . . .'

'What's it to do with me?' Sashka was getting cross. 'I didn't write it, did I?' But he was not very cross. In any case it was his own fault; he had been daydreaming during the lesson and hadn't heard the teacher's explanation. Instead, he had been imagining the Caucasus, where everything was different from life in rotten old Tomilino.

Between mountains as high as the orphanage buildings there were bread-rooms everywhere – and not one of them was locked. There was no need to dig to get inside: you just walked in, cut yourself a hunk and ate it. When you came out, there was another bread-room, also unlocked. The local people were all wearing wide-skirted

17

cossack coats with ornamental cartridge cases aslant on each breast, and they were all jolly and friendly. As they watched, smiling, while Sashka was enjoying his bread, they would slap him on the shoulder and say, 'Yakshi!' in their language. Or something else. But it all meant one thing: 'Eat your fill, lads – plenty more bread-rooms in these parts!'

It was summer and the grass was green again. Nobody was keeping an eye on the Kuzmin Twins, except perhaps Anna Mikhailovna, one of the teachers, and even she probably wasn't thinking about leaving for the Caucasus as she stared over the children's heads with her cold blue eyes.

Everything happened suddenly and unexpectedly.

Two inmates of the orphanage, two of the older, dodgier delinquents, were due to be sent to the Caucasus, but they had already disappeared – melted into space, as they say – and the Kuzmin Twins volunteered to go in their place.

The necessary documents were made out. Nobody enquired why they had suddenly decided to go, what compulsion might be driving our two brothers to such distant parts. Only the boys from the most junior intake came and stared at them; standing in the doorway, they pointed at them, 'Them two!' And after a pause, 'Going to the Caucasus.'

In fact they had a very sound reason for wanting to go, and no one, thank God, had guessed what it was.

A week earlier, their tunnel into the bread-cutting room had suddenly caved in. It had collapsed in the most visible place, and with it the Kuzmin Twins' hopes for a different and better life had collapsed too.

One evening they had left the tunnel and all had seemed normal; they had already broken through the foundation-wall, and it only remained to open up the floorboards from underneath.

Next morning they had run out of the main building to find the director and the entire kitchen staff in a bunch outside the bread-room, their eyes popping out of their heads. For – oh horror! – the ground had given way under the wall of the bread-room. What's more, they had guessed: Good God, someone's been digging a tunnel!

A tunnel – under their kitchen, their bread-room! The orphanage had never known anything like it.

One by one the inmates were hauled up in front of the director.

While he questioned all the senior boys, it never occurred to him to suspect the juniors.

Army sappers were called in for consultation. Was it possible, they were asked, for children to have excavated this tunnel on their own? The soldiers inspected the tunnel from the shed to the bread-room and crawled along it as far as the point where it had caved in. Shaking the yellow sand out of their hair, they spread their hands and declared, 'Without proper tools and without special training it would be impossible to excavate such a big tunnel. It would be a month's work for a trained soldier, provided he had, let's say, an entrenching tool and auxiliary equipment as well . . . As for children doing it . . . Well, if it really was done by children, we'd gladly enlist them in the sappers!'

'I never thought of these kids as miracle-workers,' said the director grimly. 'But I'll find that young magician, wherever he may be!'

The Kuzmin brothers were standing nearby, among the other orphanage children. Each of them knew what the other was thinking. Both knew that if the authorities started a really thorough enquiry, the clues would inevitably lead to them. Hadn't they been seen often enough going in and out of the shed these past months? Hadn't they always been missing when the other boys in their dormitory were huddled around the stove? Eyes were everywhere; if one or two people had failed to notice them, a third or a fourth was bound to have been more observant. And after their last evening in the tunnel they had left behind their home-made lamp and – worse still – Sashka's school satchel, which they had been using to carry the spoil out of the tunnel and into the woods.

It was an old and tattered satchel, but if anyone found it the brothers were sure to be caught. Obviously they had to get away, and soon; wouldn't it be better to leave officially and without fuss, by setting out for the unknown Caucasus? The authorities would be glad to see them go anyway, since this would mean vacating two much-needed places at the orphanage.

The Kuzmin Twins could not have known, of course, that in a moment of inspiration some high-up person in the administration of Moscow Province had conceived the idea of relocating the province's overcrowded orphanages, of which in the spring of 1944 there were hundreds. And even these were not enough to house all the abandoned, destitute children who were having to shift for themselves as best they could. Now, since the recent liberation of the fertile lands of the Northern Caucasus from enemy occupation, several problems could be solved at a stroke: the authorities could remove many extra mouths from the hungry region of Central Russia; they could deal a blow at juvenile delinquency; and they could, it would seem, do a good turn to the children themselves.

And, of course, to the Caucasus region.

So the children were told: If you want to eat your fill – go. There's everything there. Not just potatoes but fruit of kinds whose existence even the young jackals themselves had never suspected.

Sashka had said to his brother, 'I want fruit – all those sorts that man told us about when he came here and talked to us.' To which Kolka had replied that those fruits were just potatoes, which he knew for a fact. With his own ears Kolka had heard one of the soldiers say quietly as he left, pointing to the directors, 'He's a fine one, that old fruit . . . staying out of the war by hiding behind these kids!'

'Then we'll stuff ourselves on potatoes!' said Sashka.

Kolka had retorted that when a pack of young jackals like them were taken to a place where there was plenty, they would soon destroy it. He had read in a book that when a swarm of locusts landed somewhere – and locusts had much smaller stomachs than orphans – they stripped it bare. And because they were smaller than kids, they couldn't eat everything at once. They might eat those mysterious fruits – but *we* would gobble up the stalks and the leaves and the flowers too . . .

Even so, he agreed to go to the Caucasus.

Two months dragged by before the time came to leave.

On the day of their departure they were taken to the bread-room, of course no farther than the doorway, and given one day's ration of bread. But no more. You're going off to live on the fat of the land – so why should you have any extra bread?

The brothers stepped out of the doorway and tried not to look at the hole under the wall, the remains of their tunnel, although they felt drawn to it. Pretending to know nothing about it, they mentally bade farewell to the satchel, the lamp, and to their beloved tunnel where, by the light of that smoky wick, they had spent so many long evenings underground in the middle of winter.

Their hands clasped protectively over the rations in their pockets, the brothers were then taken to see the director.

He was sitting on the front steps of his house. He was wearing breeches, but was naked from the waist up and barefoot. Fortunately his dogs were not with him.

Without getting up he stared at the brothers and at the teacher escorting them, and only then, probably, did he remember why they were there.

Grunting, he stood up and beckoned them with a gnarled finger.

The teacher gave them a push from behind and the Kuzmin Twins took a few uncertain steps forward. Although the director never laid hands on any of the children, they were afraid of him. It was his habit to shout loudly. He would grab an inmate by the scruff of his neck and boom at the top of his voice, 'No breakfast, no lunch and no dinner for you, my lad . . .'

It was all right if he only deprived you of meals for one day. But what if he gave you two or three days without food?

On this occasion, though, the director seemed to be in a good humour.

Not knowing the brothers by name (he never knew the names of any of the children), he prodded Kolka with his finger and ordered him to take off his short, much-patched jacket, and told Sashka to take off his quilted jerkin. Then he gave the jerkin to Kolka and the jacket to his brother.

He stepped back and looked at them, as if he had done them a favour. He appeared satisfied with his work.

'That's better . . .' Then he added, 'Now – don't make nuisances of yourselves and don't steal. Don't get under the railway cars, or you'll be run over . . . Well?'

The teacher jogged the boys' elbows and they sang out discordantly, 'We won't, Viktor Vikt'rych!'

'Very well, off you go then!'

They were released.

When they were out of the director's sight, the brothers changed clothes again. In the pockets lay their precious rations. To the director, who didn't know them well enough, they may have seemed identical. But no! The impatient Sashka had already nibbled away the crust of his bread, while Kolka, ever provident, had only licked his without starting to eat it.

It was lucky, though, that he had not been made to swap trousers with any of the other boys. For in the turn-up of Kolka's trouser-leg, rolled into a thin strip, was hidden a thirty-rouble note.

That was not much money in those days, but for the Kuzmin Twins it meant a great deal. It was their sole object of value, their reserve against an unknown future.

Four arms. Four legs. Two heads. And thirty roubles.

Three

As she was instructed, Anna Mikhailovna took the brothers on a suburban train to Moscow's Kazan Station and there personally handed them over, along with their papers, to the person in charge of the Caucasus party, a balding man in a crumpled suit. His name was Pyotr Anisimovich.

He glanced at the brothers and ticked off their names on a list. Putting the list into a briefcase, which he never let out of his grasp, he sighed and muttered something about the twins' clothes. 'The Tomilino people might have given you something better than this to wear, as they're supposed to. I don't know what things are coming to.'

Only then did the Kuzmin Twins see why the director at Tomilino had so strangely made them swap jacket for jerkin. It was probably to salve his conscience about the state of their clothes. That is, if he had a conscience . . .

Waving his briefcase, Pyotr Anisimovich led the brothers along the train to the front carriages.

People carrying sacks and bundles kept coming up to him and complaining that they couldn't get a train back to their homes, begging him to help them, to fix them up with seats on a train, any train . . .

Pyotr Anisimovich gave them all the same answer: 'No, no. I can't.'

Once he flared up and shouted, 'What d'you think I am – a charity or what? I don't know what things are coming to. I've got five hundred orphans on my hands and I don't even know where to stow *them*!' Saying this, for some reason he pointed to the Kuzmin Twins. They did not much like being referred to as pieces of baggage, but said nothing.

As they passed along the train, heads were sticking out of every window, heads which shouted, whistled and whooped at every party of new arrivals, especially when they recognized someone from the markets or railway stations where they had once gone pilfering, or from one of the jails where they had done time together . . .

The Kuzmin Twins were soon spotted, recognized and followed by loud shouts: 'Hey there, louse, from Tomilino house, where're you crawling? Back to your pit – and eat shit!'

The two brothers each bagged a place on the top bunk of a three-tier set and immediately dashed over to a window, where they stuck their heads out alongside the strangers already there.

They watched the arrival of a group of children from Lyubertsy; they had not only met them in the past but had quarrelled and fought with them, and along with the others they whooped and whistled at them, each in his own way.

'Hey there, louse, from Lyubertsy house, where're you crawling? Back to your pit . . .'

In similar ways they greeted the parties from Lublin; from Mozhaisk (a real gang of cut-throats, these!); from Podolsk; from Volokolamsk; from Mytishchi (all from reception-centres for orphans picked up on the streets – such quiet, well-behaved little goody-goodies, but they would pick your pocket and you'd never notice it!); from Noginsk; from Ramenskoe; from Kolomna; from Kashira; from Orekhovo-Zuyevo . . .

Worst of all were the kids from Moscow. They were privileged in various ways: they had been better fed and were not clad in such rags as the children from out-of-town orphanages. When the boys from Moscow appeared, the entire trainload set up such a caterwauling that it drowned out the sound of trams ringing their bells in Kalanchevskaya Street outside the station.

The children roared, howled, bleated and mooed, and kept it up until nightfall as more and more parties of their fellow orphans arrived.

'Hey, Mozhaisk boys – shut your noise!'

'You lot from Kashira – don't come nearer!'

'Orekhovo-Zuyevo – back *you* go!'

'If Kolomna won't feed you – we don't need you!'

They all yelled with gusto, but there was no malice in the words – they simply yelled like that from habit.

Like Noah's Ark, the train took on its passengers two by two, a pair from each orphanage; and like the survivors of the Great Flood when the Ark came to rest on Mount Ararat, they were now faced with starting a new life in the lands of the Caucasus.

By the time darkness fell, the train began to quieten down. Every carriage was being filled to the very top, like a new box of matches. Newcomers were now less interested in whistling and screaming at the others than in looking after themselves: finding a bunk, pushing or kicking their neighbour aside in order to squeeze into enough space to be able to sit or – better still – to lie down.

Our Kuzmin Twins had already done this.

Reclining like lords on their top bunks, from this elevated vantage-point they observed the goings-on down below as if they were watching a film.

Chatter, laughter, jokes . . . Someone struck up a song:

> **Up in the Caucasus, all among the crags,**
> **Once there dwelt an old monk, dressed all in rags.**
> **He was looking there for gold,**
> **But no other monk he told,**
> **Until at last he'd found his gold.**
> **Took it to the nearest town, there to be sold . . .**

What then happened to the monk and his Caucasian gold was never known, for the train gave a sudden jerk.

Everyone fell silent and listened. Was it possible? Had they really started to move? Were they on their way? After a pause the carriage jerked again, harder this time; there was a clanking and grinding of metal and it was true – they were off! This was now clear from the slight creaking, the still infrequent bumps and the clicking of wheels on the track.

By that stage in the war the blackout had been lifted, and as the few lights slipped back into the past and the darkness, no one rushed to the window to watch the capital of the world begin to float away. Nobody cared about Moscow, especially our heroes, who knew from experience how hard-hearted that city could be.

From down below came the squeaky voice of one of the little girls saying that she felt sad.

'Why are you sad?'

'Sad about leaving.'

What was there to be sad about? She didn't really know – she just felt sad, that was all; supposing we don't come back? . . . Don't come back? To Moscow? It'll be a good thing if we don't. Obviously we won't be coming back. A fat lot Moscow's ever done for us! Stone houses – stony-hearted people . . . Damn the place, bleak, filthy, battered, where everyone only lives from one wartime day to

24

the next, bartering possessions for food to stay alive . . . and where the workers, standing over their lathes in unheated factories to forge victory over the enemy, not only fail to see the many homeless waifs that haunt the city but, by working shifts of up to twelve hours, and therefore having to sleep at the factory, have also neglected their own kids so badly that they're running wild.

As for the Kuzmin Twins, neither in Moscow nor anywhere else in the whole wide world was there another drop of their family's blood.

They had each other – on that at least they could rely.

In other words, wherever they might be taken, they depended for everything – home, family and protection – on themselves.

At the orphanage they had grown shabby, patched, ragged and infested with lice; now it was as if they were gladly running away from themselves. Flying away into the unknown, blown like seeds into the desert – and a wartime desert, what's more. Somewhere, somehow, in some crack, some chink, some little hole in the ground they might find refuge . . . where perhaps care and kindness would be lavished upon them and where they could grow and flourish, perhaps to sprout like a little stunted branch, a blade of grass; or like a tiny, flowerless potato-shoot that no one would want. Or they might not grow but simply disappear into oblivion, in which case no one would want them at all.

It would be as if they had never existed. So why go on?

This story is not just about the Kuzmin Twins, but about every one of those children who, in 1944, travelled through a war-torn country that had still not recovered from the fascist onslaught – all those, in fact, who journeyed in that extraordinary, recklessly, insanely cheerful trainload of ours!

Thanks to the peculiar selectivity of childish memory, I can still remember some of them, not only their faces but their first names and surnames, and I have tried for decades to trace them. I have sent off hundreds of those little yellow cards to the post office's Directory Service with requests for their whereabouts, but not one of them has ever produced an address . . . not so much as a scribbled note from a single one of our erstwhile companions . . .

I have now been a published author for twenty-five years, and I have openly, intentionally put their names into my short stories, novels and documentary articles, but again – never a word in response have I had.

It's a terrible thought: can I be the only one of them to have survived? Did they all vanish from the face of the earth? Did they never even grow up to adulthood?

This novel is, in all probability, my last cry into the void: so answer me, for heaven's sake! There were five hundred of us on that train! How I wish that somebody, just one maybe, of the survivors would hear me, because later so many of them – and I saw this with my own eyes – perished in that new land to which we were taken . . .

From their top bunks the twins could see – and above all hear – that the most provident ones were starting to reach into pockets, satchels, bags or rucksacks and to bring out edibles. There were carrots, beetroot, pickled cucumbers, dried fish and cold baked potatoes. One boy had a large lump of buckwheat porridge tied up in a rag . . . and there was even – oh, luxury! – a little grey patty made of fried vegetable scraps and peelings.

Then suddenly . . . that 'suddenly' was enough to tie one's stomach into a knot . . . an intoxicating smell wafted over the bunks, along the carriage, down the whole train . . . and it was like a hacksaw cutting into your guts. Someone had opened a long, shallow, oval can, glinting like gold – a tin of American Lend-Lease pork sausage-meat!

Our Kuzmin Twins only knew of this tinned sausage-meat from hearsay and by smell: twice in his life Sashka had sniffed that unforgettable smell that was like a knife-thrust between the ribs, and he had described the impression to Kolka . . .

Now both twins looked down, as one looks down into a dark well to see the reflection of a little star. And not only the twins; probably everyone in the carriage was looking and listening and sniffing, wondering if they might ever again experience such a sensation in their lifetime.

Then, as if on a word of command, both brothers turned away and exchanged looks. Each knew what the other was thinking.

Sashka was thinking: if only I had something to stuff into my mouth, to stop myself from crying out, from bellowing for the whole carriage to hear! Not about the tinned meat – to hell with that, it was unattainable anyway – but about that bastard the director at Tomilino, who had been given written instructions (which they had learned from overhearing other people talking) to give the boys bread and other rations for five days! What had the brute been thinking about that day, as he sat on the steps of his porch, scratching the pimples under his armpits; what had become of his stinking little conscience? Because he had *known* that he was sending two children

26

without food on a journey that would last several days. And his conscience had not given a single shudder, not one cell in his stony heart had so much as twitched.

Take this reproach – unspoken at the time by the Kuzmin Twins and myself – this belated, unforgiving blast from the distant nineteen-eighties aimed at *you*, you fat rats who had holed yourselves up in cushy civilian jobs, rats who infested our ship-homes of little children fished up from the ocean of war . . . One of you was called Vladimir Nikolayevich Bashmakov. Director of the Talovsk orphanage, you ruled our fates and starved us. Ah, where are you now, you mini-Napoleon with your short arms, your overbearing nature and your love of regularly torturing some wretched inmate by awarding him a few lethal days of 'dietary punishment'?

'No lunch, no supper, no breakfast, no lunch, no supper . . .'

Our hearts would shrink with aching foreboding as we heard the sentence handed out. How many times would he twist that litany around one's belly like an ever-tightening belt of hunger?

The two Kuzmins each took out the piece of bread that had been given to him. The slices were now quite tiny, reduced by the many little nips and nibbles that the twins had taken from them on the way: it was like holding a piece of mouse-meat in your hand.

Kolka sniffed, licked it and offered it to Sashka. 'Want some?'

'What about you?'

'I had enough to eat this morning,' said Kolka, thinking to himself that if Sashka had two pieces to eat he'd feel a bit fuller, and they wouldn't need any more that night, because the sense of being full was wasted at night – asleep, you didn't feel hungry.

Kolka handed his piece to Sashka and turned away. The smell of sausage-meat was killing him, blowing his innards apart like an exploding bullet. If only those beasts down below wouldn't rattle the spoon against the tin can; the sound produced cramps in his gut, as though it was the lining of his stomach that was being scraped clean. He wanted to howl aloud, to bite the wooden bunk he was lying on. He pressed his face against the dry boards, clutching his head in his hands, feeling that at any moment he would lose control. In his agony at the sounds and smells of someone else enjoying a feast, he might start to scream and roar like a wild beast for all the carriage to hear.

Sashka was clearly in no better state either. Staring exhaustedly at the roof, he said in a hate-filled whisper, 'If only we can stay alive till tomorrow . . . tomorrow, when the train stops . . .'

27

Kolka caught his meaning and sighed. 'Ye-es . . . we'll go to the market . . .'

For both of them the market meant that they might just, by the skin of their teeth, be able to survive the journey.

Their travelling companions who came from Moscow had been issued with rations for several days, and evidently their relatives had added some extra food as well. For the Kuzmin Twins, their best 'relatives' were market-stall women who didn't keep too sharp an eye on their produce.

'I've been thinking up a way to pinch some stuff tomorrow,' said Sashka, scratching his head – the place where, in its dark, unfathomed depths, his very best ideas were hatched.

'We'll do it,' said Kolka angrily, cutting him off. Talk is all very well, but you can't eat it, and both knew he would do everything that Sashka had dreamed up.

Four

The train jerked to a halt.

'Where's this? Is it Voronezh?'

As though in response to an order, the two brothers woke up at the same moment and stared out of the window. Along the grey station façade stretched the word 'VORONEZH' in brown oil-paint.

The Kuzmin Twins knew that a town of this name would be on their way, though it was not the town that interested them but the market near the station.

They rolled out of their bunks on to the heads of the kids swarming below and looked out of the window. Then they barged their way through the mob to the open platform at the end of the carriage, where they bumped into a stocky, bewhiskered conductor wearing a dirty blue railway uniform. Two flags were sticking out of the top of his boot. He was sweating and his eyes were popping out of his head as he lugged a heavy sack up the metal steps and on to the carriage platform.

'Hey, dad, are we stopping here for long?'

The conductor pushed them bodily to the far side of the platform and dropped his sack with a thud. He turned around, working his shoulders to relieve the strain, and looked at the twins.

'What d'you want?'

'Is there time to go to the market?' asked Kolka. He sounded hopeful; the man must have been to the market himself to get his sack, which Kolka could tell was full of potatoes. He made a mental note not to lose sight of that sack.

'H'mm . . . the market's right outside the station,' the conductor muttered, waving his hand towards the exit. 'But mind you're not late! The train won't stop here for long. When it gives one whistle, you'd better be nippy – the second whistle means we're off.'

The Kuzmin Twins exchanged looks. Both were thinking it was a good thing the train wouldn't be stopping for long. The sooner it

29

left again, the better for them. They had made their plans in advance, which depended on both themselves and the train making a quick getaway.

On the far side of a long wall, which ended at the half-destroyed station building – the fighting here had obviously been fierce – there was a large open square, full of people. Jumping over heaps of broken bricks and a trench half-filled with water, along with dozens of other kids from the train, the brothers raced towards the market and plunged into it at full tilt, like a dagger thrust into its victim.

Near the entrance, as usual, were peasants selling sunflower seeds from open sacks and home-made brooms of birch-twigs. Further on were the vegetable stalls: potatoes, beetroot, turnips, cucumbers . . . The vegetables here were much more plentiful than in the country-side around Moscow, and there was more milk to be had, in the form of *varenets* – slightly fermented boiled milk set out on the stalls ready to drink in glasses, topped by bubbles of pinkish froth. The stallholders were shouting, in wailing sing-song voices, '*Varenets*! Who'll buy my *varenets*?' One woman shouted it at Kolka, choosing to address him in particular because a red thirty-rouble note was peeping out of his pocket, and behind that was the blue colour of what looked like more banknotes . . . Without the thirty roubles the woman wouldn't have noticed them – and she wouldn't have called him 'my dear', either; there were too many light-fingered young rascals about the market.

The twins had left the thirty-rouble note sticking out of Kolka's pocket far enough to be seen by the whole market, while they had also stuffed in a torn-up cigarette-packet printed in the same shade of blue as the fifty-rouble note. As the boys hurried past, no one could tell from a mere glance that it was only an old packet, while the thirty-rouble note promised that there was real money in there.

Naturally the twins were running a risk: it was dangerous to put a genuine banknote where it was so visible and could easily be snatched by a pickpocket. But they had taken this into account: Kolka walked in front like a fine gentleman, flashing his money, while Sashka kept watch from behind, never letting Kolka out of his sight, ready to pounce if anyone showed too much interest in the money, or got too close.

All around them the crowd hummed, bustled and spat out the husks of sunflower seeds. The ground was carpeted with husks.

A squeal came from nearby: someone had been caught pilfering and was being beaten up. This scene was no novelty to the brothers: they too had been caught before now and had also squealed like stuck pigs – there was always a chance that someone would intervene; but if you endured it in silence, the stallholder was likely to beat you black and blue in defence of his property and no one would take pity on you. It may have been one of the other kids from the train who was yelling, but the brothers quickly made off in another direction. The peasants in this part of the market were obviously too alert.

They went about fifty paces and stopped dead: there it was! There lay the very thing they were looking for.

On a counter of flat planking – not in the middle of the counter, from which you couldn't get away easily, but at one end – were several loaves of home-baked rye bread, neatly cut into round, even slices. And alongside them was something quite marvellous, white and long: Kolka saw it and stopped, pretending to have stumbled. He stared at it, transfixed.

Sashka gave him a gentle prod. 'Why did you stop dead like that? Hey, look at that French loaf! All white, like we saw in that film . . .' As he whispered, a lump formed in his throat like a ball of clay which he couldn't swallow and couldn't spit out – and all because of this damned French loaf floating in front of their eyes!

In a pre-war film Sashka had seen a baker's shop, where someone had simply gone in and bought a white loaf like this one, and he had exclaimed, 'Look, he's bought that loaf!' Was bread really sold just like that – without ration coupons, and a whole loaf at once?

The brothers looked around to make sure that no one was likely to move in ahead of them, that no purchaser was dashing forward to secure that amazing prize. But no; nobody had picked it up, no one was proffering money . . . One or two people asked the price of the loaf and went away again. Obviously the loaf was expensive, lying there untouched and waiting for some wealthy buyer to come and claim it, with its rich golden crust gleaming in the sunlight, an uneven furrow running along its crest.

And the smell of it! The brothers ought to have caught that aroma at a hundred yards' distance; perhaps, though, they had been drawn there instinctively by their hungry stomachs, just as a bee is drawn to nectar.

They said a silent prayer: 'Oh Lord, don't let anyone else have it, but keep it there until our moment comes! Make the people with lots of money go somewhere else, oh Lord, so they can't get that wonderful white treasure before we do . . . You see, Lord, we've got a long journey ahead of us, and if we miss this chance . . . And we're so hungry, Lord! You fed the five thousand with bread (some old women had told them this) so just do the trick for us too!'

Maybe those weren't the exact words, but I'll vouch for the sense and still more for the sincerity of their prayers.

The brothers now divided the work: one turned round towards the train, the other towards the bread on the stall, where some honey in combs was also laid out for sale. The whole plan had been devised inside Sashka's little head – on an empty stomach. This was where four eyes were essential: by standing back to back, no one could pinch their thirty-rouble note, they could see all round and each only needed to move an elbow to give a warning signal to the other.

Sashka heard the locomotive give a whistle. Hoarse and plaintive, it seemed to be calling for them. 'I'm go-oo-ing!' That was the signal for action, like the Archangel Gabriel's trumpet-call, summoning our heroes to act in their righteous cause.

Now it was forward, and only forward! Forward to the miraculous French loaf, to those round rye slices and to the honey, surrounded by a little swarm of impertinent wasps . . . But first of all to that long, delicious, coveted golden loaf. Quick, Kolka – quick!

Sashka nudged his brother in the ribs, and whispered, 'Get going!'

Pulling the thirty-rouble note a little further out of his pocket to make it more noticeable, Kolka strode up to the stall. He knew he had no more than a minute or two in hand. Standing up against the counter and turning sideways so that the money could be seen, he enquired, 'Well, what've you got here?'

This was said in the tone of a passer-by who could see the goods were nothing but rubbish and not worth buying. The young woman, her glassy blue eyes starting out like buttons, turned and stared at him. She was almost broader than she was tall. Sashka would have thought at once of some quip like, 'She's wider than her counter!' Who but a market-woman could have grown so grossly fat? The little man beside her was frail by comparison; no doubt she had squashed him flat, for she looked as if she weighed half a ton.

This thought passed through Kolka's mind like a faint puff of wind as he inspected the bread with a contemptuous look.

'The junk some people try and sell . . . !' he sneered, and looked into the distance as though about to go away. 'Nothing worth buying here.'

The fat girl was stolidly cracking sunflower seeds and spitting the husks out of the corner of her mouth, firing them off in bursts like a machine-gun. But this remark touched her on the raw.

'Nothing worth buying?' she snapped, a seed-husk dangling from her lower lip. 'Call this nothing?' And she shoved the long French loaf under Kolka's nose.

Kolka pretended to move away, but stopped and took hold of the loaf, and the combination of its springy crust and intoxicating aroma brought a lump of nausea into his throat.

'What's it made of – bran?' he asked, frowning. He made it obvious that he didn't like being palmed off with any old rubbish made of bran.

'Bran yourself!' The girl flared up. 'It's a pure wheat loaf. Take a good look!'

Kolka couldn't help closing his eyes, because he felt he might be sick at any moment. If he threw up now, in front of this plump, overfed girl, it would ruin all their plans. Here was a real snag: they had worked it all out, foreseeing every move in advance, but they hadn't allowed for nausea brought on by hunger or an involuntary eruption of Kolka's gut.

He shook his head and took a couple of big gulps of air, disguising them as a yawn by putting his hand in front of his mouth. The effect was very convincing: the lad seemed to be yawning with boredom at having to stand there and look at some miserable loaf that supposedly wasn't made of bran.

'Well, how much?' he asked, casually pushing the loaf towards the girl – but not so far that he couldn't easily grab it again.

'Hundred and fifty.'

'You're joking.'

'Joking? Look – it's baked from pure wheat flour!'

'A hundred,' Kolka muttered, with a dismissive wave that meant 'Pure wheat, my foot! You can't fool me'.

'Hundred and forty,' said the girl, and began spitting out bursts of sunflower husks again.

'Hundred and twenty,' said Kolka contemptuously, starting to go. Seeming to lose interest, he took a step away without looking at the loaf.

'Hundred and thirty,' the girl shouted after him, a spray of husks fanning out of her mouth.

'All right,' Kolka condescended, turning back and slapping his pocket to make sure the money was still visible. 'Mind you, it's daylight robbery.'

Picking up the loaf, he shoved it into the pocket containing the banknote; then before the fat young woman could gather her wits again, he pointed to the sliced loaves of rye bread. 'How much are those?'

'Thirty roubles a slice. And thirty for a portion of honey.' The girl's lips worked furiously as she spat out seed-husks in all directions.

'You're robbing me, but I'll take 'em!' said Kolka brazenly, suddenly cheerful, and at once put two slices into his pocket alongside the French loaf. Without giving the girl time to object, he pushed a couple of lumps of comb-honey, wrapped in newspaper, down his shirt front. 'Oh, what the hell ... I'll take the lot!'

Now the girl seemed to smell a rat. She stopped eating seeds and her button-eyes stared at Kolka.

'Pay up! You just grab and grab – pay up, I say!'

Her puny little husband, who had been dozing until then, jumped up as his wife's voice rose to a squeak, and looked around: their produce was being hijacked before their eyes and he was not doing his duty as a scarecrow.

This was now the second critical moment: they had their hands on the loot and it was time to make an elegant getaway. As the Bureau of Information might have said in one of its communiqués: The encirclement of the enemy's group of forces around Stalingrad is complete. The moment has come to deliver the final blow.

For this, Sashka was waiting in reserve, just as the detachment led by Dmitry Bobrok had waited during the battle of Kulikovo Field against the Tartar Khan Mamai (they had learned about this in school). Mamai, in this case, was obviously the fat-bottomed girl selling bread, and the Tartars were beginning to put pressure on the Russians: the girl shouted a second time, 'Pay me!' and grabbed Kolka by the sleeve. 'Come on, pay up!'

It was then that Dmitry Bobrok, Count of Volhynia, ordered his reserve regiment to engage the enemy and to unleash the decisive armoured strike against the fascists.

Like a little imp of darkness, Sashka popped up alongside Kolka.

'Quick! Quick!' he shouted, loudly enough to deafen the fat stall-keeper. 'The train's leaving!'

Kolka turned his head and the girl involuntarily followed his movement: the train, their train, was starting to move along the track, the wheels squeaking a little as though it was stretching its legs. A mob of kids was crowding noisily around the doors as they squeezed themselves on board.

'Run!' yelled Sashka even louder, creating a sense of panic. 'Later ... we'll pay you later, at the train!'

The girl instantly came to her senses and seized Kolka's sleeve in a lethal grip.

34

'What d'you mean – *later?* Pay now!' And she squealed, 'I want my money!'

'Give her the money,' Sashka yelled, 'or we'll miss the train!'

'But it's under the loaf!'

'Then give me the loaf!'

Sashka grabbed the French loaf, but the slices of rye bread kept it from coming out. Kolka began searching in his pocket underneath the bread, pulling his sleeve away from the girl as though he needed his hand free to get at the money. The moment the girl released his arm, Kolka was away; Sashka was already ahead, racing for the train.

This was the scene: Sashka leading the field with the French loaf, followed by Kolka with the bread-girl and her husband hard on his heels. She was so hot with fury and exertion that Kolka could feel the warmth of her on his back, but this was no laughing matter: the girl may have been broader than she was long, but she could move so fast that she wasn't losing any ground, and Kolka was terrified. If they caught up with him, they would murder him; they were just the sort who would show no mercy. What's more, there were other stallkeepers all around who might join in and catch him – they looked on chasing little thieves as sport. And they would beat him to within an inch of his life . . .

A shout went up that could be heard all over the market: 'Stop thief!'

The entire trainload of children was leaning out of the carriage windows: the spectacle was as good as a pantomime. Five hundred young faces were staring from a hundred windows along the whole train of fifteen carriages, five hundred venomous little throats were screaming:

'Hey, Voronezh, you'll never catch 'em!'

'And if you do, you can eat shit!'

'Look – she's lost her husband!'

'She's no girl – she's an engine! She'd better blow off some steam or she'll blow up!'

'Hitch her up to the train! She can pull us along!'

'Wow, look at that big pair of buffers on her!'

Someone started bawling a popular song and they all took it up: ' "A train is going from Tambov all the way to Moscow, As I lie on the top bunk and hear the whistle blow . . . Whoo-whoo!" Stop thief!'

From the windows came a hail of apple cores, bottles and tin cans, which slowed the hostile advance of the fascist-tartar hordes.

In the end, as always in history, the outcome of the battle was decided by the popular masses.

First to reach their carriage was Sashka, who grasped the handrail and looked round.

Kolka missed his footing and dropped a piece of bread he was holding. As he bent down to pick it up, he dropped the other piece. Meanwhile the girl, shaking her fist at the kids leaning out of the windows, had almost caught up with Kolka and was about to grab him. Behind came her husband, followed by a hefty volunteer from one of the market-stalls, who had joined the chase for the fun of it, along with a few others bringing up the rear . . .

'Drop it!' Sashka screamed for all he was worth, desperately, loud enough for the whole of Voronezh to hear him. 'Drop it! Drop it!'

Kolka momentarily lost his head, feeling the girl's breathing right behind him – in fact it sounded less like breathing than a hissing, creaking and rattling, as if nothing less than a tank was about to run him down. Almost on all fours, he jumped up from a crouch and grabbed the narrow metal steps . . . but the girl was already pulling him by the legs.

Sashka and the conductor seized Kolka under the armpits and hauled him up, while the girl tugged at him from her end, pulling him apart like the bellows of an accordion. Kolka was giving tongue, yelling and squealing like a piglet, while the lad from the market was coming up fast.

Poor Kolka was pulled apart so hard that the girl ended up with one of his trouser-legs clutched in her fist. As the other lad joined her and was reaching out, the conductor whacked him in the face with his signal-flags, adding a kick with his boot for good measure.

'Keep off!' he shouted. 'No train-jumpers allowed! Damn' black marketeers! Scroungers!'

Another barrage of tins and bottles came flying out of the window at the pursuers, and someone tried to piss on them as the carriages slowly rumbled past, followed by a chorus of whoops and catcalls as the train gathered speed. 'Whoo-whoo! Stop thief!'

Five

The French loaf fed the Kuzmin Twins for a long time.

They sucked, chewed and licked out the soft white inside until there was not a crumb of it left. But the crust . . . the crust became their drinking vessel, a sort of magic cup. It was Sashka's idea that they should make double, triple, quintuple use of it!

At big stations and at tiny wayside halts, clutching their empty French loaf and with their trusty thirty-rouble note sticking out of Kolka's pocket, they would dash over to the market-women and ask them to fill up their hollow loaf with sour cream, yoghurt or *varenets*. Then the two brothers would put on their noisy little double act: one of them would start shouting that it was too expensive, anyway the train was leaving . . . so they would pour out the milky contents and later use spoons – borrowed from the Moscow kids – to scrape out the liquid that had stuck to the inside of the crust.

But like everything else in this world of ours, the French loaf did not last for ever. The crust gradually became thinner and more soggy until one day, sometime after leaving Voronezh, their cornucopia fell apart into little pieces; these they ate, not without regret.

The honey, too, came to an end. During Kolka's escape it had run everywhere, soaking both his shirt and his stomach. The shirt was easily dealt with: they sucked it, chewed it, and licked it clean. But Kolka refused to let his stomach be touched. 'My shirt's in holes already – I don't want holes in my stomach too,' he said.

Whenever he walked down the carriage, wasps would start circling round him. At first the kids in the lower bunks distinguished the two twins by saying that Kolka was the sweet one, while Sashka, by contrast, must be the bitter one,. These nicknames might have stuck, but because the Kuzmin Twins loved to fool people and make out that each was the other, they quickly confused everybody, especially when the smell of honey finally wore off. It was a method of self-defence which they had devised over the years.

The kids on the lower bunks would shout, 'Hey, sweet twin! Get your loaf ready, we're coming in to a station soon!'

And Kolka would reply, pointing at Sashka, 'Tell *him*! He's Kolka!'

They would also change places and wear each other's clothes. There seemed to be no sense and no obvious advantage in this. The others couldn't tell who was wearing what or who was sleeping where; but the brothers knew, and knew very well, that while this didn't matter at the moment, if something unpleasant were to happen or if they were accused of some crime it would be very important to confuse other people and so cover their tracks . . .

So although they behaved as they had behaved in the past . . . the twins were now not looking back but forward . . .

Soon other smells began permeating the carriage, blotting out all other odours such as honey, sweat or piss. The train was moving into what the schoolbooks called 'the black earth zone'.

These wartime orphans had seen too much in their short lives to be easily amazed. But now something highly unusual was revealed to them: the earth in these parts really *was* black.

Almost devoid of trees, with neither woods nor the familiar clumps of silver birches so common in the countryside of central and northern Russia, the gently rolling steppe stretched out to the horizon, and the colour of the soil was as black as the fingernails of every self-respecting orphanage kid. You couldn't, for instance, see the crows when they settled on that soil! Even the big black locomotive was lost to sight against that background.

Equally astonishing were the huge fields of fruit and vegetables growing on that black earth, unguarded and without watchmen. It was impossible to make out from a distance exactly what was growing out there, but oh! – if the train would only go just a little bit slower, if only it would come to a stop somewhere! But as if out of spite the train kept going on and on and on, rushing, pounding onward like a mad beast . . .

The kids in the carriages were begging, praying to the engine: please, please stop, just for a second, a moment, long enough for us to get a carrot or a beetroot apiece, that's all . . . Please put on the brakes and stop awhile – what difference would it make to you, dear, kind engine?

And suddenly – the train seemed to be going to stop. Had someone heard their prayer? Had the power of thought shut off the steam – right there in the midst of fields of growing corn and vegetables?

The train slowed down, hissed, and came to a halt.

The engine-driver, a taciturn old man with a grey crew-cut, turned to his stoker and growled, 'We're stopping. Plenty of fodder here for our horde of starvelings. Shut off steam for a couple of hours, let's have some hot water and we'll make tea.'

With the exception, perhaps, of the smallest, the timid ones and any who were sick, the entire trainload of little monsters poured out of the carriages to see why they had stopped. A few, without hesitating, ran straight out into the fields and vegetable plots near the railway line and began picking. At first it was only the boldest and pushiest, while the rest stayed by the track and watched; then suddenly, as if something had clicked in their collective mind, they all rushed forward like lemmings, surging towards the plots of greenery, and instantly overrunning them.

The engine-driver looked out of his cab at this scene of pillage and grinned as the horde of children flickered busily among the greenery, darting hither and thither like little beetles in the grass. He filled his enormous tin mug with hot water, and as he lifted it with shaking hands to his lips and sipped it cautiously, he added, 'Won't do Russia any harm for these kids to eat their fill for once.'

The activity in the fields was unimaginable: every child simply grabbed as much as he could, pulling up whatever came to hand. They wrenched off young corn-cobs whose grains were still white and milky. They used their teeth to bite off tiny, immature pumpkins from their stalks and chewed them on the spot, as if they were apples, skin and all. The rest they pulled out with their stalks and carried them back to the train.

Cucumbers, carrots and young beetroot were stuffed into shirt fronts or into mouths, which then spat out the black, insipid-tasting soil. They twisted off the yellow heads of half-grown sunflowers, and if they lacked the strength to do this they pulled them up by the roots and dragged them back to the train like a bundle of firewood. Some of the vegetables they found were quite exotic. Kolka shoved some enormous cucumbers under his shirt, only to discover later that they were not cucumbers at all but vegetable marrows, which were strange and horrible to eat raw. But he ate them all the same – waste not, want not!

It was at this, shall we say, unusual moment that the Kuzmin Twins first met Regina Petrovna.

The brothers were carrying back their booty and thinking of nothing but shoving it all on to their two top bunks, then running back for more.

It must be said that their teeth worked quite as hard as their hands and feet. As they were walking, both were biting the juicy, sweetish seeds out of sunflower-heads, chewing them and spitting them out into the grass.

A woman was standing by the door into their carriage.

Sashka's mouth actually dropped open in amazement, letting fall a mouthful of mushy, half-chewed, immature sunflower seeds. Kolka, too, was completely taken aback and could only stare at the unexpected sight of this woman.

Young she undoubtedly was, young and dark-haired, her long thick tresses thrown carelessly back. Her eyes, too, were black, and sparkled from some fathomless depth within her, radiating a warm, enveloping affection; and her lips – big and mobile – which seemed to live their own independent life, were not painted with lipstick: this pleased the brothers most of all. In her features there was also something of the proud, stately bearing of women of the East. She held her head high, in the way that only goddesses or queens carry themselves.

The brothers saw her at the same moment and both fell in love with her – hopelessly and for life. But they didn't admit this to each other: it was the only thing they did not share, but it was cherished separately by each as his private possession.

In any case, the two twins liked different things about this woman. Sashka liked her hair, and he liked her voice, especially when she laughed. Kolka preferred her lips and her whole bewitching appearance, like some Sheherezade, whose picture he had once seen in a book of Eastern fairy tales.

This didn't happen at once; they only came to realize it later. Now, though, the brothers simply stopped in their tracks as though the figure standing by the carriage was not a human being but an angel from heaven.

With their food-crammed shirt fronts sticking out a foot or so in front of them, with their arms laden with sunflowers, with mouths stuffed full of young seeds and still chewing them, they were spellbound by her and were suddenly aware that they couldn't live without her.

The woman looked at them and burst out laughing. Her voice was deep, velvety, and it made your skin prickle to hear it.

'Well now!' she said in a musical contralto voice, as she inspected our twins. 'Where are you two from? You're so alike! Two boots of a pair! . . . No!' she exclaimed and bent down to look at them more closely. 'No, you're like two boots for the same foot!'

And she laughed again, an amazingly light laugh that was like a shower of sparks (red sparks on a warm night!).

The brothers being reduced to a shy silence, with only a trickle of white, half-chewed seeds coming out of Sashka's mouth, the woman added, speaking to them as if they were her old and dear friends, 'I have two young men in my carriage, only they're smaller than you – much smaller. Put together, their ages only add up to seven. Their names are Zhores and Marat; they're very serious, important young men, I can tell you! You may call me Regina Petrovna . . . Can you remember that? Re-gi-na-pet-rov-na . . . So who are *you*?'

Only now did it occur to Sashka to shut his mouth; Kolka, having coughed and spat out his remaining seeds, said in a voice hoarse with excitement that they were the Kuzmin Twins.

'Is that all?' asked the woman, amused.

The brothers nodded in unison.

'It can't be!' she exclaimed with a smile, and her lips trembled, no doubt to stop herself from laughing again. 'Perhaps I should call you Kuzmin One and Kuzmin Two?'

'No,' said Kolka sternly. 'Separately we're Kolka and Sashka. Together we're the Kuzmins, that's to say the Kuzmin Twins.'

The woman shook her head as though amazed at this news; her dark hair billowed and part of it fell foward on to her temple and her shoulder.

'Which of you is which? Or "Who's who?", as the English would say? . . . But don't bother – even if you told me I shouldn't be able to tell you apart next time I saw you, each of you is a copy of the other . . . a carbon copy . . .'

The brothers didn't know what a 'carbon copy' was, but later they admitted to each other that this was the first time in their lives that anyone had ever spoken to them in a foreign language. It made Sashka come out in a sweat, and Kolka wet his pants a little, but the woman didn't notice this. She bent down really close to the brothers, until they were nearly overcome by a heady perfume, something they had never before experienced. Her wavy hair suddenly fell towards them and she lowered her voice as she confided to them, 'Look, my two young friends, we shall meet again, because I'm going to be looking after you. Yes, I am! You must always tell me which of you is which, and you won't try to trick me – all right? Because you do try to trick other people, don't you? You're so alike, you can fool anyone you care to . . . isn't that so?'

The brothers stared at the ground.

41

She was the first woman who had ever understood all about them. 'Goodbye for now, my dear Kuzmin Twins,' the woman said, and sighed. 'I'm looking after these two important young men from Moscow, and they can't manage for long without me . . . We shall meet again, shan't we? Let's say, at the next station . . . All right? That's settled then. Bye-bye!'

And off she went.

The Kuzmin Twins climbed into their carriage and unloaded all their riches on to their bunks, but somehow this no longer excited them. They at once became impatient for the train to move off, the sooner to arrive at the next station.

When they did arrive, they found that after many agonizing minutes of waiting the woman with the strange name of 'Reginapetrovna' did not come to meet them at their carriage. Nor did she at any of the other stations, and the brothers could have imagined she didn't exist at all.

The next day the train was hit by an epidemic of diarrhoea.

Six

The bewhiskered conductor could only sigh deeply when he glanced into the toilet. It was all covered in filth – the lavatory seat, the floor around the lavatory, the tap, the wash-basin, the soap-rack and the walls were spattered almost up to the ceiling. Even the open platform and the walkway between the carriages had been fouled, while some-one had actually contrived to dump a load in the carriage's heating-stove.

At the now frequent stops, the kids still ran out of the train – not to go scrumping in the fields but only to the foot of the embankment to relieve themselves. Soon they didn't even bother to go that far, but just squatted down beside the carriages or underneath them. Some of the weaker ones only had the strength to get underneath, and had to be lifted back out again.

The engine-driver, a little wrinkled man in greasy black overalls, his face smeared with soot, walked along the whole length of the train before starting off, and every so often would bend down and plead with them. 'Come on, lads! How can I get going if you're sitting under the wheels? God forbid I should crush any of you. I drove trains to the front, took troops to Stalingrad on tracks just laid on the bare earth – at night, too – and I never had one accident. And now look at you . . .'

He shook his grey, crew-cut head and called the children's super-intendent to help him.

The anxious, fussy Pyotr Anisimovich appeared, clutching his briefcase to his chest. He ran from carriage to carriage, where he would bend down and implore his charges: 'Come out of there! We've got to go! You're keeping the train waiting! Come out, or we'll never be able to move, don't you see?'

No reply came and none of the children moved. The only answers to the superintendent's plea were the loud noises issuing from a row of bare bottoms. He straightened up and spread his hands as he looked at the engine-driver, and said, 'I don't understand it!'

'It's understandable all right,' grumbled the engine-driver, 'but what are we going to do about it?'

They stopped at the next station – the name of which was Kuban – for three days. The temporary bridge across a mountain river, erected by army sappers during the advance which drove out the Germans, had been carried away by the raging elements, and the new bridge was still being built.

The train was shunted on to a siding.

The children were taken off and moved into the straw-lined boxcars of a neighbouring freight-train, which had last carried horses.

Sashka, the more impatient of the twins, had guzzled enough for two and stuffed himself with vegetables, unripe seeds, green watermelons, aubergines and more besides. He had been the first to succumb to stomach-trouble, and had followed the others, at least once an hour, to the open platform at the end of the carriage. He had managed to position himself over the creaking steel plates of the communicating walkway so that everything poured out of him, fountain-like, through a gap between the plates. After a while there was nothing left to pour out; the green had all passed, the yellow and even some black. Then followed mucus, in which were clots of blood.

Towards evening, the superintendent was accompanied on his rounds by a man and a woman in white coats, who examined all the children, including Sashka. They prodded his stomach and looked at his tongue.

Pale and silent, Sashka lay on a makeshift bed of straw.

Kolka tried to rouse him a little by telling him about the station, which in these parts was called a *stanitsa*, the Cossack word for a village, and about a yellow fruit called a mirabelle, growing in the local orchards on trees which hung right out into the street, so that you could simply pick them and eat your fill. There was another fruit, also to be had free, which grew along the railway embankment: they were called sloes. These, too, fell victim to the horde; in fact, the embankment was so thick with the pips of these and other fruit that you could hardly see the ground. The kids who were well enough to walk would put these pips on the rails and crack them with stones, making the whole station echo to the sound of them being smashed open.

'I can hear it,' Sashka tried to say, just managing to smile with

44

bloodless lips. It was as if everything had been squeezed out of him; Kolka could only stare at his brother in perplexity.

But he kept silent about one thing that he had seen at this station – some strange boxcars on a distant siding beyond the water-tower. He had come across them by chance while picking sloes on the embankment, and had heard someone calling to him from the little barred window in a boxcar on the track above him. Looking up, he saw a pair of eyes: at first nothing but two eyes, either of a girl or a boy – bright black eyes, then a mouth, a tongue and lips. The mouth was straining towards the bars and uttered only one strange sound: 'Khi.' Puzzled, Kolka showed the hard, bluish berries on his open palm. 'This?' It was obvious what he was being asked for, but there was nothing else to be had except these sloes.

'Khi! Khi!' cried the voice, and suddenly the wooden interior of the boxcar became alive. Children's hands were thrust between the bars, other eyes and other mouths appeared, which changed as though the children inside were pushing each other out of the way to get at the window; at the same time a strange, rising burble of voices started up, like the rumbling inside an elephant's stomach.

Kolka started back in amazement and almost fell over. At that moment an armed soldier appeared from nowhere. He banged, though not hard, on the wooden side of the boxcar with his fist; the sound of voices stopped at once, to be followed by a deathly silence. The hands vanished too, leaving only eyes full of fear, all of which were now fixed on the soldier.

Throwing back his head, he shook his fist towards the little barred opening and shouted what was obviously a familiar order: 'Stop that noise, you little heathens! Do as you're told! Be quiet in there!'

He strode over to the bewildered Kolka, neatly turned him round to face the station as though he knew where he had come from, and prodded him in the back.

'Go on, clear off out of it! This isn't a circus – nothing for you to see here!'

Kolka flew back to the station, clutching his pathetic fistful of sloes. If Sashka hadn't been so sick he would have told him his news then and there, and asked him what 'heathens' were . . . Were they delinquents, perhaps, or orphans – or crooks, or villains? He knew these words, but 'heathens' was something new, which needed thinking about. But Sashka was in a bad way; by the look of him, he might even be dying.

The woman in the white coat brought some more pills and some muck in a bottle. Out of pity for his brother Kolka devoured half

45

the pills himself (they might have been poisonous) and drank the nasty liquid. As he understood it, Sashka could not survive on these medicines and nothing else. He even held the thermometer in his own mouth on Sashka's behalf, for which he was well and truly cuffed. The sharp-eyed lady doctor in white separated the two brothers and ordered Kolka to go and stay in another boxcar for a while.

Kolka resisted and would not go; he even tried howling a bit, but to no avail: the doctor was adamant. Almost using force, backed up by the man in white, she expelled Kolka and ordered him not to come near Sashka, threatening that if he didn't do as he was told he would be removed from the train altogether.

After some thought, Kolka crawled under the boxcar and from there tried to talk to his brother through the floor. When the doctors weren't there, Sashka replied in a muffled voice; by putting his ear to the floorboards, he could just make out what Kolka was saying. Next, Kolka threw a heap of grass and weeds between the rails, made himself a couch there, and slept under the spot where Sashka was lying. So that his brother should know he was always with him, Kolka would bang on the underside of the boxcar with a pebble and Sashka would knock in reply.

Thus two days passed.

Their own train, standing nearby, was being disinfected. It was scrubbed, swabbed out and washed until it stank so much of bleach and carbolic that the first ones who tried to move back into the train found that they couldn't breathe and their eyes watered; so the children had to wait another twenty-four hours while the carriages were ventilated.

During that last day, Kolka made his way back to the strange freight train. Taking the trouble to approach it by a roundabout route through the bushes, he only did so out of a nasty habit typical of all orphanage jackals: to circle around something, just as wasps will always circle a place from which they are being chased away. Children know there are always likely to be some pickings there – at least something to see, if not to eat. Since we are usually charged money for a look at practically anything, for orphanage kids a sharp little eye is as good as an extra food ration.

But strain his ears as he might, Kolka could discover nothing as he sat among the sloe-bushes on the embankment. He saw a soldier – not the one who had sent him packing, but another, taller and beefier – who was patrolling the train and trying to avoid the blazing heat by staying in the narrow shadow cast by the boxcars.

In their short lifetime Kolka and Sashka had seen any number of trains of different sorts passing through Tomilino: hospital trains with red crosses on their sides; military transports loaded with tanks covered by tarpaulins; trainloads of refugees, of labour battalions, even of convicts . . . One day they had seen captured fascists being transported, with their generals conveyed separately in posh first-class carriages . . . They had later been marched in a long column through Moscow. But *this* train, Kolka could swear, carried neither refugees nor fascist prisoners-of-war. It was more like their own orphans' train; these children, too, were obviously not being given enough to eat. Orphanage jackals always managed to scrounge some food – a skill they had been learning almost since infancy – but how could you get anything if you were locked in, as these kids were? Had they robbed the director? Had they all ganged up and taken the bread-room by storm?

While Kolka was pondering these things, the engine whistled and the train started to move. The soldier took a last look along the boxcars, jumped up on the step – and immediately the sound of voices broke out again. This time it came not just from one car but from all of them: a screaming, shouting and weeping . . .

The train went off in the direction from which the orphans' train had come, but the strange thing was that the noises and the sound of voices from the boxcars hovered in the air around the station for a long time, until at last they faded away in the warm twilight. That, of course, was simply Kolka's imagination, because no one, apart from him, it seemed, heard those cries and that weeping. The grizzled driver of their engine was unconcernedly walking up and down the train, tapping the wheels with a hammer; the orphans were crowding around the carriages; and the people on the station platform were calmly going about their business, while loudspeakers boomed out the music of a brass band playing a cheerful, patriotic march: 'Oh, so boundless is my native country . . .'

Then we, too, set off – towards the unknown Caucasus.

Across the River Kuban, which was in spate and had to be crossed at a snail's pace over a rickety, swaying temporary bridge, only recently built by the army engineers, we were first met by the sight of flooded orchards and then by distant mountains gleaming on the horizon. We were as excited as though we had made the great discovery of our lives. 'The mountains! Look, those are mountains! Real mountains!'

They seemed to float like small, sparse clouds on the very edge of the sky, and it was to take us several more days to reach them. Their glittering peaks took your breath away, and at that moment it really seemed as if our orphanage dreams of plenty, of full stomachs and of a wonderful war-free life were bound to come true.

That strange encounter at Kuban station with the train of boxcars, from which children of our own age had stretched out their hands with the cry of 'Khi! Khi!' was forgotten and erased from our memories. Our two trains had for a while stood side by side, like twin brothers, without recognizing each other, and had then parted for ever; and it meant nothing to us that they were going northward while we were headed south.

Yet we were bound together by a single fate.

Seven

They were woken up early in the morning, as the message was brought along the carriages: 'We're getting out here, and don't forget your belongings – if you've got any!'

The stocky little conductor yelled out the reminder about luggage, and winked at the twins as he went by. 'Here we are at the Caucasus, my young villains – you can get out now and try it to see if it's good to eat!'

And he trotted on to the end of the carriage, his rolled-up red and green flags sticking out of the top of his boot.

The Kuzmin Twins looked at each other and then out of the window.

The train had pulled up near a range of low, bare mountain foothills, at a place where there was no station, not even a platform; it had all been burnt down in the recent fighting. Its name – 'Caucasian Waters' – was written in charcoal on a piece of plywood that had been nailed, crooked, to a telephone pole. To the right of the railway line and all the way to the horizon stretched a broad valley carpeted with morning mist; it was divided into square green fields with rows of trees lining roads, invisible at that distance, while dotted here and there among the greenery were little white houses and, no doubt, whole villages.

In the barely discernible distance at the furthest edge of the valley was a line of brownish hills, spotted with clumps of woodland, like bruises on sunburnt skin; beyond them, as though rising straight out of the air, glittered the icy peaks of the main Caucasus range. Earlier, at a halt on the way, Ilya the conductor had used his flags to point out to the Kuzmin Twins the names of the various mountains: which one was Kazbek, and which one was Elbruz with its two summits rising out of a single torso – in a word, twins.

They immediately recalled the picture on the cigarette packet held by the handsome colonel, with its zigzag of jagged peaks which

49

looked nothing like these mountains. The children had already caught sight of them from the railway during their journey, seeing them as though through gauze – real mountains, but not quite real enough yet for them to feel their physical presence. Now, on this clear morning, they could make out all the folds, gullies and ravines on the grey slopes, as well as the glaciers that ran down the mountainsides in crooked white lines. The mountains seemed near – nearer even than the brown, wooded hills over which they towered; but from here it was also obvious that those hills beyond the valley were far away – *very* far away – and that the peaks which floated above them in the heavens were even further still.

To the left of the railway line and the non-existent station, a cluster of steep bare hillocks, burnt yellow by the sun, rose straight up from the trackside. On the top of one of them stood a white, pillared, classical rotunda, which by some improbable chance had survived the war intact.

The children were drawn up in ranks of five and marched off towards the rotunda; it was obvious at once that they had no intention of keeping in formation but instead walked in clumps, grouped according to the orphanages from which they had come, making the column look like a straggle of fleeing refugees. While the children in front were already following the superintendent into a wide gorge between two hills, those at the back were still milling about near the train, unable to move away from it.

When at last they had all walked the length of a narrow but well-trodden path between several of the low, hump-backed hills, the children found themselves on a large piece of flat ground which had been hidden from the station by the intervening hills. Here were the white ruins of what had once been a sanatorium, and among the bricks and rubble strewn all over the ground they could see several square concrete pits full of steaming water, bubbling and giving off a smell of rotten eggs.

'Phew, what a stink!' said someone, and the children started repeating this and laughing loudly, the joke helping to throw off the tension of the first anxious minutes in an unfamiliar part of the world.

Pyotr Anisimovich ran panting up and down the column, waving his briefcase and telling them to stop.

They had stopped anyway, not knowing where to go next; this, it seemed, was their destination.

Pointing to the pits, Pyotr Anisimovich said, 'Sulphur water! Can't you smell it? Well, now, if anyone would like to have a wash . . . it's very good for you . . .'

The children said nothing. The stragglers at the back were still making a noise and, not having heard his announcement, they pushed against the ones in front and asked, 'Is this where we're going to live? Have we arrived?'

'You should . . . you must get into the water . . . Undress and wash off all the dirt from your journey,' the superintendent explained in a slightly louder voice and glanced somewhat uncertainly towards the pits. It was obvious that he wasn't quite sure how to wash oneself in them either.

'Get in yourself!' came the loud shout from somewhere in the crowd. 'Think we're fools? Have they brought us here to make soup out of us, or what?'

'Soup?' Pyotr Anisimovich was perplexed. 'Why soup?' He looked at the children's faces as though seeking for someone to support him, but the expressions only ranged from mockery and curiosity to mistrust or fear.

'I simply don't understand it!' he said, mopping his forehead. 'Why soup?'

'Because we'll be boiled like lobsters!' said one boy quite openly. 'That water's boiling! Look at the bubbles!'

'Aha,' muttered the superintendent with a sigh. 'Sulphur water . . . you won't have seen it before . . . Understandable, I suppose . . .'

He looked at the pits and, after a moment's indecision, walked over to the nearest of them. Without looking back at the children, as if he had forgotten about them, he began slowly to undress. He took off his jacket, folded it neatly in two with the lining outward and then, treating it like something very precious, he placed his briefcase underneath the jacket. He took off his trousers, shirt and vest and, for some reason, last of all his socks and shoes.

Wearing only his long, dark brown, knee-length rayon underpants, puffing and grunting, he went up to the edge of the pit. He put first a toe and then his hand into the water, but – like the tsar in the fairy tale of 'The Little Humpbacked Horse' standing in front of the seething cauldron in which he would shortly be boiled alive! – he couldn't bring himself to jump in.

Suddenly, with a cry, Pyotr Anisimovich slithered over the edge and into the water, sending showers of spray over the stones around the edge of the pit.

A surge of laughter ran through the crowd that had gathered

51

round to watch this circus-act, laughter which grew into shouts, guffaws and jokes.

Mimicking the superintendent's voice, someone shouted, 'I simply don't understand it!'

'Easy – we'll soon have meat broth!'

'Nice and fatty, too!'

'Superintendent soup!'

'Perhaps we should jump in and save him – there's lots of us, but only one superintendent!'

'Throw him his briefcase! He'll drown without it!'

Meanwhile Pyotr Anisimovich was splashing about and paying no attention to the children and their cheeky remarks. Snorting and scratching under his armpits, he ducked his head and came up spraying water out of his mouth like a fountain, giving a convincing impression of how much he was enjoying floundering about in the smelly water.

Gradually the jokes tailed off. Mistrust gave way to curiosity. The boldest of the children approached the pits giggling, they tested the water, but instantly jumped back. The most inquistive boy of all, who was gaping at the water from the very edge, was pushed in fully dressed. Without bothering to climb out, he began swimming around to a chorus of laughter and shouts of encouragement from the crowd.

At once several children undressed and jumped in, with much ooh-ing and aah-ing as though they were afraid of the sulphurous water, but clearly they weren't afraid of it at all, because they immediately started noisily splashing each other and spitting out the water . . . This encouraged the rest, who realized they were not going to be boiled into soup but that this was a bath and, what's more, great fun.

With a roar and shouts of 'Hurrah!' they rushed to jump into the other pits, which soon proved to be inadequate to take them all; this led to much brawling and throwing water.

Only the little girls stayed huddled to one side, watching the hubbub with a mixture of fright and curiosity. But soon Regina Petrovna appeared and led the girls off through the ruins to a large, steaming swimming-pool in a clearing among some trees, which the others had somehow overlooked. She quickly undressed two sturdy, solemn little boys aged three and four and put them, one after the other, into the pool. Squealing, as was their habit, the little girls followed them into the water.

It must have looked strange to anyone coming upon the scene: five hundred children – it was now more obvious that they *were* children, very ordinary children – were going mad among the ruins, diving into their own and other pools, splashing the warm water all over the surrounding rubble. Only Pyotr Anisimovich, having dressed again and combed back his thinning grey hair, was sitting to one side, briefcase clutched to his knees as he kept an anxious eye on his noisy horde.

Alongside him, the elderly, grizzled, crew-cut engine-driver was squatting on his haunches and smoking a hand-rolled cigarette. It was he who had told the superintendent about these unusual baths; obviously this was not his first time in these parts.

They tried, with difficulty, to persuade the young bathers to get out of the pools, in order to line them up in a column again. Some were already dressed, but others insisted on staying in the water and the effort needed to haul them out bodily was too great.

Kolka and Sashka had not wanted to go in at first, because the water smelled so horrible and made them feel sick; but when they did venture into the water they liked it, and they managed to find a small but convenient pool lined with sky-blue tiles. The brothers scrubbed each other and ducked together, wanting to see what they looked like under water, but there was nothing to hold on to, so they floated straight up to the surface again. They blew bubbles in the water, made waves, splashed some boys from a nearby pool who tried to get into theirs, and then climbed out and got dressed. They were in plenty of time for the departure because Sashka, weakened by his recent illness, could not stay in the water for long.

In wet clothes, like many of the others, the brothers stood in the middle of the column and looked up at the mountains that gleamed in the far distance. Clearly visible from that point, the mountains invited one to stare at them to one's heart's content, never tiring of the sight.

Ignoring the children still larking about in the pools, Pyotr Anisimovich called out all the names and checked them against his list. It transpired that seven orphans had been lost on the journey: some had missed the train and others, inevitably, had run away.

They took the same path back to the railway, past the station (it was now obvious why the place was called 'Caucasian Waters', although no doubt it should have been called 'Rotten-Egg Waters') and down into the valley.

As the column progressed, stretched out along the broad and dusty road between green fields, the Kuzmin Twins tried to remember which crops were growing in the fields . . . just in case; although they were not sure whether the knowledge would ever be of use, because no one knew where or how far they were going.

After a short rest, during which they all rushed off to scrounge whatever they could find (although less keenly than before, having eaten their fill on the last stage of the journey), they went on until a cluster of white cottages appeared among the greenery. They trudged along the white, dusty and strangely deserted street running through the middle of a *stanitsa* called Beriozovskaya – Birch Hamlet – although no birches grew there. Beyond the *stanitsa* was a field full of stone posts sticking out of the ground; taller than the twins, they were like the obstacles which had been put up around Moscow against the German tanks. Obviously the people here must have had to defend themselves too, the brothers deduced – look how many of these stones had been rammed into the ground. But soon their attention was drawn to the road ahead, which to all appearances was coming to an end.

Two miles beyond the village they stopped. At the very foot of the green hills, three buildings could be seen through some trees: one was a two-storeyed white house, the others were single-storeyed but longer, looking like army barracks.

Beside a green thorn-hedge at the entrance, a notice was fixed to a post, reading: 'SILKOZTEKNIUKOM'. This strange word had been crossed out with chalk, and beneath it someone had hastily scrawled, 'For settlers from Moscow Province: 500 Orphans'.

Pyotr Anisimovich looked back anxiously along his straggling column. Clutching his briefcase to his chest, he read the inscription on the notice, shook his head and turned round to the children. 'Well, here we are,' he said, wiping the sweat from his forehead. 'This is where we're going to live. There'll be discipline and all that, as you know ... No silly tricks, now – and don't ever stray far from here, because there'll be no one to come and look for you ... and that'll be the end of you.'

At that moment a rolling clap of thunder came from somewhere beyond the hills. The children looked up, but there were no clouds anywhere in sight. Pyotr Anisimovich also looked up and seemed about to say his usual 'I don't understand what's happening', but instead he announced, 'The army engineers are blowing up land-mines ... left behind by the Germans. Nothing to worry about.' Again he wiped away the sweat with the back of his hand. 'So now, you'll be shown where to find your dormitories, the dining-hall, the toilets and so on ... You're free to look around.'

54

This, it seemed, was the speech of welcome made to mark their arrival.

A bewildered little man, who until then had been in charge of a wholesale grocery warehouse, Pyotr Anisimovich knew no other way of talking. Indeed, he had nothing else to say; he was playing this role for the first time in his life. He had been told to bring the children here, and he had brought them, just as in the past he had delivered potatoes or vegetable oil to factory canteens, soap to the washrooms. That was his strong suit; he was known in his district as a good, efficient manager.

His briefcase, which had once been full of invoices, now contained the children's documents. He still had to examine these, sort them out and make sense of them – provided, of course, he could find the time for it.

As he said 'You're free to look around', Pyotr Anisimovich waved towards the buildings, assuming that the children, having arrived, would at once rush off, each one to lay claim to his iron bedstead. But he was wrong. The column stayed, motionless, where it had stopped. All of them just stood and looked at the buildings, waiting for something.

The superintendent had already noticed that in various circumstances this unpredictable, unmanageable mass was apt to behave in odd, unforeseen ways. And he had also noticed that all five hundred of them, without prior collusion, would do the same thing. At this moment the crowd reminded him of a large, prickly, silent hedgehog. Not a joke, not a laugh, not the slightest sound was to be heard from it.

The vague sense of unease, which had arisen during the long walk from the station, had not been dissipated on their arrival, but had grown even stronger. Those distant, incessant explosions were unsettling the children, too, reminding them of something which it was high time to forget. They had come to this settlement to enjoy a peaceful life, and this blessed, mountainous land should have greeted them with peace: with the golden summer sun; with an abundance of fruit on the trees; with the gentle song of the birds at dawn.

I remember that feeling of anxiety that grew in us on the way from the station to this place in the wooded foothills.

We had grown used to the train, the carriages and the railway; it had become our element. We felt relatively secure in those stations, in those markets among peasant traders and among refugees on the noisy platforms and the trains. All Russia was on the move, all Russia

55

was going somewhere, and we were a part of that human torrent, flesh of its flesh; we were its children.

Now we were being led along a hard, pot-holed road, beside which bloomed flowers that no one picked; where apple trees were ripening; where rows of tall, blackening sunflowers stood, their petals and seeds half shed. And where there was not a single human being, not one . . .

For the whole of our long trek, lasting several hours, we had not seen a cart, a car or a chance passer-by. The whole place was empty. The crops in the fields were ripening. Someone must have sown them, someone must have hoed and weeded them. But who . . . ?

We had passed through a village on our way, where people should have been living . . . yet why had this beautiful countryside greeted us with nothing but dumb, blank silence? Even the buildings of the technical college, with its hastily altered makeshift noticeboard that actually referred to us and our orphaned state, had been deserted, devoid of human life.

And we ourselves seemed like a flock of little animals, cast into a desert as part of some inconceivable zoological experiment: 'Five Hundred Orphans.' This was the official description of our breed . . .

Another explosion reverberated in the mountains behind us, and a little girl in the very middle of the column – we could all hear her – cried, 'I want to go home,' and burst into tears. Everyone shuffled, turned round and listened as the grown-ups tried to comfort her, saying, 'Now, now, what's the matter? There's nothing to be frightened of! Look – there's our new home. See? Everything here is ours from now on – the houses, the river and the mountains . . . We've come to live here!'

Once again, for the umpteenth time, there came a bang and a rumble from the mountains. We stood on the threshold of a new life, but we were in no hurry to cross it and enter. I think we all felt the same sense of unhappiness. Muddled and fleeting as our thoughts were, none of them were of 'coming home' to a place where everything was to be ours . . . Here, the only things that we could call ours were ourselves – ourselves and our legs, ever ready to run away should anything happen – and our souls, which, so we were always being told, didn't exist . . .

Why at that moment, as I distinctly remember (and I can't have been alone in this), did I feel so desperately heartsick? Perhaps from an awful premonition that no happiness awaited us in this new place. But then we didn't even know what happiness was: we simply wanted to live.

Eight

The supplies that had been provided for the journey were dumped in the courtyard, which was enclosed on three sides by the buildings and on the fourth side by a prickly thorn-hedge. These provisions amounted to a few crates of tinned food, some of which bore foreign labels; a carboy of rancid vegetable oil from a food distribution centre, which the superintendent himself had managed to secure; some strange gift packages, also with foreign labels, and a heap of old clothes.

Fortunately the two-storeyed building was already furnished with iron bedsteads and mattresses, and where there were not enough of these to go round the kids simply laid their bedding on the floor.

The little girls, fewer in number, were installed on the ground floor, the boys on the first floor, while the older ones – the thirteen- and fourteen-year-olds – were put in a wing of one of the single-storey buildings; its other wing was allocated to the kitchen and the dining-hall. The superintendent and the teachers occupied the other single-storey building, which also contained the store-room and offices.

These arrangements, however, only represented a certain semblance of order, which it took several weeks to achieve. Everything else was organized spontaneously – that is to say, it wasn't organized at all. The superintendent and three teachers comprised the colony's entire staff. No one knew anyone else, and for some time they had no opportunity to take stock of this five-hundred-strong mob that had been flung together by a caprice of fate.

There was no cook, and in any case there was nothing much to cook. The handsome American tins turned out to contain a green mush that could have been nettle soup. In the gift parcels, which were handed out to the children without being checked, were the following: a letter from the British Trades Union Council; a copy of *British Ally*, a propaganda newspaper in Russian; several packets of cigarettes; condoms; books of flat, cardboard matches; and some advertisements showing girls in highly indecent poses.

Before Pyotr Anisimovich had realized that these parcels were not meant for distribution to children, half of the orphans were smoking cigarettes or blowing up the condoms and throwing them in the air . . . The pin-up girls were duly pinned up, after someone had first written on them in pencil the names of various parts of their anatomy. *British Ally* was used as lavatory paper, and since the one and only toilet had been so fouled as to be useless from the first day, people then relieved themselves by the hedge behind the back wall of the building, and the ground became littered with pieces of the unusually strong, tough paper of our allies' newspaper. In this way it was probably more useful than anything else.

By cutting each of them in half, the tins that had held nettle soup were used for plates or bowls. The kids somehow acquired their own spoons, each person keeping his own. Many had home-made ones carved out of a piece of wood, even though at first there was nothing to eat with them. The slops that were cooked on a trivet in the makeshift, outdoor kitchen lacked any solids and were called 'scrapings': made from cornflour, water and thin cooking oil, they could be drunk straight out of an ex-soup tin. When the cornflour soon ran out, the colony was reduced to hunting for its food supplies – no novelty, of course, to the majority of the orphans, and certainly not to the Kuzmin Twins.

Having installed themselves quite comfortably in a corner of the dormitory behind the stove (it was not burning yet, but winter would come before too long, and in this the Kuzmins showed more foresight than the others), the brothers drew up an inventory of their negotiable assets.

In the secret cache which they had constructed by the banks of the nearby Sunzhi, a shallow stream of reddish-brown water, they stored some British book-matches from the gift parcels; two condoms; a beautiful transparent plastic bag; the keys to their railway carriage, pinched from the conductor's pocket while he was pointing out the names of the mountains to the twins; the thirty-rouble note, now beginning to come apart at the folds from frequent use; and a few potatoes, also filched from the simple-minded conductor.

Compared with their resources at Tomilino, they now had much more, and more is always better. The brothers had enlarged their den – made from what had once been an animal's lair – so that they could use it to stash away anything else that might turn up.

And something did turn up, although not at once.

The next thing the Kuzmin Twins did in their new life was to make a study of the colony's premises, by thoroughly exploring the grounds, all the buildings, the attics and every last nook and cranny. Out of habit they began with the bread-room, which was empty at the time. Apart from the scales and weights – which could be seen through a window – there was nothing in the room. The padlock on the door, however, was feeble and there were no iron bars on the windows.

All this the Kuzmin Twins noted as being a certain improvement on Tomilino. It amused them that the dining-hall and kitchen had carelessly been located alongside the boys' dormitory. When the need arose they would find a way of getting into the kitchen from that completely unguarded direction, although there really was no proper kitchen in the sense that the brothers understood. The slops on which they were fed were cooked by the girls out of doors, on a trivet placed over an open fire, which the twins regarded as not worth pinching.

If you wanted to, you could get into the dining-hall twice, once at each serving, especially since here, too, from the very first day the twins had managed to confuse and fool everybody by their identical looks. They would swap beds, clothes, spoons, bowls, and even their habits where that was possible, so that one day one of the other kids exclaimed in all sincerity, 'Hey, can even you two remember which one you are? Do you really know which of you is Sashka and which is Kolka?'

Without a moment's hesitation they said they didn't remember, which baffled the others even more. The dormitory burst into such roars of laughter that it even drowned out the noise of those distant explosions in the mountains, but the ones who were really laughing were the brothers themselves. It was the beginning of a general wave of fooling around, in which the Kuzmin Twins were absolutely in their element.

They carried out a reconnaissance of the superintendent's office and, in particular, of the adjoining store-room.

So far Pyotyr Anisimovich had not had time to feather his own nest, which put him at an advantage in comparison with the rogue who had been in charge of Tomilino, whom the inmates had tried to rob more than once, despite the obstacles to this in the form of the director's ferocious dogs. In this store-room, by contrast, when they managed to poke their noses into it, the only thing to be seen, apart from a few sacks of second-hand clothes, was the carboy of

59

low-grade vegetable oil – though the brothers even took note of that, especially since both the lock and the bolt were so primitive that you could open the door using no more than your fingers.

While loitering beside the store-room door, they met Regina Petrovna, who lived just around the corner. She occupied a tiny little room at the end of the building, in which were two of the same iron bedsteads used by the children and a bedside locker; but she had already hung a pretty little curtain at the window, the beds were covered with two unusually nice flowered counterpanes, there was a scrap of carpet just inside the door and a small wooden-framed mirror hanging on the wall.

When the teacher invited the Kuzmin Twins into her little home, they found all this unbelievably elegant and cosy, which they felt was just as it should be.

They stood shyly in the doorway, not daring to disturb the neat interior with their dirty shoes, indeed with their presence, so that their hostess almost had to drag them into the room by force and invite them to sit down on one of the beds. So far she had not acquired any chairs.

Explaining that her two little boys were playing in the courtyard, which, thank God, was not too crowded or dirty, Regina Petrovna spread a clean napkin on the top of the locker, and placed on it two rusks in a saucer. She then brought in a jug of tea from the outdoor cooking-fire, poured out three glasses and put in each a couple of grains of saccharine from a little white paper box, exactly like the one from which Sashka had been given his pills at Kuban station.

The brothers gulped their sweet tea and nibbled sparingly at their rusks, which melted in the mouth and only aggravated their already acute hunger.

Their hostess, after twisting her thick black hair into a bun, stood smoking by the window – a single, unbarred pane of thin glass which could have been smashed easily by anyone wanting to break into the room; Kolka's experienced eye noted this at once.

'Well, I suppose you've been baffling everybody because you look so exactly alike, have you?' Regina Petrovna asked as she looked at the brothers. 'I was sorting out all the papers just now, and although my job is to look after the little girls', I also happened to deal with yours . . . There's only one character report for the two of you. It says in it that not only your looks but your habits, preferences and everything else about you are identical. That's what it says, meaning that it's not worth writing two reports on you because the Kuzmins are really a single person in two individuals.'

Regina Petrovna was going to add something else, but changed her mind.

'All right, we'll talk about that later,' she said, after a slight hesitation. 'By the way, which of you *is* which? Who is who?'

With a sigh, Kolka looked at the remains of his rusk and said, 'Sashka here eats faster, because he hasn't much patience. I'm more patient. But he's cleverer than me, 'cos he's got a better brain. I'm the practical one.'

'I see. You *are* different . . . I suspected they didn't really know you. So you've completely fooled them. By the way . . .' Regina Petrovna remembered something and blew a stream of smoke towards the window. She smoked with such obvious enjoyment, pursing her lips into a little trumpet, that the twins also felt a desire to start smoking. 'It says in your report that you were once caught by the police . . . What for, if it's not a secret?'

Embarrassed, Kolka looked at Sashka, but Sashka was silent, nibbling the last of his rusk, so Kolka said, 'Well . . . we pinched a pickled cucumber from a woman in the market.'

'A cucumber? One cucumber?'

'No, not one – two. I took one and Sashka took the other. So that we'd have more to eat.'

His rusk finished, Sashka added, 'No, that wasn't the point. We were careless. One of us was keeping watch, that's to say if anything happened it was his job to shout "cave", while the other one pinched a cucumber out of the barrel. Then the one who was keeping "cave" decided to grab a cucumber too, and that was when they caught us . . .'

Regina Petrovna didn't laugh but gazed thoughtfully through the window. She finished her cigarette, threw out the stub and turned round to the twins.

'You must put up with the shortage of food. My two little fellows put up with it, and all the little girls in my group are just as hungry as you are. The superintendent is planning to go into the nearest town and he may bring back some food with him. In the meantime . . . come and see me, OK? If you do, I can probably find something to give you. I've still got a week's supply of saccharine, so at least we can drink some tea.'

Promising to come and see her, the brothers stood up to go, and although they didn't look at each other, each knew they were both thinking the same thought: they would not come and see this remarkably kind and beautiful woman very often, for the very reason that she was hungry too. But if they ever managed to scrounge some nice morsel, then they would come, just so that they could regally present it to her as a gift. What's more, they felt they would conduct their larcenous operations even better than before, just because Regina Petrovna was no doubt incapable of such things herself. With her gentle fingers, how could she break open a padlock? And she and her two little boys – Marat and Zhores – needed to eat too.

All this passed through their heads as they said goodbye to her. Kolka had managed to save a piece of his rusk and put it in his pocket. Later, he would give it to Sashka.

Nine

After they had investigated the buildings, the store-rooms, dormitories and attics (where they found piles of mattresses in a room behind a loosely boarded-up door); having explored every inch of the thorn-hedge, in which they discovered two concealed holes leading to the outside, the brothers turned their keen attention to the stream, to the nearby gardens and orchards and, of course, to the village of Beriozovskaya, which was three kilometres from the orphans' colony.

What they had taken for anti-tank obstacles turned out to be an old cemetery, but not at all a frightening place, as it had no crosses and no fresh graves. The grey granite headstones bore inscriptions in an unknown language, while carved on some of them were pairs of cartridge bandoliers, like the ones the twins had seen in a film called *The Swineherd and the Shepherd*, where they had been worn by a handsome shepherd who grazed a herd of sheep and sang songs at the top of his voice. As they touched the headstones and the carved bandoliers, both of them had the same thought – that, unlike their favourite film (they had seen it at least ten times), in this mountainous country there was no one to sing cheerful songs or to graze sheep.

For several days the Kuzmins reconnoitred the village and came to the conclusion that there were people living there, but somehow living in hiding, in fear and uncertainty, because they never came out of doors in the cool of the evening, never sat gossiping on the low earth walls that surrounded each plot, as people did in other parts of the country. No lights burned in the cottages at night. No one ever strolled down the street, no one was seen driving cattle, no one ever sang songs. Heaven knows how they managed to live like that, but they did, and that was what mattered.

On their first visit, the brothers went through some gardens to a field, where they found potatoes growing. They dug up a trial plant and found potatoes fully grown: they would have to come back late one evening. Creeping noiselessly up to a hay-loft, they waited and listened, only to hear a cough – a deep, man's cough – and a murmur of voices. At this they turned back; an encounter with a villager boded no good. In the market at Tomilino peasants had beaten intruders viciously, sometimes to death. People who lived in towns beat you too, but they showed more mercy.

Twice they went out in the dark after lights-out to pay calls; they dug up potatoes, filled their pockets and shirt fronts with them and crept back furtively along the village street. Once again they were puzzled at the silence, broken only by occasional muffled voices from behind closed shutters; no dogs barked, no chickens clucked, no pigs squealed as they had at Tomilino, no one sang to a battered accordion . . .

In a word, nothing.

In the past the Tomilino kids, including the twins, had occasionally watched the antics of a wall-eyed accordion-player who sold ice-cream on the station platform. He would paw any girl who came near enough, quite unembarrassed by the cluster of boys watching him, and sometimes he would sit a girl on his knees and pull up her skirt. Leering drunkenly, rolling his one eye and laughing, he would say, 'Fancy a bit of the other, eh?' The boys felt too embarrassed to reply. The man would then pull open the bellows of his battered accordion and yell bawdy songs for the whole street to hear.

In Moscow Province there was never any doubt that the houses and streets were full of life. Life went on here, too – but, as it were, furtively, surreptitiously. This was so unusual that it had the effect of making the brothers timid: how could they approach a house or sneak into a garden if they didn't know exactly who the owners were or when they might be at home?

But chance came to their aid.

One day, wandering around the village, they came across a man gathering kindling-wood. The twins were about to slip past him when they recognized him as the conductor from their train. With his moustache and short legs, but now out of uniform and wearing only a plain shirt and trousers, he suddenly seemed like any youngish man – almost like that wall-eyed accordionist, in fact.

The conductor looked at the boys and growled. No doubt he remembered how the twins had just escaped the clutches of a market-woman at Voronezh, and how he had pointed out to them Mount Kazbek and the twin peaks of Mount Elbruz. Ha! So they must have been the ones who . . . had pinched his keys, though they had probably taken them more from habit than for any good reason; the keys

64

were bright and they jangled, almost asking to be nicked. But why they did it, God alone knew – the keys can have been of no use to them.

'Coming to see me?' the conductor asked briskly, with a grin.

'We're just going for a walk,' said Kolka. Sashka nodded.

'Ye-es, too many of you lot have been going for walks around here,' said the conductor. 'And half my potatoes have gone for a walk, too! Right – you can give me a hand and carry some of this brushwood.'

'We didn't take your potatoes,' said Kolka firmly.

'Oh, you didn't, eh?' The conductor was not impressed. 'You only pinch keys. Or didn't you take them either?' And he repeated his order to carry some of the brushwood. 'OK, off we go.'

The brushwood was tied up in huge bundles, and they were given one each. They carried them as far as the road, loaded them on to a wooden handcart with rusty wheels and pushed it as far as the village. There they unloaded it at the very first house, a whitewashed cottage surrounded by a fence, with a kitchen garden at the back. The conductor went indoors, leaving the boys to wait in the yard.

The same thought came to both twins at once: the other kids had chosen this garden to scrump potatoes because it was the first house and nearest to the colony. It's always safer to pinch stuff from the edge of a village rather than from somewhere in the middle of it.

Standing there, they inspected the little yard with interest. Along the inner side of the high, solid fence ran a long, lean-to shelter; under its roof were sorted maize-stalks, brushwood, and a pile of scrap metal, among which was a copper jug with a narrow neck, green with age. The jug was an object worth remembering, although neither of them could think of a use for it at the moment. The floor of the yard was also something the brothers had never seen before: it was hard, smooth and surfaced with a layer of yellow clay. A tattered goatskin was lying on the ground in front of the door into the house.

The owner stuck his shaggy head through the doorway and shouted, 'Come on in, what're you standing there for?'

Cautiously, one behind the other, so that they could make a quick getaway if necessary, the two brothers passed through the dark, narrow little porch in which stood several brass and earthenware pitchers, and crossed the threshold into the living-room, its walls and ceiling whitewashed in the way that country people in Russia whitewash their stoves.

In the corner where an icon should have been, there hung a

65

portrait of comrade Kalinin, the Soviet president. A table without a cloth and two stools stood in the middle of the room, and in one corner was a low wooden bed; the floor in front of the bed was covered with a home-made rug, black, with a red zigzag pattern. Otherwise there was nothing else, except for a shelf by the door on which were a bachelor's few household goods: a cast-iron saucepan, two enamelled bowls, an army mess-tin and a battered mug. On the table was a soot-blackened half-gallon brass kettle.

'So this is my home,' said the conductor, grinning. 'As the saying goes – I live well but expect to live better!' And he added, nodding to the boys – who were sitting on the dirty grey blanket that covered the bed, shoulder to shoulder, not because there wasn't much room but so that they could signal to each other by an apparently chance movement – 'So we're neighbours now, are we? Fancy that!'

The brothers nodded.

'I've forgotten your names. What are you called?'

Kolka said, 'I'm Sashka.'

Sashka said, 'I'm Kolka.'

Not that there was any sense in their game of deception here; they were just playing the fool out of habit.

'Well, my name's Ilya. Call me that.'

The brothers nodded again.

'I remember you two running away from that stupid woman! I'm a runaway myself . . . And how I ran! If only they knew . . . But I'll tell you about that another time. I live alone here. Haven't got a woman. I boil my potatoes out of doors, where I've made my cooking-fire. Make tea on it, too. And I keep my eyes skinned to make sure *they* don't kick me out of here!'

Kolka immediately asked the question that had been intriguing them, 'Isn't this your house, then?'

The conductor gave a rather forced, mirthless laugh and his moustache twitched.

'Ha! Mine? . . . Even the fleas aren't ours! Know what this *stanitsa*'s called?'

'Beriozovskaya,' Sashka replied.

'Beriozovskaya! How can it be Beriozovskaya, when its real name is Dai Devel?' the conductor shouted. 'It's Beriozovskaya now, but it might as well be Osinovskaya or Sosnovskaya . . . It's really called Dai Devel. And that's a fact.'

And the conductor looked all around the room, having assumed that the boys understood what he was talking about. Kolka, however, wanted more precise information; that, after all, was why they had

66

come to Ilya's house. Purposely interrupting, he asked cheekily, 'Does that name really mean "devil"?'

'That's right – devil . . . Rotten place . . . there are devils all around here!'

Ilya the conductor shook his head, amazed at the boys' ignorance of the situation. He spoke in a whisper, leaning forward, as if they were not alone; in fact, they had already noticed his habit of constantly glancing nervously around.

'And why have *you* come here, eh? 'Cos you were bad boys?'

'We were just sent here,' said Kolka.

'Sent, were you? Where to?'

'To the Caucasus . . .'

'Ha! The Caucasus is a big place!' Ilya brushed the explanation aside scornfully. 'You were sent here to settle this land. Got it? That's why . . . Poor little tykes – you're supposed to populate this place. Like them: they've been uprooted and dumped here too . . .' And he pointed out of the window at a white house behind the green hedge across the street.

'And do they live here too?' Kolka asked.

'Yes, they do . . . like me . . . Nothing's their own, either. All other people's stuff.' And he jabbed a finger at the little carpet.

'Stolen, is it?' asked Sashka, suddenly putting two and two together.

'What do you think?' The conductor nodded, then added in something like a frenzy, 'If something isn't yours, then of course it's stolen. And you lot up at the technical school – aren't you living off stolen goods?'

Kolka nudged Sashka. Both were thinking the same thing: 'There's something fishy here. Either this Ilya's barmy, which he doesn't seem to be, or he suspects us of having nicked his potatoes. He's already guessed about the keys . . . But you aren't a thief until you're found out, so keep mum!'

'Why d'you think it was us? We don't go around pinching things . . .'

Ilya only grinned, then his expression changed and he looked at the brothers sternly.

'Listen. To survive in this place you've got to be nippy and stay one jump ahead. Now there's a store-room in your place where they keep winter clothing. It's not guarded, so the Lord above *wants* you to sneak in there, you might say. And I'll buy the stuff off you – OK?'

The brothers nodded, but uncertainly. Was this a trap? Was he saying this to tempt them, and then when they agreed he would pounce and catch them? They had learned a thing or two in their young lives, having been nabbed by the police more than once, and not just for pinching cucumbers.

Insistently, Ilya kept on. 'If you dig up my spuds, I'll wallop you. You can tell that to your mates. If you dig up other people's, though, I'm not bothered . . . But bring me some of those winter clothes, and I'll pay you. I'll pay you in potatoes . . . and more besides.'

'We'll see,' said Sashka, vaguely; he had already grasped the drift of this conversation and was no doubt already thinking up some dodge to get at that clothing. 'We'll be going now, Uncle Ilya.'

'Forget the "uncle". Just Ilya,' said the conductor. 'Come and see me again. Whenever I'm not working on the trains, I'll be here. As for all this being someone else's, listen . . .' He went out into the porch and stood listening for a long time. When the next explosion boomed out from the mountains, he said, 'Hear that?'

'They're blowing up old German mines,' Kolka said confidently. 'Ha! Mines my foot . . .' Ilya bared his teeth, but not in a smile. 'And we wretched settlers are so scared we daren't even burn lights . . . We're scared to death. What sort of a life is this?' He gave an angry kick at the old goatskin under his feet.

'Who are you scared of?' Kolka asked.

'The devils!' Ilya shouted, pushing them out of the house.

68

Ten

Muttering his usual 'I don't understand what's going on', the superintendent went off to Gudermes – the twins had no idea where or what this 'Gudermes' was – and almost at once the contents of the colony's buildings began to seep away. Mattresses, pillows and odds and ends of furniture were dragged off to the village, where the kids bartered them for potatoes and last year's corn-cobs.

They hauled a large flat stone into the dormitory (the idea was Sashka's), dropped it with a crash in the middle of the floor, and three of them set to work. One stripped the grains from the cobs on to the big stone; the second boy ground them with another, smaller stone; and the third scooped up the mush with his hand and tipped it into an empty can, in which they then boiled the crushed grain into maize porridge.

Cautiously but persistently they began robbing the fields, extending their zone of activity kilometre by kilometre outwards from the colony. Not that there was much to steal: the maize was not yet ripe, and potatoes only grew in the *stanitsa*, where the villagers had started to mount guard over their kitchen gardens.

One day a crowd of them, armed with sticks, chased the kids as far as the gates of the colony, and only by a miracle did the boys escape being beaten up. But the villagers threatened them loudly and furiously. 'Dig up any more of our potatoes, you thieving little villains, and we'll set fire to your buildings and chase you out!'

The orphans retorted, 'Clear off, you village bastards! We'll burn down *your* houses before you get the chance!'

'Beriozovskaya louse – keep away from our houses! Crawl under the bed – and eat shit instead!'

The men shouted, 'Just you watch it! You'll wake up one day and find your place on fire!'

'We'll help you!' the orphans yelled back in chorus. 'You can keep

69

your lousy Caucasus! The bugs'll get at you and eat you up! Or the mountain people will murder you with their daggers! Lousy kulaks!'
And they yelled at the tops of their voices:

> My good friend's a long sharp knife
> And my trusty dagger,
> So don't come near, you'll lose your life –
> That'll stop your swagger!

Of course the kids weren't serious about the 'dagger'; it was only part of the song. But the villagers shut up at once, went away without looking back and never returned again.

Every evening from now on there was a blaze of bonfires around the buildings of the technical college. Each orphanage inmate joined forces with a few others to light fires of dry brushwood and dead weeds and boil up a tinful of stew, mostly in empty soup tins.

The twins used the potatoes and a few corn-cobs which they had bartered for mattresses with Ilya the conductor. Shaking his head as he inspected the mattresses, Ilya had clambered up into the space under the roof, brought down a few yellow, rock-hard cobs of corn and reminded them in a serious, school-masterly tone, 'I need those winter clothes. There's piles of them up there, people tell me . . . So bring them here!' And with that he had seen them off.

One day the brothers were sitting around the cooking-fire. In a tin, with a handle made of bent wire, they were boiling up a soup made of roots of the reeds which grew in abundance by the river; the corn-cobs had not lasted long.

Scratching his dirty head, Sashka said, 'Time to get out of this place. What d'you say?'

Kolka did not ask 'Where to?' Only one road – to the station – led away from the colony. By ones and twos some of the children had been going down it and not coming back.

'Hadn't we better wait?'

'Wait? What for?'

'The super . . . to come back from Gudermes.'

'Suppose this Gudermes doesn't exist? Think of Viktor Viktorovich at Tomilino. Would *he* have gone to fetch food for us?'

'He'd have gone to fetch it for his dogs!'

'Well, yes. But this bloke . . . If you ask me, he saw what a lousy job this was, picked up his briefcase and just pushed off! He needs us like a hole in the head.'

They were silent. The weeds in their fire crackled, burning so quickly that the brothers had piled up an enormous heap of dead weeds to keep the fire fed. Around them, other fires were flickering; this time, though, the Kuzmin Twins were not sharing their fire with anyone else.

Kolka tasted the soup with his home-made wooden spoon, frowned, and suddenly said, 'What about that store-room?'

Sashka was lying on the ground and looking up at the sky.

'What about it? D'you really think there's anything there?'

'I'm sure there is. Ilya knows.'

'He knows? . . . He knows how to get other people to pull his chestnuts out of the fire for him!'

Kolka asked, 'Would it be difficult? We could break in . . .'

Sashka looked up at the sky again, which was fading into the spreading, bluish mist of early evening, but said nothing.

'We could give it a bash with a stone and the whole thing would fly open,' Kolka added.

'With a stone? We don't need a stone to do it,' Sashka replied calmly. 'There's a bolt, isn't there?'

'Yes, there is,' Kolka agreed.

'And there's a long hasp on the padlock. If we turn the padlock sideways-on . . .'

'Got it!' exclaimed Kolka. 'Got it. The bolt will have more room to move . . .'

'Any fool can work that out,' Sashka said lazily, still contemplating the sky. 'But you're like our jackals – they'd try bashing away at the lock with a stone. You'd only dent it . . . you thick-headed bashers.'

The brothers said no more. Talking won't fill your belly when what you need is bread! Today, after dark, they would go to the store-room . . . Meanwhile they had to eat their soup and then make sure that no other jackals had forestalled them with a raid on the store-room. As we all know, ideas have a way of floating through the air, and if the store-room had not been robbed so far, that was no reason to be complacent. You might go there today and find that a dozen young crooks had had the same thought about the bolt. Such is the way of the world.

The twins quickly gulped down their soup, hid the tin in a safe place, and then concealed themselves until twilight in some bushes from which they could keep watch on the store-room door.

Nobody came to try and force it open. Perhaps the brothers were the only two in the colony to have the hare-brained idea that the room contained anything useful. Perhaps someone had already been in there and cleared it out – legitimately; after all, it can't have been by pure chance that Pyotr Anisimovich had taken an enormous sack with him to Gudermes. His briefcase and a sack: did this mean he had taken those winter clothes to sell?

But everything turned out as they had foreseen.

At a cautious jog-trot, glancing around them as they went, the Kuzmin Twns made their way to the store-room. Kolka turned the lock into a horizontal position, pushed the bolt hard to the left and . . . the miracle took place that had first arisen in Sashka's brilliant brain: the bolt slid out of the catch and the door opened.

For a moment the brothers stared dumbstruck into the black hole, unable to believe it had been as simple as 'Open, Sesame!'

But there it was!

'We've done it!' Kolka whispered excitedly – and therefore rather too loudly – and slipped through the store-room door, into its mysterious, enticing depths. Sashka quickly slid back the bolt and replaced the lock in position. Glancing around to make sure he wasn't being followed, he ran away and sidled into the bushes to keep 'cave'.

Of course he was longing, positively itching to take a quick look to see what was in the store-room, to feel himself, if only for a moment, the owner of a whole wagonload of clothes. Not that he wanted it all for himself: what was the use of so much stuff to one . . . well, to two boys? He just wanted to feel like a real person – he who owned absolutely nothing and had nothing in his stomach but half a pint of reed-root soup. And suddenly – to possess all this! To walk around as master of one's own kingdom, to handle it all, to try on this and that, to know that if you wanted to you could take this thing or, if you felt like it, something else. Perhaps he wouldn't take anything but would just devour it with his eyes and leave it all behind.

At that point Sashka stopped himself short: there was absolutely no point in taking nothing. They must take a certain amount, but within sensible limits. Kolka would decide what those limits were . . . provided no one came along and disturbed them.

Sashka knew there was a rule in life: if you don't want something to happen, don't think of it, don't summon up a mental image of it; he had broken that rule by imagining the possibility of someone disturbing them . . . and sure enough – people were coming. The little girls were coming, their high-pitched chatter audible from far away: they were talking about the superintendent and his trip to Gudermes. They imagined Gudermes as some kind of promised land, where loaves of bread grew on trees. But Sashka knew that in the real world loaves of bread grew in that store-room.

The girls' noise had just died away when Regina Petrovna, the twins' beloved, appeared with Marat and Zhores. She sat down on the steps of the store-room to watch her two boys playing. And of course the little lads had to push their way into the very same bush in which Sashka was hiding, where they almost trod on his head. Please God, don't let them look round ... or there'll be trouble! Worse still, Kolka might start to hammer on the door from inside; he couldn't see that Regina Petrovna was sitting on the steps right in front of that door.

Looking thoughtful, Regina Petrovna lit a cigarette and stared into the distance for a while; but before she had finished her cigarette, she called her little boys, got up and walked away. Suddenly Sashka felt deeply, terribly sorry for her. This quite remarkable woman was forced to kick her heels in this dreadful, absurd orphans' colony, suffering considerable privation. Why should such a beautiful woman have to live – in want – in a dump like this among this uncouth horde of little ruffians? What had brought her here? The orphans were a different matter; they were rolling stones, pushed hither and thither by the whims of fate ... Someone had once said of his brother Kolka, 'You're the original rolling stone ...'

If only Kolka, cooped up inside the store-room, had been able to see how sad Regina Petrovna had looked, he would have pinched something to give to her too!

Sashka was startled out of his thoughts by an unexpected sound: the girls were coming back. They were arguing, their little voices audible at a considerable distance, and telling how a cart driven by one of the older boys had been sent to the station to fetch the superintendent, who was due to return from his trip. The boy, no fool he, had jumped aboard a passing train, and the horse, with the cart behind, had simply plodded back home ... without the boy – and without the superintendent either.

The little girls went by, to be followed by three lads from the senior boys' group; Sashka had never imagined that so many people would be passing this spot. What's more, the boys had evidently come for some ulterior purpose. Glancing around furtively, they went up to the store-room door and tugged at the padlock; one of them then produced a large nail and began using it to hack at the lock.

The hairs stood up on the back of Sashka's neck. His hands and

73

feet went numb. What if Kolka thought it was Sashka tampering with the lock, and started to call out to him from inside?

Fortunately, shouts were heard nearby. The boys abandoned their assault on the lock and walked away, whistling a tune as though they were just out for a stroll.

Sashka felt a surge of relief. Although he had been a bit scared, he had also thought contemptuously, 'Fools! Think they're grown-ups. Their arms and legs may have grown, but their heads haven't. They ought to use their brains, not nails!'

Soon after the noise had stopped, Kolka knocked three times. He knocked softly, but to Sashka it sounded as if his brother was drumming away for the whole colony to hear. He ran to the door and tried to turn the padlock on to its side, but it wouldn't move. Obviously the boys had damaged the lock with their nail and it was stuck in one position.

'Open it!' Kolka whispered through the door. 'Hurry up!'

'OK, in a moment!' Sashka was growing nervous as he found he couldn't make the beastly lock move. And he could hear voices coming nearer.

He leaped away from the door, glanced around and immediately went back again: no matter what might happen, he couldn't leave his brother locked in the store-room. Kolka was no longer whispering but hissing loudly and furiously, 'Open up! Stop messing about, or we'll be in real trouble!'

Sashka gave the lock a final despairing wrench, loosened it and slid the bolt open. The force of his pull almost made him fall over backwards, and in his haste he caught his finger in the lock. The skin broke, and it started to bleed.

When Kolka bounded through the doorway, Sashka didn't recognize him: this was a Caucasian bandit, in a long coat reaching to the ground, a fur hat that came over his eyes and an enormous pair of boots – a fairy-tale character, but not Kolka; if Sashka hadn't known who it was, he might have been quite scared.

Having bolted the door shut, before they had gone three paces from the store-room they saw Regina Petrovna coming towards them – and not her alone but with all her little girls.

She bumped into the Kuzmin Twins, amazed. The little girls stopped and stared at them.

'Why, here are my two little friends!' said the teacher. 'Good news, boys. The superintendent's come back. Why haven't you been to see me?'

The brothers shifted from foot to foot, unable to reply or to look

Regina Petrovna in the eye. The girls began to giggle, at which the teacher turned her attention to Kolka's weird garb and burst out laughing. At any other time the brothers might have done the same, but now they were in no mood for laughter.

'What are these clothes? Who dressed you like this?' Regina Petrovna asked firmly as she inspected Kolka. 'And by the way, who are you? Are you Sashka or Kolka?'

'Sashka,' mumbled Kolka.

He didn't want to deceive her, but he just had to.

Sucking the blood from his pinched finger, Sashka added, 'And I'm Kolka.' This was in case he might have to cover up for his brother.

'There, girls – remember which they are . . . if you can,' said Regina Petrovna cheerfully. But she at once changed to being serious, even stern. Bending towards Kolka, she said:

'I'm sorry for being so silly, I didn't recognize you in your new coat. A coat *and* a hat . . . Where did you get them from?'

'From the store-room,' Kolka blurted out cheekily. Sashka gulped, and cleared his throat. Now was the time to make a dash for it, before the grown-ups cottoned on. But the teacher was too naïve to understand about the store-room, and said kindly, 'That's good. It's time you were given some new clothes.' She turned to the girls and said, 'Go on, I'll catch you up.'

The little girls ran off.

'These things are a bit big for you, of course,' said Regina Petrovna as she examined 'Sashka', who was really Kolka. She turned out his coat collar and straightened his hat. 'Room for you to grow into them . . .' she added thoughtfully.

She seemed to be about to go, but something was keeping her.

'Don't wear them until it gets cold, though,' she advised. 'It's warm now . . . hot, in fact, wouldn't you say? People will think you're in fancy dress . . .'

'Yes, it is hot,' said Kolka, as though confessing something.

Regina Petrovna gave them a last glance as she turned to go, then quickly walked away.

The brothers instantly dived into their hiding-place in the thorn-hedge. Regina Petrovna was right; it would be too risky to cross the courtyard in this fancy dress. Ten minutes later, having folded coat, boots and hat into a bundle, they set off for Beriozovskaya, discussing their adventure as they went.

Kolka burst out, 'When I got in there . . . Lord, there were great heaps of clothes everywhere! I was so amazed, I didn't know where to begin . . . Then those voices . . .'

'That was the girls . . .'

'Yes, well, I was so scared I dived head first into a pile of that clobber! Sat in there till it was quiet again. I started pulling stuff out, then I heard someone banging at the lock . . .'

'That was the jackals . . .'

'It was all right for you – you could see what was happening. But I was shaking all over . . . I'd put on the coat, but it dragged on the floor and tripped me up . . . the hat was over my eyes . . . and the boots made walking difficult . . . I thought – just get out quick! Doesn't matter if the coat is too long, got to get out somehow. And you wouldn't open the lock. Was I sweating!'

'The lock was jammed!'

'Jammed? But I was boiling in there! . . . And when Regina Petrovna asked which of us was which, I was sweating so much my back was all wet. I wanted to dive straight into the bushes. I just couldn't stick it out any longer. I thought we were done for anyway.'

'Why did you tell her you'd got the stuff from the store-room?'

'What else could I say?'

'You should've thought up something!'

'Well, so I did! I told the truth for once – and she didn't suspect anything, did she? I couldn't think of anything else!'

'Even so, it was a terrible risk . . . Is Ilya expecting us?'

'Maybe, maybe not. But he's always at home. He never goes out after dark.'

'Is he scared?'

'Yes, he is . . .'

'I'm scared, too,' Sashka suddenly admitted.

Kolka gave a whistle of surprise and looked at his brother.

'What're you scared of?'

'Don't know.'

'How can you be scared, if you don't know what you're scared of?'

'Well, you can . . . And if everyone else is scared, that makes it even worse.'

'OK,' said Kolka, 'we'll dump the clobber right now, get some food for it and stuff ourselves! Then you won't be scared any more!'

76

Eleven

With a keen glance at the bundle, Ilya invited the twins indoors.

After drawing the curtains over the windows and lighting a kerosene lamp, he produced fried potatoes and some thick pancakes made of cornflour, which he called *chureki*. It turned out that the rogue also had some bacon, which he cut into slices. No host had ever offered the Kuzmin Twins such a rich spread – but the brothers weren't just kids any longer: they were merchants, owners of goods which they had brought to sell. How could a proper deal be struck without a bite and a drink?

Ilya also put a bottle on the table.

'This calls for a drop of the hard stuff, my lads. Made it myself. If you live in a sawmill, you've got to eat sawdust!'

He poured out some of the moonshine vodka into three mugs and invited them to help themselves to food. The brothers looked at each other; both realized they were terrified of the effects of strong drink, but that to disgrace themselves would be an even worse fate. It was the first time in their lives that they had been offered such hospitality and treated as equals, the first time that anyone had ever poured out drinks for them as if they were grown-ups.

Ilya reached for his mug. 'Well, down the hatch, as the soldier said. Here's to a successful partnership! OK?'

Each brother picked up his mug and sniffed it. It made their guts turn over, like the smell of dirty washing-up water. They only wished he had offered them a sweet drink, like the fruit cordial they had once been given, which had been delicious ... not like this stuff ... But they gave no sign that it disgusted them – on the contrary, they clinked mugs with Ilya as if they had done nothing all their young lives but drink moonshine. They watched him closely as he casually tossed it down in one, wiped a stray drop from his chin and sniffed at a crust of bread. You could tell at once he was an old hand at the game.

Noticing that the brothers were hesitating, Ilya said encouragingly, 'Knock it back, then! One drink's as good as another, I suppose, as the kitten said when they took him off to drown him . . .'

The brothers gave a rather forced laugh. Kolka shut his eyes, took a sip, then another, and almost threw it all up again. Mastering himself, he took a few more sips until he began to cough and tears started from his eyes.

Ever thoughtful, Ilya was already offering him a piece of bacon, slipping it to him so adroitly that it went straight into his mouth. Kolka began chewing the salty meat, but the tears kept flowing and his throat was gripped by spasms that made him unable to breathe or speak. Suddenly, though – he had no idea how it happened – he began to feel really good. A glow of well-being flooded through his body and a warm flush spread all over his face. He looked at Sashka with new eyes, aware that his brother didn't yet know what a fine thing grown-up drinking was. Poor Sashka was still suffering, shaking his head and curling his lips.

'What did you think it'd be like to drink? Honey?' said Ilya mischievously. He slapped Sashka on the back, at the same time offering him a piece of bread spread with white, melt-in-the-mouth bacon fat.

'Eat, while your stomach's ready for it! If you don't eat now, it'll never look at food again!'

He then produced a matchbox and began to show the brothers how railwaymen measured out their vodka: if you stood the box longways up against the side of the bottle, that amount of liquor was called an 'engine-driver'; if you put it on its side, that was a 'driver's mate'; and if you laid it flat, the width of the narrow side gave you the measure known as a 'stoker'. So whenever railwaymen sat down over a bottle, someone would ask how much each person wanted: enough for an engine-driver – or his mate?

In chorus, the brothers asked for an 'engine-driver'. They liked this game.

Half an hour later, red-faced and much bolder, they were acting as if they were the hosts, sometimes even shouting at Ilya. And the wonder was that he put up with it all and only ever smiled . . . you didn't need binoculars to see what a splendid bloke Ilya was – a real chum, one of us! He just kept filling up the mugs and offering more titbits, never once looking at the twins' bundle . . . treating it, in fact, as if it didn't exist.

'It's just a load of old clobber,' he said as he cut another slice of

78

bacon. 'I didn't invite you in because of what's in that bundle, but so's you'd both feel at home here.'

Which showed how much he liked them, didn't it?

Ilya proposed a toast – an 'engine-driver' apiece, of course – to the bold brothers, not because they were seven bold brothers, like in the film, but because each one of them was worth seven! He was sure such splendid lads could do any little job he might suggest. A second visit to the store-room, perhaps – and then there was another thing he had in mind . . .

'Anything . . . the shtore . . .' Kolka tried to say in reply, but found he couldn't get the words out properly. He was hearing everything and taking it in all right, but his lips didn't seem to belong to him any more and were being as disobedient as his wooden tongue. 'Any . . . shtore . . .'

Sashka didn't even try to talk, but just nodded his head.

'That clobber now . . . Still plenty of it there?' Ilya kept asking them. Suddenly his face divided into two, into three, multiplied and swam in front of Kolka's eyes. 'Lots more to nick, is there? Eh?'

'He's not Nick,' said Kolka muzzily. 'I'm Nick . . . Nikolai, that is . . . and he's Sashka.'

Sashka nodded in agreement, then suddenly his head dropped on to his arms folded on the table and stayed there.

As he took all this in, Ilya's tone of voice and his whole behaviour changed, as though he hadn't been drinking at all.

'Silly little fools . . . green as grass, you are . . . So what am I going to do with you now?' he muttered. 'You won't make it back to your kids' home, that's for sure . . . Will you?' And he shook Kolka by the shoulder.

'Yes, we will . . . but first . . . an engine-driver each . . .' Kolka shouted as he stood up, then collapsed forward on to the table and knocked over his mug, spilling the dregs of vodka. Surprised, he wetted his finger in the puddle, licked it and immediately felt sick.

Ilya lifted Kolka up and dragged him to the door.

'And I say you're more than ready,' said Ilya in a different and far from friendly voice. He hauled Kolka out into the yard and, leaving him there to be sick on his own, went back for Sashka. Then he led both of them to the lean-to where he kept his hay.

'You can kip there, you two. Engine-drivers, indeed! I'll wake you up tomorrow.'

He went back into the house and firmly locked the door. Inside, he picked up the bundle and tipped its contents on to the floor, lifting up each item and inspecting it separately. Slowly and carefully

79

he folded them all and laid them out on his bed, then examined every garment again in the reverse order, feeling them, trying them on, estimating the market value of the overcoat, the fur hat and the big, solidly made boots. The woollen overcoat almost new, had a foreign label, but the fur hat was Russian, made in Kazan of lovely smooth fur – soft to the touch, like stroking a kitten.

As he stroked it, a thrill ran through him. Everyone likes nice things, but somehow they don't always like us. Ilya's life had been an up-and-down sort of affair – more down than up, on balance – but now he felt sure: this time he had really struck lucky. He mustn't let this chance slip through his fingers.

Twelve

If you live among wolves, as they say, you learn to act like a wolf.

Ilya was orphaned in 1930, when his parents were branded as *kulaks* and deported from their village. Soon afterwards they perished, probably somewhere on the way to far-off Siberia. He had been left with his grandmother, to eke out a pauper's life. From childhood he had fetched and carried on the collective farm – and a very poor farm it was, since all the most hard-working peasants had been labelled *kulaks* and forcibly removed. Before Ilya had time to grow and fill out properly, the war came. Too puny and undersized for the army, he was considered quite fit enough for Labour Corps service, despite being well below the average weight for his age. Skinny and short, he was so undernourished that not even all his adult teeth had come through.

He and his ilk were called up from all parts of the local military district, loaded into cattle trucks and dispatched all the way across Russia, in the footsteps of his parents, to distant Siberia. They were so hungry on the journey that they ate the hay which covered the floor.

At Omsk they were given their first meal in a filthy station dining-room. Ilya noticed that the more experienced of his companions ate only a little and saved most of their food for later. They kept crusts of bread in their boot-tops and buckwheat *kasha* in handkerchiefs.

They were taken to a camp near Novosibirsk and there – predictably – they were simply dumped. For a month they just idled the time away: there was no work and no one to tell them what to do. Nor were they fed. They ganged up into robber-bands, organizing raids on the big freight sledges that were used to transport bread, potatoes and vegetables. They would jump on them, grab what they could and scatter.

Ilya now looked upon the twins and their fellow-orphans as being in exactly the same situation. Russia's a big country and there are lots of nice places in it, as they say, but wherever you may be – in his experience – it's every man for himself and the devil take the hindmost.

Ilya decided (his surname being Zverev – from '*zver*', the word for 'beast' – he was known, despite his small size, as 'Ilya the Beast') to join up with three of his pals and make their way home; life in this 'Labour Corps' didn't suit them. They jumped a passing freight train and set off, but they were careless, made little attempt to keep out of sight and were caught while changing trains at a junction just east of the Urals.

They were locked up in a gangers' hut beside the tracks and a sentry was posted to guard them. Through the window they saw a stationary coal train, and asked to be allowed out to relieve themselves. The sentry was young, and let them out. They immediately nipped round to the back of the hut and made straight for that train. No one saw them.

By now, they had grown more cautious. Whenever the train was approaching a junction they would jump off, make a wide loop round it on foot and wait for their train at the outbound signal. By these tactics they successfully crossed the Urals.

Of course, they were half starved for most of the time. Here and there they begged or stole food. One day they managed to pinch a suitcase from a man in a passing train. There was nothing to eat in it but it contained a set of underwear, an officer's tunic and a pair of good-quality uniform trousers. When they tried these clothes on themselves, they were all about six sizes too big and useless even as fancy dress.

Ilya recalled this, too, as he examined the overcoat brought by the twins.

His fellow runaways sent Ilya with the uniform to a nearby village, but he wasn't as foolish as the twins had been. He bartered the trousers for food – lumps of frozen milk, eggs, cottage cheese – and swapped the tunic for a shirt in his own size.

Near Tutayev – a place known as Romanov before the revolution – they fell asleep after eating their fill and were caught again. They were put into a penal colony for young delinquents until their case came to court; this colony was behind barbed wire and well guarded.

> Coming to Tutayev,
> It's enough to make you wail!
> Tell us what you saw there –
> Parade ground, hospital and jail . . .

So ran the song they used to sing about the colony, and it exactly described how the place looked when seen from the nearby river Volga.

By the time Ilya arrived in the penal colony, there were about two thousand young people in it. There was near-famine: by the time they had screened you and dealt with your case, you were most likely to have turned your toes up.

One day Ilya and his companions decided to run away. Every day a horse and cart would bring a load of supplies to the colony, and the gates were opened to let it in. They planned to rush out in a bunch through the open gates as the horse was leaving, then – scatter. Some lucky ones were bound to get away to freedom.

They waited until the feeble old nag arrived, bringing a load of the rotten fish used by the cooks to make a horrible kind of fish soup. When the cart had been unloaded and the gates were opened, the little gang rushed out, shouting to keep their spirits up.

Shouts, screams, the tramp of boots, rifle-fire.

At once Ilya realized that because the other lads were all running in one direction, he must go the other way, towards the Volga.

It was May and the water still ice-cold, but he didn't notice it. Soon, though, he realized he would never manage to swim across, and he felt himself sinking . . .

When he came to, he was lying, covered with a sheepskin, on a big, brick stove. Ilya raised his head and looked around: a peasant's cottage. An old man and an old woman were sitting at the table and talking about him. The old woman was saying, 'Come on, let's hand him back. They do say there are murderers and all sorts in that colony. Supposing he's one of them?' And the old man answered, 'You silly old fool! How d'you know he's a murderer? And what if he isn't? Suppose our son was in trouble somewhere, and people refused to help him?'

Ilya soon recovered. The old man told him that he worked on the Volga, keeping the navigation buoys in good repair. He had been out in his boat, seen someone struggling in the water, and it was obvious even from a distance that he was drowning . . . He'd been surprised to see anyone bathing so early in the year, so had rowed over and found Ilya, already unconscious and about to go under . . .

They dressed him in some of their son's old clothes, gave him bread and a slab of bacon. As they said goodbye, the old man made the sign of the cross over him and led him out of the house into the dark.

'From here it's not far to Yaroslavl,' he said. 'It's nearer to Rybinsk, but I don't know if you'll be able to cross the bridge at Rybinsk. There are guards on the bridge, they may catch you.'

By now Ilya had acquired a lot of experience. He went to the station at Rybinsk, found an engine-driver who was ready to take him on as a stoker, and by that means he got past the guards.

He arrived at his native village to find the house derelict and no grandmother; she had died. He crept next door to a neighbour, Aunty Olya. It was night, and he was covered in coal-dust. When she saw his black face in the window, Aunty Olya was convinced he was the devil and screamed so loudly that the whole village came running.

Ilya stayed there for a day or two, and everyone advised him to settle down in the village and get married. But Ilya felt restless: if he stayed he would have to register for military service and they would call him up again. So off he went once more to ride the trains all over Russia and pinch suitcases. He had already learned the tricks of the trade: he found his prey in crowded flea-markets, or when crowds were struggling to board a train. Sometimes he would lie on top of a carriage-roof and fish for luggage off the rack with a hook through an open window. Small he may have been, but he was smart – and successful!

The inevitable day came when he was caught, and again he was slammed into a prison camp for delinquents. By now, though, like any hunted animal, he had become hardened; he knew how to swing the lead – that is, to malinger.

Ilya smashed a window-pane with a brick, ground the glass into powder and inhaled it deeply. He might have used granulated sugar, but in those days there was no sugar to be had, so he filled his lungs with broken glass until he began to spit blood. He was put into the camp hospital, and from hospital the way to freedom is always shorter and easier. He must have breathed in a lot of glass, because he went on spitting blood for nearly six months.

Near Ostashkovo in Kalinin Province he got a job as a lumberjack, sawing timber. It was monotonous work: you pulled the saw towards you, then pushed it away, and so on for ever... Then one day, when he and a pal were walking to work, they saw some German prisoners-of-war, who worked at felling trees in the nearby forest. The Germans lived almost as free men, in a dug-out hut on the edge of the village. There they sat, these Fritzes, eating bacon. When they saw the two young Russians they shouted, '*Russ, schnell – komm her!*' meaning 'Come over here and have a bite'.

84

The lads refused the offer of bacon, but it really needled them to see these fascist bastards so well-fed that they could give it away.

On their way back from work that day they couldn't resist having a look at the Germans' quarters. They went into the dug-out hut and it was empty; the occupants were no doubt paying calls on the peasant women in the nearby cottages. The thought made the lads wild: What is this? We live in leaky huts and get fed on slops, while the Fritzes are in the warm, shacked up with our women!

They pinched everything they could lay their hands on, mostly grub – meat, bacon, tinned food . . . They took a forty-pound sack of flour, but because it was so heavy they hid it by hauling it up on a rope into the branches of a pine tree, intending to retrieve it later. From there they went to an old woman they knew and asked her to cook the meat and other food for them. 'We're celebrating a victory,' they said. 'Today we've surrounded and defeated the German fascist aggressors, and these are our spoils of war!'

The old woman couldn't understand what they were talking about, but she cooked their supper for them. They ate and drank their fill and flopped down to sleep.

That night Ilya was woken up by a strange feeling, as though someone was gently nibbling at his bare toes . . . He jerked his foot, and the response was a fierce growl. He leaped up: God almighty – there was an Alsatian dog in the room, and alongside it were several soldiers and the local policeman!

They interrogated the two lads and the old woman, and searched her house. She showed them all the stolen food that hadn't yet been eaten, except for the flour: 'I never saw no flour . . . never did. Never seen forty pounds of flour in my life.'

Ilya and his mate were put into the big police sledge and driven into town. On the way, they drove through the same wood the lads had been through on the day before. As they passed the tree, Ilya said, 'Hey, mister, stop the sledge. You wanted to know where the flour was, didn't you? Well, it's hanging from a branch up in that tree.'

At first the officer was furious, convinced this was part of a trick by Ilya to escape; but then he saw the sack and shouted at him, 'All right – up you go! You hung it there, so you can get it down!' But Ilya answered him back, 'No, mister . . . You should thank me for showing it to you. I'm not going to need it for a long time. Thanks to you, I'm going to be living on fish soup from now on. So if you want it, you can climb that pine tree!' And the officer got down from the sledge.

So far nothing had happened to Ilya, and he had even had a bit of fun out of the episode; soon, though, he was sentenced to a year in a prison camp. During his first month, he extracted the coloured lead from a grease-pencil, ground it up and threw it in his eyes. It blinded him for six months, which brought him a long spell in hospital, a shortened sentence, and – freedom.

Ilya's whiskers had started to grow, and he was beginning to look older. He decided to lead a new life. One of the prisoners in his camp, who was in there for teaching wallets to fly from one pocket to another – one of the light-fingered gentry, in fact – had told Ilya that there were land and houses to be had for the asking in the North Caucasus. Go there, he had said, and they'll give you a house, a plot of land with tools thrown in, and all for free. Only make sure you spin them the right yarn: tell 'em you're a refugee . . .

Well, what was Ilya? He was on the run and seeking refuge, wasn't he?

He got a job as a conductor on the line that runs south to the Caucasus, working on the trains that were carrying the new settlers to that region, and settled there himself without any difficulty or red tape. It was all that he'd been told: a house, a plot of land . . . with potatoes, sown by God knows who, already growing there, and sunflowers and ripening maize.

At first he didn't realize he had fallen – as befits a little wild beast – into a trap; this time his instinct had failed him. He had wanted to make a clean break and earn an honest living, but instead he had landed up in a dodgy situation yet again – and how!

He should have run away, but he was tired of being on the run. What's more, he needed money if he was to get away. And then, lo and behold, the Kuzmin Twins had turned up.

It was late when the brothers woke; the sun had already passed the meridian, and the hay was smelly and stuffy. Overcoming their languor and stiffness with an effort, they went into the house, where Ilya had already prepared breakfast: tea and pancakes, and again – a bottle of moonshine vodka.

The Kuzmin Twins shook their heads: they couldn't even bear to look at the hooch, still less drink it; the very sight of the bottle made them queasy.

Slowly sipping tea from tin mugs, they kept glancing surreptitiously at Ilya, who was being particularly solicitous and talkative. 'Haven't you washed yet? . . . You haven't? And quite right too. It's bad for you to wash too often. I read about it in some book. You can always wash after breakfast . . . Ever heard the story about the cat? You haven't? Ha! Well, I'll tell you, then. A cat caught a bird, you see, and he was just settling down to eat it – but the bird was a smart bird and he said to the cat: "Look, cat, you're not going to eat me without washing first, are you? That's a nasty, mucky thing to do." Well, the cat opened his paws to wash himself and the little bird was off and flew away. So ever since then cats only ever wash themselves *after* they've eaten . . .'

Once more the zealous host tried to pour them out some vodka, as though nothing had happened yesterday . . . Or was he right? *Had* anything happened? The brothers could only remember the start of it; the rest was shrouded in a sort of fog. Someone had been boasting and shouting, someone had called to them . . . And then again perhaps nobody had shouted and called them, and really it had all been part of a nightmare they had dreamt – a nightmare about something nasty and dangerous, something to do with horses, in which people had come galloping from somewhere on horseback, and the sound of that galloping had made their hearts stand still. They found it hard to separate dream from waking, but one thing was certain: there couldn't have been any horses in reality.

Then Kolka remembered about the clothes in the bundle. He looked over to the corner and then at Sashka, who had also been thinking about them.

Ilya caught their exchange of glances, and quickly asked, 'What's the matter? Lost something?' He gave an odd sort of laugh, and his moustache twitched.

'Where's the overcoat?' Kolka enquired.

'And the fur hat?' Sashka added. 'And those . . . boots'

'Oh, so that's what you're worrying about!' said Ilya in fake astonishment. 'They're far away. You won't catch up with them now!'

'What do'you mean . . . won't catch up with them?' asked Kolka, looking at Sashka. Both stared back at Ilya, who was still smiling an innocent smile. But the smile faded, and he enquired anxiously, 'But . . . you gave me those things, didn't you? Or didn't I understand you aright yesterday?'

'*Gave* them to you?' Sashka repeated.

The brothers stared at Ilya as though seeing him for the first time.

'What? Don't you remember giving them to me?'

Ilya could see perfectly well that the twins were flabbergasted at this news. He stood up, poured them out some more tea, gave them each another pancake, then sat down and shook his head despondently.

'You gave them to me all right ... d'you want me to remind you?' The brothers said nothing in reply, so he began telling them what had happened the day before: how he had bargained with them, offered them a choice of potatoes, maize or money in payment, and how Sashka had asked for bacon. And when they had finally agreed that he'd give them a slab of bacon and a bucketful of potatoes, Sashka had suddenly announced, 'Oh, go on – take the lot for free! We'll bring you some more tomorrow.' Naturally Ilya had flatly refused this offer, but then Kolka had joined in on his brother's side and insisted on persuading Ilya to take the stupid junk and get rid of it, all because they were such good friends. It wouldn't be any trouble for them to break into that silly old store-room again, where, as Sashka had explained, they only had to twist the bolt a little bit and slide it open ...

Listening to Ilya, the brothers stared at the floor, unable to look at each other. Neither of them could remember anything of the sort. But since Ilya knew about the bolt ... in that case ... they must have been so drunk that they had simply given away the goods ...

Ilya offered to boil the kettle and make a fresh pot of tea, but the brothers were in a hurry to get back.

'Aha, I understand. Can't wait to get on the job, is that it?' Ilya at once brightened up, and the brothers got up to go. 'You can always rely on me ... like one of the family,' he said, as he followed the boys out into the yard. 'If you nick the stuff, I'm ready to do my bit! But I'm not taking any more presents from you – got that? You slide back the bolt, get the stuff, and then ... it's strictly cash! Agreed?'

Kolka and Sashka nodded uncertainly. They were depressed. Instead of doing a deal they'd got drunk, and instead of settling up they'd come away with nothing. At the gate Kolka looked round with a sigh, and avoiding Ilya's eye, he asked in a plaintive voice, 'All the same ... maybe ... couldn't we have a little bacon to take with us?'

Sashka said nothing, but looked away, not wanting to see Kolka's humiliation.

Ilya had already turned to go back. With a look of surprise he said, 'Bacon? You ... bacon?' He paused, staring at the brothers. 'But you scoffed it all yesterday, you little piglets! All I've got left is the rind and the salt I used to cure it!'

The brothers relapsed into gloomy silence. Apart from the slice that Ilya had given them as a snack between drinks, they remembered nothing about eating all the bacon.

88

'You're big eaters, I must say . . . eat enough for four you do!' And Ilya sighed, to show how much he hated having to disappoint his best friends. Suddenly he perked up 'Ha! Wait a moment! I'll have a look – there may be . . .'

He positively oozed generosity and kindness: how could he let such good friends go away empty-handed?

He went indoors and came back with a small lump of bacon, about half the size of the palm of his hand. He picked a dock-leaf and wrapped the bacon in it, doing it slowly and hesitantly to make it obvious that he was giving away his last piece – tearing it out of his heart, as they say.

And say so he did, as he handed it to them: 'There you are – for friendship's sake . . . I'll manage somehow . . .'

The brothers chorused a 'thank you' and went.

Ilya watched them go. Suddenly he shouted, 'Hey, piglets!'

The Kuzmin Twins turned round. He was looking at them silently, clearly hesitating whether to say something else, then he suddenly said in a low but urgent voice, 'Look, kids – you should get out of this place. I'm telling you straight. Get out – run away while you can. And run for all you're worth!'

Thirteen

They did not go back to the colony.

Even if the superintendent had brought some food from the town and the cooks had boiled up some hot slops, the Kuzmins were already too late for the meal. Their portions, meagre as they were, would have been given to other kids.

As soon as the village was out of sight, the brothers turned off the hot, dusty road into a field and beyond it to where the little river Sunzha ran through banks overgrown with bushes. There by the riverside, on an open patch amid a thick growth of prickly brambles and wild olives with their little pointed silver leaves – Sashka noticed that no birds ever perched on those shrubs – they lay down on the grass.

Neither of them felt like talking.

After some time, Kolka spoke. 'My head's splitting. Is yours?'

Sashka remained plunged in gloomy silence.

'It's splitting *and* buzzing . . . like a wasps' nest. I'm never going to drink again – ever . . . I had no idea it was like this, and I . . .'

Without finishing what he was about to say, Kolka went down the bank to the river, began scooping up water with his hand and splashing it over his face. Cupping his hands together, he drank his fill; then holding as much water as he could, even though some of it dripped through his fingers, he carried it to Sashka and tipped it over his brother's face. As Kolka splashed the water over him, Sashka didn't turn away; he was preoccupied and seemed not to notice it.

Without opening his eyes, Sashka asked, 'Know what a dog-box is?' Drops of water were glistening on his nose and forehead and trickling down his temples.

'A what?' Kolka asked without curiosity. 'A dog-box?' Then he guessed that something important must be brewing in Sashka's clever head. 'No, I don't know.'

'A box . . . a sort of iron box,' Sashka went on, his eyes still shut; he might have been describing something he had dreamed. 'It's slung under a railway-carriage . . . Once when we were standing at a station, I spotted one under a train that was standing on the next track. Ilya pointed to it with his signal-flags and said it was a dog-box . . . before the war, or some time, they used to carry dogs in those boxes. Nowadays *people* sometimes get in and ride in them.'

'He's a crafty one, is Ilya,' Kolka sighed.

'A bit too crafty,' said Sashka. 'Anyway, I climbed in and tried it for size . . . He was right, you could ride in it.'

Kolka now saw what Sashka had in mind.

'You mean – it's time we were getting out of here?' he asked, looking at his brother. 'What about the colony?'

'Well, we've tried that, haven't we!'

Sashka had once told a joke about a man who saw a piece of shit in the road. Not knowing what it was, the man had bent down, tried it on his tongue, and exclaimed, 'Good thing I tried that stuff and found out what it was like, or I might have fallen in it!'

Kolka didn't laugh. He had covered his face with a dock-leaf and was basking in the sun. It was no laughing matter, anyway; they had both fallen in it, like the man in the joke might have done . . . they'd fallen in the shit with the orphans' colony . . . and with Ilya too.

But Sashka was getting impatient. An idea was spurring him on.

'Let's go to the station,' he suggested.

'What – now?'

'Why not?'

'Maybe we should first . . . perhaps have another go at the store-room? Like Ilya said . . .'

'He's not called "Ilya the Beast' for nothing. He *is* a beast,' said Sashka harshly. 'Shall we go? Don't imagine we're going back to do his dirty work today!'

Kolka realized that Sashka must have a good reason for urging him to go to the station.

'Can't we rest here a bit longer?' he asked. 'My legs are still all shaky when I walk.'

'Then I'll go without you,' Sashka announced briskly. 'By the way, there's a cart over there . . .'

He had just noticed a farm-cart, which meant they could get to the station before evening. Otherwise, if they had to walk, they might not make it that day.

They ran across the field to the road, jumped out in front of the cart and shouted to the driver, 'Going to the station?'

'Yes, I am,' said the man, and gestured to them to mount the cart. 'Hop on! With a bit of luck we may get there – this old nag of mine goes like an express train!'

The man wasn't old or grey, the brothers noticed, but was older than Ilya. His faded ex-army tunic, bleached by the sun, had white buttons that had come off a pair of old underpants and he wore a peaked cap pulled down over his eyes. He sat half-dozing on the driver's seat, occasionally glancing at the road with his bright blue eyes before sinking back into a reverie. He paid no attention to the two brothers seated beside him, until they were approaching the station, when he asked, 'You'll be from the colony, I suppose?'

'So what if we are?' Kolka countered suspiciously.

'Running away, are you?'

'Running away? Where to?'

'Anywhere . . . Stands to reason: where you all run away to – home!' the man said, clicking his tongue to urge the horse on.

'Maybe, if you have a home to go to . . . Some people haven't!' Kolka snapped, looking at him; but the man evidently didn't want a quarrel and had not meant to accuse or provoke the twins. He answered gently, 'Right you are. Some have – and some haven't. It's this war, I tell you, what's turned everyone upside down and given us such a terrible shaking. Seems like heaven and earth, live people and dead ones, they've all got mixed up . . . But lately everyone's suddenly noticed the war's almost over . . . and they're starting to talk about home . . .' He paused, not expecting a response, and seemed to sink back into his own thoughts. Suddenly he began again: 'So far they've not been thinking about their lives nor how to live them, but only how to get through it all . . . Not about eating well but just staying alive, that's what they've been thinking. How to come out of it in one piece.' He tapped his whip-handle against his leg and it made a wooden sound. Only then did the brothers notice the man had no legs; he was a disabled war veteran.

He went on: 'I gave up part of myself and I was ready to give up all the rest, too. Like I didn't need myself, sort of. But then with the war coming to an end, I started feeling sorry for myself . . . Supposing I come through after all, thinks I? So where'm I going to live, I ask myself? Where's my home? Nowhere – it's gone . . . They killed all my family and burned my old house to the ground. When I heard about it, I didn't go back to my village. Going back there'd be like trying to live in a cemetery, I'm telling you. Like bleeding to death a little bit every day. You'd end up killing yourself . . . So I decided to come here, to Beriozovskaya . . . see if

92

I could settle down ... You're little, you've still got time to grow some wool on you. I haven't, though. Came here not hoping for anything ... But lately a bit of hope's turned up. Over there, past the station, that's where I work – on the land that belongs to the railway. If you ever want anything, ask for Demyan ...'

Having said his piece, he seemed to retreat into hiding again behind the peak of his cap.

When the brothers got down at the station and thanked him, Demyan came to life once more and nodded, saying, 'So long!' He flicked the reins. 'And if you don't run away, come and see me ... Myself, I'm not running anywhere ... Trouble is, people here are afraid. But it doesn't bother me; I'm not afraid. My fearing days are over ...'

The brothers said 'thank you' again and set off, walking a bit bandy-legged because the cart's hard driving-seat had given their bony little behinds a real pounding. When they reached the sulphur baths, they jumped in, splashed around for a while and felt better. Much better, in fact – as though these smelly pits were full of the life-giving waters they had once heard about in a fairy tale.

For once upon a time, long, long ago in the olden days, ladies and gentlemen from the northern capitals of St Petersburg and Moscow had come here to take the waters ... Moustachioed officers and fine ladies in white dresses with brightly coloured parasols had driven up in elegant carriages just to take the cure by drinking the mineral water of the Caucasus ... A military band had played for them, the lush wistaria had bloomed; and after bathing in the hot waters the fine ladies and gentlemen used to climb up the hill to the rotunda, to 'contemplate' (as Regina Petrovna had put it) the distant mountains in the golden light of the setting sun ...

The brothers never could decide whether it had really been like that, or if their teacher had made the story up. The waters were here all right – they were still flowing for the Kuzmin Twins to enjoy; but as for ladies and gentlemen coming all this way from Moscow to bathe in them – and before there were any trains, what's more – this the brothers frankly doubted. To come for the local pancakes, potatoes or mirabelles, now – that was another matter ... If people are hungry, they may go anywhere, any distance ... But water is water. You can't eat it; and if you drink it, it's still just water.

No trains had come yet, though any approaching train could be seen in the distance from the mound where they stood. The brothers had climbed up to the top of the hill where the little classical rotunda

93

gleamed snow white, although when they reached it the rotunda didn't loo⸱ quite so white. The paint was peeling, the floor was deep in filth and all the pillars were covered with graffiti – written in Russian and, presumably, in German.

Sashka sat down on the stone steps and looked out over the valley, just as the fine ladies and their gentlemen escorts had also once gazed out. Kolka found a sharp stone and scratched on one of the pillars, 'The Kuzmin Twins from Tomilino. 10.9.44.'

He grinned as he looked at his inscription. People in the future would know that they too had taken the waters here and contemplated the sun setting in the mountains. The twins might come back here in ... well, say, in twenty years' time, as old men – as old as Demyan – and show the rotunda to a party of orphanage brats: look, Sashka and I were here ... The band played, he would say, and the young ladies with parasols sighed with delight ...

Before Kolka had time to finish his imaginary scene, a puff of smoke appeared behind a distant outcrop of the bare mountainside. The brothers galloped down to the railway line and reached it just in time to see the train pull up at the station.

Sashka walked past the stationary train, looking under the carriages; when he finally found what he was looking for, he called his brother.

'Look,' he said, pointing.

Under the middle of the carriage, suspended above the track, was a dirty, rusty, oblong metal box, about as long as a coffin.

Sashka lifted the hinged lid and told Kolka to climb in.

'Won't the train leave and take us with it?'

'So what if it does?' said Sashka.

Puffing and grunting with the effort, Kolka climbed into the box, followed by Sashka. It turned out that the pair of them just fitted inside if they lay down head-to-foot. Round openings had been made in the sides of the box, and you could look through them with one eye. All around were rails, sleepers and grass. The only frightening thought was that the box might come loose and fall off while the train was moving; then it really would become a coffin.

'An iron coffin with music!' Kolka said into one of the openings. 'From the northern capitals ... In a carriage, to take the waters ... Two gentlemen, the Kuzmin Twins, have just arrived!' And he blew out his cheeks: 'Boom, boom, boom ...' A military band was playing in honour of their arrival in a dog-box.

Sashka said, 'How about it, eh? In here, you could go anywhere you like for free.'

'Where d'you want to go?' Kolka asked. 'Boom, boom, boom . . .'

'Anywhere,' said Sashka, 'only away from here. And I never want to come back.'

'Wouldn't it be worse?'

'Worse than it is *now*?'

'Yes – worse than now.'

The engine hooted and the carriages gave a jerk, shaking the box violently.

Kolka sang his march-tune even louder.

Sashka suggested, 'Shall we stay in here and go with the train?'

'You mean – now?'

'Why not?'

'What about Regina Petrovna?'

Sashka was silent.

Kolka shouted, 'She'd be alone here with her little boys. Won't you feel sorry for her?'

Quickly Sashka opened the lid and jumped out. Kolka clambered out after him, stumbling on the sleepers. They watched the train go, taking with it the carriage and its box that had already become their box. It was like saying goodbye to a dream.

They spent that night in a half-burned-out freight car on a siding, and it was only in the evening of the next day that they knocked on the door of Regina Petrovna's room. Before that, though, they had first gone to the store-room to make sure that the lock with the special bolt was still in place.

Regina Petrovna did not open her door at once, and when she saw the brothers she invited them in but signalled to them to be quiet, because her little boys were asleep.

The Kuzmin Twins crept in on tiptoe, glancing round at the bed where the two young ones were lying, head to toe, in different attitudes. Zhores was on his back with his arms flung out, while Marat had curled into a ball with the blanket pulled up to his head. Now one could see plainly that Zhores was the older of the two.

Regina Petrovna herself was wearing a bright, button-through pink dress that reached to the floor and glittered like gold. Shining, her long black hair let down, she struck the brothers as even more beautiful than ever – truly a queen.

'Sit down. I've been expecting you. What brought you here? Are you hungry?'

'No,' Sashka answered for both. 'We've already eaten once today.'

Kolka put down the bacon, wrapped in a dock-leaf, on her bedside locker.

Regina Petrovna looked at the bacon without touching it, then at the boys, and shook her head.

'No, no thanks. I won't deprive you of it.'

As the brothers stared at her in perplexed silence, she gave her reason: 'You earned it, so you eat it. And how, by the way, did you earn it?'

The twins exchanged glances.

'Ah, well,' said Regina Petrovna, 'I think we understand each other, don't we?'

Sashka nodded. He had a quicker imagination than Kolka, although at this moment imagination was hardly needed: Regina Petrovna had already guessed, when she had seen Sashka outside the store-room, that they had been stealing clothes, and this was why she had been waiting anxiously to see if they would come back. But the chief thing was – she hadn't given them away!

Meanwhile she went on: 'I was looking for you, asking where you were. You didn't sleep here last night, did you? Everyone agreed you must have run away, because someone saw you at the station. But I didn't believe it. I knew you wouldn't run away like that. And I was right.'

Regina Petrovna got up and reached into the pocket of her overcoat hanging on the wall and searched for something, but then, not finding it, she returned and sat down again.

'Lord, it's awful not having anything to smoke . . . I'd even smoke dried herbs or something . . . Oh well, never mind . . . Now I'll tell you why I was looking for you: in a few days' time we're going to start work at a canning factory. Pyotr Anisimovich has signed a contract with the manager. The senior boys will work there – classes five to seven. But I've put your names on the list too . . . At least you'll be able to get some extra food there. Got it?'

The brothers nodded uncertainly; their plans had not included working in a factory.

'So please don't get in a muddle and let me down: although you're in class *four*, I've put you down as being in class *five* . . . The juniors are being sent to a collective farm to pick apples . . . Now off you go to bed.' And she called after them as they were leaving, 'The bacon – don't forget your bacon!'

Silently Kolka picked up the bacon in its dock-leaf; then, as though at a word of command, the two brothers turned round in the doorway, and Sashka said, 'The fact is . . . today . . . we were thinking . . .'

'What? That you would . . . ?'

96

'Yes. Today we almost got on a train to run away!' Sashka blurted out.

'What, run away altogether?' said Regina Petrovna in a dull voice. All her brightness was suddenly dimmed.

'Uh-huh.'

'And what about us? And the others?'

The boys could find nothing to say, although it must have been obvious that their reason for not running away had been their affection for her.

'My dears . . . Wait a minute!' Regina Petrovna quickly recovered herself. 'Look, we'll go to the canning factory together . . . and give it a try, shall we? Who knows, you may like it. I'm sure everything will work out fine. It will. You'll see.'

Kolka said nothing, because he was not too quick at guessing what lay behind people's words. Sashka, though, frowning and looking at the floor, answered for both of them. 'Well, you may be right. We'll wait and see.'

He sounded almost like a grown-up as he said it.

'Well, that's settled.' Regina Petrovna brightened up a little.

'And I've got a surprise for you. I almost forgot. Come over here.'

From her bedside locker she produced an enormous shaggy, Caucasian sheepskin hat, and inside it was a metal-studded leather strap.

The brothers stared at the hat. 'What's that?'

'It's called a *papakha* . . .'

'Where did you get it from?'

'From the box-room . . . It was left over from some amateur theatricals, I suppose. Or maybe it came from the village – I don't know. There's a lot of these things in there. The boys found it when they were looking for some fancy dress . . .' Regina Petrovna paused, listening to the children shouting in the courtyard. 'I grabbed this and kept it for you . . . Like it?'

The brothers looked at each other, both thinking what a blunder they had made. How had they missed the box-room when they'd been scouring the attics? Supposing there had been some *food* there?

Intrigued, Kolka asked, 'Were there any of those Circassian coats with embroidered cartridge-pockets?'

'I didn't see any,' said Regina Petrovna. 'There was a dagger, but it was broken, and there was this little strap . . . I thought you might like to have it too.'

But the boys were not interested in the strap. They took it in turns to try on the *papakha*. It came right down over Kolka's head

97

as far as his shoulders and in a deep voice he started singing a song, forgetting that the little boys were asleep:

> Whatever lands I'll go to yet,
> Whatever roads I'll follow,
> One friend I never shall forget
> Because we met in Moscow!

'Quiet!' said Sashka, pulling the fur hat off him and jamming it on his own head. 'I'll be Hadji Murat, and you . . .'

'And I'm Budyonny,' Kolka shouted, grabbing the *papakha* back. 'Budyonny was for the Reds, and your Hadji Murat was for the fascists!'

'Was Hadji Murat for the fascists?'

Regina Petrovna brought the argument to an end by taking the fur hat away from them.

She smiled, and said, 'I've just had an idea . . . I'll cut it up and make you two caps for the winter. They'll be really useful. And you, Kolka – you are Kolka, aren't you? – can have this strap and use it as a belt to keep your trousers up, instead of that piece of string.'

The brothers stared at the strap, a narrow piece of leather adorned with silver rivets and a tooled pattern, as well as a lot of shorter strips of leather dangling down from it.

Kolka tried on this novelty, approved of it, and announced, 'I'll hang my spoon from it . . . and other things, too . . .' The keys they stole from Ilya would have looked good on it, but then it would also be too easy for someone else to pinch them. Some corn-cobs, perhaps? Kolka imagined himself strutting around the Tomilino orphanage with corn-cobs hanging from his belt like hand-grenades. And a *papakha* on the back of his head! What a figure he would cut: back from the Caucasus after eating his fill of corn, and even bringing some back with him! He would unclip his corn-cobs and hand out one apiece to all the starving orphange kids . . . The thought prompted him to burst into song again:

> For I am sure that we will meet again,
> And then, dear friend, we'll go together . . .

Regina Petrovna gently pushed the boys towards the door. 'Off you go and sing in the courtyard!'

And off they went.

She shut the door and once again felt in the pockets of her

overcoat, collecting as much loose tobacco as she could find. Along with some fluff and dust she gathered a little heap of tobacco, clumsily rolled a home-made cigarette with a scrap of newspaper, lit it and went outside. For a long time she stood on the veranda and watched the children playing in the courtyard, trying to spot the Kuzmin Twins among them. Some of them wearing *papakhas*, from the many they had found in the box-room, the kids were playing at soldiers and chasing each other with sticks. One was wearing a huge, moth-eaten *burka*, the Caucasian horseman's cloak, his bare heels occasionally showing under the heavy felted material as he scampered about.

Regina Petrovna finished her cigarette and went back to her room. She lay down and tried to sleep, but couldn't. Several times she got up and looked out of the window. Finally she decided to do something to occupy herself, picked up a pair of scissors and began cutting the *papakha* into two equal halves. Thinking about the Kuzmin Twins and about the splendidly warm pair of fur caps she would make for them out of this big shaggy hat, she quite lost track of time. Nor did she notice one of the shutters opening slowly and noiselessly as though of its own accord, and the black muzzle of a gun pointing at her through this gaping space.

From the darkness three men watched her as she cut the *papakha* into pieces . . .

99

Fourteen

The pandemonium in the children's dormitories went on late into the evening. Regina Petrovna was right: having been well fed, the orphanage inmates had come to life again; clearly, for them a square meal was an event – and what an event! This was why they were going wild: howling, squealing, bleating, grunting, mooing, barking and making every possible noise to express their high spirits.

Somebody had the idea of singing a song – out of tune, but very, very loudly:

> My pal and I went out together,
> My pal and I went out together,
> We wandered o'er the mountains wild,
> O'er the mountains wild!
>
> A rock came rolling down, ohoho!
> A rock came rolling down, ohoho!
> A rock came rolling down, and down my pal did fall!
> Down my pal did fall!
>
> I took him by the hand, ohoho!
> I took him by the foot, ohoho!
> I took him by the foot, but my pal could not get up,
> My pal could not get up.
>
> I spat into his face, ohoho!
> I spat into his face, ohoho!
> I spat into his face, but the lad did not spit back,
> The lad did not spit back!

In the next verses, as might be expected, a pit was dug and the singer buried his friend. 'And then the earth did move, ohoho,' his

100

friend emerged from it and . . . 'the lad spat in my face!' In other words, he answered back – having been alive all the time. What a joke! They all exploded with laughter. They then struck up a convict's song about prison life, but without finishing it because the words were too tearful to suit their mood.

There followed a string of scurrilous ditties – underworld songs: market traders' songs (very pathetic, these), orphanage songs, cripples' songs, prison-camp songs, songs about railway stations and trains, Siberian exiles' songs, songs about life's trivia, Odessa songs, thieves' songs (at once both cruel and sentimental), hooligans' songs, songs of prisoners in labour-gangs (pre-revolutionary) and songs from films . . .

But the sing-song was not as organized as that description makes it sound: groups would strike up their own songs, the result was a general cacophony and the singing soon died down altogether.

The explosion came towards morning, when it was still dark.

The Kuzmin Twins woke up simultaneously. Both thought a bomb had fallen; it was something they well remembered from the first months of the war.

A fiery glow shone in at all the windows, painting the walls a quivering blood-red. From downstairs they could hear one of the little girls screaming and shouting. At once several voices raised the cry: 'We're on fire! We're on fire!'

Having no mattresses, the twins were sleeping fully dressed as some protection against the grid of iron springs pressing into their bodies to the very bone. Hardly aware of what they were doing, they joined all the others in a panic rush to get out of the dormitory. The doors were wrenched off their hinges. Those behind trampled on those in front, who fell, creating a heap of bodies. In the dark, someone's fingers were crushed, another boy had his nose broken.

The Kuzmin Twins were lucky to escape with a slight jostling.

They all poured down to the courtyard, into a whirlpool of voices, people rushing about, bright, hot light – a scene of hectic, dangerous panic.

There was a lot of aimless activity, as at first nobody understood anything, and the children simply ran around shouting. Soon it became clear that the building containing the store-room was on fire.

The twins' first thought, however, was not for the store-room but for Regina Petrovna and her two young sons . . . Where was she? Had she managed to get out in time? Looking around, stupefied, both twins were thinking about her – although thinking comes hard when you've just been fast asleep – until they caught sight of her. Frantically clutching her little boys, she was standing alone amid the chaos as though dumb and petrified, her big eyes full of terror.

'Regina Petrovna!' the twins yelled, and ran straight towards her, bumping into people on the way, pushing others aside. 'Regina Petrovna – we're here, we're here!'

Although she must have noticed the twins as they shouted to her, she gave no sign of having seen or heard them but just kept staring at the fire, leaping flames reflected in the dilated pupils of her eyes.

Pyotr Anisimovich came running up, shouting to no one in particular, 'Where are the buckets? Bring some buckets! I simply don't understand what's happening' – and he vanished, only to reappear again a moment later, this time with a bucket of water.

Shielding himself from the heat with his briefcase, he strode towards the burning building; unable to get close, he could only spill the water to the ground, where it instantly turned into steam.

Now that the first fear and sense of danger had passed, the children – even the little girls – had stopped squealing with fright and were tearing around the courtyard; fascinated by this extraordinary sight, they were finding the fire great fun.

Shooting vertically upwards, the flames looked like a gigantic Roman candle, roaring and spraying out a rain of big sparks. The building's carcass was laid bare by the light from within; there came a moment when it seemed to be transparent, with every individual beam of its skeleton clearly visible, reddened by fire.

Only the few most frightened of the little girls were clinging to the still motionless Regina Petrovna as though to a life-raft.

Pyotr Anisimovich shouted to her, 'Did you see? Did you see anything?'

Regina Petrovna did not turn towards the superintendent, apparently not having noticed him. It took a little time for her to realize that someone was asking her a question.

'What . . . ? Did I see . . . ?' she said slowly, as though in a dream, without looking away from the fire.

'I'm asking you!' shouted Pyotr Anisimovich, still shielding himself from the flames with his briefcase. 'Did you see the explosion? Did you or didn't you? And then those men . . . on horses . . .'

'On horses?' mumbled Regina Petrovna. 'What horses?'

'I simply don't understand what's happening!' Pyotr Anisimovich started to scream, but immediately stopped: he had just realized that Regina Petrovna was very unwell. One of the other teachers, Yevgenia Vasilievna, ran up, thrust a piece of ammonia-soaked cotton-

102

wool under Regina Petrovna's nose and massaged her temples. Suddenly Regina Petrovna groaned, threw her head back and started to collapse. She was at once led away to the girls' dormitory, where her two little boys had already been taken.

Kolka bent down and picked up a spent cartridge-case. The shiny brass case was not hard to spot where it lay in the grass. Sashka took the case from his brother, turned it over in his hand and put it in his pocket; it might come in handy at some later time.

'How did you guess?' Kolka asked, and searched the ground again, but there was nothing more to be found.

'How? Well, it's obvious – if it was them, they would have been here . . . What fools they were, though, to ride right into the courtyard! It's a trap!'

'Who are "they"?'

'I don't know.'

'D'you think they were shooting as well as setting fire to the place?'

'I don't know,' said Sashka, and looked up at the mountains.

A new day was dawning, the sky bright and quite cloudless. High above them, the mountains shone in the rising sun, their snowy peaks gleaming.

No fires, no night-time alarms had the power to disturb that timeless, unearthly beauty.

'It's going to be a hot day,' said Kolka, adding thoughtfully, 'I expect they'll be starting school now back in Tomilino . . .'

The brothers looked at each other, both thinking that although Tomilino was a horrible dump and life there had been hungry and uncomfortable, at least it had been simpler and quieter than here, amid these spectacular mountains.

Fifteen

At lunchtime on the same day, two policemen and an army officer arrived on a motor bike and sidecar.

While the children crowded into the courtyard to inspect this exotic machine and argue about it, the officers went to see the superintendent, talked to him and the teachers, walked around the burnt-out building and then drove away, raising a plume of white dust that could be seen from a great distance.

None of the children, including the Kuzmin Twins, were asked any questions; but even if they had been questioned, the two brothers would not have said a word about their find.

During lunch it was announced in the dining-hall that no explosion of a bomb or a shell had taken place, but that the fire in the store-room had started from an unknown cause; a canister of petrol had exploded for no apparent reason, and this had caused the whole building to burn down. This statement was made by Pyotr Anisimovich as he stood in the middle of the dining-hall, clutching his briefcase and wiping the sweat from his brow with his free hand. He looked extremely worried.

After the announcement, he suddenly added, 'I just don't understand what's happening,' which set all the children laughing.

The Kuzmin Twins were in the dining-hall at the time, having wormed their way in for a second meal, to make up for having missed their lunch the day before; the soup, made with rice, was much to their taste. When the director mentioned the petrol canister that was supposed to have exploded, they exchanged meaningful glances and went on spooning up their soup.

The superintendent also added that tomorrow a lorry would come from the local canning factory and would take the children from the senior classes to work at the factory. The juniors would go on foot to the collective-farm orchard to pick apples; they would also be fed there . . .

104

With that, the affair of the fire seemed to be closed.

The charred remains of the building were dismantled, the blackened beams were sawn up for firewood and the orphans, covered in soot from head to toe, were sent to wash it off in the Sunzha river, where they rubbed themselves clean with sand.

The brothers learned that Regina Petrovna and her young sons had temporarily moved into the kitchen, where a corner was screened off for them with a blanket. She herself, however, was not to be found. The little girls said that she had been taken to hospital; she had asked the girls to look after the little boys, with a special request that the Kuzmin Twins should help them.

The brothers nodded agreement.

'When will she come back?' asked Kolka.

'In a few days. Why do you ask?'

'No special reason. Is she ill, then?'

'No,' said the girls. 'She just had to go.'

The brothers walked away, discussing whether the girls were lying and whether Regina Petrovna would really have left her little boys if she were not ill; but if she indeed had promised to be back soon, then it wasn't too bad. The only trouble was that without Regina Petrovna's influential help, the Kuzmin Twins wouldn't be allowed to work at the canning factory, because they were so small for their age and couldn't pass off as belonging to a senior class. Then they would have to prove that they were old enough but were undersized from a lack of salt: their legs and arms and teeth simply hadn't grown enough . . . nor had their heads.

It is always a problem in wartime to get salt, matches and soap; housewives know this well enough. The orphanage inmates used to do a nice line in fake soap: they would get a piece of wood and coat it with a thin layer made from scraps of soap they scrounged in the communal bath-house, then flog it as a bar of real soap. Instead of matches there were tinder-boxes, with flint and steel and some pieces of tinder. But no one ever managed to acquire any salt, so they would sneak into a nearby cattle-pen, where there was a huge lump of rock-salt. Down on all fours they would lick the rock-salt as if it were a great delicacy, and no force could drag them away from it.

In size, the senior boys were not in fact much bigger than the Kuzmin Twins, but they differed from them in appearance and behaviour. Their hair-style, for instance, was different: most of them sported a carefully cultivated quiff. They smoked like grown-ups, inhaling the smoke. They despised the little girls, calling them

105

'stupid cows', and they would spit on the ground through their gappy teeth. Their adult teeth refused to grow properly.

One of them, a friend of the brothers called Mitek, had a pronounced lisp from his lack of teeth.

'Lasht night I shlept badly and got up at sheven, went down to breakfasht and when I shaw what they were sherving, I broke out in a cold shweat . . .'

Everybody laughed at his lisp, and they used to imitate him: 'Mitek shweated when he shwallowed his shoup on Shaturday!'

Next morning very early, when the fields were fresh and dewy and there was very little dust on the roads, a brand new Lend-Lease Studebaker truck drove right into the courtyard, still bearing American markings on the sides, the roof and cab doors. In the back, the sides let down to form slatted wooden benches along the whole length of the truck.

With a loud slam of the cab door, a young woman jumped down: she was dressed like a man in trousers, a quilted jerkin and a jaunty, battered, peaked cap. But the children saw at once that she was a woman, and within minutes they all knew her name was Vera.

After that she came to fetch them every day; she was always laughing as she watched the children scrambling over each other to climb into the back of the truck. She was a naturally cheerful person and would yell at them, hooting with laughter, 'Come on, lads! Let's see how tough you are – we're off to do some *real* work! The old conveyor-belt'll grind to a halt without you!'

Only later did the children find out what a conveyor-belt was and how it worked, but every last one of the boys immediately fell in love with Vera the truck-driver, even though she wore men's clothes, including – worst of all – trousers. They would talk about her in heartfelt tones, each one sure that she liked him and secretly hoping that he might perhaps marry her when he grew up. And of course, from then on each boy – and the girls too – wanted to be a truck-driver like Vera.

On the first morning, as the Kuzmin brothers had predicted, the staff tried to turn them off the truck when they attempted to get on board, especially since a lot of the other, younger kids were trying to pile in too. After that it was filled to bursting every morning, and every morning a teacher had to come and remove the under-age stowaways who hoped to go along just for the ride to the factory; they were quite happy to come back on foot.

The teacher always managed to remove the stowaways – except for the Kuzmin Twins. Both yelled that they were old enough, even though they slept in the junior dormitory, that they only looked small because they didn't get enough salt to eat and that height wasn't everything. Singly, they might have been hauled out of the truck along with the other stowaways, but the two of them were another matter, especially when they clung together and made an almighty fuss. So the teacher would give up the attempt and wave the truck off.

Laughing approvingly, with a conspiratorial glance at the Kuzmin Twins, Vera would check that her passengers were all seated, climb into the cab and start the engine. The truck then leaped forward and kept up a furious speed all the way. The orphans howled with delight at this headlong, daredevil dash. They shouted, whistled and roared triumphantly from thirty cast-iron throats, and Vera, bubbling with laughter and glancing in the rear-view mirror to keep an eye on her bandits, as she called them, would gun the engine even harder.

The truck flew rather than drove along the little-used road, between hedges and bushes covered with white dust, leaving behind it a long, smoky-white plume. They arrived at the factory on the first day whooping and howling in a surge of excited emotion.

People looked out of the little office at the entrance-gate and said to each other, 'They've brought the orphans.'

Vera jumped down from the cab, pushed her cap on to the back of her head and shouted cheerfully, 'All right, lads! Out you get! Now I've got to sign for every last one of you.'

But nobody ever counted them or checked the numbers. Vera drove the empty truck through the big wrought-iron gates into the factory yard, while the children were led on foot through the narrow door of the employees' entrance.

They found themselves in a huge courtyard, cut off from the outside world by a high stone wall. The yard was stacked with bushel-baskets and crates full of fruit and vegetables. There were tomatoes, plums, apples, pears and those funny little marrows that our twins had once eaten by mistake, thinking they were cucumbers. None of this bounty was guarded. Some worried-looking women in grubby blue overalls passed through the courtyard, glancing around the noisy bunch of children, and disappeared into one of the long factory buildings. They had probably come to cast an eye over the orphans who had been sent to help them. There were no more than a dozen or so men in the whole factory.

Cautiously, glancing round to make sure they were not seen, the children started pinching fruit from the baskets – a plum here, a

107

tomato there – and tried to stuff them whole into their mouths and swallow them. But a woman came past, saying as she went, 'Go on, eat as much as you like! Don't be shy! All that stuff has been washed down with the hose . . .'

This set off such a rush that it could have been dangerous. Everyone threw themselves at the baskets and began grabbing and shoving fruit into their mouths, into their trouser pockets and even down their shirt fronts. They scooped up apples, pears, plums and tomatoes – whatever was closest at hand. The kids swelled and instantly put on weight. They filled their bellies and clothes, stuffing themselves to the point where it was nearly coming out of their eyes and ears.

But still nobody hurried them up or scolded them for this unseemly orgy. The only thing that annoyed the children was that although there was such an abundance of everything, there always seemed to be plenty left. It proved to be impossible, with the best will in the world, to eat their way through all the baskets or take enough fruit away with them – even though the orphans firmly believed that for them, where eating was concerned, nothing was impossible.

There was a limit to what they could eat on the spot, their stomachs being small, but having digested it they could come back for more. And take some back to the orphanage for the others. And build up a store for themselves against a rainy day . . . by drying the fruit or by some other means . . .

So reasoned the Kuzmin Twins as they filled their shirt fronts with plums. Later, though, these plums got squashed into a mush, and had to be carefully removed and thrown away.

They tried to imagine the scene if the young jackals at Tomilino had been shown so much as a single plum, let alone a basketful! Even the ones crushed into a pulp!

They were all set to work, as it happened, on grading and selecting plums. Each day the factory-workers put out huge glass one-hundred-litre carboys, into which the orphans had to drop the plums after selecting them for ripeness and cleaning off any dirt. The carboys were then filled with some stinking liquid, after which the plums began to turn a nasty white colour and became inedible.

It was explained to the orphans that in this way the plums could be preserved at least until winter, and when the rush of harvest-time was over they would be processed and boiled up into jam and plum sauce. But what sort of jam, the children wondered, could be made from these ruined white plums? Although this was explained

108

to them, the kids still didn't like the idea that the product of their labours was being artificially spoiled before their very eyes. Since the plums couldn't be eaten after being soaked in that poisonous liquid, it meant they were being spoiled, and it was impossible to convince them otherwise.

The orphans preferred sorting tomatoes and apples. These were not doused and spoilt; instead, several hefty Jewish lads came and carried them into the factory.

Everyone knew they were Jews. They were over six feet tall, blue-eyed, fair-haired and cheerful. It was child's play to them to heave a basket on to each shoulder, all without complaining or getting tired, as the Kuzmin Twins noticed.

The brothers therefore decided that Jews were a strong, good-natured people.

But they did not like Zina, at least not at first, who used to stand at the factory door through which the Jews carried the fruit. She was elderly and peevish, dressed in dirty blue overalls and a white headscarf knotted behind her head.

Zina kept a beady eye on the orphans. She would chase the bolder ones away from the door and shout for everyone in the yard to hear, 'Little skeletons! Where did they get such starvelings from? It's a crying shame – why, I can see all their ribs!' She had a piercing voice, which could be heard all over the factory.

But one day, after shouting that, she suddenly beckoned to Sashka, who was standing nearby, and asked him, 'Where are you from, sonny?'

'Me?' Sashka asked, keeping away from her, not knowing what to expect from Zina. 'I'm from Tomilino.'

The woman nodded, as though she knew where Tomilino was.

'Where are your parents?'

Sashka shrugged his shoulders and turned away. He never answered such questions.

'So you're alone, are you?'

'Alone?' he snapped. 'There are two of us.'

'Two of you? You and who else?' the woman persisted.

'Well . . . me and my brother.'

'You don't say,' said Zina, looking in the direction that Sashka was pointing. Kolka was sitting beside one of the fruit-baskets and eating a tomato. 'Are you twins?'

Sashka nodded.

'Tell him to come over here,' ordered the woman.

She looked Kolka up and down angrily and shook her head.

109

'All right. I'll be able to tell you two apart now,' she muttered to herself, beckoning to them both: 'Come along with me . . .'

At that time the factory doors were closed for the lunchtime break, but Zina led them into the forbidden kingdom, where a row of huge cauldrons stood, each as high as a single-storey house. They were hissing. Fastened to the side of each cauldron was a steel ladder, leading to the open top of the vessel.

Zina sat them down on a box at the bottom of the ladder, and fetched a jar filled with a yellow mush that looked like the excreta of a child with diarrhoea.

'Eat up – here are a couple of spoons. Don't go wandering about the place. Got it?'

Staring at the jar the brothers nodded.

Before going out, Zina explained, 'It's called aubergine paste. Usually people eat it with bread, but there isn't any. So you'll have to eat it as it is.'

She went out, and the twins plunged into the stuff with their spoons. It disappeared so quickly that before they knew where they were it was finished. You didn't have to chew the stuff, just suck it – warm, delicious, with a lovely smell that made you feel dizzy.

The Kuzmin Twins scraped the jar with their fingers, taking turns to put them in, until the greenish glass was so clean that it shone. And within the minute or so that Zina was away, they were sitting and staring hungrily at the empty jar. They wanted more.

Zina looked at them and at the jar, and groaned with a mixture of annoyance and amazement.

'Well, you're champion eaters all right!'

She handed Sashka a red ribbon.

'You can wear this so that I can tell which one you are. Not you' – this to Kolka. She regarded Kolka as something secondary who was only a carbon copy of his brother but otherwise might not have existed.

She took the ribbon from Sashka's hand and tied it round his neck.

'That's right. And there's no more aubergine paste. But there will be . . . There'll be another day. Off you go now and work.' And she pointed to the yard.

Sashka could not quite understand what she meant by 'There'll be another day', and Kolka explained: she was saying she'd give them some more of the stuff tomorrow.

Next day, though, Zina appeared not to notice the brothers. Sashka kept strolling past her, and even said 'good morning' to her,

110

but in vain. Zina simply nodded sternly and said nothing, but screamed at all the children in the yard in her high-pitched voice, 'Hey, you midgets! Wretched little skeletons! Don't touch that basket! Let the Jews carry it!'

Nor did Zina pay the brothers any attention on the second and third day either. By the time they had stopped thinking about her, she suddenly found them during the lunch-break, sitting behind a crate and eating tomatoes (which they now detested) and she invited them to follow her into the factory.

Having seated them on the box under the familiar steel ladder, she gave them a jar and went out. This time, though, there was something else in the jar – not 'perjeen' paste, as Sashka had renamed it, having forgotten its proper name: this jar was brimful of sweet, sweet, aromatic plum jam. Once again the brothers, try as they might not to hurry, devoured the lot in a matter of seconds. But Zina was obviously keeping a motherly eye on them, because she brought them a second, and then a third jar.

With the third jar Kolka and Sashka could not keep up the same rate of gobbling and began to slow down. Of course, this did not mean they couldn't finish the jar, nor that they would have, shall we say, refused a fourth jar... It was just that they were now eating slightly more slowly, or, as some people like to put it, they were *savouring* the jam. They might have savoured a fourth jar too, but they were not given it.

The lunch-break was not yet over, and Zina sat down beside them and asked, 'Well, champions? Was it tasty?'

The brothers nodded agreement and exchanged meaningful looks.

The fact was that Sashka and Kolka had changed clothes the previous evening. They had done so as part of their general tactic of confusing people, not Zina in particular, but now Kolka and not Sashka was wearing the red ribbon.

Zina stared hard at them and suddenly prodded Sashka with her finger. 'Why've you taken off your ribbon? Think I wouldn't notice, did you? I'd recognize you anywhere! You're different!'

No one else had ever been able to tell the brothers apart, but old Zina had guessed which one of them was which. This amazed them. They sat in front of her with full stomachs, grateful and slightly ashamed.

But Zina did not scold them. She asked, 'In that place ... Tomilino ... where you used to live ... What did they feed you on?'

The brothers were nonplussed. It was a strange question. As far

111

as they knew, orphans were fed everywhere on the same stuff, if they were fed at all: skilly.

'Skilly!' said Sashka.

Zina generally turned to him for answers to her questions.

'What's skilly?' asked Zina. 'Is that a sort of broth?'

The brothers were embarrassed. How could anyone not know what skilly was? Skilly is skilly! Murky-looking slops, in which you might find a few bits of black, frost-bitten potato if you were lucky, or . . . or a lump of undissolved semolina: horribly delicious. But rice, which they had eaten the other day in rice soup, was something they had tasted then for the first time.

'Did they give you polenta?' Zina asked again.

'Po . . . lenta?' queried Sashka. 'No . . . they gave us slops.'

'Slops?' Zina enquired. 'Well, I s'pose that's like polenta, only more runny . . .' And she sighed. 'They brought us out here too, you know, like they brought you . . . we're from Kursk province.'

The brothers stared at Zina. At first they could not grasp how grown-ups could be brought here; grown-ups did things for themselves, they thought, and couldn't just be shoved around.

But Zina went on: 'Some bossy fellow came along and told us to pack our things . . . though my sister was ill and my daughter was in a bad way too – she wasn't right in the head since a fascist raped her. So we tied up our bundles – nothing much to pack, everything we had was on our backs. And we cried our eyes out at leaving. Not that there was much to leave . . . the village mostly burned down and empty, grass already growing everywhere, and German mines still all over the place . . . Not a cow or a piglet, even the cats had been eaten . . . we'd been living in holes in the ground. They put us in cattle trucks and brought us here. We just kept on weeping. And the bossy fellow says, "Stop that bawling, girls, I'm taking you to paradise . . ." When he said "to paradise" we were sure he meant we were all gong to be shot, because they'd been hunting for traitors everywhere – anyone who'd slept with a German was called a traitor . . . And my daughter had, even though she'd been forced to do it . . . Lord, the weeping and the wailing! You'd think the wagon was going to burst with all that noise . . .'

Zina looked around. The lunch-break was over and people were starting to bustle around as they came back to work. She stood up.

'So then they brought us to paradise – to this place, I mean. It's not bad here, though. You can even live quite well here. If it weren't for *them* . . .'

112

She didn't say who she meant by 'them', but made a sweeping motion with her arm, as though flourishing a sword.

'We're so afraid . . . so frightened of them . . . They've been down our way once already . . . But you're young, you don't need to be bothered about them . . .'

As Zina started to walk away, Sashka looked at her and asked, 'But tell us – who? Who are they?'

Zina looked around, pushed the brothers further under the ladder and whispered hurriedly, 'This is Chechen country! The people who lived here are called Chechens. When the Germans were in these parts, the Chechens welcomed them – they were traitors like us, or so we're told. Maybe their girls played around with German soldiers, but who's to know if they really did? So they packed them all into cattle-trucks, like they did us, only they didn't even give them time to pack their bundles, it seems . . . They brought us here to the Caucasus and took *them* off to paradise in Siberia . . . or so we've heard . . . But some of them . . .' – here the twins could hardly hear her voice – ' . . . some of them didn't want to go, so they hid themselves up in the mountains. And now they're making all the trouble they can. They come down here robbing and killing, that's what!'

Having rapidly said her piece, looking round her all the time, Zina pushed the boys out from under the ladder, saying, 'Off you go, now! You'll find out more, and you'll soon be old before your time. Off you go!'

Sashka resisted, not wanting to go outside.

'So it was they who set fire to the store-room . . . with a bomb!' he exclaimed, astonished at his discovery.

Zina looked round in terror, and suddenly shouted, 'What are you gawping at, eh? Never seen a factory before? Go on – back to work! This is no time to be chattering!'

With that, refusing to listen to any more questions, she pushed the brothers out into the yard.

113

Sixteen

Suddenly the orphans were told they were to put on an amateur concert. For the collective farm.

Relations with the local population had become very strained.

The villagers had been keeping a watch on the water-melon plantation, where they had caught several children scrumping and then thrashed them until they were half dead. In revenge the orphans captured a young man and a girl near the orphanage – they had been making love among the maize-stalks – and tied them, naked, back to back. They then led them in that state down to the village. When people came running up, the boys melted into the bushes . . .

And the trouble started.

Pyotr Anisimovich came back from the collective-farm office looking very sad, clutching his briefcase to his chest and repeating, 'I just don't understand what's happening . . .'

He called a meeting of all the staff, told them everything he had heard in the farm office and ended by making a suggestion:

'Perhaps we could . . . Perhaps we could meet the collective-farm people and talk to them? Or sing them something? Like the songs the kids are always bawling in the dormitories?'

'They can sing and dance all right,' was the answer. 'They're all performers – especially at conjuring. There are plenty of conjurors among those kids: they can make something out of nothing!'

But the superintendent was in no mood for jokes. Pressing his briefcase to his chest like a mother with her baby, he begged in a pained tone, 'So why not . . . Why don't we form a choir? And they could recite poetry. I'll tell the village people that we'll put on a show for them and they can . . . Well, offer us some food . . . In other words, make peace between us.'

Peace and friendship were notions that meant nothing to the orphans. The idea was a dead duck, as they understood it. They had long been stealing food from the collective farm and would go

114

on doing so. But as for being offered a meal in exchange for putting on a show – that was another matter. Immediately a large number of volunteers came forward.

The Kuzmin Twins, too, offered to perform, saying that they had once sung in a choir, and they offered to represent the Tomilino contingent by singing a song. They were enrolled. The rest were auditioned in groups, according to their previous orphanages. The auditions took place in the dining-hall.

The children from Mytishchi offered a choir – it was a large group. Their proposed repertoire included 'Stalin's iron will inspires us to knightly deeds' and 'Fly, my song of victory . . .' – these two were proposed as starters, to get the audience singing along and warmed up. Then they would sing the sad and sentimental 'Traveller's Song', to introduce a soulful note. The first song was approved, the second received special praise, and everyone knew and loved Dunayevsky's 'Traveller's Song'.

'We'll certainly sing Dunayevsky,' the Mytishchi kids replied, 'but we know a better one than that.'

They all stood up to attention, put their right foot forward and tapped it on the floor in time to the tune, which they hummed in unison: 'Tum-ta, tam-ta, tum-ta . . .'

Everyone liked this introduction; it was a clever imitation of the clicking of a train's wheels. Then came the words:

> An officer was sitting in a train,
> A dandy with much charm
> But little brain.
> A mere lieutenant though in army rank,
> As lady-killer he's
> A Tiger tank!
> The journey was long
> So he sang her a song:
> About perversion, total immersion,
> Thuggery and buggery,
> Spanish fly and beaver pie!

'What is this?' I just don't understand what's happening!' Pyotr Anisimovich exploded as he stared at this strange choir. 'What was that about tanks and, er . . . thuggery?'

The choir relapsed into despondent silence.

'Perhaps they can go on?' enquired one of the teachers.

115

'*Go on?*' Pyotr Anisimovich was amazed at the suggestion, and waved his briefcase in dismissal.

The choir, however, interpreted his remark and his gesture as an instruction to continue. Once again, as though on a word of command, the Mytishchi lads put their right foot forward and began tapping it rhythmically as they hummed, 'Tum-ta, tam-ta, tum-ta, tam-ta!'

Against the background of this accompaniment, one of the soloists began singing with langorous melancholy:

> **The train was coming to its destination,**
> **And peeping through a crack –**
> **Sensation . . . !**

Hoping to please the superintendent, the choir then roared out:

> **The officer and she were coming too!**

'That's enough! Enough!' cried Pyotr Anisimovich, jumping up and pressing the briefcase to his chin. 'That song will *not do*. Only the first one. About the knightly deeds . . .'

'And the other ones?' asked several voices from the choir.

'What other ones? Have you got any more?'

'Lots!' came the reply. 'For instance, there's "Hey Valya, you whore, what's your price?" . . .'

'No, no!' said Pyotr Anisimovich. 'None of that!'

The choir went away disappointed, to make way for the boys from Lyuberets, who sang and danced to the traditional tune 'Little Apple', a simple refrain to which each singer makes up their own words: 'Hey, little apple, you've rolled a long way, Down to the Caucasus – let's hope we don't stay . . .'

'You can dance to it, but don't sing the words,' said Pyotr Anisimovich with a sigh. 'You can do it without any words.'

The children from Kashira – the group consisted entirely of girls – sang a little song about a girl who followed her soldier-lover all the way to his position in the front line. When they had sung it, one of the boys waiting to be auditioned shouted, 'She came to the position a girl, and when she got up from her position she was a mother!' But nobody reacted to this outburst, and the song was approved.

Two orphans from Lyublino proposed to sing a parody.

116

'A parody?' The teachers livened up and showed interest. 'Well – off you go!'

They began by singing with great feeling about a crane that has flown a long way, migrating to a distant country: 'Here under a foreign sky I'm an unwanted guest . . .' At these words they pointed out of the window, up to the sky. This place was obviously the 'foreign sky' – in other words, the song was about themselves, orphans who had migrated to a far country where they were unwanted. After that verse, they suddenly struck up another song, in the cracked, drink-sodden voice of a beggar:

> Dear mothers and fathers,
> Please give what you can,
> A rouble, two roubles,
> To a poor crippled man . . .

This was followed by a very different song, about a little girl writing to her father who is fighting at the front:

> Dear papa, writes little Olya,
> Mother doesn't love you any more;
> A colonel by the name of Kolya
> Comes and lays her down upon the floor . . .

These songs were considered unsuitable; they would do better to stick to the migrating crane. The boys from Lyublino agreed, but said they would like to add another song, a funny one about Hitler, sung to the tune of 'Tout va très bien, madame la Marquise'. The song about Hitler was approved without an audition.

The children from Ramenskoye proposed to declaim Pushkin's poem 'Beneath me the Caucasus', and a passage from the long narrative poem about a nobleman by the name of Luka who loved a merchant's wife – a tragic story.

Luka was rejected, the other poem was accepted.

The Kolomenskoye contingent offered to sing kolkhoz folk-songs, specially chosen to appeal to the people in the village . . . something like the songs that were sung by the Pyatnitsky National Choir.

Forewarned by the bitter experience with 'Little Apple', Pyotr Anisimovich asked them to sing one of these songs. Adopting the rather quavery, metallic tone typical of Russian folk-choirs, they struck up a verse to the well-known tune of 'A Lad Walks Past My House at Sunset':

I went working on the fa-arm
Earned myself a rouble piece!

Stuck the rouble up my backside,
Left the hole in front wide open!

'No, no, that won't do for a collective-farm audience,' Pyotr Anisimovich said hastily. He sighed with relief. 'Is that all? Any more for
auditions?'

At that moment Mitek turned up and lisped, 'I'd like to do an act
on shtage too.'

'You?' Pyotr Anisimovich was amazed. 'I jusht don't undershtand
what'sh happening . . .' Without meaning to, he was lisping himself.

'What don't you undershtand?' Mitek asked, puzzled. 'I do conjuring tricksh.'

'What?' The teachers sounded interested.

'Tricksh,' said Mitek.

And without waiting for permission, he said to Pyotr Anisimovich,
'Your watch, for inshtanshe . . .'

Pyotr Anisimovich protested limply. 'No, no. Leave my watch
alone.'

'But here it ish,' said Mitek, producing the superintendent's watch
from his own pocket.

'I don't understand what's happening,' groaned Pyotr Anisimovich. 'All right. But in the farm club you mustn't do that trick with
any of the farm workers. Otherwise there'll be trouble . . . They'll
think all we ever do is steal things from them.'

'Who'sh watch shall I take then?' asked Mitek innocently.

'Anyone's you like,' said the superintendent, 'except for the farm
people's.'

'All right,' said Mitek, with a meaningful glance at Pyotr Anisimovich's briefcase.

Just then several more orphans approached the audition panel,
each one shouting. 'I can do, er, tricks, too!'

'I'll chew a glass, if you like.'

'I'll chew a light-bulb!'

'If you like, I can make them all cry!'

'I can tell fortunes by reading their palms.'

The superintendent lifted up his briefcase as though protecting
himself from the onslaught and shouted, 'Next time! You can chew
glass *next* time! Anyway, there aren't any glasses. And we've enough

to cry about already, without you making us burst into tears. That's all! The audition is over, comrades!'

Seventeen

A week passed. All the orphans, except the girls, were transferred to jobs inside the factory, where they were put into different departments. A few were given the task of washing jars. Another bunch of children, including the Kuzmin Twins, were set to work on the conveyor-belt, as predicted by Vera the truck-driver. The children were taken to the conveyor and shown how it worked. A wide rubber belt crawled out of a huge tank, in which floated the tomatoes that had been tipped out of the baskets. Standing on both sides of the belt, the boys had to be handy enough to remove, stalks, leaves or rotten tomatoes and extract anything else superfluous. They were kept under the watchful eyes of two women who stood at the end of the belt.

Standing beside the conveyor all day was boring, but in fact it did not function all day: sometimes the belt would get stuck or there would be a hold-up in the supply of tomatoes . . . the steam would occasionally be shut off or there might be a total power-cut. In fact, if the belt didn't get stuck, somebody was likely to poke a stick into the works to stop it! And then the children, headed by the Kuzmin Twins, would hurry over to a far corner of the building where, next to the place where the jars were washed, plum jam was being cooked in huge cauldrons fenced off by steel barriers. The orphans flew towards that smell of jam like bees to a honeypot – with the Twins, naturally, leading the swarm!

Aubergine, or 'pergeen', paste, was undoubtedly good – you could devour it by the bucketful – but after a while you got sick of it.

The apple sauce was sour, and was quickly rejected.

Stuffed peppers were very acceptable – you could fill yourself with the stuffing until you burst – but these were only prepared occasionally.

Jam, though . . . that was the food of the gods. Stick your head into one of the big jars, and you could suck it all out until you were oozing sweetness! None of the cooking processes, in fact, took place without attracting the keen attention of a gaggle of orphans.

The tall Jewish lads would climb up the ringing steel ladders to the very top, where they would tip a load of plums from their heavy baskets into the cauldron – the same plums that had been cleaned and sorted in the yard by the little girls. Then from the tops of those same ladders, which shook and resounded from their heavy male feet, the Jews would pour out granulated sugar, noisily ripping open the greyish jute sacks above the cauldron and throwing them down, empty, on to the floor.

The orphans would grab these sacks and scrape the remaining grains of sugar from them. Occasionally one of the men, as though by accident, would tip a sack outside the rim of the cauldron, and then the manna from heaven would pour into the children's cupped, waiting hands: oh, that white stream of utter sweetness! They would gobble the sugar with unspeakable pleasure, then fill their pockets with it – which soon brought the wasps and bees swarming around them.

But the most solemn moment came when the jam was run off from the cauldrons. Thick, sweet-smelling and oily-brown, it came pouring out of the narrow opening into the sterilized, steam-heated jars. If one of them happened to burst, the orphans would grab the fragments of glass, still scalding hot and thickly smeared with equally hot jam, and quickly devour it at the risk of cutting or burning themselves. Miraculously, though, no one ever suffered a cut or a burn!

Filled with jam, the jars were then capped with metal lids that shone like gold. Mitek, lucky fellow (the one who used to 'shweat because of the shoup') was given the job of keeping up the supply of lids to the man who screwed them on. This work, too, made him sweat, and the other orphans envied him for getting this special and responsible job.

The Kuzmin Twins carefully studied and learned the entire process of making jam – from cauldron to stock-room. This was no mere idle curiosity. They reckoned that jam, especially in airtight jars, could be a useful item to keep in reserve for the hungry winter months. To be exact, the thought of a winter stock only came to them later; for the time being, they were only concerned to purloin a few jars to hide in a secret cache. For themselves and – of course – for Regina Petrovna and her two little boys.

With this in mind they came to an arrangement with the simple-minded Mitek. As soon as the section was empty except for himself

121

and the jar-capper, and the jars had accumulated on the long, metal-topped table behind the capper's back, Mitek began whistling loudly the tune of that uplifting song 'Dear Comrade Stalin, come and visit our Collective Farm . . .'

Taking it in turns, the Kuzmin Twins left the conveyor-belt and hurried over to the source of the melodious signal, with considerably more haste than Comrade Stalin was ever likely to show in visiting even his favourite collective farm . . .

The main objective was to hide the jars near the conveyor-belt, in a place where they would not be seen by any of the grown-ups.

The Jews were not included in that category; they used only to laugh when they caught the eye of an orphan stuffing a jar into his pocket; now and again one of them would even screen the lad from view with his hefty frame.

Sashka had divided Operation Jam Jar into three phases: phase one – remove them from the boiling-room and hide them in a safe place; phase two – smuggle them past the sharp-eyed Zina and conceal them securely in the yard; phase three, the most important – transfer the jam to a hiding-place in a thick hedge outside the factory.

Within a few days of the start of the operation, the Kuzmin Twins had abstracted and hidden seven sealed jars of jam.

All around the conveyor-belt there were innumerable pipes and complicated metal components forming such a labyrinth of nooks and crannies that anyone who wanted to could have hidden not seven but seven thousand jars. No detective could have found them if a search were ever made.

In the matter of concealment our two brothers, to say nothing of the other orphans, were unsurpassed experts.

As a means of smuggling the jars past the eagle eye of Zina, who, although she wasn't malicious, was terrified for her job and therefore doubly vigilant, Sashka proposed that the twins should embrace wherever they went – going to the conveyor, coming away from it, into the canteen, out into the yard . . .

'Won't it be a bit hot, clutching each other all the time in this weather?' said Kolka, failing to grasp the reason.

'You'll just have to put up with it!'

'But why?' Kolka repeated.

'Because!' Sashka teased him. 'When we do it, you'll understand why! Don't you see? There's just the right amount of space between us!'

Kolka got the point, and asked, 'Do you suppose . . . those loving couples who walk out of the factory together – are they carrying stuff on them too? They're always going around with their arms round each other. I've seen them myself!'

Sashka thought for a moment, then said, 'Heaven knows. Anyway, who cares?'

From now on they went everywhere clasping each other around the shoulders. The women in the factory would look at them and say, 'Just look at those two, how fond they are of each other! Blood's thicker than water, they do say . . .'

Who could have guessed that if anyone *had* succeeded in separating them they would have found two jars of jam: one under each shirt. They rehearsed their act in a nearby maize-field and tested it inside the walls of the orphanage. When they walked side by side, embracing, it was impossible to spot the hidden jam jars, unless someone were to have prodded them – but who would do that?

It was true, however, that Zina did suspect something on the first day they started smuggling jam. Previously it had not mattered how many times they had walked past her embracing; she had never once stopped them or questioned them. But now – perhaps her woman's intuition was at work – Zina shrieked at them piercingly for all to hear, 'Hey, you!' This, of course, was aimed at Sashka; she recognized him at any distance, even without his red ribbon. 'Come here, I say. Why do you two keep walking up and down like that? . . .'

They went over to her, without relaxing their embrace. The jam jars felt cold against their bodies, the smooth glass rubbing their skin every time they breathed in and out; occasionally the jars chinked softly against each other.

Zina looked at the twins, and said, 'Why are you two clutching each other like that?'

Kolka said nothing. Zina wasn't asking him; she didn't recognize his existence at all. In any case, Sashka was quicker at thinking up what to say to her and how to say it.

Sashka answered at once, in a conciliatory, confidential tone, that they preferred walking around the yard like this because they had secrets to tell each other, and it was easier to whisper into each other's ear.

Sashka was not really lying: they had a secret all right, though their ears did not come into it.

'Fancy that!' said Zina, baffled. 'Secrets, eh? And supposing I find out what your secrets are – what then?' She stared hard after them, but noticed nothing.

The brothers sauntered away for as long as she could see them, then nipped sharply round the nearest corner.

There, in a deserted backyard behind one of the buildings, where the factory-workers never went, was a rubbish-tip. It was a sizeable heap of broken jars, smashed crates, broken handcarts, old barrels and general garbage. This was the safe place they had found for hiding their jam.

It now only remained for them to spirit it out of the factory grounds.

As a test, although they hadn't much faith in this method, they tried going through the normal pedestrian exit. But although the security guard – an elderly woman reservist with an unloaded rifle – was not as bright or sharp-eyed as Zina, she nevertheless shouted at them, 'Hey, you two – why are you hugging each other like that? Walk separate, like normal people, like everyone else does!'

'We can walk like everyone else does,' the brothers thought, 'but if we do, we'll never get any jam jars past the guard!'

Sashka could think of only one other method: to throw the jam over the factory wall. Unfortunately it was a solid stone wall and about twelve feet high.

One day after work, Kolka ran ahead of all the others, and Sashka threw him several empty jam jars over the wall of the yard.

Of five jars, Kolka caught only one. They changed places, but the result was no better: Sashka failed to catch any. And he had nothing else to suggest; it was as if his brain had stopped working.

After that, Kolka slipped a pinch of granulated sugar into Sashka's food; he had heard that sugar made your brain work faster – just as it helped to cook the jam in the cauldron. But it had no effect on his brother, who grew depressed and gloomy, went into a decline and actually lost weight. He would wander around the courtyard alone, or have long talks with Zina. Kolka wondered what his brother found to discuss with her; there was no hope of talking her into helping with their plan, of that he was sure. The jars were still under the rubbish-tip, and time was passing . . . The orphanage might stop sending them to work at the factory: every day here might be their last!

One day Sashka said, 'They were here, too, you know.'

'Who were?' asked Kolka, but he had already guessed what his brother meant. 'You mean the devils?'

'The devils' was what they called the Chechens.

'Yes, the devils. They came galloping through on their horses,

124

with rifles . . . they blazed away and then disappeared back into the mountains. Zina saw them. She said she nearly died of fright.'

'Did they kill anyone?' asked Kolka.

'I don't know. But why do you suppose Regina Petrovna won't say what happened to her on the night of the fire?'

'Why?'

'Because she saw them. And it made her ill. Zina says that can happen sometimes if you've been very frightened.'

'Regina Petrovna isn't afraid of anything,' said Kolka.

'But what about her kids? And what about the explosion? Wasn't that enough to scare anybody?'

The brothers were sitting on upturned crates in the backyard, near the place where they had hidden the jam. In the grass at their feet a stream ran through the yard and out through a large pipe let into the base of the wall. A lot of the factory's effluent went into this stream; as a result, it was a dirty yellow in colour and stank horribly.

'Well? Have you thought up something?' Kolka asked.

'Something? About what?'

'You know what! Are we going to sit on our store of jam here for ever?'

Sashka scratched his head and said, 'Oh, an itch is bugging me . . .' In orphanage slang this meant 'a bug is making me itch'. And apropos of nothing at all he said, 'Let's push off from this place, shall we?'

'What – now?'

'Well, tomorrow. Zina says she would have gone long ago, only she has a family . . . All the people who work here were mobilized, like soldiers, and they're forced to stay here. But nobody's forcing *us* to stay here!'

'But what about Regina Petrovna?'

Sashka thought for a while. 'Supposing she doesn't come back?'

'She'll come back,' Kolka said firmly. 'Her two little kids are here.'

'And what if she died?'

'No,' Kolka insisted. 'We must wait for her to come back and collect enough jam to feed us when we do push off. So whatever happens, we've somehow got to get those jars out of here.'

Sashka was silent, staring up at the distant mountains, which were now hazy and barely visible in a pale blue mist. A weak sun was shining and it was quiet enough to hear the rippling of the stream and the buzzing of wasps.

125

'Maybe there aren't any devils at all?' Kolka wondered hopefully. 'Surely the police will catch them, won't they? They used to let off bombs and things, but now the explosions have stopped.'

Kolka did not say this because he believed it. He was enjoying life in the Caucasus.

As well he might: the starving orphans' age-old dreams of food had been realized. Where else could he stuff himself full of sugar, 'pergeen' paste and jam? Zina had said they were being taken to paradise, and for Kolka this factory *was* paradise.

He saw no cause to complain at being forced to work in the factory; indeed, it was Kolka's dream that the orphans might never be released from this place. When he grew up he would ask to be allowed to work here for ever. That would be the good life! They would carry sacks of sugar, as the Jews did; nobody who did that job would ever go short of food again.

Sashka looked at Kolka and realized what his brother was thinking. 'All right,' he said, 'we'll wait a bit.'

'But the jam? What are we going to do about the jam?' Kolka insisted.

Sashka stared hard at the mountains and at the wall where the stinking stream ran under it through a culvert. 'We'll float them out.'

'What?' Kolka did not understand him.

Sashka laughed. 'We'll put the jars into the stream, see?'

'How?'

'How . . . I don't know. We'll think of something,' Sashka promised. He leaned back, turned his face to the sun, closed his eyes and began thinking.

Sashka's idea was brilliant: tie each jar of jam to a stick and float it down the stream. And then, of course, catch it on the far side of the wall . . .

They tried it once; the stick sank, because the jar was too heavy for it. They found a plank, but the plank was no good either because it was so clumsy and unmanoeuverable that it got stuck in the reeds.

Sashka gave up the idea of using a plank, and spent the whole of his lunch-break loafing around the yard, peering into corners and looking for something. What he was looking for he didn't even know himself. Finally, he found a galosh on the rubbish-tip – a galosh so big that it was impossible to imagine anyone actually wearing this monstrous object, except perhaps Gulliver himself.

Sashka took the galosh to the stream; put into it a stone about

126

the size of his fist; and launched it downstream. The galosh nego-
tiated all the waves and all the obstacles, sailed through the hole in
the wall and out on the far side, where Kolka was waiting for it.
Then Sashka filled a jam jar with sand and put that into the galosh;
it capsized and the jar sank. Sashka again loaded a sand-filled jar
into the galosh, and this time he tied it firmly in place with string.

The rubber vessel sailed away, scudded downstream and emerged
at the far end. A little of the sand had been lost, but the brothers
decided that this didn't matter; the jam wouldn't fall out or get
washed away, because the jar would be tightly shut. What mattered
was that it should float and not sink, because it could never be
salvaged from the bottom, whereas if the current carried it into the
reeds they could always find it and rescue it.

On a certain evening, straight after work, Kolka went through the
factory gates with all the other kids and set off at a run to the stream.
The orphans always had to wait outside the gates for a long time
before the truck came to pick them up. The spot where the stream
flowed out through the wall was a piece of waste land at some
distance from the gates. That was why he had to run as hard as he
could: the wall around the factory stretched for half a kilometre.

Kolka gave a whistle, the agreed signal that he was in position on
the far side of the rapids and Sashka could launch his vessel. Having
whistled, he started to wait, lying down on the grass the better to
see the opening of the culvert.

Time passed. The empty minutes dragged by, as empty as the
surface of the water.

Suddenly, when he was about to abandon the wait and had stood
up to shake off the grass and dirt, he saw it: the black galosh, like
a gift from the gods, emerged from the hole in the wall and came
floating towards him, looking like a British dreadnought that he had
once seen in a picture-book! It was floating, turning from side to
side in the current, but in it was all that mattered – its precious,
brass-hatted passenger!

Kolka untied the jar, and in a rush of emotion he kissed its golden
head, and its cold, damp bottom, then held it to his cheek and to
his ear, listening to the sound of the viscous jam as it slopped from
side to side.

Here, in freedom, the jar looked different: inside the factory
grounds, it somehow didn't yet belong to them.

And Kolka stroked the galosh as though it were a live creature,
saying as he did so, 'You lovely little galosh . . . so clever, so brave . . .
You're our very own girl and your name's Glasha.'

127

So from then on the brothers, between themselves, started to call it Glasha.

One day the Kuzmin Twins went into the girls' dormitory. Embarrassed, they asked if they could take Regina Petrovna's two little boys for a walk.

The girls gave their permission, but they were not to take them for long and they must not go far . . .

Keeping a look-out to make sure they were not being followed, the brothers took their little friends to the bank of the yellow river Sunzha, extracted a precious jar of jam from their cache and opened it. They sat the little boys down on the grass and began to feed them. There was only one spoon, so they ate in turn: one spoonful for Zhores, one spoonful for Marat.

The little boys ate seriously and without hurrying. They licked the spoon carefully each time, occasionally glancing into the jar to see how much was left. Although it was obvious that they greatly enjoyed this heavenly food, they never asked for more but waited until it was given to them.

All of a sudden there was no more left.

They sighed, took a last look into the jar and asked, 'Will there be more?'

'There will,' Kolka promised. 'Glasha will bring some, and then we'll have more.'

'Who's Glasha?' asked Zhores.

Sashka looked at Kolka, and said, 'Glasha is . . . well, Glasha. She's good and kind.'

'Is she your mama, maybe?' asked Marat.

'No,' said Kolka, and sighed.

'We miss our mama,' Marat complained. 'It's horrid without her.'

'Yes, of course it is,' Kolka agreed.

'Will your mama come here?'

'I don't know,' said Kolka, and began closing the jar, licking some drops of jam from the edge of the lid as he did so. He didn't look at the little boys.

'Everybody's mama comes here,' they said.

The Kuzmin Twins took the young lads down to the water's edge and washed their lips, cheeks and hands, which were all sticky. On the way back to the orphanage they warned them not to say a word to anyone about the jam that Glasha brought . . . otherwise Glasha would be upset. The little boys promised; then they were taken back to the girls, looking nice and clean, rosy-cheeked and very content.

And Kolka asked, 'When is Regina Petrovna coming back?'

'She's coming back,' said the girls. It was clear they were not telling all they knew.

Meanwhile Glasha continued to deliver the jam regularly and efficiently, and one day Kolka thrust his hand into their cache and counted the jars by feel. It turned out that they had accumulated no fewer than eleven jars.

'Eleven!' he whispered to his brother, who, as usual whenever they crawled into their secret den, was keeping watch outside.

If only the kids at Tomilino could see their hoard! They would have gone crazy at the sight of such riches. There, they sold themselves into slavery for a scrap of saccharine; they would risk their necks to climb up a linden tree in spring to lick the sweet, sticky juice off the leaves ... They ate frost-bitten potatoes – not just because they were hungry but for the sweetness. Chocolates and other sweets were mere legends; no one had ever seen them, and no one had ever seen any jam, either.

'Eleven!' Kolka repeated, savouring the effect. 'And a couple of empty sugar sacks, too!'

They had pinched the sacks to carry their belongings in when they ran away.

Eighteen

Jackals are called jackals because they see everything. The brothers had four eyes; the jackals had a hundred and four, and each one of them had the ability to see not only straight ahead but round corners. And they kept note of what they saw.

However careful the brothers were, and try as they might to keep Glasha's voyages secret, they were spotted and found out. Not by the grown-ups, of course; they were so dim and stupid that one wondered why nature had bothered to give them a pair of eyes. No, the twins were spotted by their fellow-jackals.

One day Kolka was hanging about at the edge of the stream, waiting for Glasha to appear, when he saw one of the orphans running towards him. To be on the safe side, Kolka lowered his trousers and squatted down to make this intruder think he had come round here to relieve himself.

'They're looking for you!' shouted the boy.

'Who's looking for me?' asked Kolka, glancing at the stream out of the corner of his eye – please God, don't let Glasha appear now, or the game's up!

He had no idea that the others had long since discovered what they were up to and that a plot had been hatched against them.

'Your brother's looking for you! The other Kuzmin twin. He's round there in the backyard. Sashka, isn't it?'

'*I'm* Sashka,' said Kolka.

He pulled up his trousers, threw a last glance at the stream, and set off around the wall at a run. As he reached the factory gates, Sashka was coming towards him.

'Did you send for me?' Kolka panted, out of breath.

'Me? Send for you?' Sashka was surprised. 'No, I didn't. But where's Glasha?'

'Glasha? You mean you sent her off?'

'Didn't you get her at your end?'

They stared at each other. No words were needed; they had clearly been caught out.

They strolled over to where the orphans were boarding the truck. Kolka asked casually, 'D'you think they'll give it back to us?'

'The jackals?' Sashka grinned and snorted. 'I don't mind about the jar . . . but they've ruined the whole operation . . . don't you see?'

With that he was silent. Sitting in the truck, he did not look around him or try to guess from the jackals' faces which one of them had played this trick on them. Thinking about it objectively, the twins only had themselves to blame. The first rule for any orphanage inmate is to fool others and not to let them see what you're up to.

If you want to survive, that is.

And everyone wants to survive.

Jackals, above all, want to survive . . . so they had gathered into a pack and pounced . . .

They handed back Glasha the galosh, of course, but they did not return the jam. They had shared it out among themselves there and then, while waiting for the truck to arrive, and licked the jar clean. As if they hadn't just left the factory, where they could have eaten their fill anyway; but no: a jar of jam eaten outside the factory gates was doubly sweet.

From now on, the orphans started pilfering many more jars than before. They took them out in their trousers and behind their shirt fronts, for which purpose, imitating our twins, they joined up into couples and also started walking around with their arms around each other's shoulders.

The women factory-hands found this very touching. 'How our little orphans do love each other! Lord, don't they look sweet, clasping each other two and two . . . Regular little angels, they are!'

The little angels kept on pilfering more and more – it wasn't wings they were sprouting under their shirts, but jars of jam . . .

Before long they thought up the idea of loading the jars into baskets. From time to time the bushel-baskets, empty sugar sacks and scrap packing-materials had to be taken out in order to clear a space in the yard . . .

Sashka saw what they were doing and groaned: it showed the advantage of the collective mind at work. He had failed to hit on the idea of using baskets, but the jackal-pack had done it. They were now taking all their booty to the backyard, where they had set up whole storehouses beneath the rubbish.

The galosh was kept working round the clock. The jackals

131

renamed it 'The Magic Galosh', after the title of a fairy story that one of them had read. But no fairy-tale galosh could compare with this real-life galosh: it was not the source of mere fantasy but of a delicious goodness that was thoroughly tangible, multiplied to the nth power by all those jars of sweet jam with their golden lids!

At first the twins agonized over Glasha; Kolka in particular was worried that she might sink, get lost or torn . . .

One day, though, Sashka said to the jackals, 'Take the galosh and keep it! Do what you like with it!'

Kolka heard this and almost rushed forward to snatch the galosh away from Sashka. He even burst into tears. Why was his brother giving away their very own darling, precious Glasha for nothing, without demanding anything in return?

Kolka was so furious that he shouted, 'Are you off your rocker?' And he tapped his forehead with his finger, to show how much Sashka must have lost his head and gone crazy.

'Do I look crazy?' Sashka asked innocently.

Kolka wiped away his silly tears and looked hard at Sashka. No, he didn't look crazy. He was smiling just like the old Sashka and the look in his eyes was the same as ever. It was just that something must have happened to his brain: perhaps it had started to work backwards because of eating too much jam! Kolka had, after all, been cramming the stuff into his brother lately . . . Perhaps his brain was getting gummed up from too much sticky sweetness?

'But Glasha's ours! *Ours!*' Kolka shouted at him in despair. 'How can we *live* without her?'

'Quiet . . .' said Sashka, and both brothers glanced around them. But no one had overheard their argument. They were in the back-yard, where no one else was in earshot. The stinking stream was burbling away; weeds were peacefully sprouting through the piles of old crates which had been lying there for years and years, probably since before the war.

Sashka puffed out his cheeks and breathed out loudly. 'We'll manage as we always have. Without Glasha. We've finished with her.'

'Finished?' Kolka was astonished. 'But we . . . we've only just begun!'

'And now we've finished,' said Sashka calmly. 'It's time to stop and fade out of sight.'

He said this with such certainty that Kolka bit back the angry retort he was about to make.

Kolka always had faith in his brother's foresight and mental agility.

132

Always. Now, perhaps, was the first time that he felt any doubts. Sashka looked at Kolka and read his unspoken thoughts.

'They've gone completely barmy, don't you see?' He was referring to the jackals. 'Haven't you noticed that they're pinching far too much jam for their own good? They're burning their bridges as they go, and they're not thinking about the future! I'll be a son of a bitch if they don't go to the bottom along with our poor old Glasha . . .' And he added, 'Ibesobamyl . . .'

Decoded, 'IBESOBAMYL' meant: 'I'll be a son of a bitch all my life.' Sashka then tapped his front teeth and his throat with his thumb; this in turn meant: 'You can pull out a tooth and cut my throat . . .' It was a most solemn oath. For grown-ups the initials of the word were supposed to stand for: 'I'll bear the Soviet Banner all my life'. That was all right; the 'son of a bitch' version, however, was frowned upon and therefore all the more popular.

Sashka seldom swore this oath, so when he did Kolka could believe him.

But Kolka asked, 'Shall we tell them?'

'Tell them what?'

'Well, that we ought to stop pinching jam. That it's time to lie low or there'll be trouble, and we will all . . .'

'*They* will all,' Sashka corrected him.

'And *they* will all . . . you know . . . get it in the neck.'

'Tell them if you like,' said Sashka calmly. 'I suppose they'll believe you . . . But why didn't you believe me, eh? You were talking just now like the greediest, stupidest jackal.'

Kolka sighed. It was really hard to give up all those delicious free goodies which had come floating down the stream right into your hands.

And where was the orphan who would give them up – and just before the start of the hungry winter, too, which they knew from experience would shortly be upon them? The work at the factory, which would last for another month, or two months at most, was the time when they should be feeding themselves up! And after that? Take one's teeth out and put them on the shelf?

But Sashka kept firmly to his decision. The jackals had abandoned all restraint; they lacked the chief characteristic that distinguishes the decent thief from the jackal . . . They had no sense of proportion, no conscience. Conscience has to play a part in thievery, as in every other social activity. When you take something, you leave something for others; you must know when to stop when you abstract your share from someone else's property. If you take just a little from a

133

lot, that isn't theft – it's sharing! So said a great writer, though Sashka had forgotten exactly which one it was; that didn't matter – he had absorbed that writer's experience of life.

The jackals, on the other hand, pilfered shamelessly. Once a jam jar even fell out of a boy's shirt when he was already in the truck. They floated their booty through the wall almost for all to see. Once they took out a whole crateful of jars, which the remarkable Jewish porter had thrown over the wall for them.

Vera the truck-driver smiled and joked, pushing back the peak of her cap: 'Aha, you pirates, you robbers! Been hard at it, have you? I can tell my truck's going to have to work hard to pull *this* load!'

Vera saw everything, but never reported it – or as the orphans said, she never split on them.

About two weeks or so had passed since Sashka and Kolka had given up pinching jars of jam. They behaved as quietly and meekly as model children; they didn't pilfer any more, but nor did they hinder the others. The whole affair blew up one day when two orphans were seen hauling a basket, covered in sacking, out of the factory building and into the yard.

The keen-eyed Zina stopped them. 'What're you humping those sacks for? Leave them, I'll do it myself later . . . You should be doing your proper work!'

'We're helping!' The orphans could hardly get their tongues round the words. The basket was heavy, very heavy: out of greed they had overloaded it, shoving in about fifteen jars. They now stood there, going red in the face from strain and not knowing what to do next . . .

'We don't need your help!' said Zina. 'I'll carry it myself.'

Completely nonplussed, the orphans just stood there dumbly. The basket, too, was already creaking and starting to give way under the strain. Suddenly its bottom gave way with a loud clatter and the jars flew tinkling on to the concrete floor, the reflected sunlight from their bright golden lids flashing in all directions.

There were a lot of jars. They rolled over the uneven floor, and one stopped right at the feet of the factory's chief engineer, who happened to be passing. The old man bent down, picked up the jar, adjusted his steel-rimmed spectacles on his nose and looked at the label. 'Plum Jam. Ministry of Food Production. Factory No. 36–72. Russian Soviet Federated Socialist Republic,' he read, and glanced around him; the entire section had stopped work and was looking at him. The last of the jars was still rolling across the floor of the

134

section, as though running away, just as an orphan might take to his heels after such a disaster.

'Is this theft?' asked the engineer, watching the jar as it rolled away. 'This looks to me like a serious case of theft.'

At that point the two jackals dropped the basket and ran for it – out through the steel factory doors, across the yard and through the gates . . . No one tried to catch them; in any case, there was no point in just chasing two: they might be caught, but the rest would get away with it, and that would be that.

The orphans were barred from working in the factory.

Nineteen

That Sunday evening the children marched in a column – although it was far from being the seemingly endless column which had disembarked from the train a couple of months before – to the club in the village of Beriozovskaya to meet the local inhabitants.

The amateur show, which the orphans were to put on, coincided with the scandal at the factory – or rather, the orphanage superintendent decided to bring the concert forward in order to defuse the resulting ill-will between the collective-farm workers and the orphans. In the two months that they had been in those parts, the orphans had succeeded in antagonizing everyone.

The little clubhouse was in the very middle of the village, a single-storey brick building with pillars along its façade. The pillars still bore traces of shell-splinters, which had been hastily plastered over and whitewashed.

The hall was spacious, with folding wooden chairs set out in rows. There was no curtain in front of the stage; steps led up to it, left and right, from the auditorium. On the two large pillars flanking the stage on either side could just be seen some inscriptions written in a language that wasn't Russian; they had been painted over with oil-paint, though not quite thickly enough, and were partly concealed by portraits of the Soviet leaders. As a result, the leaders seemed to be shyly concealing their own slogans, but slogans written in another and now undesirable language: Chechen.

To the left of the fore-stage, almost at its very edge, stood a plywood rostrum painted a dirty purplish red.

Strangely enough, a lot of people had turned up. Most of them – peasants forcibly relocated from different parts of Russia – were slightly drunk; they talked loudly and animatedly, shouting to each other across the rows and creating much noise in the hall.

The orphans filtered through the crowd to take whatever empty seats they could find; but with the age-old defensive instinct of homeless people in a strange place, many of them stayed in a bunch, pushed their way forward and sat down on the floor between the front row of seats and the stage. Those for whom there was no room on seats or on the floor stood strung out along the side aisles, their backs pressed against the walls (another instinctive attitude of self-defence).

Clutching his inseparable briefcase, the superintendent of the orphanage, Pyotr Anisimovich, climbed up on to the stage; a few of those who saw him applauded. He went over to the rostrum. Inevitably, he already had a nickname: behind his back the orphans called him 'Mr Briefcase'. They would say, 'Mr Briefcase has ordered the dormitory to be searched.' Now one of them commented aloud, 'Mr Briefcase is going to give a report on our achievements.'

The jackals, sitting in front, laughed; their achievements were all too well known.

When the noise and laughter had died down, the superintendent began to speak. He spoke without notes. He congratulated the newly arrived collective-farmers on their first, difficult months spent in territory recently liberated from the enemy; he wished them success in getting in the harvest and in the start of their new lives, especially as the German fascist invaders had been beaten, were in retreat and soon, very soon, would face the hour of final retribution. As the Leader of the World Proletariat had predicted: 'Our cause is just, the enemy will be defeated and victory will be ours.'

Everyone applauded – not in honour of 'Mr Briefcase', of course, but of the Leader.

'Our young orphans,' the superintendent went on, 'have also come here to settle these fertile lands and, after a life of privation and homelessness, to begin a new, hard-working and constructive life, as enjoyed by all Soviet working people . . . These children will soon be starting the new school year, but they will also be helping our agricultural workers to bring in the harvest . . .'

'They already are helping,' came a voice from the audience. There was a burst of good-tempered laughter.

'And those who leave the orphanage on reaching fifteen years of age will join the collective farm or go to work in the canning factory,' the superintendent continued, pretending not to hear the remark. 'So we are going to live together with you as neighbours for a long time to come. I believe that today's get-together will help us to understand each other and to make friends . . . For a start, the collective farm has allocated some land to us as an ancillary small holding for us to cultivate – admittedly it's rather far from the

137

orphanage, but that doesn't matter. Our lads and lasses have young legs and they will easily cover the distance . . . And so we now have a basis on which to produce some of our own food; there are arable fields there, calves and goats . . . and so on . . . For that – thank you!'

There was a thin spattering of applause from the hall. The remark about living together as neighbours for a long time aroused no enthusiasm, especially as the farm had been obliged to hand over a parcel of land and several head of cattle. Everyone perked up, however, when the superintendent added, as he was leaving the rostrum, that the orphans were a lively and talented bunch, and had prepared their first amateur concert for the entertainment of the collective-farm workers.

First to come on stage were the dozen or so lads who formed the choir from Mytishchi. A teacher, Yevgeniya Vasilievna, announced that they would sing a song about Stalin. The superintendent nodded approvingly. The choir launched into the stirring ditty:

> **Oh, let our song of victory reach the Kremlin's very towers,**
> **Oh, let our people show their pride in Russia's fertile fields!**
> **When kolkhoz barns are bursting with the harvest that is**
> **ours,**
> **We're proud to know that Stalin, too, will smile to see those**
> **yields . . .**

The boys in the front row of the choir suddenly broke into a little dance, in time to the song, depicting collective-farmers gathering the harvest, and the audience loved this. There was generous applause, and the choir bowed awkwardly. But since the clapping didn't stop, and no more of their songs had been approved for performance at this show, the boys from Mytishchi stood and waited. Suddenly, all together, every choir-member put his right foot forward, tapped it in the 'train-wheel' rhythm, starting humming, 'Tum-ta, tam-ta-tum-ta, tam-ta . . .', and then:

> **An officer was sitting in a train,**
> **A dandy with much charm**
> **But little brain . . .**

The superintendent stood up and began to push his way through to the exit.

The boys, of course, thought he was leaving because he didn't

138

want to listen to the song he had censored as unsuitable. But this was not the reason; or at least, not the only reason.

No one knew about it, but he was driven by Vera back to the orphanage for an urgent appointment: he was to take part in a search of the orphanage premises. He would conduct the search, and then, if possible, return to the concert before it was over. It was assumed that after the concert the collective-farm management, in the spirit of friendship that Pyotr Anisimovich had stressed in his speech, would invite the orphans to the farm for supper.

Like the rest of the children, the Kuzmin Twins for once had no inkling of what was happening back at the orphanage. Even the perceptive Sashka was in quite a carefree mood; he was only concerned to know when it would be their turn to go on stage. The twins were waiting impatiently in a narrow little room backstage, more like a corridor than a room, while Yevgenia Vasilievna called out the names of the next performers as they were due to go on: 'The Kashira girls . . . Quickly! Quickly! . . . Are you ready, Lyubertsy? . . . After that it's the Lyublino group . . .'

'What about us? When are we going to sing?' the Kuzmin Twins asked her.

'What's your name?'

'The Kuzmins.'

'Both of you?'

'What d'you mean, both of us?'

'What are your separate names?'

'We're never separate.'

'Aha . . .' said Yevgenia Vasilievna. 'So you're a family duet? Wait here. I'll tell you when it's your turn.'

The brothers looked at each other and did not reply. Although they were brothers, they didn't like having the word 'family' applied to them. In fact, they had already met Yevgenia Vasilievna, but she had obviously forgotten them. It had happened once when they had gone to see Regina Petrovna, who had been drinking tea with Yevgenia and the superintendent. The grown-ups had turned round, and the Kuzmin Twins, as though they were being put on show, had stood uneasily in the middle of the room, feeling it would be rude to go straight out again.

Regina Petrovna had laughed, pointed at them, and said, 'These are my two little friends. It's impossible to tell them apart, so they're simply known as the Kuzmin Twins. There's no need to remember which is which, because they'll only try and fool you . . . You do, don't you?' she asked the brothers, and they nodded. Everyone had

139

laughed, including Regina Petrovna, though not like the others, who were merely amused, but in a kindly way as though she were one of the twins' family.

But the Kuzmins did not remind Yevgenia Vasilievna of that occasion; they were only concerned that no one should forget about the turn they were to perform in the concert.

At the same time several people, including the chief engineer from the factory, the superintendent and a soldier with a mine-detector, were searching the orphanage courtyard. So far all they had found was scrap-metal in the form of some rusting bits of old machinery, but there was no sign of what they were looking for.

Somebody suggested going back to the senior boys' dormitory, where everything had already been turned upside down. They searched the place several times from corner to corner, but without result. They were just about to leave the dormitory when the soldier reported a faint buzzing in his earphones, indicating the presence of a small quantity of metal.

Once again the soldier passed his 'frying-pan' on its long handle over the floor of the room, then took off the earphones and pointed to the far corner. A crowbar was fetched, and they began trying to prise up a large, thick floorboard. It refused to give way.

The superintendent, who had been watching the whole procedure with increasing dubiousness, glanced at his watch and asked the soldier: 'Are you sure you're not mistaken?' And he said to the others, 'I just don't understand what's happening! Will somebody please tell me how they could hide anything there? They haven't any tools . . .'

'All right,' the chief engineer agreed and adjusted his steel-rimmed spectacles. 'This will be our last attempt. If we don't find anything, we'll call the search off. That means your young lads are cleverer than we are!'

'Or more honest!' said the superintendent. 'And it will prove they didn't steal anything.'

'Apart from those sixteen jars that fell out of the basket at my feet . . .'

'Yes, apart from those . . .' the superintendent agreed with a sigh.

Meanwhile a youth from Ramenskoye was on stage, reciting Pushkin's poem 'The Caucasus' with great feeling:

The Caucasus beneath me: there upon a peak

Above a precipice I stand, amid the snow;
An eagle, launched from distant rocks on wing-beats slow
Now hovers at my height his prey to seek . . .

Sashka said to Kolka, 'It's a poem about comrade Stalin!'

'Why?' Kolka was always slow to grasp such things.

Crossly, Sashka explained, 'Don't you see? It's him standing on the mountain . . . All alone, like a monument, got it? He's a great man, that's why he's all alone on the summit . . . And the eagle, you see, isn't flying higher than him – it's afraid to, so it keeps on the same level. He's standing up there and looking down on the Soviet Union. That way he can see all of us – got it?'

The youth continued reciting:

Below me there is little but sparse moss, dry scrub;
But lower flourish groves of pine, flow torrents clear,
Where birds are singing and where browse the speckled deer.
There, too, stand simple huts, where dwell the mountain folk . . .

At this point in the poem a special, heavy silence settled on the auditorium. The inspired reciter, however, was not aware of it, and went on bellowing out the familiar verses:

. . . Here sheep do graze upon the meadows, steep yet lush;
A shepherd there descends, past stream and bush,
To where the Aragva flows within its shaded banks.
A ragged horseman shelters in a rocky cleft . . .

A strange rustling sound passed through the hall. Suddenly words began passing from row to row, but it was hard to catch their meaning. Only one insistent refrain was clearly audible: 'The poem's about the Chechens! It's about them – the brutes!'

The adults in the audience were so excited and disturbed that they forgot to applaud. Only the orphans clapped.

The huge nails creaking and squealing, the floorboard was at last levered up and an underground pit was revealed to the searchers, at the bottom of which glittered the golden lids of countless jam jars. At first it was impossible to estimate whether the cache numbered hundreds or thousands. The jars were piled on the ground in heaps, each lid being marked with a letter and a number indicating its owner, to avoid any confusion later.

Grunting, the chief engineer lowered himself into the pit, adjusted his steel-rimmed glasses, and peered around, still unable to believe his eyes. He looked up at the superintendent and asked him to hand him down paper and pencil.

'We must draw up an official report. There's more stuff here than there is in the factory warehouse,' he said. 'So shall we just enter them in the stock-book and say no more about it? Well, Comrade Meshkov?'

Pyotr Anisimovich, who had turned pale at the sight of this hoard, reached eagerly into his briefcase and produced a sheet of paper. In a lifeless voice he said, 'I just don't understand what's happening . . .'

When it came to the Kuzmin Twins' turn to go on stage, there was already a tense silence in the hall. The brothers looked down at the floor where the orphans were sitting, then stared into space and began singing:

> Upon an oak, above the plains,
> Two keen-eyed falcons high did perch:
> The people knew those falcons well . . .

It was, of course, a sad song; one of the falcons was dying, and the other said to him . . . I swear an oath to follow your path and from it I shall never turn aside:

> He kept that oath, that warrior's oath,
> And made the people happy, too,
> The people of the land he loved . . .

The romantic image of the two falcons was, of course, an allegory for Lenin and Stalin, as the audience well understood. The twins ended the song on a high note, having sung it all very touchingly, and so for a more cheerful finale they belted out a familiar old song about a coach pulled by galloping horses, which was also well suited to two-part close harmony. The twins acted out the words of the song and went off to a loud and approving reception from the audience.

As they were leaving the stage, they caught sight of Pyotr Anisimovich, the superintendent, clutching his briefcase to his chest and pushing his way to his seat through the cluster of orphans sitting on the floor. They could not help noticing that his face was not just sad: it was grey in colour and stamped with a look of despair.

He sat down with a deep sigh and prepared to listen, unaware that the concert was almost over.

'Tricks and sleight of hand!' Yevgenia Vasilievna announced from the stage; with a wave of her hand that was holding the list of performers, she summoned Mitek to centre-stage.

Mitek had wrapped a long scarf round his head so that he looked like some oriental fakir, but the orphans recognized him and immediately started giggling. 'It's Mitek! It's Mitek! The shoup made him shweat!'

Mitek pretended not to have heard, and kept up a convincing act as a magician. He raised his arms, made a few passes in the air, and there in his hand was an apple. Mitek took a bite out of the apple, and the orphans in the front of the audience commented, 'That's an easy one! Can you produce a jar of jam?'

At this the superintendent shuddered and looked fearfully around him.

Mitek finished eating the apple with evident enjoyment, made some more passes, wriggled his fingers, and there in his hand was a bright, golden lid from a jam jar. Then came a lot more lids, which fell on to the stage, and two of them fell into the auditorium.

'He must have pinched those lids from the factory!' said a loud male voice from the audience, but he was quickly hushed by the others:

'Don't spoil the show!'

'Now for my chief piece of magic!' Mitek warned them, and stared into the auditorium. 'I shall now remove an object from one of you who ish shitting in thish hall . . .'

There was a rustle of excitement in the hall, and people began checking their pockets.

The superintendent fidgeted uneasily and cast a nervous, wary glance at Mitek. He was no doubt regretting that he had allowed the boy to perform.

The magician glanced around the hall, found the superintendent, stared hard at his briefcase and even stretched out his arm towards it, which made Pyotr Anisimovich clutch it even more tightly to his chest.

Mitek smiled a wise, knowing smile. In his hand was a sheet of paper.

'There!' he cried, waving the paper in the air. 'Thish hash come from a shertain well-known briefcashe.'

143

'Show us!' roared the audience, and Pyotr Anisimovich glanced uneasily at his briefcase. Both locks were firmly shut.

'May I? May I show it?' Mitek asked him.

'You may, you may,' replied the superintendent wearily, still firmly clutching his briefcase.

'I shall now read it,' said Mitek; he looked intently at the sheet of paper and began to read the contents aloud.

'Today, the fifth of October 1944, a shearch wash carried out in the groundsh and premishesh of the orphanage, in particular in the shenior boysh' dormitory . . . In the dormitory a floorboard wash removed and a shecret hiding-plashe dishcovered, in which . . .'

'Stop!' screamed Pyotr Anisimovich, and jumped to his feet in anguish. 'That document is mine!'

'Go on! Go on reading, magician!' shouted the audience.

' . . . A shecret hiding-plashe dishcovered, in which were five hundred jarsh of plum jam produshed at the local canning factory . . .'

'Give me back that paper,' begged the superintendent, 'and I will explain . . .'

But the orphans were already pushing their way towards the exit, no doubt hoping to save at least some of their buried treasure. In any case, what the hell was the point of staying at a concert supposed to promote friendship, when they searched your home behind your back?

The people from the collective farm were also starting to get up, laughing and joking among themselves. These lads were conjurors all right if they could pinch five hundred jars of jam from their neighbours, just to show how friendly they were – and without so much as a 'thank you'!

Amid the noise and the clattering of chairs, a man's voice was heard shouting from somewhere in the back rows, 'Quiet! Keep quiet, will you?'

Puzzled, the people fell silent, looking around at the place where the voice was coming from and wondering why he was shouting so desperately. Perhaps the magician had cleaned him out too!

In the ensuing silence, from somewhere very close there suddenly came a rapid clatter of hooves, the neighing of horses and shouts in an unknown, guttural language. There was the roar of an explosion, apparently from the roof of the hall; the walls shook and lumps of plaster fell from the ceiling. For a moment it seemed as if the whole roof was about to fall in. People instinctively crouched down, and some threw themselves flat on the floor.

144

There was a tense silence. Everyone listened and waited, glancing nervously upwards, but nothing happened. After a while they straightened up, began to move and look about them in perplexity. Suddenly they all started to head for the doors, without jostling or shouting; they just disappeared without a word, leaving the orphans in the semi-darkened hall.

'So our new friends have faded away, have they?' said a cheeky voice from somewhere amid the silence. At this moment Pyotr Anisimovich recovered his authority.

'All orphanage inmates to stay in the clubhouse!' he shouted, looking round at the door. 'We will all leave in an orderly fashion, when . . . when . . . when.'

'Mr Briefcase is so scared, the needle's got stuck on his record!' Sashka whispered.

Kolka nodded. But he, too, was staring at the door.

Everyone jumped when a sharp cry was heard from the street. 'They've blown up the truck! Our Vera was in it! And a house is on fire!'

'What about the people?' the superintendent asked in a hoarse, cracked voice. No one knew what 'people' he meant; the people who had been in the club and were running away in all directions, or . . . the people . . . who . . . ?

'Hey! Is there somebody out there?' The superintendent's voice rose to a squeak and broke off.

An orphan repeated the news about the truck and Vera . . . and about the house that was on fire.

Pyotr Anisimovich went cautiously up to the door and looked out, listening to the sounds coming from the street. Clearing his throat hoarsely, he said in an indecisive voice:

'We will . . . that's to say . . . go outside . . . I just don't understand what's happening . . .'

The orphans began to move towards the exit, but no one was in a hurry to push forward.

The street was deserted and dark; not a single window was showing a light. Perhaps everyone had managed to get away in time.

On the square in front of the clubhouse the Studebaker truck was blazing furiously – the same truck that used to take the orphans to the factory. Rooted to the spot, the children stared at the fire, many of them no doubt thinking of Vera.

Without stopping, and appearing to ignore the burning truck, the superintendent strode forward, followed by all the orphans. Somewhere on the edge of the village, behind some trees, huge pink

145

tongues of flame were leaping and flickering. As they drew nearer, it was clear that a house was on fire.

Kolka shuddered and said, 'Look – it's Ilya's house!'

Sashka asked, 'Do you think he's inside?'

'How should I know?'

'I hope he managed to get away . . . or . . . maybe he didn't?'

The brothers looked at each other. Red flames were dancing in Sashka's eyes as he stared at the fire.

The superintendent looked around him and shouted, almost hysterically, 'No one . . . anywhere near . . . Keep away from it! Stay with me! Got it?'

And because he shouted so loudly and in such an unmanly voice, the children seemed to huddle together and were very quiet.

The picture, then, was like this: the superintendent was walking forwards, his briefcase held out in front of him like a shield, his gait was not exactly hesitant, but somehow unsteady and jerky, as if he had forgotten how to walk. No doubt he felt the support of the children behind him. And they, too, felt that by keeping close behind him they were better shielded and protected.

None of them, thank God, could see his face at that moment.

The thick darkness seemed especially gloomy after the bright glare of the fire.

We walked on, clustered into a tight, silent mass. Our eyes were not used to the black night; the light of the leaping flames was still imprinted on our retinas. The whole experience was so unfamiliar that it seemed as if tongues of flame were shooting out at us from the surrounding blackness. We even did our best to tread carefully, so that our shoes should make as little noise as possible. We held our breath and tried not to cough or sneeze.

The children at the back kept glancing behind them and tried to push forward into the middle of the bunch, where it felt safer. Everything around us was a threat: the night; the dense, heavy darkness; the impenetrable thickets of maize on either side of the road, which rustled in the faint breeze.

What did we know, what could we understand of the danger that threatened us? We knew and understood nothing whatsoever. There had been only secrecy and hushed muttering about certain things that we could only guess at, such as the unfortunate fire in the orphanage . . .

But then we were gullible, carefree; it had not yet dawned on us that we were mortal, and even the danger, the nature of which was

146

still not quite clear to us, seemed to be little more than a game. The war had taught us to fight for our existence, but it had by no means taught us to expect death.

Later, as adults, those of us who survived were to recall that night over and over again: the neighing of horses; guttural, unfamiliar voices; explosions; the truck burning in the middle of the deserted village . . . and the walk back through the alien night.

We were frightened, but not because we might die. It was the feeling experienced by a caged animal who is suddenly imprisoned by some mechanical monster that admits no light from outside. Like little wild animals, we sensed through our skin that we were being inexorably caged in by the night, by those endless walls of maize, by those explosions and fires . . .

But these are just words. Words written forty years after those events of the autumn of 1944. Sitting in a comfortable Moscow apartment, can anyone conjure up from within themselves that sense of unrelieved terror that was all the stronger the greater our numbers were? It was as if each individual's fear was multiplied by the number of those in our group; we were together, but each one's fear was his own, personal yet increased by the fear felt by all the others. It gripped you by the throat.

I have only recalled it here in mental retrospect; yet the memory is still in my skin, and it is as real as it is possible to be: how our legs weakened and buckled with fear but could not stop walking and running, because escape seemed our only salvation.

There was a chill in one's stomach and chest, there was an insane desire to hide somewhere, to disappear, to go away – and not with all the others but alone! And we were, of course, on the very edge of crying out. We kept silent, but if one of us had suddenly shouted, or howled like a hunted wolf, then we would all have howled and shouted, and we might have literally gone mad . . .

At all events, that walk through the deadly night was our break-through into the harsh reality of life, a rite of passage of which we were unaware. With our guts, our hearts, our arms and legs we wanted to live . . .

Not all of us were to be so lucky . . .

Twenty

That same night the Kuzmin Twins decided to run away. The panic gripping the entire orphanage, from Pyotr Anisimovich down to the youngest jackal in the junior classes, had also affected the two brothers.

What had shocked them was neither the explosion that took place in the village that evening nor the blazing Studebaker truck (although they could not understand how steel could burn like that), but the fire that destroyed Ilya's house: he it was who had been the first to warn them of danger, yet despite his own warning the silly fool had been the first victim.

To the twins it seemed like a grim reminder that no one can escape their destiny: a crafty little man he might be, yet fate had caught up with him and he had presumably been burned to death inside his house. Even so, while aware of this, at the same time they couldn't help feeling sorry for him: they forgot that he was a cheat who fenced stolen goods, and only remembered how he had poked his signal-flags into the face of the man at Voronezh Station when they were being chased by that screaming market-woman. Here, too, in this inhospitable village, who but Ilya had invited them into his house . . . and had said, as he saw them off, 'Get out of this place while you can, because there's going to be big trouble!'

It was easy enough to say that, but where could they have gone . . . ?

Now, though, with their large stock of jam, it was a different matter; now, any conductress would let them stow away on her train in exchange for a jar of jam; perhaps she might even let them travel in a compartment, so they wouldn't have to ride the rods or suffocate in the dog-box slung under the carriage, but they might even make the trip like gentlemen, reclining on a luggage-rack!

The brothers knew without looking at each other that they were both thinking along the same lines. Everything around was burning,

148

and only someone who was blind or stupid could fail to sense that the fire would soon engulf the orphans too . . . indeed, it was already singeing them.

Neither the twins nor anyone else slept much that night.

The senior boys went straight to their dormitory with its ripped-up floor. They looked glumly into the deep hole they had dug; it was exuding a cold draught that smelled of rats. It was a heart-rending sight; their feelings must have been something like the emotions of a field-mouse when, in late autumn, just before the start of a hungry winter, he finds his store of grain has been ransacked.

The Kuzmin Twins had not known about the under-floor cache, but they had guessed there must be one somewhere; the huge flow of jars out of the factory would obviously have required a large storage-space. When underground agents are infiltrated into the enemy's rear area, they never operate in groups of more than three, in order to minimize losses if a group is discovered. But just as the jackals hunted in a pack and hid their booty in one enormous pile, so they were caught wholesale – and lost the whole lot at once!

That night, however, our two brothers were not worried about the other boys' stockpile, but about their own.

They decided that as soon as all was quiet they would pack their booty in two sacks, sling them over their backs, hot-foot it to the station . . . then jump on a train, and escape, escape, escape! The light of the fire that night had made one thing absolutely clear to them: they must get away in order to save themselves.

After midnight, when the orphanage inmates had finally sunk into a light, restless pre-dawn sleep – if they were sleeping at all – the brothers slipped out of the building, crawled through their prickly gap in the hedge, which now seemed especially awkward and difficult to negotiate, and made their way to the bank of the little river.

On their way, they saw through the bushes the flicker of headlights and heard men's voices.

Their hearts began to beat faster and a shiver seized them from head to foot: they felt certain the men had found their cache and were raiding it. If they had found one under the dormitory floor-boards, then why not by the river-bank?

But when the twins came a little closer, they realized that these men were not concerned about their hoard of jam, which was causing them such obsessive anxiety (the man with fleas thinks of nothing but the bath-house, as the saying goes!): a party of soldiers had driven up on motor cycles and had stopped for a rest by the river. They had not lit a fire, but were using the headlamps to provide light, and were cursing as they busied themselves around their machines. Even at a distance there was a strong smell of petrol.

The men were talking loudly about a ravine in the mountains where they had been ambushed by bandits, who had blocked the road with boulders and then opened fire from behind a mound. Although a motor cycle and sidecar had been wrecked, the soldiers had managed to escape from the ravine, but one of them had been wounded in the head and shoulder.

The Kuzmin Twins could now see the wounded soldier. The others were giving him first aid. At first he only groaned and swore, but then he screamed in a piercing voice, making the twins jump, 'Those damn' rebels! Ought to be put up against a wall and shot! They've been robbers and cut-throats for a hundred years and they still are. The only thing they understand is force, the mother-fuckers . . . Shoot the lot of them, I say! Comrade Stalin knew what he was doing when he kicked the bastards out of here! He should have cleaned out the whole Caucasus while he was about it! Damn' traitors! Sold themselves to Hitler!'

When the wounded man had been bandaged, he fell silent. His comrades went into the bushes to piss, where they began talking about how the war was nearly over, complaining about their bad luck – while their pals at the front were storming westward into Europe, here in the Caucasus they had to mess about attacking tumbledown Chechen villages in the mountains, fighting old women and children!

When the soldiers had finished talking and began settling down to sleep, the brothers realized these men were not going to leave. This meant that the escape would have to be postponed to another day. To leave without their jam would be inviting disaster; wherever they might go, without their food-supply they could only expect hunger, begging or theft . . . and then, inevitably – the police!

And anyway, who would voluntarily give up such a treasure?

Kolka said as much: he announced that he would rather lie down and die than move a step away from their secret store. Better to die here on the river-bank beside the cache than abandon it!

They decided that on the whole they should wait until morning – a time of day which, if the Russian proverb is to be believed, is wiser than evening.

Dawn, however, was already approaching; the twilight was fading from the invisible mountains. There was already a slight freshness in the air and gusts of breeze were making the maize-stalks rustle.

At breakfast that morning it became known that Regina Petrovna

150

had returned from hospital. When the Kuzmin Twins heard the news in the dining-hall, they exchanged glances. Both of them thought the same: what a piece of luck for them; it's an ill wind, as they say.

They ran quickly to their cache by the river-bank. The soldiers had already gone; a bloodstained wad of cotton-wool, scraps of bandage and several fag-ends were scattered on the grass.

Kolka thrust his hand into their hiding-place: intact! The jam was all there! He counted all the jars – smooth, chilly to the touch, and even slightly heavy in feel. If the soldiers had only known how near they were to such riches as they snored away!

There was now an urgent necessity to see Regina Petrovna before that night, when they were planning to escape. Although she had returned, and the girls insisted that they had seen her, she did not put in an appearance; nor was she to be seen in her little room behind the kitchen, however often the boys tried to peer through the little window.

They loafed around all day, looking in frequently, but in vain.

That evening, Kolka said it was time to run away and that he simply could not wait any longer. Suddenly Sashka announced firmly that without Regina Petrovna, at least without having seen her, he, Sashka, was not moving from the spot. Kolka might be pining for their stock of jam, but he, Sashka, wasn't going anywhere until he had seen Regina Petrovna. And to hell with the jam! To hell with all eleven jars of it and the two sacks! They could *not* leave without Regina Petrovna and her little boys, and that was that! Otherwise, the twins would be saving themselves and leaving a person like Regina Petrovna to almost certain death ... how *could* they?

They had to escape together; that was how Sashka saw it.

And so another night was lost for their escape plans.

Already, though, the initial sense of alarm, the profound panic felt by all the orphans had worn off, and fear – desperate, clinging, relentless fear – had also begun to lessen and melt away. Even the funeral of Vera the truck-driver, two days later, failed to galvanize the twins.

That morning, a decrepit old Zis truck, which rattled like a farm-cart, came to fetch the boys from the senior classes. The benches in it did not let down from the sides but were placed across the load-platform and wobbled dangerously because they were not fixed to the floor.

Everything, in fact, seemed unfamiliar to the orphans: the grim, taciturn old driver; those uncomfortable benches; and even the way

151

in which he drove, slowly and cautiously as if his passengers were made of glass – so different from the way in which the dashing Vera had driven them!

The children sincerely mourned poor Vera: she had almost been one of them. She had not behaved like a bossy grown-up, because she had known all about the orphans' misdeeds yet had never given them away. *And* she had driven a truck! *And* she was pretty and cheerful with it! *And* such a good sport! Anyone might think she had spent half her life in an orphanage too!

But strangely enough, none of the children wanted to go to the funeral, and none of them could properly explain their reluctance to go. Only when it was announced that they would all be fed in the factory canteen, and the meal would even include a dish of meat, did the children agree to go. It was a fact that apart from this one occasion they had never yet been given meat to eat.

The Kuzmin Twins went too, because in addition to the promised meal they had their own reasons for going: they might be able, with luck, to look and see whether a few extra jam jars were still intact under some old crates in the backyard, where they had hidden them before all the fuss had blown up.

If only they could manage to grab them and add them to their store – and in time for their escape, too!

The funeral ceremony, as was expected, took place in the main factory yard.

The coffin was hidden behind a crowd of women, who were clustered around it; all were wearing clean white headscarves, and some of them were crying.

Seeing the orphans coming in through the gates, several of the women turned around and moved aside to let them through.

Although they hadn't wanted to, the Kuzmin Twins found them-selves right in front of the coffin, a rectangular box knocked together from rough planks and unpainted. The top of the coffin was just at the boys' eye-level. Standing on tiptoe and staring into it with a mixture of curiosity and fear, they could see lying in it a beautiful woman with tightly shut lips, her reddish-gold hair framing a calm, unfamiliar face.

The woman was nothing like their cheerful truck-driver in her peaked cap and men's clothes.

It was another Vera, not theirs; the brothers saw this at once, and looked away. With downcast eyes they stared at the legs of the table on which the coffin had been placed. The table, its steel top now covered with a sheet, was familiar to them from the factory: it was

152

the one on which the jar-capper had stacked the glass jars of jam, which they had then pinched from behind his back.

The two brothers longed for this depressing ceremony to be over, so that they could sneak round to the backyard where their jars were hidden.

The tears, the sighing and snitfling, the ritual lamentation that was coming from the crowd of women was starting to make the twins' heads ache, causing the same kind of headache they had felt in police stations when they had been caught pilfering from market-stalls.

At last the old chief engineer came out of the factory, still wearing the plain blue coat that he wore at work. He looked at the dead woman's face as he began telling them all about Vera. He said that Vera was a very young girl, only nineteen when she died, but who in her short life had experienced a great deal, especially since she had lived through the German occupation. The fascist invaders had driven Vera's family away into slavery in Germany, but they had been unable to catch Vera . . . Three times she had escaped during deportation and three times she had returned home. On the last occasion she had hidden in a wardrobe, and the enemy had had to drag her out of it . . .

The brothers couldn't help finding it very funny, as they imagined Vera sitting inside a wardrobe. But everyone was looking at the chief engineer and listening with serious faces.

In her work at the factory Vera had been a Stakhanovite, even though she had done such tough, man's work as driving a five-ton truck; it had been her job to carry the finished products to the railway station and bring the children to and from work . . . As he said this, the old man pointed at the Kuzmin Twins, and they felt very embarrassed. As they saw it, driving a truck was not hard work at all but fun.

'Rest in peace, Vera dear, we shall not forget you,' said the old man, and bowed his head. His short grey hair was silvered by the sunlight. The women started to sob, and the loudmouthed Zina burst into a ritual, keening lament for the departed. It turned out from her words that she and Vera had come from the same village; they had been brought here together and put to work at the factory . . .

The Jewish stevedores pushed their way through to the coffin. With inscrutable faces they lifted Vera as easily as if she were a speck of dust and carried her over to the truck that had brought the orphans.

A band consisting of a drum, cymbals and two trumpets struck up; the muffled thumping of drum and cymbals made the twins' hearts turn over, and they felt sick and miserable.

Alongside the table bearing the coffin, several women, including the wailing Zina, took their seats in the back of the truck, and the vehicle drove away.

Everyone began to leave by the factory gates, except for the old chief engineer, who remained standing in the middle of the yard and said to the orphans, 'Off you go! . . . We're not working today!'

So there was no meal and no meat for them; apparently there had been no such invitation. The brothers set off on their way back to the orphanage.

As they walked along the road they discussed what they had seen. Both agreed that Vera had not looked like her real self and wasn't young at all. By the Kuzmin Twins' reckoning, nineteen was almost old age; after all, they were not little children any longer, and if you added their ages together they would be slightly older than Vera.

Kolka also told how he had heard someone just behind his back whispering that Vera had apparently been sitting in the truck, waiting for the concert to end in order to take the orphans to the supper that had been arranged for them. She had not noticed the horsemen coming. No doubt they had not spotted Vera either, and had only seen the truck. But when they threw a grenade at it, Vera had managed to jump out of the burning vehicle and run a few yards before falling down. It emerged later that one fragment of the grenade casing had lodged right in her heart . . . So how had she managed to run when her heart was pierced?

Sashka was pondering the question and did not reply. To Kolka he only growled, 'I don't believe it,' and fell silent again.

'What don't you believe?' asked Kolka. 'That she was hit in the heart? Is that what you don't believe?'

Sashka said nothing.

'Do you think they made it up? . . . About her heart, I mean?'

Still Sashka said nothing.

'Or about . . . those people . . . the bandits?'

By taking a short cut across the fields, they had reached the bank of the Sunzha river and were now sitting on the grass.

The mountains, indistinct and mirage-like, glittered in a bluish-white haze. They seemed to exist, but in such a way that it was quite impossible to perceive them as concrete reality.

'I don't believe anything,' Sashka said suddenly. Then, after another long silence: 'I can't understand it all. There was Vera: she used to drive us to work, shout at us and make jokes . . . Then all of a sudden she's not there. So what's become of her?'

Kolka was surprised, and objected, 'But we know where she is . . . They've buried her!'

'No, I didn't mean that.'

Sashka screwed up his eyes and looked into the distance. The reddish-brown water was dancing over the pebbles, a butterfly fluttering above it.

'Those, now . . .' Sashka pointed up to the mountains. 'They appear and disappear again, but they're always there. Isn't that so?'

'Well, what . . . ?' Kolka was about to ask.

'And this stream . . . It's always here, too . . .'

'Well?'

'But what about people? What happens to them?'

'Are you talking about Vera?'

Sashka frowned. 'I'm talking about everybody. About you and me and all the rest. Did you feel frightened when you were standing by the coffin?'

'No,' said Kolka. 'Not exactly frightened. But . . . I felt sort of uncomfortable.'

He could not find a better word, but only gave a shiver.

'And the other night, after the fire, when we were all walking back from the village past the maize-fields? Did you feel frightened then?'

'Yes, I did,' Kolka admitted.

'So did I. Only I don't know *what* I was afraid of. I was just afraid.'

'Were you afraid . . . of *them* . . . the devils?'

'No,' said Sashka, and sighed. 'I wasn't afraid of them. I was afraid of everything. The explosions, the fire and the maize . . . I was even afraid of you.'

'Me?'

'Uh-huh.'

'*Me?*' Kolka asked again, astonished.

'Well, no, not just you, but all of the others . . . And you. I was just afraid of everything and everybody. I felt that I'd been left completely alone. D'you see?'

Kolka did not understand, and remained silent. That evening they went to see Regina Petrovna.

Twenty-one

At first they decided to take a jar of jam with them, then they changed their minds and left it. There was too much talk in the orphanage about that jam, and it might not be the best moment for the twins to appear with their jar.

They went in the evening after the funeral and found Regina Petrovna at home. She had settled into a distant corner of the kitchen, screened off by a yellow-striped, government-issue flannelette blanket.

Regina Petrovna was sincerely delighted to see them. 'My dear Kuzmins,' she said as she admitted them to her corner and sat them down on the bed. 'Who's who?' she asked in English, pointing to Sashka, who this time was wearing the silver-buckled belt she had given them, and said, 'You must be Kolka, aren't you?'

The brothers laughed, and she realized she was mistaken.

'All right,' she said, 'you win. I've been busy doing the washing since I got back. It had piled up . . . Although my little boys were being looked after by the girls, they had got pretty filthy. But I'll get rid of it all while you're here . . . We'll have some tea in a moment . . . With sweets! I've brought some real sweets!'

The brothers exchanged looks and nodded at the same time. At once, Regina Petrovna asked, 'Or are sweets no surprise for you?'

She picked up a basin full of soapsuds and carried it out. When she came back she sat down opposite them, and asked, 'Well, were you mixed up in the jam business? Did you nick a lot of it, as your pals would say? Did you? And stash it away somewhere? Am I right?'

'Well, so what if we did?' mumbled Sashka. 'Yes, we have stashed it away.'

The two brothers were thrilled to hear her amazing, deep laugh, which sounded to them like a favourite song.

They had already managed to scrutinize their teacher, noticing that she had grown thinner and that a yellowish pallor was showing through her naturally dark-olive skin. Her hair, though, had become thicker, longer and more luxuriant; it was hardly hair any longer but a black, unruly mane carelessly knotted into a bun. As the Kuzmin Twins watched her, she looked at her reflection in the window – her mirror had presumably been destroyed in the fire – and with a single, slight movement she pulled a large comb out of her hair. It cascaded on to her shoulders like a dark waterfall, making her face look even paler, her features slightly more pinched.

'I'll let my hair breathe for a while,' she said, throwing her head back so that it fell down on her back. 'And I'll make tea. Then we'll have a chat.'

Regina Petrovna brought in a teapot, glasses and a saucerful of sweets that looked like brown beetles. 'Help yourselves.' She pushed the saucer towards them. 'They're called "cushions", and they're quite delicious with tea.'

The brothers took a sweet each. Sashka put his into his mouth at once and ate it, but Kolka only licked his and laid it aside.

'Now I see that you weren't trying to fool me about who was who.' Regina Petrovna laughed again. 'Sashka really is Sashka, even though he's wearing Kolka's belt. Now tell me ... You did have something to tell me, didn't you?'

Sashka looked at Kolka and nodded.

'How have you been getting on, my dears? I was afraid you'd run away. You did want to run away didn't you? Own up, now!'

'Yes, we did,' said Sashka.

'You were frightened, weren't you?'

The brothers did not reply; the answer was obvious.

Regina Petrovna gazed at them with a long, thoughtful stare and they looked down, embarrassed.

'I was frightened too,' she said simply.

'Did you ... did you see them?' Sashka stared at her.

'Yes, I did.'

'There!' Sashka exclaimed. 'I knew it!'

Regina Petrovna poured out tea for the twins and herself. She then went over to the window and lit a cigarette; as she was doing so, the twins noticed that her hands were shaking.

'Thank God I managed to get some cigarettes while I was in hospital,' she said, looking out of the window and inhaling the smoke deeply. 'Well, when it happened ... I didn't go to bed for a long while, and my light was burning all the time. Suddenly they appeared outside my window ... Three men. And there was a boy with them too. The window was wide open, as this one is now, and I couldn't

157

really understand what was happening. The three were just standing there and watching my hands as I was cutting up and sewing that fur hat into caps for you two. I looked up at them . . . and then . . .'

Regina Petrovna took another lungful of smoke, got out another cigarette, lit it from the first and threw the end out of the window.

She smoked for a while in silence, stubbed out the cigarette in a saucer, came back and sat down again at the table.

'My dears – why aren't you eating some sweets?'

'We've already had some,' Kolka replied for them both. 'What happened then?'

Biting her lip, Regina Petrovna thought for a while. Then, as though remembering herself, she looked at the brothers. 'Yes. Yes . . . Only you must not tell a soul, all right?'

The brothers nodded.

'The police told me . . . ordered me not to tell this to anyone. Anyway, they aimed a gun right here . . .' She pointed to her forehead. 'But the little boy jogged the man's elbow – I think it was his father. And the shot missed me. The boy shouted something to him, and the man looked at me and yelled in Russian, 'Get out! Clear off! And take the children.' I ran to the door, then came back and picked up the boys in my arms. All the time they kept the gun pointed at me – wherever I went the gun went too . . . maybe they were afraid I would start shouting. Then when I ran out into the courtyard, there came the explosion . . . The whole building went up in flames . . . and your fur caps were burnt too. After that, I must have lost consciousness. I don't remember anything more. Only those words of his stuck in my mind: "Get out!" And that gun following me all the time. I can see it now.'

'They killed Vera,' said Kolka. 'She was sitting in the cab of her truck. They got her right in the heart, and she ran a bit, then fell down.'

'And they spared me . . . why? I wondered about it all the time I was in hospital. When the police questioned me, they ordered me not to tell anyone, not to talk about anything. They said the bandits would be caught and that would be an end to it. Only I think . . . We shouldn't have touched that fur hat.'

'Why not?'

'I don't know. We shouldn't have, that's all. They looked at it . . . in such a funny way . . . as if I were cutting up something that was alive . . .'

'There were soldiers here,' said Kolka, 'who were chasing those men.'

158

Sashka asked, 'Those . . . well, those three men . . . were they frightening?'

'I didn't understand, you see!' For some reason Regina Petrovna looked out of the window again. 'They were just ordinary people. One was in civilian clothes, the other two were in some sort of uniform . . . But without any badges or shoulder-straps. And the boy was about your age . . . Dark, with black hair . . . He kept staring at me . . . His father took aim' – again she pointed to her forehead – 'and the boy jogged his elbow . . .'

'Did they have horses?'

'I didn't see any. They may have done.'

Sashka looked at Kolka and produced the brass cartridge-case.

'There.' He put it on the table. 'It's one of theirs. From when he fired that shot at you.'

Regina Petrovna gave a frightened look at the cartridge-case from a distance. Looking the twins straight in the eye she asked anxiously, 'So you're planning to run away . . . Where to?'

The brothers looked at each other and said nothing. Kolka wanted to go back to the countryside around Moscow, but Sashka was proposing to head south, towards the mountains. Between them they agreed that they would get on the first train that passed through.

Regina Petrovna stood up and lit another cigarette. 'You'll come to grief!' she said sharply. 'We'd better all go together. But not yet; I couldn't go now. I still feel very unwell.'

She threw away her cigarette without finishing it. The brothers had noticed how frequently she was lighting and throwing them away. Her supply would not last for long.

Standing by the window, she asked, 'Have you heard about the little farm that the big collective farm has given us?'

'Well?' said Kolka, and Sashka nodded.

'They're sending me there. To recuperate. The place has a couple of cows, some goats and a few calves . . . Would you like to go there? With me?'

'What would we do there?' asked Sashka, though he already knew that he would go anywhere with Regina Petrovna. And if he went, Kolka would go too. And then the pair of them together would push off for good.

'We'll tend the animals, look after them and feed them . . . They think it will be restful for me. But I'm afraid of going there on my own!'

'Is it far?' Sashka asked again. He had really wanted to ask something quite different.

159

'It's a little way up in the mountains, but not in these mountains . . . It's on the other side of the railway.' Regina Petrovna said hastily, realizing at once what Sashka was implying. 'There's no one in those parts. They never go beyond the station . . . Or they haven't so far!'

Kolka, however, was chiefly concerned about their store of jam. 'But will we be able to come back here?'

'Back here?' Regina Petrovna was trying to light another cigarette, but match after match was failing her. 'Yes, of course. We shall even have our own transport. We'll use it to bring milk and other things to the orphanage.'

'A Studebaker?' Sashka exclaimed.

'It's a secret,' said Regina Petrovna.

Kolka was not worried about the type of vehicle but about their secret hoard. It was not a good idea to be separated from their cache for a long period of time. It wouldn't take long for them to lose it. Here, though, it was close at hand; you could go down there, touch the jars, count them, and it set your mind at rest. But *there*, on a distant farm beyond the railway line . . . You might be sleeping soundly, dreaming of eleven jars of jam, each lid gleaming like a gold coin, each one a passport to paradise – and they could come along with a mine-detector and steal your treasure, as they had done with that cache under the floor . . .

While Kolka was agonizing about their hiding-place, Sashka asked about the little boys: what about them?

'They'll come with us,' said Regina Petrovna. And she insisted, 'I'd be terrified to be out there alone with them. But if you come, we'll all live together. Just like a family . . . Do you see?'

The brothers did not understand about living like a family. It was something they could not understand. The very word 'family' was in some way alien, if not hostile to their way of life. To them, the whole world was divided into people who lived in families and those who didn't. And so far those two halves of the world were incompatible.

Twenty-two

After leaving Regina Petrovna (Kolka was still clutching the 'cushion' he had saved), they had an argument before going to sleep. Not a serious one, but a slight argument all the same.

Both of them wanted to run away; on that they were agreed. But Kolka wanted to run away at once. He was against going out to this farm. What use were cows and goats?

Sashka, on the other hand, advised waiting until Regina Petrovna was ready to go. She was still weak – she had said so herself – and could not leave immediately. When she was stronger, they would all go together.

And imagine the riches they might be able to scrounge from the farm to add to their secret store. They hadn't expected to get anything from the factory – they'd been glad enough to eat a few plums – and look how it had turned out for them!

As usual, Sashka proved to be the cleverer of the two; he had thought it all out and weighed up everything in advance.

Kolka sighed and reluctantly agreed.

He was also well aware that no one was waiting for them – anywhere – when they ran away. And there were lots of trains. If you didn't get on one, you could catch the next one . . . The beggar has nothing to lose; if one village burns down, he moves on to the next.

Before leaving to go to the farm, they went into the village to look at Ilya's house.

Everything had been burned to the ground: the house itself, the yard, the sheds, and the trees around the house. The kitchen garden was empty. No doubt the neighbours had dug up the potatoes – and the orphans had probably lent a helping hand.

Among the weeds, covered in a fine, dust-like layer of white ash, they found the handcart with rusty wheels, which Ilya had used to carry firewood.

Kolka went up to it and kicked it. The little cart rolled away. He kicked it again . . . Then he bent down, found the rope and pulled the handcart behind him.

'Drop it!' said Sashka. 'What do you want that thing for?'

'But it might come in handy.'

'What for?'

Kolka had no answer; but he pulled the handcart to the bank of the Sunzha, hid it in some bushes and asked Sashka, 'Why don't you want it? It doesn't get in our way, does it?'

'No, it doesn't bother me,' snapped his brother.

'Well, then – it's no trouble to us, so let it stay there.' And he added, 'It doesn't need feeding . . .'

Unlike Sashka, Kolka lacked the ability to calculate things in advance and explain his reasons; his brain didn't work like that. But he did know that if something is lying around, you should pick it up; you can always think of a use for it later on.

The brothers felt sorry about Ilya and his house. Ilya had been a rogue, but a cheerful rogue – almost one of them, in fact.

Poking around in the ash with his foot, Kolka said thoughtfully, 'He had a feeling they were going to burn his place down.'

'But why?' Sashka asked. 'Why did they go for him but didn't touch any of the others?'

'Perhaps because his house was on the edge of the village . . .'

'Well, so what? They set fire to the truck right in the middle of the village.'

'Maybe they guessed he was a cheat and a thief?'

'How?'

'Simple,' said Kolka. 'There was the kitchen garden, for instance: Ilya never once touched a spade; he only ever picked what others had planted.'

'But what about the other people in the village? Don't they do just the same thing?'

'They work on the collective farm . . .'

'What's the difference?'

'But why do the devils burn things?'

'Why do the fascists burn things?'

'The fascists! There's no comparison . . . The Chechens aren't fascists!'

'What are they, then? You heard what that wounded soldier was shouting about them, didn't you? He was saying they were all traitors to the country! Stalin ordered them all to be put up against a wall and shot.'

162

'But what about that young boy . . . the one Regina Petrovna saw through the window? Is he a traitor too?' asked Kolka. Sashka had no answer to that, and the argument ended without the brothers coming to any agreement.

They rummaged among the ash, glancing around to see if they were being watched, but no one was showing any interest in the burnt-out remains of Ilya's house.

The twins fetched the handcart from its hiding-place and went back to the orphanage.

They left early in the morning, before the sun was up. A little grey donkey with sad eyes was standing in the middle of the courtyard, harnessed to a two-wheeled cart. Into it they piled their luggage, saucepans, sacks of oatmeal and a large bottle of cooking-oil.

The superintendent, clutching his everlasting briefcase, came out to see them off. He looked as if he hadn't slept all night.

He looked at Regina Petrovna and at her two little boys, who were whining because they had been made to get up so early.

The Kuzmin Twins were there too, yawning and shivering.

'What about these two?' enquired the superintendent, nodding towards the twins. 'Are they going with you?'

'Yes,' said Regina Petrovna. 'They are the Kuzmin brothers. I told you about them.'

The superintendent frowned and fingered his briefcase. 'Kuzmin . . . Kuzmin . . . Where are they from?'

'From Tomilino,' Sashka mumbled. He should have lied and said 'From Ramensk', but Regina Petrovna was there . . . He looked at Kolka, realizing what his brother was thinking. 'Mr Briefcase' had reason enough to remember them. Now was no time to delay, but to get clean away before Pyotr Anisimovich's memory started working. After rummaging in his briefcase, however, the superintendent was still unable to find what he was looking for.

'I thought there was a letter here . . .' he said. 'About . . . something about a kitchen . . . No, I don't remember!'

'Look for it, if you like. We'll wait. Who knows what some people may write about . . .' said Regina Petrovna. She looked kindly at the twins, who were standing by the cart, shivering and hopping from foot to foot. *They* knew what that letter was about! And what it would mean if it were found. Better not to remind anyone about it!

The superintendent searched again in his beloved briefcase, but luckily found nothing.

'All right . . . It will be two less mouths to feed,' he said. Then to

163

Regina Petrovna: 'Here are your papers from the collective farm . . . There's a man there who will show you everything . . . Are you sure you'll manage all right . . . with these two?'

'They're good lads,' said Regina Petrovna. 'They'll be a great help to me.'

The superintendent looked up at the sky and sighed.

'Ah, if only I were free . . . I'd leave this place too. But where would I go? I must go to the factory this morning, to try and persuade them to take the children back to work . . . Then I've got to go to Gudermes again, to see about teachers . . . It's time to get the children's schooling organized . . . I just don't understand what's happening!' he said finally, and spread his hands in despair.

What was it that 'Mr Briefcase' didn't understand, the twins wondered: the food supplies, the school . . . or the factory? It was as clear as day that the factory would never allow the orphans to work there again; the superintendent was the only person who didn't realize this. Obviously the jackals would only rob the place again and strip it bare.

'Come over and see us whenever you're free!' Regina Petrovna invited him, as she began to get ready to leave. 'We'll give you a glass of fresh milk . . .'

'I'll send you a party of jackals to harvest your maize. And come back when it gets too cold for you! Goodbye and good luck!'

The superintendent waved and went off to the kitchen, where the girls had already started the day's work.

Regina Petrovna settled the little boys in the cart so that they could go back to sleep, folding up some clothes to put under their heads. She took hold of the donkey's bridle and they set off on their way.

At first Regina Petrovna, followed by the Kuzmin Twins, walked ahead, being afraid that the donkey might get it into its head to wander off the road and into the fields; but the donkey pulled his load obediently along the road, doing nothing more rebellious than twitching his long ears, and soon Regina Petrovna fell back and walked alongside the cart. Now and again she would stop to light a cigarette, waving her arm to signal to the twins that they should keep going and she would catch them up . . . But they, instead, would stop the donkey and wait for her. Although they were on a road, there was undergrowth on either side of it, from which lurking enemies might leap out at them.

In the twins' view, Regina Petrovna was dressed rather unusually for the journey. She was wearing a brightly coloured man's shirt

164

with rolled-up sleeves and dark – also clearly male – baggy Turkish trousers. The Kuzmin Twins had never seen a woman teacher dressed like this, but they didn't disapprove of it; after all, Vera the truck-driver had been dressed much more outlandishly.

When they were out of earshot of Regina Petrovna, Kolka said to his brother, 'That letter is about the tunnel we dug at Tomilino ...'

'Do you suppose he really has lost it?'

' "Mr Briefcase" doesn't lose things! He carries everything with him – in that briefcase of his!'

Sashka bent down, picked up a stone from the road and threw it aside. 'Well, let him! We're going to run away soon!'

'But what about our secret cache?'

'We'll take our store of jam ... and then we'll run away.' He looked round at Regina Petrovna, and said, 'But only when Regina Petrovna is well enough.'

Keeping up a steady pace, they reached the railway station by lunchtime.

A goods train was standing in a siding, and a party of soldiers was unloading military equipment: a number of small field-guns, painted bright green, several jeeps and some horse-drawn wagons.

The twins slackened their pace and stared at the guns. Even though they had seen plenty of artillery at times during the war, and a lot of captured German guns had been put on show in a park in Moscow, no real man could let such a sight pass without looking at it. For some reason, guns are always fascinating. These little field-guns were handsome things.

Standing beside the sloping planks used for unloading the guns from the flat-cars was a group of soldiers, smoking and talking loudly. When they caught sight of Regina Petrovna, they all turned round in her direction as if obeying a word of command.

The boys inspected the guns, while the soldiers stared at the beautiful young woman.

The Kuzmin Twins did not like this.

'What are you stopping for?' Sashka yelled at the donkey, and whipped the beast with a switch. 'It's only an army train and some soldiers.'

Bumping noisily over the sleepers, the cart began to cross the tracks.

'Look! Natives!' the soldiers shouted after them.

The brothers exchanged looks, but did not answer back. To think that these were soldiers and didn't realize that Regina Petrovna, her

165

boys and the twins were not *natives*! 'Natives' went about naked or wore feathers: you could see them in any geography textbook.

Along the path that led to the foothills of the mountains, past the rotunda, they climbed up to the ruins of the sanatorium and there stopped to rest.

Each of the two brothers chose a separate pool for his bathe, and undressed. Regina Petrovna dipped her two little boys in the warm water and left them to play by themselves, while she went a little further to a huge square swimming-pool; there she splashed around on her own, having wrapped her head in her shirt turban-fashion.

When they heard her shout, the twins could not see her for steam and assumed that she was simply calling out to them, so they yelled back in reply as they ran from pool to pool, whooping as they dived in.

Suddenly they heard her clearly: 'Boys! Boys! Help! Come here! Quickly!'

The twins hastily pulled on their clothes over their wet bodies and raced off towards the sound of her voice. Their immediate thought was that their teacher was being attacked by Chechens.

But there were no Chechens.

A soldier was standing on the edge of the swimming-pool and staring fixedly at Regina Petrovna. She herself was sitting in the water up to her chin at the far end of the pool and watching the soldier with a look of fear.

He had obviously followed them here from the station.

First to run up was Sashka, who had managed to pick up a lump of paving-stone on the way. He stopped between the pool and the soldier, so near that the brass buckle of the soldier's belt was flashing straight into his eyes.

'What do you want?' he shouted, throwing back his head. 'Why are you snooping on us? Who asked you to come here?'

At that moment Kolka ran up alongside him. 'What are you doing here? Eh? Clear off, or we'll call your officer!'

The soldier was amazed to find himself faced with two identical boys shouting at him in identical voices. He took it calmly, however, and ignoring them he turned aside to stare at Regina Petrovna; then wrinkling his nose in the way that little boys do, he sighed and started to walk away. As he went, though, he looked round several times – not at the twins, whom he appeared not to see – but only at the woman in the pool.

'Go on! Clear off!' Sashka shouted after him, and swung his arm

166

back as if to throw the lump of stone. And Kolka, imitating a sailor he had seen in a film, unbuckled and took off his beautiful belt.

Suddenly the soldier stopped, and the brothers were sure he would come back and beat them up . . . it had been a mistake to shout at him once he had started to go.

The twins, of course, had a method for dealing with attackers: one of them would creep up and tackle him from behind while the other butted him in the chest . . . and the enemy would turn a backward somersault in the air! The trick, though, was hardly likely to work with this soldier.

Biting was another matter. They had proved it in practice. At Tomilino they had once been beaten up by a full-grown young thug from the criminal inmates, who had lain in wait for each of them separately, at the time when they had been taking turns to dig their tunnel. One day, in desperation, the twins had hurled themselves at him and bitten him so hard that he ran away from them as if they were a couple of mad dogs, after which he would walk a mile to avoid them.

The soldier, however, did not come back and fight. Not without regret, he looked at Regina Petrovna for the last time and sighed again. When Sashka shouted at him, he only shrugged his shoulders in perplexity and quickly, very quickly ran off.

Could he have been frightened by Kolka's threat to call his officer?

While the twins were standing there bristling defensively, Regina Petrovna jumped out of the water, pulled on her trousers, and ran over to her little boys, who, all unsuspecting, were playing beside the cart.

After this incident she seemed to liven up, to become happier and more talkative. Perhaps the hot water had had an effect on her. She kept making fun of her own fear, saying how silly she was to have squealed so much that she had frightened everyone else.

'Did I scare you a lot?' she asked the twins. Then she said, 'Now you're my knights in shining armour! My protectors! My defenders!'

The brothers felt hot with embarrassment.

Never before had they come to anyone's defence other than their own, and the new experience had turned out to be a pleasant one.

'What did he want?' asked Sashka grimly. He had still not cooled off after the episode. 'Did he want to steal something, d'you suppose?'

Regina Petrovna looked towards the direction in which the soldier had departed, and smiled a strange smile. 'I don't know. He looked rather a nice lad . . . Why did I have to scream my head off and frighten him, I wonder? Like a little girl . . . And I think you two put the wind up him, too! You brave lads!'

The twins looked at each other and blushed. If only Regina Petrovna knew how terrified they had been for one moment!

The teacher reached into a saucepan and produced a paper-wrapped parcel, which contained slices of bread and butter. 'These are for you, instead of medals,' she said with a laugh, looking red-cheeked and exceptionally beautiful.

The brothers fell upon the bread, and although the butter had long since melted, it had soaked into the slices and made them utterly delicious. The two little boys were given one slice to share between them.

The road was asphalt-paved for several kilometres onward from the sanatorium, then changed to cobbles and finally to chalk-white, scorched, rutted earth.

The mountains were not like the mountains which rose up immediately behind the orphanage. They were bare of either trees or bushes; the only things that flourished here were weeds and dry grass, and nothing but thorny, prickly plants grew beside the streams that ran down narrow gullies. The twins sighed as they looked around them; although the mountains behind the orphanage had been out of bounds, they were more beautiful and better provided with plants and trees: walnuts, wild pears, cherry-plums. Here there were wild olives, but they were very small and so bitter that they made the inside of your mouth pucker if you tried to eat them.

Regina Petrovna, who had grown more lively – and was even, the twins noticed, smoking less – was also looking around in astonishment. Several times she repeated the words 'a biblical wilderness'. The twins had no idea what that meant, but they guessed it was 'empty'. Sashka explained it to Kolka: 'It means there's not a damn' thing here. It's a grown-ups' word, and a rude one, too.'

Regina Petrovna laughed and said that the Bible was a big, big fairy tale . . . and that the Jews had written it.

'You mean the porters wrote it?' Kolka asked.

'Why the porters?'

'The porters at the factory! They're Jews!' said Sashka.

'They're *good* Jews,' Kolka insisted.

'And why should Jews be bad?' Regina Petrovna enquired with interest. She thought for a moment, then said, 'There are no bad peoples, only bad men and women.'

'But what about the Chechens?' Sashka retorted. 'They killed Vera.'

Regina Petrovna did not reply.

Meanwhile the cart had taken the last bend in the road, and the travellers, who had been on the move for the best part of ten hours, were vouchsafed the sight of a flat valley between hills, where greenery flourished and two little white houses could be seen in the distance.

After a while it transpired that it was in fact only a single house, and a tiny one at that, made of whitewashed adobe. The other was simply a lean-to, where the cart could be kept.

Under this lean-to they found an iron trivet standing on bricks, and a heap of tools of all kinds: rakes, scythes, spades and – more than anything else – mattocks.

'We've arrived,' said Regina Petrovna, looking around. Nobody was there to meet them. 'This is where we're going to live,' she added hastily lighting a cigarette. She was obviously nervous.

A man appeared. The brothers at once recognized him as the ex-soldier who had once given them a ride in his horse and cart. Now he was no longer wearing an old army tunic, but only a shirt and no cap; he was bald and he walked with a limp.

With his rolling gait he came towards the new arrivals and recognized the twins as inmates of the orphanage. Holding out a hand to the brothers, he introduced himself: 'Demyan'. He only nodded to Regina Petrovna from a distance.

'So you've arrived, have you?' he said to the twins as if they were grown-ups, appearing to ignore Regina Petrovna.

'Yes, we have.' Sashka answered Demyan in the tone of an equal. 'We're going to work on this farm.'

And Kolka added, 'Tending the animals.'

Unlike the superintendent, Demyan showed no surprise that the boys should be coming here to farm. He nodded approvingly. 'Good for you . . . In the army we used to say: "Fighting's all very well, but a job in the supply-train is better!" I'm leaving you two cows, seven calves and three goats . . . Can you milk?'

'We'll learn,' said Regina Petrovna, and came closer, cigarette in hand.

Demyan looked at her hand holding the cigarette and at her baggy trousers, and stroked his bald head. 'Excuse me, lady, you'll have to *work* here . . . slog your guts out, as we say . . . not puff out smoke!'

'And we're going to slog our guts out,' Regina Petrovna said

169

ingenuously, smiling at the Kuzmin Twins. But she put out her cigarette. And went off to look after her little boys.

'Are there no working men at the orphanage?' Demyan asked the twins. 'Is that why they send the female sex up here?'

The boys liked talking in this man-to-man way, but they could not tolerate hostile remarks about their Regina Petrovna. They were, after all, her protectors and defenders!

Kolka frowned, and Sashka looked at Demyan as though seeing him for the first time. 'Regina Petrovna has been ill,' he said, 'since one of our buildings was burnt down . . . She's just come out of hospital, and they sent her up here to get better . . .'

'But *we're* going to work!' Kolka put in. And to make it sound more convincing, he lied, 'The superintendent ordered us to help her. You, he said, are our only hope . . .'

Demyan seemed embarrassed. He nodded his head a great deal, and turning to Regina Petrovna he explained that he had cut a lot of hay and reeds. They would do best, he suggested, to sleep in the adobe house – it would be warmer in there. But they would have to cook on the trivet and burn compressed dung as fuel. There was a hand-mill in the farmhouse for grinding maize-flour. There were still some tomatoes in the vegetable beds and some cucumbers, but many of them were rotting; then there were pumpkins, cabbages, beetroot and potatoes . . . There was a vineyard, but the vines had been neglected and had run wild; untrained, they were simply creeping over the ground . . . And Demyan had planted sugar-cane . . . 'You'll find it all . . . in time,' he concluded.

Towards evening, Demyan harnessed up his horse and said goodbye. Then he took out a tobacco-pouch, and skilfully, with a single movement of his hand, rolled a long, home-made cigarette. He handed it to Regina Petrovna in a gesture of reconciliation.

'There you are,' he said, but without looking her in the face. 'Though I can't put up with women who smoke . . . It's a fashion that started in the war . . .'

'You don't have to put up with it,' Regina Petrovna replied with a smile. 'But they do . . .' And she pointed to the Kuzmin Twins.

'Supposing I come back?' Demyan reported mischievously. 'What will you say then?'

'We welcome everybody here,' said Regina Petrovna, and lit the 'goat's leg' (Demyan's name for roll-your-own cigarettes), holding it at the bend, like a pipe. She was going to add something, but started coughing.

Demyan burst into delighted laughter. 'Tickles, does it?' he

170

exclaimed in satisfaction. 'None of your Moscow rubbish! This is good old home-grown stuff – fetches the skin off the back of your throat! Grew it, cured it and cut it myself!' Taking a sheet of newspaper out of his pocket, he tore it in half and tipped into it a handful of brownish, coarse-cut shag from his tobacco-pouch.

'You can smoke this,' he said, handing it to Regina Petrovna. 'When life gets boring.'

He shook the boys' hands in farewell.

'You two sang really well, like professionals . . . I nearly died laughing at your song – in the collective-farm club that night . . .' Then changing his tone and frowning, he added, 'But it was a bad business about Vera.'

He hobbled over to the cart, jumped up on to it with a skilful sideways leap, crammed his grubby old cap on to his bald head and clicked his tongue to the horse. The animal ambled off and Demyan drove away without looking round, as though nothing at the farm was of interest to him any longer. For a long time a faint cloud of dust hovered above the road, gilded by the setting sun.

Twenty-three

Regina Petrovna and her two little boys settled into the house; somehow all three of them contrived to sleep in one bed. She made up beds for the Kuzmin Twins on the floor, but they declined them, feeling that the room was too crowded and stuffy. They threw down a pile of brittle but pleasant-smelling reeds in one corner of the lean-to and made themselves a bed on top of them. The walls of the lean-to were plaited from dried reeds, which rustled at night.

Next morning, the first thing they did was to find the cane that Demyan had called sugar-cane. They gave some to Regina Petrovna and the little boys. They approved of these tasty sticks, which you could chew and spit out all day long, and decided to make the most of it while it was still plentiful.

They also found the grapevine. It had spread over the ground, and if you lifted up the branches you found the bunches of reddish-brown grapes on the ground beneath them.

Sashka picked one, tried it and pulled a face. 'It's so sour, it'll twist your jaw off!'

But Regina Petrovna thought otherwise. She asked them to pick as many grapes as would fill a basket. Then the boys watched as she tipped all the grapes into a basin, washed them and began crushing them with a cobblestone. A muddy-looking juice came out, which the brothers tasted by dipping in a finger and licking it: the stuff set their teeth on edge.

'That will be wine when we next have a celebration,' she said.

'What sort of a celebration? What for?' the twins enquired.

'I don't know,' she said. 'We'll think of a reason.'

'Can you invent your own holidays?' asked Sashka. 'I thought they were fixed and happened automatically.'

'Sometimes they do . . . and sometimes . . .' Staring hard at the twins, she asked, 'When were you born?'

172

'What?' The brothers asked in unison. They didn't understand the question.

'When is your birthday?'

The brothers looked at each other and back at Regina Petrovna. 'you mean – were we born during the day? Why daytime? What if we were born at night?'

'But don't you see?' she said with a smile. 'Absolutely every living creature in the world – even an animal, like a cow or a goat or a calf – was born on a particular date of a month in a certain year . . . You were, too. Only you've forgotten when it was – is that it?'

Kolka smiled and looked at Sashka, who had the better brain: let him see if he could remember. If Kolka had been asked, say, how many jars of jam were hidden in their cache, he could have said it. But this . . .

Sashka, however, could not give an answer either.

'Well, we'll think up a date ourselves,' said Regina Petrovna. 'And we'll have a party! How about that?'

Kolka asked obtusely, 'When will it be?'

Regina Petrovna did some silent calculations, moving her lips. 'Well, let's say in a week's time. October the seventeenth. Does that suit you?'

'I don't know,' said Kolka. Sashka, too, said, 'I don't know.'

'And when will we leave?' Kolka enquired.

'Leave? Where to?'

'Anywhere?'

'But don't you like it here?' asked Regina Petrovna, addressing Sashka, who squirmed uneasily.

He was thinking to himself, 'I like it here. We may not like it somewhere else . . .'

He had imagined that Mr Briefcase would leave them here for ever. They wouldn't have to go to school, but like Demyan they would learn to roll their own cigarettes, grow tobacco, make hay and chew sugar-cane. Then one of them would marry Regina Petrovna and would feed the little boys with buckwheat porridge. But wait a moment, no – the boys would no doubt grow up too. They would tend the animals.

'All right,' said Regina Petrovna. 'First we'll celebrate your birthday, then we'll decide about leaving. Agreed?'

Her voice and her warm affection appeased the twins. They agreed to wait until after the birthday party. From their orphanage experience they knew how official holidays were celebrated: they would

173

be summoned to the dining-hall, given one dry biscuit and a handful of sunflower seeds. And that's it – off you go . . .

If the brothers had wanted to have a celebration, they could have done so on their own. Sashka was a bright lad and could invent any number of excuses for a party; there was no need to dream up this business about 'birthdays'.

Anyway, it was probably a myth that children without families, such as orphans, were *born* at all. They probably just spawned themselves like fleas, say, or lice or bed-bugs in a dirty house: one moment they're not there, the next moment they're crawling out of the woodwork. They swarm everywhere like little beetles; you can tell them by their dirty faces and by their reflex grabbing movements: gottit! They belong, of course, to none other than that pestiferous breed, the homeless – the source, it is claimed, of all infection, vermin, epidemics and rashes of every kind . . . And of course they are the reason why there's a shortage of everything all over the country and why the crime-rate is forever rising. So it's high time to eradicate these nasty little creatures with flea-powder, a good scrub with disinfectant or a dose of paraffin, just as you deal with cockroaches. And as for the greedier ones – off to the Caucasus with them! Not forgetting to disinfect the railway tracks with derris dust or bug-killer, so that no trace of them is left and there's no chance that they'll come back. There – that's got rid of 'em! Everyone is greatly relieved, and their consciences are clear: the little creatures came from nowhere and back to nowhere they have gone. As for them being *born* and having birthdays . . . Really!

The twins had survived everything possible in their lifetime so far, and no doubt they would survive a birthday too. They had lived through much worse! In any case, it was unlikely to happen again.

It was strange how slowly time had passed in the orphanage; they had had little to do but loaf around until the next mealtime. Now, though, the days flew by, like the carriages of a train as it flashes past you.

And all because the Kuzmin Twins were kept busy with real jobs to do.

They took it in turns to go to the spring at the foot of the mountains to fetch water for the household. One could wash there too, but this the brothers frankly disliked. In any case, it was harmful to wash in cold water: it could wear your skin away and soak your clothes. Besides, what was the point of it?

Driving the animals out to pasture was also their responsibility, though Regina Petrovna would not let them milk the cows. They had secretly tried to do it once, but it hadn't worked. The cow had kicked the bucket over ... it was pure luck that it hadn't been one of the twins' heads!

The cows were called Zorka and Mashka, as Demyan had told them.

Zorka was big-bellied, brown and good-tempered; she was the one that the twins had tried to milk. Mashka, by contrast, was black and white in patches, nasty and capricious; it wasn't safe to approach her, although in time she grew used to them and would allow Regina Petrovna, Sashka and even the little boys to come near her, although even they still had to do so cautiously, keeping a wary eye open. Kolka was the only one she would not tolerate. Whenever she caught sight of him in the distance she would stretch out her neck, turn her wet nose in his direction and snort. If he tried to come closer, she would start to paw the ground with her fore-hoof, lower her horns and bellow; this was her way of swearing at him.

Kolka was seriously offended by Mashka; he would shake his fist at her from a safe distance and go away.

The twins tried to confuse the cow by changing clothes and pretending to be the other, but it proved impossible to deceive the cow, just as they had been unable to fool Zina.

The two brothers also had to grind maize into flour with the two round millstones, one on top of the other. You turned the top one, pouring the grain into the hole in the middle of it, and white flour would come out of the gap between the two stones. You shook it through a sieve and there was your flour and groats – in a word, food.

With it you could bake pitta – a coarse, pancake-like bread – or make maize porridge. All this, especially when it came to eating it, the brothers quickly learned to do. The only thing they didn't like was turning the millstones.

At first they took it in turns to do the grinding. Then Sashka did it alone. Kolka, as he himself announced, hadn't the patience for this job.

On the other hand, he liked collecting firewood and dried cow dung, whereas Sashka couldn't bear the sight of cowpats. He would rather give the millstones a hundred turns than pick up a cowpat. The locals, he said, might call it '*kizyak*', but in proper language it was still shit. If he had known about this back at the orphanage, where the orphans used to shit behind the hedge, think how much fuel they could have gathered! Enough to keep the fires burning for a hundred years!

175

As long as the rice lasted, they cooked rice pudding with milk, then they changed to pumpkin.

The first pumpkin they rolled into the house from the kitchen garden was as big as one of the little boys, and the twins danced around it in excitement while Regina Petrovna chopped it into yellow slices with an axe. They each grabbed a piece, took a bite, chewed it – and spat it out. They had thought it was going to be like melon; instead it was more like the root vegetables used for cattle-feed. It looked delicious but tasted like wood.

They announced to Regina Petrovna that they were not going to eat this mangel-wurzel.

'It's not mangel-wurzel, it's pumpkin,' she corrected them.

'Doesn't matter. Let Zorka and Mashka or the calves eat it. They're stupid, they don't know any better.'

Regina Petrovna laughed, and shook her finger in mock threat. 'I warn you – you'll be asking for a second helping!'

'No, we won't!' The brothers were equally certain. 'Just look at all the space those mangel-wurzels are taking up in the garden! They're big but useless – full of seeds and stuff like orange cotton-wool!'

Regina Petrovna put some slices on the griddle and held it over the glowing coals of the stove; as they cooked, she made some magic passes over them and kept a cunning silence.

At lunch she gave the twins a slice apiece. 'There, try that – you fusspots!'

The twins considered the matter and tried a sliver. Then more slivers. The slices of pumpkin had acquired a rosy flush, had become sweet and aromatic. Sticky honey oozed over the skin . . . it was, in a word, delicious.

The brothers finished their slices and looked at the griddle: how many slices were left? Regina Petrovna wagged a finger at them, but gave them a second helping, the twins being too proud to ask for it themselves. Now *this* was what they called a celebration – a sheer feast, in fact.

Kolka licked his fingers and declared, 'It's a good thing mangel-wurzels like this grow in the Caucasus!'

Coming from him, this was high praise, both for the Caucasus and for pumpkins.

Sashka said nothing, but mentally noted that they had made a blunder; they had disgraced themselves. Regina Petrovna also made sour cream and cottage cheese from milk, hanging the curds in a muslin bag, and gave them the whey to drink. Things made from

176

milk, though, were not to the twins' taste; they drank it, frowned, and tried to get down from the table.

'You are silly boys,' Regina Petrovna said in an attempt to persuade them, as she poured them out mugs of hot milk. 'You don't know how lucky you are! This is the best drink that nature has to offer you!'

'We can manage without nature,' said Kolka obstinately. Sashka nodded. 'We're used to looking after ourselves.'

'But you're a part of nature yourselves . . . I'd even call you a force of nature!' Regina Petrovna laughed and sat down to drink her milk. She broke a piece of pitta into pieces, one for each. 'Please tell me – why is it that when there are a lot of you in a bunch you're so uncontrollable? You're like a sandstorm: there's no stopping you, no way to restrain you . . . But when it's just the two of you' – she gave them each another piece of pitta – 'you're different, and better. Not altogether good, of course, but much, much better . . .'

'It's good without the jackals,' Sashka explained. 'But if they came, they would simply nick everything. Pumpkin, milk, pitta . . . the lot . . .'

'And talking of nicking things – what about you?' Regina Petrovna asked. She wiped her two little boys' white lips and noses. They were lapping milk from saucers, like kittens.

'What – *what* about us?'

'Why pretend you don't know what I mean?' said Regina Petrovna.

Sashka was about to say that he really didn't know, but checked himself. Yesterday, he and Kolka had started to make another secret horde of food. They had stolen three pittas and a jarful of flour, thinking that Regina Petrovna hadn't noticed.

Regina Petrovna swept the crumbs from the table, but it was obvious that she was expecting an answer from the twins. She had drawn her black eyebrows together, which meant that she was angry. Frowning, she sat down, rested her cheeks in her hands and stared past the twins. Then she told them how she had hoped they would all live together as a family, having everything in common and sharing everything . . . Some people, however, were behaving like jackals – in other words, they were stealing from themselves. Or nicking stuff, as jackals called it. And that was something that she, Regina Petrovna, would never be able to understand. How could people steal from their own table?

Without a word the twins got up and went out. First out into the meadow for a brief conference, then to their hiding-place.

177

They came back and put all their booty, the pittas and the jar of flour, on the table.

And no more was said about it.

The day before the twins' 'birthday', Regina Petrovna made the mixture for a cake. She also asked the two brothers to bring in the ripest pumpkin from the garden, and to look after both the animals and the little boys.

She then harnessed the donkey to the cart and drove to the station. After quite a long time she returned and produced two metal tins of stewed pork. She had bartered them for milk with the passengers on a passing train. To be more precise, one of the tins contained stewed pork; in the other, an oval tin with a key attached to its side, was American preserved sausage-meat.

The twins already knew that you had to put the key into a little metal tag, turn it, and the lid opened along a seam. And beneath that lid . . . now this was something worth celebrating! If it meant having one of these tins, they were prepared to put up with having a birthday every day!

The Kuzmin Twins could not tear themselves away from the table. They kept looking at the tins, sniffing them and stroking their cold, gleaming sides. They even tried licking them, but the taste was simply metallic and only made their tongues tingle.

Suddenly Demyan arrived on his cart, although no one had invited him. He knew nothing about the birthday celebrations, of course, but he had brought a slab of lard wrapped in a rag, and a jar of jam that he had acquired from friends at the factory.

Regina Petrovna gave Demyan a rather cool welcome, but was delighted by the jam: this would help make the cake really delicious!

The twins, on the other hand, were not very impressed by the jam; they longed to be able to add a tin of pork stew to their secret cache, or sausage-meat in an oval tin complete with its little key! As it was, with Demyan at table too, the food for the party would disappear all too quickly! He certainly had a keen nose – he had made a bee-line for the stewed pork.

Meanwhile, although Demyan had ostensibly come to discuss practical matters, he was hanging around in the kitchen and getting in Regina Petrovna's way. He was telling her something about his private kitchen-garden – how he was pickling water-melons and planting potatoes; he was scathing about the local apples while praising the variety, the Antonovka, which grew in his native region of Russia.

'I'm a handy fellow, I can turn my hand to anything. What I lack is a woman,' he was saying, looking at Regina Petrovna's back. 'I can do my own work and woman's work too, but even so home without a woman keeping house is like a house without a stove. Everything's there, except the warmth. And I reckon it's not so easy for you on your own with two little ones . . . Isn't that so?'

Busy with cooking over her little stove, Regina Petrovna said nothing and did not turn round. Suddenly she asked Demyan for a smoke. 'Roll me a . . . what d'you call it . . . a "goat's leg" . . .'

Her hands were covered in dough, and when Demyan had rolled her one of his home-made cigarettes he put it into her mouth and lit it with a taper made from a dried reed. As he did so he looked questioningly into her eyes.

As Regina Petrovna puffed out smoke, she glanced towards the Kuzmin Twins, who were keeping a watchful eye on her. 'I was an airman's wife . . . Do you know what that is? It's a profession in itself,' she said. 'In the small town where we were stationed before the war, we used to say that: her profession is "airman's wife". See him off . . . and wait. Then see him off again . . . Whenever we used to get together, we airmen's wives were all very alike: some women talk about clothes, or jewellery or make-up – but we talked about aircraft and flying. Whose husband was flying to the Far North, whose was flying to America . . . That was fashionable at the time. And the talk was also about war. Because those planes carried bombs – that's why they're called bombers, after all – and although it was all supposed to be a military secret, we knew everything about the aircraft: how many bombs they carried, their speeds, and what their targets would be if and when war came . . .

'Then when it all started in earnest, the squadron was transferred to an aerodrome near Leningrad and they flew on a mission to bomb Berlin. The distance was shorter from there. He came back from that first raid. My little boys were quite tiny then. And we wives of the men who came back had to go and visit the families of those who *didn't* come back. That was the custom. I can tell you it was terrible to go into a house where they didn't yet know. And to pretend you'd just happened to drop in . . .

'Then came the second bombing raid. Stalin personally ordered it. For effect. By then the Germans were ready for them – on the first occasion it had never entered the fascists' heads that we would dare to bomb them . . . And this time the other airmen's wives came to visit *me* . . . Our summertime airbase was transferred to the rear, the Germans were advancing on us, and there was no point in my moving east with the other airmen's families any longer . . . a widow, and with a burden like this into the bargain . . .'

Regina Petrovna spat her cigarette-end out on to the floor and stubbed it out with her foot.

'So I went to work in an orphanage. It was easier to manage my own kids where there were others . . . though we nearly starved, the food situation was so bad . . . Then I decided to come with them when they were moved down here . . . I thought things might be easier here . . .'

There was a hissing sound as water spilled over the edge of a saucepan, and Regina Petrovna groaned. 'It's boiled over! Oh well, that's what comes of talking too much.'

She leaped up and dashed over to the stove, and Demyan trotted after her, offering to help. 'Let me hold it! I'll hold it!' he kept repeating, fussing around her. 'I'm a handy fellow! I do all my own cooking! Don't worry!'

Regina Petrovna dealt with the fire, wiped her forehead with the back of her hand and asked, 'Can you peel potatoes, Demyan Ivanych?'

At once the bald Demyan was made to sit down behind a pile of potatoes, while the Kuzmin Twins, who had been jealously watching the tins of food on the table – and simultaneously keeping an eye on their fussy, restless visitor – were sent off to collect dry sticks and cow dung. Today's culinary operations required a great deal of fuel.

'Just look at him!' said Kolka, glancing round, when they reached the far side of the garden and were far enough away. 'I bet you he saw that tin of stewed pork and that's why you can't get him away from the kitchen . . . "I'm a handy fellow! I'm such a handy fellow!" ' – Kolka mockingly imitated Demyan – 'We're all handy when there's stewed pork in the offing! He's so handy, it sent him bald!'

'Bald men are always extra crafty,' Sashka assured him.

'Well, let him keep his hands to himself!'

'It's not the tin of pork that he's after!'

'Isn't it? Then what? A pumpkin, d'you suppose?' asked Kolka.

'No-o-o . . . We're the pumpkin-heads for not realizing it! When he started whining about what his home was like . . .'

'Well, so what?' Kolka asked in surprise. 'He was just saying his place was shabby and he didn't have a stove . . .'

'Shabby it may be,' Sashka said. 'But when he started going on

180

about the stove, I rumbled him straight away . . . He wants to get married!'

Kolka stared dully at his brother. He had even forgotten about the dried cowpats that he was supposed to be collecting, so astounding was Sashka's revelation. 'Get married? Marry who?'

'*Who?* Oh, come on! Who d'you think?'

Kolka relapsed into bewildered silence as he digested this piece of news, from which he drew the somewhat unexpected conclusion, 'But he's old, isn't he? He must be at least thirty . . .'

'Well, so what? How old d'you suppose she is?'

'Regina Petrovna's different,' said Kolka firmly. 'She's beautiful. She'll marry a general . . . Or a marshal . . .' Kolka thought for a moment, then corrected himself, 'No – of course *we're* going to marry her.'

'She wouldn't have us.'

'Why not?'

'You are a fool, Kolka!' Sashka shouted angrily. 'How could you marry her when you're not grow-up yet?'

'But I'll grow bigger,' growled Kolka, obstinately.

'By the time you've grown bigger, that crafty little man will have come here again and again, and he'll prance around her and talk about stoves and potatoes . . . and then he'll put her on his cart and carry her off!'

'I won't let him!' said Kolka. 'I'll kill him!'

'Who? Demyan?'

'I'll poison him. I'll put deadly nightshade in his food,' Kolka insisted obstinately. 'And I'll poison his horse, too!'

Looking past the bushes at the plume of blue smoke rising from the kitchen, he shouted at the top of his voice:

You're lucky you've only got one leg instead of two,
You never wear your socks out and you only need one shoe!

Demyan, of course, could not hear him from so far away, but Kolka's outburst did make the twins feel better.

Twenty-four

A holiday is always a holiday, though, so they agreed to put up with the 'birthday party' idea.

Besides, when the twins returned and saw how pretty Regina Petrovna looked in the dress she had put on – and how she was paying no attention to the bald Demyan but only had eyes for Sashka and Kolka – they both thought, 'What, marry? *Him?* Not a hope! Handy he may be, but he's wasting his time here – he'll be sent home with his tail between his legs!'

And the Kuzmin Twins would stay here with her.

At first they were so upset that they didn't notice the table she had set for them. Now that was a spread for a party! If the whole of their secret store had been laid out to the last jar, it could not have compared with the sight they now saw before them.

On the table, which had been covered with a white sheet, all kinds of unheard-of delights were laid out in little bowls and on large dock-leaves – no doubt Regina Petrovna and her little boys had thought up this one. There were rosy maize-meal pancakes; bacon, in grains of sea-salt, decorated with rounds of sliced onion; American sausage-meat from that tin, cut into thin, pink slices; pickled cucumbers with sprigs of dill; tomatoes; garlic; and slices of their favourite pumpkin, baked to a turn, with little pieces of charcoal still sticking to the outer skin and oozing with sticky honey.

Also on the table were piles of lump-sugar, glistening like the snow-capped Mount Kazbek, together with a scattering of coffee-flavoured sweets and a bowl of jam.

And a cake, which deserves a separate description . . .

It was a round, many-layered and therefore tall cake, still warm – or, as they say, still breathing!

The top of the cake was decorated with sliced plums and apple rings all around the outer edge, and in the middle, written in thick, sugared, whipped cream it said in big letters:

182

KOLKA
SASHKA
17.10.44.
HURRAH!

In place of candles, eleven golden-yellow stalks of reeds had been placed in a circle around the edge.

No doubt there was more that the boys managed to see at one glance before they were invited to sit down – first, as the guests of honour! – at this unbelievable, magic table.

Suddenly they felt timid and shy!

Normally they were never flustered by the sight of food; if it were laid on the table, you were meant to stuff yourself, or more simply scoff the lot as fast as you could – because if you weren't quick, there'd be none left. Now, though, they stared and did not know where to begin.

Shivers ran up and down Sashka's spine and he went cold with excitement, while Kolka was so mesmerized by this scene of unearthly delight that he almost sat down on the floor instead of on the end of the bench.

Finally they took their places; the little boys were seated opposite them, while Demyan, who was hindered by his wooden leg, arranged himself sideways-on to the table.

Smirking, he conjured a bottle of moonshine vodka from some-where behind his back (although he hadn't known about the birthday party, he had nevertheless come provided with a bottle, thus proving Sashka's dictum about bald men being extra crafty!) and poured out a glassful apiece for himself and the hostess, who did not decline it. He was about to pour some for the twins too, but Regina Petrovna at once said, 'No. They mustn't have any.'

If only she had known that Ilya had once given them an 'engine-driver' to drink!

She went down into the cellar and brought back a large jar full of juice, wiped it off with a rag and poured out the liquid into two mugs for the twins. Before giving it to them, however, she first took a sip out of one of the mugs.

183

'Now that's the stuff for them!' she announced. 'Drink it, but not all at once – OK?'

The twins nodded in unison and looked into her eyes – dark brown, twinkling, huge and profound, with something about them that took the twins' breath away as they stared into their very inmost depths. But Regina Petrovna withstood their gaze and smiled calmly in reply. In just the way that she always smiled.

And it was as clear as could be that Old Baldy was not wanted in this household. He had set his sights on the wrong target! Come here as often as you like, but we can manage very well without you, thank you very much! That was what she should say to them all – the bald, the lame and the mangy . . . every last one of them!

Regina Petrovna lit a spill from the fire and with it she lit all the little reeds that she had stuck into the cake. Then she said, 'Now blow!'

'Do . . . what?' asked the twins.

'Blow out the flames!' she said loudly. 'Well, go on!'

The brothers stood up, puffed hard and blew them all out, leaving only a wisp of smoke hanging over the table.

'Done like real men!' Regina Petrovna said solemnly. With an emotional gesture she raised her glass. 'Well, boys, I wish you a happy birthday. Be good, healthy, happy boys, just as you are now, and I will always love you! My brave defenders!'

The twins looked at each other. This was exactly what they had wanted to hear. She loved them. And she didn't love baldies. And they began to drink the slightly sourish wine. Suddenly they found themselves liking it so much that they downed it all and asked for more.

'But that's not fruit juice!' cried Regina Petrovna. 'It's wine! You don't drink it by the bucketful, you know!'

'But we do!' Kolka shouted in reply. 'Will it be like this every month? Will it?'

'Like *what*?' asked Regina Petrovna.

'A party? Like a birthday party?'

'Listen to them!' Demyan exclaimed, slapping his wooden leg and laughing. Regina Petrovna laughed too. 'No, my dears,' she said. 'It only happens once a year . . . But then, it comes *every* year.'

'Every year?' Kolka enquired. 'Even when we're twenty years old?'

'Of course. And when you're thirty and forty . . .'

'We'll be old then,' put in Sashka. 'We'll have forgotten all about it.'

'No, you won't.' Regina Petrovna jumped up as lightly as a little

184

girl, disappeared into the lean-to and came back almost at once, carrying something. She put a parcel wrapped in newspaper on each of the twins' laps. 'That's from me . . . and from the little boys too.'

She sat down, looking at the two brothers with sparkling eyes. She really was dazzlingly beautiful today, in her smart dress, with her hair attractively curled into a bun. Around her neck she had hung a necklace of red beads made of some dried red berries that she had gathered . . . Even Demyan grunted with approval as he looked at her, and to hide his embarrassment he began rolling himself a long cigarette with his home-grown tobacco.

At any other time this would not have escaped the twins' attention, but now they were too busy with their packages.

They had never before been given presents, except for the occasion at the orphanage when they had all been given a dry biscuit and a handful of sunflower seeds apiece and were told it was in honour of a public holiday . . . They had devoured the biscuit without even chewing it and cracked the seeds with their teeth, and this had made the holiday so memorable that they had wanted more! But nothing more had been forthcoming.

Now, though, they did not know what to do with their parcels. Should they unwrap them or not? Or perhaps they should quickly take them away and stow them in a hiding-place before they were taken away again?

Regina Petrovna understood everything that was passing through their minds. 'Let's all look and see what's in them . . . now.' She took the parcel from Sashka, who was sitting nearest to her, and unwrapped the newspaper.

There, on top of the little pile, was a new, blue, high-collared Russian shirt complete with buttons. Underneath it was a pair of trousers, also blue. With pockets. There, too, was a pair of ankle boots in yellowish-brown leather, with yellow laces and broad tongues. And a scarf, chequered in squares like an arithmetic exercise book; finally came a little round hat, like a skull-cap, decorated with coloured embroidery. The hat was called a *tyubeteika*. Sashka immediately said, 'Tutubeika', and everyone laughed.

Kolka, though, was frowning and whispered very, very quietly – almost in a squeak – into his bowl, 'What about me?' He seemed to have forgotten that there was a similar parcel on his knees.

Once again everyone laughed and helped him to unwrap his parcel. In it there turned out to be the same set of clothes, only in green.

The twins asked permission to try on their presents.

185

Sighing with intense anticipation and glancing around them, they went out and around the corner, where they changed into the new clothes.

And although neither of them spoke while they were changing, they both knew exactly what the other was thinking and feeling.

Sashka's back was itching from excitement, so much so that Kolka noticed his brother had broken out in red blotches. And Kolka's left leg suddenly began twitching so hard that he could not get it into his trouser-leg.

In a dispirited voice he said, 'You go first! You're the clever one!'

Sashka replied, 'You're no fool yourself. Why should I go first?'

'I'm scared,' Kolka confessed. 'I've never been dressed like this before.'

'Nor have I. Do you think she'll be able to tell us apart now?'

Kolka looked at Sashka and frowned. Nothing would induce him, he thought, to go around dressed like this all the time. It was too dazzling. In any case, it was not the right dress for an orphan – it would get pinched in no time. Anyone who saw them in this get-up would think they were not orphans at all but a couple of successful crooks. Could any normal person wear so much good stuff? If they showed themselves like this, it would be nicked off them and then flogged in the nearest flea-market! Black marketeers would simply rip it off their backs!

Kolka, however, said none of this aloud; it was as if he were standing outside himself and looking on. With a sigh he said, 'You look fine.'

'So do you!'

'It's like you're not you at all but a baron or something.'

'Does yours crackle?' asked Sashka.

'Where?'

'Everywhere. And it's still a bit tight . . . Maybe we should take the buttons off?'

'We could,' said Kolka, after a moment's thought. 'But it'd be a pity. They're so lovely and shiny.'

They might have gone on talking like this for a long time, to put off the moment when they showed themselves off, but the others came out to look at them. Demyan spread his hands in perplexity and said something wonderful. He said, 'Ye-es. You look like a real couple of innerlekchals!' The little boys froze with delight. Regina Petrovna clapped her hands and did a little dance on the spot.

'Well, boys!' she exclaimed. 'Now you really are twin brothers.

186

Now I'll never tell you apart! Are you Kolka?' And she prodded Sashka with her finger.

The boys laughed, but Regina Petrovna was not a bit embarrassed. This time she was only joking.

'Everyone come to table,' she said brightly, looking hard at the twins as though afraid they might now run away. 'As soon as you two start eating, I'll know ... "who's who",' she finished with her familiar expression.

Hearing her say these words in English, Demyan for some reason looked embarrassed and suggested having another drink.

Later they all went for a walk, and when they came across the little herd of goats Demyan did a trick for them. He lit a roll-your-own cigarette and showed it to a goat from a distance. The goat at once ran to him and took the long, burning cigarette in its mouth. Smoke streamed out of its nostrils ... then it ate the cigarette and smoke continued to pour out of its nose!

'Oh, why do you make fun of the poor animals?' asked Regina Petrovna. But she was good-tempered and said it without intending any reproach. 'I know something better – let's think up names for our calves.'

She invited the twins, as the birthday boys, to be the first to invent some names.

Without hesitation they named the greediest of the young bullocks 'Jackal', the other one 'Scrounger', and they called the two heifers 'Slag' and 'Thickhead'.

Regina Petrovna did not approve of these names, but said nothing. They had given them the only kinds of names they knew. As a contrast, she suggested calling the other two bullocks 'The Kuzmin Twins'.

'But can you do that?' asked Sashka.

'Why not? They're just calves. Friendly and sensible. If they wander off, they always come back. All in all, they're nice calves.'

While they were arguing, Demyan winked at Regina Petrovna and limped off to a thicket at the far end of the garden. After a few moments he emerged from it, carrying an enormous water-melon.

At first the twins thought it was a pumpkin, then when they looked closer they saw it was striped. It was a water-melon! A real water-melon!

They all began to dance with excitement and the little boys jumped up and down, begging to be allowed just to touch it.

'Where did you get it from?' Regina Petrovna asked, pleasantly surprised. 'Have you got a secret hiding-place too, eh?'

Demyan smirked and shook his bald head. 'Well, you see, I forgot to tell you about the water-melon bed . . . When I left, I reckoned that these two . . .' – he nodded towards the twins – ' . . . would either find it, or they wouldn't. And although they're good hunters, they missed it!'

The twins looked at each other, both simultaneously thinking what fools they were to have failed to find the water-melon bed. Now that really was disgraceful! They had sniffed out everything else: the sugar-cane, the walnut tree and even the berries that had gone to make the beads for that necklace. Apparently they came from a bush called berberis. But water-melons – and such water-melons . . . Well, Old Baldy had really taught them a lesson! He had made the twins look fools in front of everybody! But then . . . perhaps he was lying and had really brought it from his own garden at home and was now telling a fib!

Demyan, though, realized that he had been overdoing it by claiming that there was a secret melon-bed. He carried the water-melon to the table, cut out a slice for everyone and gave the twins the sweetest bits from the very middle.

'I'll bet you've never eaten one like this!'

'So it's not made of iron, then?' Kolka asked for a joke.

'What? A thing like this made of iron? It's a water-melon like any other!'

Then the brothers said they knew a joke which they could tell, about a conversation between two liars . . .

'All right, please tell it,' Regina Petrovna asked them with happy anticipation.

The twins then stood up and faced each other:

KOLKA: Ah, the places I've been . . . I tell you, I've been everywhere!

SASHKA: *Have you been to Paris?*

KOLKA: Yes, I have.

SASHKA: *Did you see the Awful Tower?*

KOLKA: I didn't just see it – I ate it!

SASHKA: *You can't have eaten it. It's made of iron!*

KOLKA: Yes, well . . . Have you been to the Caucasus?

SASHKA: *Yes, I have.*

KOLKA: And did you drink *kumis*?

SASHKA: *What?*

KOLKA: I said – did you drink *kumis*?

SASHKA: *No, I didn't . . . You can't. It's made of iron!*

The twins and everyone else laughed, and even though the little boys didn't understand, they clapped their hands. Regina Petrovna congratulated the twins, but also corrected them: it's not the *Awful* Tower but the Eiffel Tower. It was built by someone called Eiffel.

They had had their revenge for the hidden water-melon, and the brothers devoured it with pleasure. From now on they would not overlook the secret melon-patch. They would clear away every last reed if necessary, but they would find those water-melons – provided, of course, that Demyan wasn't lying. And if he was lying, then that joke had been aimed right at him!

Regina Petrovna realized this, but she wanted to make sure that this happy day ended peacefully, so she proposed a sing-song. No celebration was complete without a song or two.

The twins agreed at once, and boldly launched into the first song:

> The salt tears so gently are falling
> And run down my thin, haggard face,
> As sadly I sit here recalling
> The mem'ries brought back by this place . . .

But Regina Petrovna felt this song – a prisoner's lament – was unsuitable. With a wave of her hand she brushed aside the brothers and their song, and started singing one of her own:

> The cossacks were galloping home from the fair:
> They'd kidnapped young Galya and snatched her away!
> Once Galya, young Galya, was free as the air –
> Now they have enticed her, and she's gone astray!

At this point Demyan coughed, cleared his throat and joined in with the song – but in such a piercing, delicate, high tenor voice that it took the twins' breath away:

> Come ride like a cossack,
> Fly with us on horseback,
> Far better than home you will find your new life –
> Come live you with us as a young cossack's wife!

And the twins and Regina Petrovna joyfully chimed in with the chorus:

Once Galya, young Galya, was free as the air –
Now they have enticed her and she's gone astray!

Demyan disappeared for a moment and came back with a balalaika. It was an unusual balalaika, of a kind the twins had never seen before, with a long, long finger-board.

'Found it in the house,' Demyan boasted, as he strummed on the three strings. 'The Chechens used to play on it, and people say they called it a "wooden accordion" . . . Lord, some people are ignorant! How can it be an accordion, if it's a balalaika? It's a difficult instrument, this – needs a special touch to play it.'

Grinning tipsily, he plucked the strings again, producing a series of short, muted notes; then suddenly he struck it with all his fingers, rolled his eyes upwards and sang in his high, true voice:

Beyond the deep river and under the mountain
The forest grows green and there springs a clear fountain.
Beneath that high mountain, beside the deep river,
A little white farmhouse has stood there for ever;
A nightingale, charming the woods with his song,
Sings out from the treetops so loudly and long.
A pretty young widow lives there quite alone,
Lamenting past joys, all – alas! – long since gone . . .

Demyan came to the end of the song, paused and looked at Regina Petrovna. He gave another slightly drunken grin, and his eyes were sparkling.

Demyan had not sung the song loudly or boisterously, but the effect was cheerfully jaunty. He seemed to have been singing about Regina Petrovna, about himself and about this little house of theirs, where he had come – as if to the 'little white farmhouse' in the song – to pay a visit . . . The Kuzmin Twins were so envious of Demyan that they stood on tiptoe and stretched out their necks as they tried to see into his mouth, in a vain effort to discover just how he managed to control his beautiful voice with such power and smoothness. And in his hands the three-stringed Chechen balalaika played a delightful, Russian-style accompaniment in chords that ran up and down the scale. It was wonderful!

At that moment the twins forgave this crafty little peasant for everything: for the hidden water-melon, for feeding the goat with a lighted cigarette and even for his attempts to make up to Regina Petrovna.

What really amazed them was the fact that it was possible to make them shiver to their very bones with a song like that, about a widow, instead of with one of those maudlin prison songs which made up most of the twins' repertoire.

Never before had they heard or felt anything like it. The ending of the song, especially, had made them feel sad. Both of them might easily have burst into tears, but that would have been overdoing it in front of the grown-ups ... This was provoked by the verse in which the young widow invited the merchant and the fisherman to sit at her table; the two men vied in singing songs to her, while the young man who really loved her was looking in at the window, and he tolerated it patiently until ... until he could bear it no longer and murdered them all! Just like a Chechen might have done. And Demyan's song had ended like this:

> That farmhouse is empty, no one's there to sing songs,
> And only the nightingale sings loud and long ...

They had all sat in silence, either upset by such a terrible story or shattered by the thought of a young man so bold and desperate that he had killed the widow out of jealous love ... Regina Petrovna took her little boys off to bed. And came back. It was the evening hour of sunset, when everyone was feeling a little sad, langorous, warm, subdued and in a good mood. In a word, they were happy. Our twins, however, had not yet discovered whether they were ever happy or not; they would, perhaps, discover it later in their lives ... if they ever did. If, that is, they were granted enough time in which to discover it.

My God, how short life is, and how painful it is to think of the future and guess what it will bring – especially when we already know everything ...

I remember, how I remember that magical evening in our little white farmhouse, somewhere deep in the foothills of the Caucasus. Strange as it may seem, the day invented by that sorceress Regina Petrovna as our birthday became my birthday for the rest of my life. I sometimes wonder whether perhaps I was not really born until that day. I remember looking around and trying to identify the nature of the striking change that came over the world. But everything was simply as it was: the sky, fading in brightness as the evening drew in, but still clear and cloudless; the grass, still warm from the heat of the day; the dry smell of wormwood, that bitter-sad exhalation of the harsh soil of those parts. And Demyan's docile horse, grazing nearby – a dark silhouette against the mountains, though not flying, limbs outstretched, like the familiar picture on the packet of 'Kazbek' brand cigarettes, but with its muzzle peacefully bowed low – completed the idyllic picture of our day. I knew for certain that things were never really like this, and if they were, it was a bad sign, because it was all too good not to become much worse later. But it was at that very moment, when I had a vague premonition of all kinds of evil to come, that I suddenly realized for the first time that I was alive, that I really and truly existed and that one day I would die. That nagging feeling of the transience of existence, which I had just come to understand, has affected me for all my subsequent life, like being struck by lightning, like that grenade-fragment that pierced the very heart of Vera the truck-driver. But my God – how I longed never to die! Only later did I realize, when I was reading some scientific article, that in that moment the 'death-gene' had been awakened within me, which is inherent in all living human beings but does not reveal itself until a certain time, and only in early youth at some special moment . . . After which it is lodged in our consciousness for the rest of our lives. But a child – as I was until that moment – lives without any awareness of the transience of existence, and that is why children are immortal.

Twenty-five

Next morning, very early, when the first rays of the sun were only just glinting past the mountain-tops, Demyan started to get ready for his return journey. He spread a layer of reeds on the bottom of his cart and loaded it with two big yellow pumpkins.

Noticing his preparations from her window, Regina Petrovna went out, hastily buttoning up her shirt on the way. 'Could you take the Kuzmin Twins with you?' she asked. 'We need some more supplies.'

She was keeping a little distance from Demyan, and avoided looking him in the face. This was because of what had happened the previous night, when Demyan had asked to sleep inside the house, ostensibly because of the cold; he had then crawled into Regina Petrovna's bed (pretending to be so drunk that he was doing it by mistake) and she had kicked him out – right out of the house and into the lean-to, where he was obliged to bed down on a pile of reeds alongside the sleeping twins.

He spent all night puffing away at his home-made cigarettes, waiting for the dawn. He recalled the day when he had been in the military hospital at Biisk and had gone to the nearby river, intending to drown himself: he had just received a letter telling him that his wife and two little children had been burned alive in their house by the fascists. Being by then a one-legged cripple, Demyan felt he was of no more use to anybody, so . . .

He had walked down to the river with a rod and line, as though going fishing; the water there was fast-flowing, turbulent and full of whirlpools, not like the placid, smooth rivers of the flatlands of central Russia. The noise of the rushing water could be heard all over the hospital grounds.

As he leaned over the river-bank, his head was spinning. What was the sense of living any longer, when the whole of his life had gone up in flames?

Suddenly he caught sight of the woman doctor who had sawn off

193

his leg. He had shouted aloud when she did it . . . How did she happen to be on the river-bank? Was she out for a walk? Anyway, she saw him and spoke to him. 'Would you like some vodka, Demyan Ivanych? Come on, I've got a little stock of it.' He agreed. He knocked back a glassful and felt better. He lit a cigarette and she poured out another glass. 'Drink up, don't be afraid. Where are you going to when you leave here?' He drank another half-glass of vodka, and muttered, 'Don't know.' And he thought to himself, 'Nearly kicked the bucket . . . almost dived head first into the whirlpool.'

Suddenly she said there was rich farmland to be had for the asking in the northern Caucasus. They needed men there. Why didn't he give it a try? Thirty was no age; for a man it was little more than adolescence . . .

'So that's that,' she insisted. 'And you can start another family – you can raise up a dozen of them.'

The woman doctor was Jewish. Quite young, and married. Her husband was a political exile, but was allowed to live with her – or more likely she had managed to get transferred to this area where he was forced to work as a lumberjack, felling timber. Their life wasn't exactly a bed of roses, either, when you came to think of it. But Demyan was a free man, and he could, it was true, pull up sticks and go anywhere he wanted to. Things couldn't be any worse for him than they were at present – what did he have to lose, after all? So he went, and was amazed at the unfamiliar sight of mountains and at the rich, fertile black soil; you only had to push a stick into the ground and it would start sprouting.

He was allotted a house that had once belonged to someone unknown; he cleaned it up and improved it by excavating and building a cellar, laying a stone-flagged path to the front door and planting poplars along both sides of the path . . . He repaired the yard, cleaned out the well and distilled himself a carboy-full of moonshine, as he had done back in his home village. He looked around; everything was in place, yet he felt that something was missing. What did he lack? All he needed every day was a handful of maize and a crust of bread. What the place lacked was living beings: children running about; cows mooing and chickens clucking; and being met on the doorstep by someone with a jug of water who would then pour it into a washbasin and watch while Demyan snorted and spluttered as he washed the sweat from his face after the day's work.

He began drinking. And always alone. Again he had visions of swirling river-water. He closed his eyes and there was nothing, just as before. And that was the whole trouble: it was just an illusion, a

194

fiction that he was alive . . . He was only imagining it . . . Although that doctor had been a wise woman, even she had not been able to cure the most deep-seated element of his problem. He had come to the end of his tether. When he had first gone to the outlying farm, he was constantly glancing at the railway line all the time to see how often a train passed by. There were no whirlpools here, but there were the rails: he could lie down across them and he wouldn't have to wait long. Especially since the train passed by at speed and the only sign of it was the echo thrown back by the mountains.

And then suddenly the farm was inhabited by a teacher from the orphanage and her little children.

'So will you take them, Demyan Ivanych?' she asked, blinking in the light of the early-morning sun.

She was a good-looking woman, well proportioned and sturdy: shapely breasts, arms and legs, and long witch's hair that she could wind into a bun. No make-up on her face, either; it was only a pity that she was fool enough to smoke. But she could be taught to give that up. With a whip, or by some other means.

'What about you? Why don't you come?' he enquired rudely. 'Or have I scared you, and you don't trust me? You think Demyan's not to be relied on, don't you! That he's just an old goat – is that it?'

'Why do you say that? . . . I trust you, Demyan Ivanych. I know I'm stupid, but it's the way I am, I'm afraid . . .' she said, still frowning in the bright sunlight and avoiding his look. 'And one of my little boys isn't well this morning. He overate yesterday, and he was up all night being sick. Otherwise I'd come with you myself. In fact, I very much *don't* want to send the twins. I'm afraid for them!'

She looked guilty, and he felt sorry for her. 'I'll bring you what we call a "belly-bag",' he said. 'My old woman taught me how to do it: you dry the lining of a chicken's stomach and grind it up. That's why it's called a "belly-bag"; it'll cure any troubles in your gut . . .'

'Thank you,' Regina Petrovna said quietly.

She still stood waiting.

'Of course I can take the boys with me. My cart's big enough. But how will they come back?'

'Couldn't you bring them back?'

He did a quick mental reckoning. 'They'll need a whole day to go there and back. I can't bring them back, because they won't let me take off so much time from the collective farm.'

'But you could bring them as far as the station, couldn't you?'

195

Regina Petrovna begged urgently. 'At least take them as far as the station, and then I'll fetch from there with the donkey and cart . . . how about that?'

Demyan grunted and scratched his bald head. He turned on his heel and walked towards his cart. Without looking round, he barked as he went, 'All right, go and wake them up. Only I can't waste any more time waiting here.'

Regina Petrovna hastily went off to get the twins up. They, too, had eaten and drunk too well the day before, and were so sleepy that they couldn't make any sense. She shook them, poured out water for them to wash themselves, and told them to eat something. But they refused any sort of food.

She stuffed a couple of hessian sacks into a bag, instructing them to fetch buckwheat in the sacks and bread in the bag. She also put in some slices of bread and butter and a bottle of milk. If possible, they were to use this bottle to bring back a supply of sunflower-seed oil.

'Can you remember all that? You won't forget, will you?' She asked the twins.

They nodded, yawning as they went. They just could not wake up properly. Each one of them had a parcel under his arm; they were taking yesterday's birthday presents with them.

'Why are you taking those?' Regina Petrovna asked in surprise. 'Do you want to leave them at the orphanage?'

The twins shook their heads. They weren't such fools as to take treasures like these to the orphanage!

'Are you going to hide them in your secret cache?' she guessed – correctly.

The twins did not reply. It was obvious they were taking them there.

'You'd do better to leave them here,' Regina Petrovna advised them. 'No one will touch your things. I promise you . . . Well?'

The two brothers exchanged looks and handed her the parcels.

'Off you go, then . . .' She patted each of them on the head, one with her left, the other with her right hand. 'If the superintendent asks you, tell him we're all getting on fine here and we have all we need. He can send some of the children up here to help with the harvest . . .'

'We don't want *them*!' said Sashka, turning away. Kolka nodded in agreement.

Regina Petrovna led the brothers to the cart and installed them in the back end. 'Keep an eye on them, Demyan Ivanych . . . One

196

never knows what may happen down there . . . And I'll come and fetch them tomorrow, as we agreed.'

Demyan burrowed in the straw, dug out his battered little cap and slapped it down on his forehead. He stared hard at Regina Petrovna from under the peak. In the morning light his eyes were a transparent, childlike blue.

'Don't worry. Things down there are normal now. When I was driving up here, I saw what was going on and weighed it all up by what I'd learned in the front line. They were bringing up so many troops, it was like they were throwing a circle around Stalingrad all over again. And they were carrying back those . . . you know . . . Chechens . . . in carts . . .'

'In carts? Why?' Regina Petrovna asked, suddenly turning pale. 'Alive, I hope?'

'All dead!' Demyan gestured dismissively. 'I didn't want to tell you yesterday. There wouldn't have been any point. As I see it, they're better dead . . . Life here'll be a lot quieter . . .'

Regina Petrovna frowned. 'Forgive me, but you sound as if you were glad of it . . .'

'Why should I cry over them?' He suddenly flared up. 'Better for us to get them before they can get us. Or do you want to have it different? Didn't those brutes give you enough of a fright?'

Regina Petrovna shook her head and looked at the twins. 'Personally I don't want anything. But why does there have to be all this killing?'

'Because it seems they don't know any better. They sold themselves to Hitler! And Hitler made a Chechen into a general in the German army. Killing Russians is a sort of national disease with them.'

'But suppose *you* were turned out of house and home?' Regina Petrovna asked quietly.

'I *was* turned out of my house,' Demyan suddenly gave a nonchalant smile, although he can hardly have found it funny. 'I was sixteen at the time. And all because of a horse. It was during the collectivization. Because my father owned a horse, he was listed as a *kulak*. But I gave the horse to the collective, and glad of it. At least it made life a bit easier for me. Now I use a collective-farm horse. And I'm still alive. Not like some of those people who refused to hand over their livestock or slaughtered it . . .'

'Yes, but . . . We're not talking about that,' Regina Petrovna sighed. 'The fact is, the war has made you hard. Everyone has become harder and more callous. That's why it's so frightening . . . So you will take care of them won't you?'

Demyan turned away and clicked his tongue at the horse.

Sitting on the tailboard of the cart, their legs dangling over the end, the twins watched Regina Petrovna.

'I'll be at the station at lunchtime tomorrow to fetch you!' she shouted after them and waved her hand.

The twins shouted back, 'All right!'

Demyan, though, said nothing and did not look round, as if this were no concern of his. Now and again glancing at the road from under the peak of his cap, he drove the cart in silence.

He remained silent all the way.

The two brothers guessed at once why he was silent: he had been turned down! He might be a fine singer, but as a husband he didn't measure up. It was obvious . . .

When the twins jumped over the roadside ditch and went in among the maize-stalks for a piss, Kolka said, 'She's given Old Baldy the boot!'

'I feel sorry for him,' Sashka replied. 'He's a grand singer!'

'D'you think the super will give *us* the boot today?' said Kolka, changing the subject. 'He's still got that letter about us from Tomilino!'

'I'm sure he's forgotten about it . . . He's got other things to worry about besides us.'

'The main thing is to get the jam out of our hiding-place,' said Kolka. 'I reckon it's time we pushed off.'

'But Regina Petrovna?'

'What about Regina Petrovna? After all, she promised we could leave after the birthday party.'

'Supposing she won't go with us?'

'Well – so what?'

'I feel sorry for her . . .'

'Well don't! There are plenty of others to feel sorry for her and look after her now!'

Sashka began doing up his fly-buttons, but was so nervous that he tore off the top button. As they went back to the road he said to Kolka, 'You can do what you like, but I'm not going to leave her.'

'Never?'

'What, d'you mean – never?'

'Never?' Amazed, Kolka repeated the question. 'Do you mean you wouldn't leave if I did?'

Sashka nodded.

198

They had said it. For the first time in their lives it had come out that they might part – voluntarily – and go their separate ways.

Kolka did not believe his ears; even if it had been spelled out to him by a third person, he would not have believed it. It was impossible to separate them; together, they were what is called in arithmetic a prime number: a quantity that is indivisible . . . an expression that might have been invented to describe them.

As Kolka saw it, Sashka had gone off his rocker. It wouldn't matter if this didn't last long, but if . . . He rejected the grim thought, and said to Sashka, 'We'll decide when we get back. Agreed?' And he gave Sashka the silver-buckled belt that Regina Petrovna had given him, so that his brother could keep his trousers up.

'Agreed,' said Sashka. He may well have been thinking that it wouldn't be himself but Kolka who would change his mind. But he took the belt and buckled it on.

Then they both lay down in the cart, with an arm around each other, and went to sleep.

When they woke up it was twilight, and at first they couldn't remember where they were.

The horse had been unharnessed and was grazing alongside the cart among the maize. Demyan, for some reason, was sitting on the ground and looking watchfully around on all sides. His face looked worried and had turned pale.

The twins raised their heads, scratching themselves as they looked around them.

'Hey!' Demyan called out softly and beckoned them to him. 'Come here . . . only be quiet, very quiet!'

Reluctantly the brothers jumped down from the cart and went over to Demyan. 'Where's the orphanage?'

Demyan, though, only made a strange movement with his hand, indicating that they should come nearer and sit down.

'Aren't you well, or something?' Sashka asked, surprised at this behaviour.

And Kolka added, 'I must have eaten too much yesterday. My tummy's making awful noises – like a brass band!'

The boys roared with laughter, but Demyan looked round and hushed them. 'Be quiet! Quiet, I said! . . . The orphanage is over there.' And he pointed out the direction. 'Only the whole place . . . is empty!'

'Empty?' the twins retorted, staring at Demyan. 'What d'you mean – empty?'

'Empty, that's all,' he said in a whisper. 'Go and have a look, if you like. Only don't walk on the road and don't show yourselves . . . Got it?'

'All right . . . But why?'

'I'm telling you to be careful, see? Have a look and then come back. I'll wait for you here.'

The twins stood for a while, trying dully to absorb this news, but they couldn't make head or tail of the situation. Without further discussion they turned and set off, walking unconcernedly, as if out for a stroll; they were now on familiar ground. Most of all they were longing to go straight to their cache, to make sure that their precious hoard was still there and intact.

After about five or ten yards the maize thinned out and they could see the orphanage: there was the central two-storey building. They were surprised by how quiet it was. Not a single voice was to be heard, yet normally the place resounded to yells, shouts and squeals audible for miles around.

'Are you going to crawl through?' asked Sashka, pointing to their secret hole in the hedge.

'What about you?'

They were talking in whispers, although there was nothing to be afraid of; it was simply that talking loudly amid this silence seemed out of place. As for Demyan, the twins' last impression of him, sitting in that funny attitude on the ground, was that he had been drinking again to get rid of a hangover from yesterday and was not quite himself. Perhaps he had not only imagined that the orphanage was empty, but was seeing little green devils as well!

Puffing, the twins clambered through the gap in the hedge and emerged by the rear wall of the two-storey building.

It was absolutely quiet; nobody was to be seen through any of the windows. Were they all at supper? Were they out in the fields, helping with the harvest?

They reached the end of the wall, turned the corner and froze.

Kolka, who was walking behind his brother, bumped into Sashka. Together they stared in amazement. It was a strange sight. The whole courtyard was littered with junk, as if the place had been evacuated. It looked as though the inhabitants had intended to abandon the place for good: they had, it seemed, piled up all the furniture – beds, mattresses, chairs and tables – into great heaps, and then had simply left it all and gone away.

And it was silent. There was a kind of deathly quiet everywhere. The only sound came from above, as though from the sky – a noise

200

like the regular tolling of a bell: dong, dong, dong . . . The twins shivered; it sounded horribly like a funeral.

Slowly and cautiously they walked across the courtyard, broken glass crunching under their feet. All the windows in the buildings had been smashed and the window-frames knocked out. Doors, torn from their hinges, lay flat on the ground.

Up on the first floor, the blue-painted head of an iron bedstead was protruding from one of the gaping openings, and the wind was making an empty window-frame bang monotonously against it; this was the source of the dismal sound that they had taken for a bell.

Sashka bent down and picked up a tin bowl, made out of an empty American tin that had contained food. He turned it over and threw it away. It rolled across the broken glass and the bare ground, rolling on and on for a long time with a metallic tinkle, as if it were running by clockwork. About ten paces from the spot where it finally stopped, something dark was lying on the ground.

'Hey, look,' said Kolka, turning something over in his hand that he had picked up from the ground. 'It's a buckle . . . a buckle from . . .'

He was going to say, 'A buckle from a briefcase,' but he had no time to say it, because the dark object lying on the ground was the briefcase itself.

It was that famous briefcase – familiar to every inmate of the orphanage, with bulging, faded sides and two gleaming buckles on the front, one of them had now been torn off – which Pyotr Anisimovich used to carry: the briefcase he had always carried, and which he had never, never under any circumstances, ever let out of his sight!

The twins looked at the briefcase, and an awful fact was borne in upon them, shattered though they already were by the scene of destruction.

If the briefcase was here, and the superintendent *wasn't* here, then it meant that nothing less than a catastrophe had occurred.

Had there, perhaps, been a bombing raid? Had the Germans maybe mounted an air-raid from somewhere? Was it . . . ? Could it . . . ?

Fear began to take hold of them; at first groundless and unreasoning, it redoubled itself because they could not understand what had happened.

Sashka squatted down and cautiously touched the briefcase, as though it were not a briefcase but a living creature.

201

Suddenly from nearby came a deafening crash, and Kolka yelled wildly, 'Come on! We're getting out of here!'

And they tore off at full pelt, dashing over broken glass, over plywood doors, over mattresses whose straw fillings were spilling out of their innards . . . around the corner of the main building and through the hole in the hedge – miraculously without being jabbed by a single thorn. They charged into the thick of a maize-field, knocking over the crackling stalks as they went.

Neither could explain what it was that had so scared Kolka – indeed both of them – unless it had been the noise made by the wind suddenly tearing at a sheet of corrugated iron . . . and tearing their nerves to shreds at the same time!

The further they ran, the more panic-stricken and terrified they became. They already had a nasty feeling that they were alone and that Demyan had disappeared. What on earth would they do then?

Fortunately, though, Demyan was still sitting where they had left him. He turned around, sharply and fearfully, when the twins appeared. Without getting up or changing his position, he looked at them intently from under the little peak of his cap.

'Well? Did you see it?' he asked them, and began rolling himself a cigarette. His hands would not obey him, and spilled the tobacco over his clothes and on to the grass.

The two brothers stared at his hands. Both boys were out of breath from fright or from running. Breathing hard, they watched the uncontrollable twitching of his hands.

Finally Demyan lit his cigarette, took several deep drags of the smoke as he stared at a point somewhere behind the boys. Then he threw away his cigarette and stood up nimbly without any help. 'We must get out of here,' he said in a hoarse croak.

It wasn't clear whether he was talking to himself or to the twins. Without another word he plunged into the thicket; he seemed to have lost his limp.

The boys wanted to follow him, but stood there in perplexity, looking dubiously at the cart and their bag, and at the horse, which was grazing untethered.

Demyan looked round and waved to them. 'Forget it,' he muttered, again talking to himself rather than to the twins. 'We haven't got time to bother about those things. We've got to save our skins!'

'Our . . . what? . . . Why?' asked Sashka.

But Demyan only put his finger to his lips as a signal to them to be quiet, and set off into the field of maize, doing his best to avoid every gap between the rows of stalks, every bare patch. He moved

202

cautiously, keeping a constant look-out, no doubt in the way that scouts do in war.

The boys realized at once that he was heading for the village – in other words, for home. He was no longer paying any attention to the twins, and seemed to have forgotten about them.

Only once, when Sashka carelessly caused a maize-stalk to snap loudly, did he turn round and shake his fist. 'Quiet! Don't make a sound!'

At that moment Kolka stumbled and crashed into a dry stalk with a loud noise.

Demyan came back to them, beckoned the boys to him, pressed their heads painfully to the ground, and hissed angrily right into their ears, 'You little fools! Are you tired of living? If you want to die, go by the road! They'll catch you and knock your heads off!'

'Who will?' Sashka asked, his eyes wide with fright.

Never in his life had he seen a grown man so furious or, rather, terrified. He had always thought that grown-ups, especially men who had been soldiers, were never afraid.

'Who! Who!' said Demyan in the same angry whisper. 'Don't you understand? They're *here*! Right near us.' And he looked all around him.

He let go of the twins and started to hobble off again, though now more slowly. He was evidently tired, as indeed they all were.

Kolka, what's more, was suffering from a severe bout of diarrhoea. Back at the orphanage they would have said he was so scared he was shitting his pants. Every few minutes he had to stop and squat down, grunting, staring imploringly through the deepening twilight at the disappearing Sashka. Although Sashka knew that he would never abandon Kolka, he nevertheless hurried on after Demyan, trying not to lose sight of him, constantly turning his head to look now back, now forward.

Demyan, meanwhile, seemed to be unaware of Kolka's agonies, and had apparently ceased to notice the twins altogether. He was creeping furtively through the maize, dropping down every so often and peering around like some kind of thief.

It was at one of these moments that it all happened.

Demyan was in front, when he suddenly took a sideways leap and disappeared. Kolka, who was squatting down in pain from an attack of diarrhoea, although not a drop was coming out of him any longer, saw Sashka hurl himself after Demyan. There was a flash from the silver buckle of the belt which Kolka had given him, then Sashka vanished from sight.

Then Demyan appeared again. He was hobbling along at speed, stamping hard with his wooden leg, making no attempt at caution. He turned and shouted, presumably to Sashka, 'Don't stay in a bunch! Scatter! It'll be harder for them to catch us!'

He crashed noisily into a thick clump of maize and disappeared. Sashka, too, had vanished. Kolka was left squatting there alone.

All this took place in a moment, and Kolka did not have time either to collect his wits or to pull up his trousers. Suddenly, above the tops of the maize-stalks, a horse's muzzle appeared. From his squatting position he looked up at the animal, which stared back at him with one red, mistrustful eye. Then, above the horse's head, he also noticed the dark shadow of the rider and heard his piercing, guttural cry: 'Khey! Khey! Khey!'

That was the moment when Kolka understood.

He hit the ground with a thud and shut his eyes.

He could hear the horse coming towards him, noisily pushing its way through the maize-stalks. It snorted, breathing right down Kolka's neck, and as he half opened one eye he saw, right in front of his face, the horse's restless leg and its stamping hoof as it crushed a brittle stalk. The stalk rebounded and lashed Kolka painfully across the face, and lumps of earth flew into his hair and on to his back.

He had to get up and run. He realized that they had found him, and would seize him at any moment. But no sooner did he make a move to stand up than the horse suddenly took fright, whinnied and made a violent jump sideways.

Although his legs were as numb and stiff as crutches and he was trembling all over, Kolka ran off through the dense thicket of maize at a brisk trot, clutching his trousers. Somewhere behind him, very near, he could hear a man's guttural voice and his barking cry: 'Khey! Khey!'

Then came a crashing and splintering of maize-stalks, the clatter of hooves in thundering pursuit.

He ran, prancing along in a ridiculous gait as he tried to keep his trousers from falling down. He didn't know for certain whether they were chasing him, or for how long, because he could hear nothing but his own breathing and the crackling of the maize that he crushed as he ran. Then his breathing stopped and his strength came to an end. He fell into a little hole in the ground and found he could no longer move. Gripped by a kind of paralysis, he drifted into unconsciousness.

He did not hear the horse passing near him, smashing down the stalks, nor did he hear it move away until it disappeared altogether.

204

When he came to, it was dark. There was complete blackness all around, as if his eyes and ears were glued shut.

He felt the little trench into which he had fallen, but was still unable to get up. Then, using hands and feet, he began to dig himself further in. With his fingers he clawed away the heavy earth, smelling of rich humus, and like an animal he threw it out by kicking it away with his feet.

How long he did this for, or why he did it, he didn't know. Indeed, he knew nothing about himself. When he was worn out, he lay down, pressing himself against the earth, deeper into the little pit that he had dug; again he vanished from this world and tumbled into oblivion.

Twenty-six

It was morning – warm, without a trace of cloud, without a breeze. The nearby mountains were etched sharply against the blue, clean-washed morning sky. Every wrinkle on them could be clearly seen.

A grey bird, its wings flickering in rapid movement, was hovering over the field as it tracked its prey. Grasshoppers chirruped, little birds were twittering. A black swarm of starlings swooped past with a rustling sound.

It was all so ordinary, so peaceful that the events of yesterday evening now seemed like a bad dream. Had it not been for the horse's hoofmarks stamped deep into the narrow corridor that the animal had driven through the maize, Kolka would have felt sure he had dreamed it all.

If only he could have woken up at the farm, lying on their bed of reeds with Sashka snoring gently beside him. Kolka would have punched him in the side to waken him and tell him about his dream: '... It was like we were being chased by one of those ... you know ... Chechens, on horseback! And I nearly lost my trousers running away from him! What a laugh!'

Yet even the incident with the horsemen no longer seemed as terrifying as it had been at the time. Everything was so clear, blue and peaceful now; it was unthinkable that anything in the least bit evil could happen on a morning like this.

Kolka brushed the earth from his trousers and looked around; he even tried jumping up in an effort to see over the top of the maize and find out where the village lay. But of course he could see nothing.

He attempted to work out his position from the mountains and from the sun, and having chosen what seemed to him the right direction, he set off, without trying to hide himself or to bend double. Sashka and Demyan couldn't have gone far, and if they were sensible they too would head for Beriozovskaya.

206

Indeed, they might even be there already, sitting by the well and drinking cold water. Kolka was also very thirsty.

He walked on and on, brushing the thick cobwebs away from his face which had been spun between the maize-stalks, and scaring several fat, black birds as he went.

Once a grey hare shot out of a thicket and bolted off, the soil spraying up behind its back legs.

Kolka was not frightened by the hare, and thought to himself, 'Supposing they weren't chasing after me at all but were hunting hares? And there were we, fools that we were, shaking with fright – just as frightened as that hare, I expect!'

On one maize-stalk, shorter than the rest and quite green (obviously self-sown late in the season) he broke off a corn-cob that was still soft and milky and ate it whole, core and all. He tried to find another one like it, but there were no more green stalks to be found. The dry, ripe cobs were so tough that you couldn't even dig the corn out with a stone, let alone get your teeth into it.

Having given up hope of ever finding a road, he suddenly came out on one. It was a dry, white cart-track, covered in fine dust. Clumps of camomile, small and bushy, were flowering on the verges and butterflies were flitting back and forth. But there was not a trace of a cart having passed that way.

Kolka looked up at the mountains again and wondered whether he had already passed beyond Beriozovskaya and should turn back; otherwise he would be walking towards the station, and on foot that was a whole day's journey. Anyway, why did he need to go to the station now, if Demyan and Sashka were waiting for him? They must surely realize that Kolka would look for them in Beriozovskaya. First, though, he had to find a well and have a long drink of water.

He wondered what sort of fibs they would tell in describing how they had run away from the horsemen. Each would probably lie and say he hadn't been scared at all but had only run away because the others had run . . . Sashka would say he had followed the lead of Demyan, who had been the first to plunge into a thicket, and Demyan would say it had been Sashka who had confused him and created a panic.

They could spin whatever yarns they liked, if that amused them; Kolka had no wish to recall how he had lain under the very hooves of that horse – it was only by a sheer fluke that the animal hadn't trodden on him – and then how he had plunged through the maize clutching his trousers, with the sound of crashing and pounding close behind him . . . though perhaps it was he himself who had

207

been making all that noise! And then there was that hole . . . He certainly wouldn't tell them about the hole. Kolka himself was mystified by the way he had feverishly tried to dig himself deeper into the hole, without being aware of why he was doing it.

He rounded a corner; here the maize-stalks thinned out, and through them he could see kitchen gardens with pumpkin and marrow patches, the tops of poplar-trees and the roofs of houses.

Kolka quickened his pace until he was almost running.

Somehow he believed he would reach the village at any moment and would at once find Sashka and Demyan. If he didn't, he would make enquiries; people were bound to tell him where they had seen them and which way they had gone.

But first he would drink his fill of water.

His throat was dry and there was not even enough saliva in his mouth to swallow. There was nothing but dry dust on his teeth, which crunched if he bit on them.

No doubt Kolka was too careless; otherwise he would have noticed as he approached the village that there was no one in it. But he was thinking only about Sashka, and hardly looked around him at all.

Only as he drew near to the first house did he notice that here, too, as at the orphanage, the windows had been smashed in, and there were only black holes against the background of white walls, like the empty eye-sockets in a skull.

In the middle of the road was a well, surrounded by a round concrete well-head and above it a slightly battered pail on a hook.

Kolka leaned over the black hole, where far at the bottom was the oily glint of water. He took hold of the bucket, but suddenly noticed that it was smeared with something thick, red and sticky . . . and he started back in horror.

At that moment he saw Sashka.

Kolka's heart gave a bound of joy: Sashka was standing at the very end of the street, leaning against a fence and staring hard at something – perhaps at the crows which were circling around near by.

Kolka put two fingers into his mouth and whistled.

Anyone familiar with the twins' habits could have told them apart by the way they whistled. Kolka only used two fingers, but he could make a sound capable of intricate modulations. Sashka, on the other hand, employed four fingers, two from each hand, and he could whistle louder than Kolka, so loud that it made your ears ring, but only on one note.

Now Kolka whistled and grinned to himself. 'Aha! Sashka must have gone deaf – he can't hear me whistling! He's standing there like a statue.'

Kolka ran along the village street, straight towards Sashka, thinking what fun it would be to creep up on Sashka while his brother was still watching the crows; he had done this before – he would creep alongside the fence and then bark at the top of his voice, 'Hands up – I'm a Chechen!'

But as he came nearer, he slowed his pace in involuntarily: there was something very strange about Sashka, but at first Kolka could not make out what it was.

Either Sashka had grown taller, or he was standing in an awkward attitude – what's more, the fact that he hadn't moved for so long was beginning to seem suspicious.

Kolka took a few more hesitant steps and stopped.

Suddenly he felt cold all over and sick and short of breath. His body froze, down to the very tips of his fingers and toes. His legs gave way under him and he dropped down to the grass, though without taking his gaze off Sashka, his eyes wide with horror.

Sashka was not standing; he was hanging, impaled through his armpits on the spikes of the fence, and from his stomach there protruded a yellow corn-cob, its silky 'floss' waving in the breeze.

The other half of the corn-cob had been rammed into Sashka's mouth, its thick end sticking out, giving Sashka's face a silly, even stupid, expression.

Kolka remained sitting on the ground, overcome by a strange feeling of aloofness, as though he were not in his own body but was nevertheless seeing and remembering everything. He saw, for instance, that the flock of crows, perched on a nearby tree, was watching his every movement; he saw some nimble grey sparrows taking a dust-bath; and he saw an ugly chicken leap out from behind the fence, chased by a hungry, feral cat.

Kolka made an effort to stand up, and succeeded. Walking forward, he did not go to Sashka but around him, without going either nearer or further away.

Now, standing directly opposite his brother he saw that Sashka had no eyes; the crows had pecked them out. They had also pecked at his right cheek and ear, but not so hard. Below his stomach and below the the corn-cob and tufts of grass that had been stuffed into it, Sashka's intestines – black with clotted blood – were hanging out down his trousers, and had also been pecked by the crows. Clearly the blood had also run down his legs, which were so oddly raised above ground level; it was hanging in large clots from the soles of his feet and from Sashka's dirty toes, while the grass under his feet was a single, jelly-like mass.

Suddenly Kolka noticed, sharply and in every detail, how one of the crows – the most impatient of them, or perhaps the most predatory – dropped down to the road and began moving slowly towards Sashka's body. The bird paid no attention to Kolka.

He scooped up a handful of sand and threw it at the crow. 'You horrible beast! You brute!' he shouted at it. 'Go away, filthy thing!'

The crow jumped back, but did not fly away, as though it realized that Kolka wasn't strong enough to be a real threat to it. It stood in the road at a slight distance and waited expectantly. This was more than Kolka could bear. He yelled, howled and shouted, and hurled himself blindly at the crow as though at a detested enemy. He chased it down the street, now and then bending down to pick up sand and throw it at the bird. He must have shouted loudly – so loudly that he could have been heard in the whole village, across the whole valley; if a single living creature had been nearby, it would have run away in terror at the sound of that inhuman shriek.

But there was no one to hear it.

Only the carrion crows took off from their perch in fright, and flew away.

And Kolka kept on running down the street, still shouting, hurling sand, lumps of turf and stones – whatever came to hand. But his voice gave out, he tripped and fell in the dust. He sat up, shaking the dirt out of his hair and wiping his face with his sleeve. Even now he could not understand why he had been shouting and why he had run all the way to the very edge of the village.

Barely able to drag one foot after the other, he went back to his brother's body and sat down by his feet, alongside the big clot of blood, to rest and get his breath back.

Everything that he did from then on was seemingly deliberate and logical, although he acted with little conscious thought, as if he were standing to one side and watching himself.

Rested, he went up to Sashka, slithering on the clotted blood, put his arms around the body and pulled it towards him. Sashka immediately collapsed to the ground and seemed to shrivel. The corn-cob fell out of his mouth, but the mouth stayed open.

Kolka went round to his brother's head, picked him up under the armpits and dragged him to the nearest house.

The door had been wrenched off its hinges. A pile of maize lay inside the large, glassed-in porch.

Kolka laid his brother on the maize and covered him with a

quilted jacket that was hanging there on a nail. Then he lifted up the door and used it to block the entrance, so that the crows could not get into the house.

Having done all this and rested a little, Kolka set off along the road to the orphanage, without attempting to hide or take any precautions against being seen.

He knew that the very worst that could possibly happen to him had already happened.

Twenty-seven

A few hours later, when it was starting to grow dark and the sun was setting behind the distant mountains, Kolka returned, pulling behind him the handcart which they had found at Ilya's house.

The cart had been hidden in the bushes near their secret storage-place, and Kolka had found it at once.

The store, too, was intact: the jam, the sacks, the thirty-rouble note and the keys from the train – everything was still in place.

Kolka pulled out the sacks and a half-litre jar of jam. He opened the jar with a stone and ate two spoonfuls, but it immediately made him sick.

He went down to the river, where he washed himself and ducked his head under water to freshen up a little.

On the way, pulling the handcart behind him, he turned into the maize-field where they had left the horse and cart the day before. He soon discovered the spot: there were the wheel-tracks of the cart, and nearby was the half-smoked butt of one of Demyan's cigarettes.

On reaching the house in Beriozovskaya, Kolka dragged Sashka out into the street again and put him into the handcart, after first laying the two sacks on the bottom of the cart for padding, lest his brother find the ride too bumpy. Then he rolled up the quilted jacket into a makeshift pillow and put it under Sashka's head.

Next he took a leather strap, which he found in a corner of the porch; it was thick but rotten, and it broke in two, so he had to double it over to make it strong enough. While doing this, he noticed that Sashka was not wearing the silver-buckled belt; it had obviously been lost somewhere. Kolka pulled one end of the strap under the handcart and tied it in a knot over Sashka's chest. He tried not to touch his stomach, so as not to hurt Sashka too much.

Having tied the strap, he stopped and looked at his brother. The expression on Sashka's face was peaceful, even slightly surprised,

212

due to the fact that his mouth had stayed open. He was lying with his head facing forward; Kolka thought this would be the most comfortable way for Sashka to travel.

While he was making these preparations, the twilight – brief, gentle, golden – had set in. The mountains dissolved in a warm haze; only the bright, topmost peaks glowed on for a while like dying embers on the jagged skyline and then were soon extinguished.

Exactly twenty-four hours had passed since they had woken up at sunset in Demyan's cart, but it now seemed to Kolka that it had been long, long ago when they had walked into the devastated orphanage courtyard, then had run through the undergrowth to find Demyan sitting on the ground and trying to light a cigarette with shaking hands. Where was he now? *He* was the one who had known what might happen to them; it was they, the twins, who had been the stupid ones.

Kolka gave no thought to the farm, to Regina Petrovna and her two little boys. They were now beyond the horizon of his life, his feelings and his memory.

He sat down and rested awhile, then stood up. He fastened the handcart's rope in such a way that it wouldn't cut into his hand, and set off, pulling it down the street.

He had no idea whether pulling the little cart was hard work or not. In any case, how could he tell how heavy it was, when he was giving a ride to his brother, from whom he had never been separated in his life? They had always been together, each a part of the other, so it was really as if Kolka were pulling himself.

Beyond the village the surroundings were a little more open and the light seemed a little brighter, but not for long.

The air seemed to grow dense and black, merging into the impenetrable walls of maize on either side of the road. Soon nothing could be seen at all, and Kolka could only feel the road with his feet. Ahead, where the lines of maize should have merged, there was just a hint of a slightly brighter gap between them against the background of the inky-black sky.

Kolka was not afraid of the dark nor of the solid, unrelieved blackness of the road, empty of people or traffic of any kind.

If Kolka had been more aware of the reality of his situation, and if someone had asked him what was the best and most convenient way for him to transport his brother, he would have asked for exactly this: that he should meet no one on his way and that no one should prevent him from reaching the station. Anyone he might encounter now – be they Chechen or anyone else, even kind, well-disposed

213

people – would inevitably be a hindrance to him in the task he had set for himself.

He pulled his handcart through the night and talked to his brother as he went, saying to him, 'Well, it's ended up so that *I'm* giving *you* a ride. We always used to take it in turns to pull each other along in one of these, didn't we? But don't worry about me. I'm not tired and I'll get you there. Maybe you'd have thought of a better way of doing this – in fact I'm sure you would. You always understood things better than me, because your brain worked faster than mine. I was your hands and feet when you were alive – that was the way things were shared out between us – and you were my head. Now our head's been cut off, and they've left the hands and feet. I wonder why they did, though . . . ?'

Kolka changed hands whenever one arm grew numb, but before starting off again he would feel Sashka, to make sure he was lying comfortably and the rolled-up jacket hadn't slipped out from under his head. He noticed that Sashka seemed to be getting stiffer and colder, that his body was hardening, his arms and legs were becoming wooden. All the same it was still Sashka, his brother; having made sure that he wasn't being bumped about by the pot-holes in the road and that he was finding the ride comfortable, Kolka would then set off.

And their conversation continued like this: 'You know,' said Kolka, 'for some reason I was just remembering the time at Tomilino when they once brought in a big basket of blackcurrants from a collective farm. I was ill in bed at the time. And you crept under the cart and found a bunch of blackcurrants and brought it to me . . . You crawled under my bed in the sick-room and whispered, "Kolka, I've brought you a bunch of blackcurrants. They're good for you. Eat them, and you'll get better, OK?" And I *did* get better . . . And at that station in the Kuban, when we all got the shits and you were lying in the carriage all doubled up, you got over it and you were fine. You got up and you made it to the Caucasus! . . . Did you and I drag ourselves all the way here just so they could cut our guts out and stick a corn-cob in us instead? It was like saying, "Stuff yourself with *our* food – so much that it's coming out of your mouth!" '

Just then Kolka heard the sound of a cart on the road ahead of him. As the creaking of wheels and the murmur of men's voices drew nearer, he hastily turned aside into the maize-field and hid – as an animal hides at the approach of man.

But he kept his gaze fixed on the road, and kept a sharp look-out (now there were only *two* eyes to do duty for both of them!). It was

214

a small column of soldiers: there was a clinking of weapons, the rumbling of army carts and the flash of torches throwing beams of light over the verge. Although they were not talking loudly, Kolka could make out from what they were saying that they had been ambushed in the mountains; some of their attackers had been shot but others had broken through to the valley and carried out a massacre. Those villagers who survived had run away. Now the order was to spare no one, and if a Chechen tried to hide in a house or in a field, then he was to be killed by setting fire to the house or the crop ... If the enemy wouldn't surrender, he was to be destroyed ...

They passed on. The lights dissolved into the darkness. All was quiet.

Kolka stuck his head out, cocking his ears first in one direction then the other, to make sure no one else was behind the soldiers, and waited until he was sure the coast was quite clear.

He went back to Sashka, felt him to make sure he was lying comfortably, and dragged the handcart out on to the road again. He gripped the rope in both hands and set off.

'There you are,' he said, 'I expect you heard what those soldiers were saying ... They're going to kill the Chechens. And they'll kill the one who crucified you, too. But you know, Sashka, if I met that man I wouldn't kill him. I'd just look him in the eyes to see if he was a wild beast or a man. And if I saw anything alive in him, I'd ask him why he goes around robbing and burning, why he has to kill everyone he sees. Have we ever done him any harm? I'd say to him, "Listen, Chechen, are you blind, or what? Can't you see that me and Sashka aren't fighting you? We were brought here to live, so we've just been living here – and in any case we were going to run away from this place soon. And now look what you've gone and done ... You killed Sashka, and the soldiers have come to kill *you* ... Then you'll start killing the soldiers, and so everyone – you and them – will just die. Wouldn't it be much better if you lived and let them live – and let me and Sashka live too? Can't we make it so that no one upsets anyone else and everybody stays alive? Just like we in the orphanage live alongside each other?" '

Although Kolka was busy with this conversation, it was then that he heard sounds which told him he was nearing the station. He noticed the noise first, then the road came out on to open ground and he could see what was happening. Lights were shining along the line and a train was standing in a siding. The scene was lit by floodlights, there were sounds of horses neighing, wagons rumbling; another army unit had arrived.

Kolka moved a little further towards the station, but only far enough so that if necessary he might quickly dive for cover. He pulled the handcart off the road and put it behind a bush.

'We've arrived,' he said to Sashka. 'We were here not so long ago, you and I, wondering how we could run away together, remember? Now we'll wait for the next train. I'm a bit tired, and I expect you are too. You stay here, and I'll go off and do a bit of scouting. Don't worry, I'm not leaving you – I'll be back when I've had a look at what's going on at the station . . .'

With Sashka safely hidden behind a bush, Kolka moved closer to the lights and the railway line.

He saw only soldiers, busily engaged in unloading the train; they were hard at work, with a lot of shouting and rumbling of army wagons as they lowered them down planks sloping from the flat rail-cars to the ground.

Kolka realized that the trainload of army equipment was no obstacle to his plan. As soon as the next regular train arrived on the main line, it would block the view from the siding and prevent the soldiers from seeing the twins.

He went back to Sashka, and said to him, 'There – you see, I came back. There are soldiers there at the moment. They've come to kill the Chechen who stuffed the corn-cobs into you. But when the next train arrives, the soldiers won't be able to see us. You know I'm not too bright, and it took me a long time to work it out. But I thought it out all the same. Now I see how hard it must have been for you to rack your brains and dream up ideas. *Why* didn't you dodge those Chechens on their horses, though? But then I was thinking just now that maybe you went out to meet them yourself, because you were sure they wouldn't do anything to you, just as they didn't kill Regina Petrovna even though they pointed a gun at her – was that it?'

Kolka peered out at the station from behind the bush and added thoughtfully, 'It'll probably be morning soon. If only the train comes before it's light . . . otherwise you and I are going to have problems by daylight . . .'

At that moment a train appeared, its lights strung out against a distant hillside like Sashka's lost silver belt, its locomotive looking like the buckle of the belt with its two gleaming jewels.

Why was Kolka again reminded of that silver belt? He could not get it out of his mind. The belt had been the last thing he had seen

216

when they were separated; Sashka had plunged into the maize-thicket, only the belt glinting in the twilight . . .

Could it have been the belt, made long ago by a Chechen crafts-man, which had betrayed Sashka and cost him his life?

Was it the *belt* that had caused Sashka to be murdered?

When they had gone to look at the wrecked orphanage it had been Kolka, not Sashka, who was wearing that belt. Only the incident with Sashka's top trouser-button had changed the situation . . .

The train was drawing nearer. The dull click of the wheels could already be heard, reflected back from the hills on the far side of the line.

Kolka jumped up and set off at a run across the field, pulling his brother in the handcart behind him. They reached the railway line at the very moment when the train braked sharply and stopped, with a hissing sound from under the carriages.

Kolka left the cart among a clump of burdock at the foot of the embankment, then ran along the line of carriages looking for one with an underslung luggage-box. Neither the first nor the second carriage was fitted with one of these boxes, but he found one under the third carriage.

He opened the steel lid and felt inside the box to make sure there were no passengers in it already. Then he ran back, pulled the handcart along the embankment to the third carriage and untied the leather strap. He spread out the quilted jacket on the bottom of the box, then gripped Sashka under the armpits, praying that the train would not move off. Sashka was now so stiff that none of his limbs would bend, but he seemed lighter than before.

Panting with exertion, Kolka heaved Sashka up and tipped him into the luggage-box, face upward. He arranged the sacks along his sides and on top of him, so that he wouldn't be cold; the box, after all, was only made of thin metal and wasn't heated.

He kicked the handcart with its rope down the embankment and into the long grass. It had done its job; they had no more need of it now.

As the train still hadn't started to move, Kolka went back to the luggage-box, squatted down in front of it on his haunches, and said to Sashka through a hole in its side, 'Well, you'll be off soon . . . You wanted to go to the mountains, didn't you? . . . But I'll stay here for a while. I would've gone with you, but Regina Petrovna and her little boys would be left alone. Don't worry, Sashka, I'll be thinking about you all the time.'

217

Kolka tapped on the box so that Sashka shouldn't feel lonely and frightened.

As he was walking away, he saw the guard jump down from one of the carriages. The man was just about to walk past Kolka, when he stopped. 'Aha! Hallo there!' he shouted, showing all his teeth in a wide grin.

Kolka looked closer: it was Ilya. 'Hallo!' he replied. 'Weren't you burned up with your house?'

Ilya laughed. 'Ha! I don't burn! Non-inflammable, that's me! I'd already guessed what sort of trouble was on the way, so I went back to work on the railway. I'm on this train now, as you can see. I'll take you wherever you like to go.'

'No,' said Kolka. 'I can't go.'

'Which one are you? Are you Kolka or Sashka?'

After a moment's pause Kolka said, 'I'm both.'

At that moment the engine whistled.

Ilya shouted, 'Ah! We're off. You'd do better to come with me and get away from all this trouble, wouldn't you?' He ran back to his carriage and jumped up on to the steps.

'Yes, perhaps I would,' Kolka nodded with a sigh. Ilya could no longer hear him. The train started with a jerk and a clanking of buffers, then picked up speed as it moved off towards the still-invisible mountains. And Sashka went off with it, leaving Kolka alone on the dark embankment.

Twenty-eight

Kolka stayed sitting on the track.

When it began to get light – which it did quickly, as if someone, somewhere, had flicked a switch – and yellow flecks of light began to crawl along the grey-blue steel of the rails, Kolka got up, made a detour around the station and climbed the hill to the white rotunda.

He sat down on the steps and looked down; staring into the valley, he began to weep. It was the first time he had cried since he had seen Sashka impaled on the fence. His tears blurred the beautiful view of the mountains and the valley which was being revealed as the sun rose.

After a time he had no more strength left for crying and fell asleep. He dreamed of mountainsides as sheer as walls and cleft by ravines. He and Sashka were walking on the summit; Sashka went to the very edge, and he didn't see, didn't see it . . . Sashka slipped on the ice and began sliding downwards, slowly at first, while Kolka tried first to grasp his sleeve, then his coat-tail . . . But he couldn't catch him! Sashka rolled headlong down, further and further, and Kolka's heart ached because he had let his brother go, and now his arms and legs were broken and he would be smashed to fragments. On and on rolled the little black ball . . . Kolka woke up in a paroxysm of fright.

He felt his face. It was wet with tears; he had been crying again in his sleep.

As he looked down into the valley, he suddenly remembered a poem they had once been taught. He had never recalled this poem before and did not even know that he remembered it:

> *One night a little golden cloud did rest*
> *Upon a lonely mountain's rugged brow;*
> *Next day, departing for the plains below,*
> *It floated free and sailed towards the west.*

Yet high upon the mountain's summit bare
That cloud left drops of dew where it had lain.
The mountain wept, and flowing to the plain
Its tears of grief brought plenty to the earth.

Perhaps, Kolka thought, this hill is that mountain, and this rotunda is the little cloud . . . He looked around and sighed. Or perhaps the cloud was the train that had carried Sashka away with it. Or maybe not. At this moment the mountain was Kolka, and he was crying because he had turned to stone with grief and had grown old, as old as the Caucasus mountains themselves . . . And Sashka had been turned into a cloud . . . 'Who is who?' We are clouds . . . We are drops of dew . . . We are here, and then we vanish, float away . . .

Kolka felt he would start crying again and stood up. He found the inscription that they had made on the tenth of September, and with a sharp flint he added underneath it: 'Sashka went away. Kolka stayed. 20th October.'

He threw away the flint, watched it bouncing down the hill and set off to follow it. First he washed his face in one of the pools of hot water, then took the road towards the farm. He did not know what he would say to Regina Petrovna.

When Kolka, approaching the farm, had already turned the corner around the last hill, he had still not decided whether to make up a lie or tell the truth. He didn't want to frighten Regina Petrovna or the little boys. They were in no danger if they stayed here; they could tend the animals and bake pumpkin pie in safety. But he didn't want to live here any more. He would say, 'Sashka has gone away, and it's time for me to go too.'

He would, of course, give them all the jam from the secret store, keeping one jar for himself to eat on his journey. And he would keep the thirty-rouble note; it was the twins' joint fortune. Back at Tomilino, they had run great risks to acquire and keep this precious banknote for their very own. Now Sashka didn't need money any longer. He was travelling free . . .

From now on, he would always be a non-paying passenger.

Kolka went up to the lean-to, but saw no one. They must be asleep, he decided. He tapped on the window and looked inside. There was no one there either. The bed was made – neatly, as with everything Regina Petrovna did – and all the household belongings were in place. Only the inhabitants were missing.

It occurred to Kolka that they had perhaps gone out to milk the

220

cows. He went back to the lean-to and searched among the utensils until he found a saucepan full of maize porridge, which he scooped straight out with his hand and stuffed into his mouth. Only then did he realize that he was ravenously hungry. He devoured handful after handful, and quickly ate it all. But he was still not full. He scraped the saucepan clean, then found some cottage cheese and ate that too. Regina Petrovna would scold him when she came back, but then she would forgive him, because he hadn't eaten it out of greed but because he was genuinely starving.

He had a drink of water, lay down on his and Sashka's bed of dried reeds and instantly fell asleep.

Towards evening he was woken up by the silence. He was alone, except for the birds twittering loudly on the roof. He went over to the spring, drank his fill and splashed water over his face.

The silence and loneliness made him feel vaguely uneasy. He went over the kitchen garden, and then to the meadow, where the animals were grazing.

Only a little while ago they had all been standing here and giving names to the bullocks and heifers. And the goat had swallowed a lighted cigarette until the smoke came out of its nostrils. Now the whole herd turned towards him; the goats recognized him and bleated, and the bullock they had named Jackal came trotting towards Kolka . . . Strangest of all, the bad-tempered cow Mashka, who had once been in the habit of lowering her horns at the sight of Kolka, suddenly gave him a kindly, welcoming 'Moo-moo-oo'. She had acknowledged him at last. But what was the good of it? If only she had been able to tell him what had become of Regina Petrovna and her little boys . . . Then he suddenly remembered: the donkey and the little cart were missing!

But of course – she had gone down to the orphanage to fetch the twins! Sashka would have grasped this in a flash. No doubt she had driven to the station, had failed to find them there and gone straight to the orphanage. And here he was, loafing around and dozing!

How much Kolka *didn't* want to go back through the village to the orphanage! But then he had a mental image of the abandoned, ransacked houses, and among them the perplexed, frightened Regina Petrovna, looking for him and Sashka. For she had gone into that devastated place, where the Chechens were still charging about on their horses, while he, Kolka, was still dithering and agonizing over whether or not to go and find her!

Who was there but Kolka to save her now?

He looked around for the last time, trying to find what was making

221

him reluctant to leave. He had found it very hard to overcome his unwillingness to set off to find Regina Petrovna, despite the inner promptings which urged him to go; something was holding him back, and he could not understand what it was.

Only after he had been walking for half an hour down the road, its surface still warm from the heat of the day, did he remember: he had meant to look and see whether their birthday presents, the beautiful clothes, were still intact. The pair of yellowish-brown leather boots, the shirt, the trousers and the brightly coloured *tyutyubeika* . . . Had they been pinched? Now that he and Regina Petrovna were both out looking for each other, it was highly likely that someone might steal them . . .

Darkness was rapidly closing in as he passed the station. The trains bringing the troops and equipment were no longer there, but there were plenty of wheel-marks on the roadway and a lot of maize-stalks on the verges had been crushed and broken.

Further on, there was a strong smell of burning. Kolka couldn't understand what this meant; Sashka would have guessed the answer at once; he would have put his mind to it, and announced, 'Don't you see? They're burning the crops! They're doing it to smoke out the Chechens who are hiding among the corn!'

Only later did Kolka realize that *he* had worked this out, and that *he* and not Sashka had thought of it.

The smell grew stronger, and already smoke was creeping over the surface of the road, like a ground-wind. Kolka's eyes began to water painfully. He wiped his eyes, and when it grew unbearable he lay face down in the grass and it eased the pain.

Bare, burned-out patches appeared in the fields of maize. On either side of the road, and especially ahead, the red glow of fires could be seen flickering across the sky, and even on the road the glow was strong enough to make the light seem brighter.

Soon Kolka came across, fire that was still burning: the smoking, smouldering remains of the roadside grass, and sunflower-stalks like glowing, burnt-out poles. The heat was so fierce here that Kolka had to pull up his shirt and cover his face to keep his eyebrows and hair from catching fire. His eyelashes, too, felt sticky and had no doubt been singed.

Then he lay down on the ground and began thinking: should he go to the orphanage or not? If he went on, he might be burnt to death; if he didn't, it would look as if he had abandoned Regina Petrovna and her little boys amid all this fire and danger.

Having rested awhile, he felt better. He decided that he must go on and find Regina Petrovna. He *had* to. Sashka would have gone.

The fire was now blazing away on all sides, and the smoke was beginning to make Kolka feel sick. He had almost got used to the ash and smoke; what worried him was that amid all the fire around him there were no people.

Before, when he had been pulling Sashka to the station, he hadn't wanted to meet anybody. Now, though, he longed just as strongly to see another human being.

If only just once.

Anyone, no matter who.

Now if only he were to meet Regina Petrovna leading her donkey! With the frightened little boys in the cart and she herself looking to right and left, in fear of the fire . . . And Kolka would shout to her, ' "Who's who?" Don't be afraid! I'm here! I'm with you now! No need to worry when we're together! I know how to pass through the fire! I'll lead you and the boys back to the farm, and there we'll be in paradise again! We'll all live to be a hundred and there'll be no fires and no Chechens!'

Kolka came to his senses to find himself lying in the middle of the road; he had been temporarily overcome by fumes, although he had no recollection of falling down. His head was splitting and nausea was rising to his throat. He tried to get up, but could not. His legs refused to move. He looked ahead: thank God, there were the roofs of houses. Beriozovskaya! There it was! Just a stone's throw away! He would get there, even if it meant crawling on his hands and knees . . .

Here there were gardens, trees and bushes; the fire would not penetrate past them. How he dragged himself to the well, Kolka couldn't remember. He let down the bucket on the end of its chain, but lacked the strength to haul it all the way up again. Twice he pulled the bucket half-way up, but the chain slipped out of his hands and it fell back.

Kolka leaned over the edge of the well-head in order to breathe in the cold, damp, smoke-free air. Afraid of falling in, he wrapped the end of the chain around his leg and lay for a long time bent over the parapet, with his head down the well and his legs outside.

Feeling better, with only a slight touch of nausea, he went on further into the village. As he was passing the cemetery, he suddenly had a hallucination that these were not granite headstones but Chechens standing in rows . . . A silent crowd had frozen into immobility at the sight of Kolka and they were following him with their

223

eyes. Of course, it was some kind of delusion. Or was he starting to go mad? He shut his· eyes, passed his hand over his face and looked again: they were gravestones and not Chechens at all. But he quickened his pace, just to be on the safe side, and kept his eyes firmly fixed on them, in case – God forbid – they turned into Chechens again! The fire had not spread in the direction of the orphanage; here there was no need to cover his head with his shirt, nor to press himself to the grass. The only harm done to Kolka was that he was black all over; he couldn't see himself, but anyone who had come across him then would no doubt have decided that the devil himself had popped up from hell. But what Kolka had been through *was* hell.

He couldn't remember how he reached the Sunzha. He lay down in the shallow, yellowish-coloured little river, ducking his head in and out of the water.

He lay like that for a long, long time, until the air grew clearer around him. Then, to his amazement, he realized – it was morning. The sun was shining. The birds were twittering. The water was rustling. Out of hell and straight into heaven . . . But he had to get to the orphanage as soon as he could; Regina Petrovna was waiting for him there. He must get her out of that place, and quickly, before the fire spread that far. And here he was, enjoying a nice bathe!

Kolka sighed and started out, without bothering to wring out his wet clothes. They would dry by themselves. He didn't go into the orphanage through the gates, but crawled through his own private hole in the hedge; he was more used to that way and it was safer.

Nothing had changed since he and Sashka had come here, except that there was a smashed army-supply wagon lying on its side in the middle of the courtyard; beside it was a mound of earth. At one end of the mound a plywood board had been rammed into the ground, and someone had written on it in indelible pencil: PYOTR ANISIMOV-ICH MESHKOV 17.10.44.

Kolka bumped into the piece of plywood. He read the lettering twice before he realized: it's the superintendent! His grave! If they had written 'Mr Briefcase' he would have grasped it sooner . . . So that was what had happened. They had killed him. This meant that they might kill Regina Petrovna too . . .

He stood in the middle of the courtyard and shouted for all he was worth, 'Reg-in-a Pe-trov-na!'

Only the echo answered him.

He ran through every building, to every floor, tripping on things

224

scattered everywhere, without noticing them. As he ran he repeated in desperation, 'Regina Petrovna . . . Regina Petrovna . . . Regi . . .'

Suddenly he stopped, rooted to the spot. He had finally realized: she wasn't here.

She was nowhere in the whole place.

He began to feel miserably lonely, as though he had thoughtlessly blundered into a trap. He ran out of the courtyard, but came back, aware that he simply lacked the strength to go through the fire again. He might have gone through it with Regina Petrovna and her little boys . . . For their sakes, to save them, he would have gone. But on his own – he couldn't face it . . .

He went into one of the buildings and lay down on the floor in a corner, without putting down anything to lie on, although there was a mattress and even a pillow lying around nearby. He rolled himself up into a little ball and sank into oblivion.

From time to time he awoke, and then he would call for Sashka and Regina Petrovna . . . There was no one else in the world for him to call for. He imagined they were nearby but couldn't hear him; he shouted despairingly, and then got up on all fours and whimpered like a puppy.

It seemed to him that he had slept for a very long time and simply could not wake up, except on one occasion in the night, when he woke up, not knowing where he was, and heard someone breathing rapidly and hard.

'Sashka! I knew you'd come! I've been waiting . . . waiting for you!' he said, and burst into tears.

Twenty-nine

He opened his eyes and saw Sashka, who was prodding him in the face with a tin mug. Kolka shook his head, and water spilled out of the mug and over his face.

Pronouncing the words strangely, Sashka said, 'Khi . . . drink, or you quite die . . . must drink water . . . khi . . . you see?'

Kolka swallowed a few mouthfuls and fell asleep again. He had meant to tell Sashka that he was talking in a funny way, but he was too weak. He lacked even the strength to open his eyes. What did it matter if Sashka was speaking so strangely . . .

Sashka covered his brother with something warm and vanished, to return some time later with his mug.

Once Kolka opened his eyes and saw an unfamiliar face. Or rather, the face was familiar, because it was Sashka's, but when this person prodded Kolka's lips with his tin mug, his face suddenly looked strange and swarthy, with wide, prominent cheekbones . . . Before, this hadn't bothered Kolka at all; Sashka was so clever, he was capable of inventing any kind of face for himself. Now, though, Kolka took only one look and realized that this wasn't Sashka at all. A strange boy wearing a singed quilted jacket that came down to his knees was squatting in front of him and muttering something.

'Khi, khi,' he mumbled. 'You drink . . . or you die . . .'

Kolka shut his eyes and again the thought came to him that this wasn't Sashka. In that case, where was Sashka? And why had this dark stranger taken on Sashka's new face, why was he talking so oddly in Sashka's voice? Kolka failed to answer any of these puzzling questions and fell asleep again. When he woke up, he immediately asked, 'But where's Sashka?'

He could not hear his own voice, but he heard the stranger's voice in reply, 'No Sask. Alhuzur here. That my name . . . Alhuzur . . . see?'

'No,' said Kolka. 'Tell Sashka to come here. Tell him things are bad for me without him. Why is he being silly? Why doesn't he come?'

Kolka thought he was saying this; in fact, he didn't say anything at all, but only groaned a couple of times. Then he slept again, but he also seemed to be seeing Alhuzur, the dark stranger, feeding him with grapes, one at a time, and putting bits of walnut into his mouth. First he would crack a walnut with his teeth and then give it to Kolka.

One day he said, 'Me, me Sask . . . you call me Sask if you want . . . I can be Sask . . .'

He cracked another nut and pushed some grapes, one at a time, through Kolka's lips. 'Me Sask . . . And you live . . . you live . . . you get better . . .'

For the first time, Kolka nodded. He was on the way to recovery.

Alhuzur liked the name 'Sashka' and happily answered to it. Kolka was lying in a corner on a mattress, to which Alhuzur had dragged him and covered him with another, thinner mattress.

One day Kolka could hold back no longer; he looked Alhuzur in the face and asked him, 'Sashka wasn't here, was he?'

Alhuzur looked sadly at his sick friend and shook his head.

'Soldier here,' he said, 'Me afraid him . . . run away . . .'

'Afraid of a soldier? One of ours?'

Alhuzur looked nervously out of the window and did not reply. His prominent cheekbones stood out sharply and his eyes glistened.

'And the fire?'

'Fire? What fire?' Alhuzur repeated, staring at him.

'I mean – the burning maize.'

The other boy nodded, pointing to the many holes and scorchmarks on his jacket. 'Many fire . . . corn burning . . . can't go there . . . Much smoke in me . . . ?'

Kolka looked at the despondent Alhuzur and giggled. It sounded so funny: 'Much smoke in him'.

Alhuzur turned away, and Kolka said, 'Don't be cross, I didn't mean to be unkind . . . Do you have a pencil?'

Alhuzur looked sideways at Kolka but said nothing.

'Or a piece of coal . . . I need it!'

Without a word Alhuzur went out and came back with a piece of charred wood.

Kolka turned it over in his hands. 'It's from the superintendent's house,' he said with a sigh. 'When they threw a bomb and set it on fire. It burned all night, can you imagine . . .'

Alhuzur nodded, as though he knew about the fire.

227

Kolka was surprised.

'You mean – you saw it? Did you really?'

'Me not see it,' said Alhuzar sharply. He turned away and stared out of the window; he seemed to know something that he wouldn't say, though Kolka may have imagined this.

He moved over to the edge of the mattress and began to draw a plan on the floor with the piece of charcoal. He drew the orphanage, the little river and the cemetery. Alhuzur looked at the lines sketched on the floor and jabbed at the cemetery with his finger: '*Churt*!'

'All right, call it "*churt*" if you like,' Kolka agreed. 'But we call it a cemetery. And the whole place is Beriozovskaya.'

Alhuzur rubbed out the word 'Beriozovskaya' and wiped his hands on his jacket. 'No Perozovsk . . . Is called "Dei Churt"!'

'Why?'

'Dada . . . Father . . . Father grave . . .'

'Father's grave?' Kolka guessed. 'Is your father's grave there?'

Alhuzur thought for a while, no doubt remembering his father. 'No my father . . . Father of all . . . ?'

Kolka now began to understand: the name of the village was 'The Tomb of the Fathers'. '*Churt*' meant 'cemetery' in Chechen, and the village was 'Dei Churt' . . . That must have been why Ilya had always been droning on about 'chort', the Russian word for 'devil'. It certainly sounded just like it.

Kolka turned back to his drawing, propping himself up a little so that he could see it better. He drew a picture of a bush beside the river, and then a hole alongside the bush.

'Can you find it? Can you?' he asked urgently.

He would never have revealed the secret of his cache to anyone. It was like surrendering to an enemy. But now Alhuzur was Sashka, and Sashka knew where their treasures were kept. Kolka could not get to the place himself; he lacked the strength. 'When you find it . . . Take a jar of jam and bring it here.'

So saying, he fell back on his mattress. This long conversation had exhausted him.

Alhuzur took another look at the drawing and disappeared, as if the ground had swallowed him up.

After what seemed a long while, Kolka began to think that his adopted brother had vanished for ever. Had he found the secret store, rifled it and run off? After all, he didn't need Kolka any more, did he? Kolka, sick and helpless? Alhuzur was rich now! . . . Kolka rejected the idea; despite himself, these thoughts came into his head,

228

but he consciously banished them . . . yet why was Alhuzur taking so long . . . ?

The hours passed, seeming like an eternity . . . until finally there was a loud crash and Alhuzur burst into the room, his face distorted with fear. He tripped, fell, jumped up, fell again and this time lay there, staring at the doorway and shuddering at the slightest rustle.

Kolka raised his head. 'What's the matter?' he asked. 'Have you hurt yourself?'

Alhuzur did not reply but pulled a mattress over himself and lay there in silence.

'Are you deaf, or what?' Kolka shouted angrily. He waited a short while, then crawled over and lifted up the edge of the mattress: Alhuzur was lying underneath, his eyes shut, as though expecting to be hit. Suddenly he began to cry, repeating the word '*Churt* . . . *churt* . . .'

'Oh, stop it,' Kolka begged him. 'I'm not going to touch you, for heaven's sake!'

Alhuzur turned over with his face to the floor and covered his head with his hands, as though preparing for the very worst.

'Well, stay there if you like!' said Kolka, and tried to stand up. Swaying with weakness, he dropped on to all fours and crawled over to the smashed window. He pulled himself up, sending fragments of glass tinkling to the floor.

In the evening twilight, he made out a group of soldiers in the courtyard. They were trying to move a cart which had got stuck and which was loaded, as Kolka recognized at once, with long gravestones. 'Surely they can't have brought them from the cemetery?' he wondered. 'Where to? What for?'

The cart was obviously stuck fast. One of the soldiers made a gesture of impatience and looked around him. 'We need a crowbar . . . I'll go and see if I can find one.' After a glance at the buildings he headed for the one where the boys were hiding.

Seeing this, Kolka started back, but could not manage to reach a mattress to hide under. He remained sitting on the floor, like a helpless fledgling that had fallen out of the nest.

At first the soldier did not notice him. He took a few steps, looked round the room, and suddenly caught sight of Kolka. He actually shuddered with surprise. 'Oho! And what are you doing here?' he asked in astonishment. The soldier was ash-blond, freckled and blue-eyed. He wrinkled his nose at the unexpectedness of this meeting.

'I live here,' Kolka answered hoarsely.

229

'You live *here?*'

'Here, in the orphanage . . .'

The soldier looked around him and suddenly his face brightened. 'The orphanage, you say?' He squatted down on his haunches to see the boy better, and wrinkled his nose again. 'Where are all the others, then?'

'They've left.'

'And why didn't you leave? Are you alone here? Or aren't you?'

Kolka did not answer.

The soldier had sharp eyes. He had already noticed that the mattress over Alhuzur was twitching, and he glanced at it several times while he was talking to Kolka. 'Who's hiding under there?'

'Where?' Kolka asked.

'Under that mattress.'

'Under what mattress?'

He was spinning it out, in order to give himself time to concoct a good story. Sashka would have thought of something at once, but after his illness Kolka was feeling particularly dense and his brain refused to work properly.

He just blurted out the first thing that came into his head. 'Ah – under that mattress . . . That's Sashka. My brother . . . His name's Sashka. He's ill.' And for plausibility's sake he added, 'We're both ill, in fact.'

'So they left you two sick ones behind!' the soldier exclaimed, and stood up. 'I thought I heard people talking in here yesterday . . . I was on sentry-duty . . . Yet we'd been told there was nobody here . . . Why did they abandon just the two of you?'

He went over to where Alhuzar was lying and looked under the mattress. 'Of course! He's got a high temperature. Probably malaria. Look how he's shivering!' The soldier stared at Alhuzur for a little longer, then covered him with the mattress again. He turned to go out, but stopped and said to Kolka, 'Back in a moment.'

Kolka was suspicious. Why should he come back? Had he guessed that Alhuzur wasn't his brother?

The soldier returned with a hunk of bread and some wheatmeal porridge in a familiar-looking tin can that had once contained stewed pork. He put them on the floor in front of Kolka.

'There you are . . . This is for you. Give some to him, too. And here's some medicine for you.' He put six yellow tablets beside the tin can. 'Those are quinine tablets, see? Lots of our lads get sick with malaria, and quinine saves them . . . What's your name?'

'Kolka,' said Kolka. There was no longer any point in switching names now. Anyway, what other name could he use? Alhuzur?

'And I'm Private Chernov... Vassily Chernov. From Tambov.' The soldier stood over Kolka, reluctant to go. He wrinkled his nose and looked pityingly at the sick boy. As he went out, he said, 'Now mind, Kolka – don't eat it all yourself... Leave some for your brother... I'll be sending the medics to see you... Tomorrow. Keep well. So long!'

Alhuzur did not peep out from under the mattress until it was dark. He wanted to make quite sure the soldier had gone.

Kolka shouted to him, 'You can come out!... There's nothing to be afraid of. Look how much Private Chernov has brought us! He brought it for you and me...'

Alhuzur peered out, saying nothing. The mattress above him twitched.

'Don't you want some?' asked Kolka. 'Kasha?'

Alhuzur poked his head out a little way and turned it to look at the can.

'It's wheatmeal porridge!' Kolka added, enticingly. 'And bread. Have you ever eaten wheatmeal before?'

Alhuzur emerged a little further, looked at the can and sighed.

'Go on – eat,' said Kolka in the commanding tones of Private Chernov. 'He ordered us to eat it.'

Alhuzur squirmed and sighed, but could not make up his mind to creep out, so he crawled towards Kolka, holding the mattress above him and pulling it along as he went, so that in case of danger he could immediately hide again; no doubt it made him feel safer.

Kolka broke the bread in half and divided the tablets; there were three each.

Pointing to the bread, he asked, 'What do your people call this?'

'*Bepig*...'

Alhuzur greedily attacked the bread.

'Don't be in such a hurry, eat the porridge first,' Kolka advised him. 'It's always more filling. And then we'll fetch some water from the Sunzha...'

'Solzha...' Alhuzur corrected him. 'Is two rivers, one name...'

'Are there really *two* rivers?' Kolka asked, surprised, as he sampled the porridge.

'One, but like two.'

'One river flowing in two beds?' Kolka was amazed. 'Just like Sashka and me... used to be. We were two people like one... A Solzha, in fact!'

231

They scooped out the porridge with their hands, ate it all and cleaned the can with their fingers. They should have done this with a crust of bread, but they had already eaten their crusts. Satisfied, they looked at each other.

'Now you are my brother,' said Kolka after a moment's thought. 'You and I are like the Solzha ... When they come and fetch us tomorrow and ask for our surname, you say that your name is Kuzmin ... Will you remember that? And the two of us are the Kuzmin Twins ... You and I call bread *bepig*, but for them bread is bread ... Take care not to get it wrong ... Sashka Kuzmin, that's who you are now!'

'Me Sask,' Alhuzur said firmly. 'Me brother Sask ...'

He sighed and asked, 'Where other brother Sask?'

'He went away,' Kolka replied. 'He took a train to the mountains.'

'I go too,' Alhuzur announced. 'I run away ... from soldiers ...'

'Why?' Kolka didn't understand him. 'The soldiers are kind. Private Chernov gave us the porridge.'

Alhuzur closed his eyes, 'Soldiers break *churt*.'

'You mean those gravestones? Well, let them. What does it matter to us?'

But Alhuzur insisted: 'Bad to break *churt* ... very bad ...' He rolled his eyes upward to show just how bad this was.

'Why does it upset you so?' Kolka shouted. 'All right, so it's bad. But a gravestone can't be hurt! It's dead!'

Alhuzur pursed his lips and spoke in a kind of sing-song, making himself look terribly silly. 'Stone gone, *churt* gone ... Chechen gone ... Alhuzur gone ... Me – what for, what for?'

'But I'm telling you again,' said Kolka, starting to lose his temper. 'If *I'm* here, then *you're* here too. We're both here and alive. Don't you see? Like your Solzha.'

Alhuzur looked out of the window at the darkening sky, pointed up at it and then pointed to himself. 'In Chechen, Alhuzur mean bird. He fly ... to mountains. Dada – boom! Mama – boom! Alhuzur not fly mountains and he ... boom ...' He made an expressive gesture with his index finger, imitating a pistol.

Thirty

In Moscow, in the Lefortovo district, behind the student hostels of the Moscow Institute of Electical Engineering, there is a four-storey brick building, the public sauna baths. Every Wednesday a collection of people meet there who enjoy taking a good steam bath – students, pensioners, army officers.

One day a friend of mine, a colonel, took me there with him. It was in early March. He introduced me to a man of pensionable age, sturdily built but with a pot-belly, saying, 'There, Viktor Ivanovich . . . We must show him (that is, me) our baths – and properly, with all the trimmings!'

Viktor Ivanovich was wearing a small knitted cap and a pair of plastic sandals. He handed me two little hand-brooms fashioned out of oak twigs – he had made them himself – and led me into the steam-room, showing me on the way how I should dip them in a basin of cold water and then shake them well so that there was no surplus moisture left on them. Pressing these twig-brooms to your face enabled you to breathe when you were enveloped in the intense, sticky heat of the steam-room. All the people in there knew each other; stretched out on the broad wooden shelves, they would shout back and forth, 'Viktor – let's have some more! I could do with some mint! Eucalyptus! Vitya! Haven't you got any eucalyptus?'

After the steam-room they laid me on a tiled slab and Viktor Ivanovich and my friend the colonel made some magic passes over me, Viktor Ivanovich doing it with particular gusto. He brought in two tubs of hot water and a third full of soap-suds. He dipped two twig-brooms into the hot water and briskly applied them to my body. Pressing them to my sides, back and spine and heating my skin painfully, he whispered, 'Bear it . . . bear it . . .' And he continued to heat my skin to the point where, if he had done it only a little longer, I could not have borne it; but therein, evidently, lay the whole art of it – to know exactly the limit of what a person could stand.

Then they rubbed me, soaped me, stroked every muscle and tendon in my body, massaged my arms from wrist to shoulder and my legs from toes to knees, and then my forehead and cheeks, gently, from nose to temples. Afterwards they doused each part of me with water, first hot (as hot as I could bear but never too hot) and then cold, also at the limit of tolerance.

Then they applied hot twig-brooms to the small of my back; this was a special treatment and was the reason why I had come to the baths; I had lately been suffering agonies from lumbago.

My lumbago is a story on its own. I have had it for a long time . . . since that day in my childhood when I lay in a hole in the ground in a field of dry maize-stalks . . . We were being chased by men on horseback. One of the horses passed about a centimetre away from me. Through the back of my neck I could feel the movement of its hoof and its noisy breathing ruffling the hair on the back of my head . . . But it was twilight, and the rider couldn't see why his horse was stamping its hoofs on one spot. Then from a distance came a long drawn-out call for help in their guttural language – they had caught someone. And he galloped away, spurring on his sluggish mount.

Ever since then I have been troubled by this relentless pain in the small of my back . . . It has only been relieved thanks to the bathhouse, thanks to Viktor Ivanovich, my saviour.

In the cooling-off room, blissfully tired, my new friends brought out a bottle of vodka and bought some beer from the attendant at a rouble a bottle, while Viktor Ivanovich produced some cold pork chops, chives and a jar of pickled cucumber . . . And quietly and peacefully, wrapped in sheets, we ritually took turns to drink from one glass.

Viktor Ivanovich told us about the oak-twigs, which he would break off and put under a press, then dry on his balcony and keep in a polythene bag . . . enough to supply him with twig-brooms till the next season!

'Till summer?' asked my friend, the Tank Corps colonel.

'Ah, you youngsters!' said Viktor Ivanovich, shaking his head. 'You spend all your time studying but you don't know anything! Till Trinity Sunday! Ever heard of it?'

We went back into the steam-room for the final touch. Then we finished our beer, got dressed and went outside. But that was not the end of the ritual, as I discovered. They took me back into the

234

bath-house, but by the side entrance. Viktor Ivanovich went through a shabby-looking door, but soon reappeared and beckoned us to follow him. 'Come on! This way!'

There, in an untidy little semi-basement room, two men were drinking, seated at a plywood-topped table; we had seen them earlier, in the baths . . . Beside them was a little man wearing a winter cap with ear-flaps and a quilted jacket.

'Well, Nikolai Petrovich, have you got something for us?' my friends asked him.

'Certainly,' he replied obligingly. 'In here, or in the other room?'

'We would rather be in the other room . . . if possible,' said Viktor Ivanovich in an authoritative tone.

We were led through a corridor heaped with carpenters' tools, timber and assorted rubbish, and shown into another lumber-room, bigger than the first. Here, too, sheets of plywood did duty for tables and crates for stools. Nikolai Petrovich went out and came back bringing a bottle and glasses.

As he poured out the drinks, Viktor Ivanovich nodded towards the corridor and said, 'They're a couple of *ours*. One's a lieutenant-colonel, and I've forgotten what the other one is . . . used to be a quartermaster, I think . . .'

'And what were you?' I asked him.

He didn't reply at once, but produced his army discharge papers. 'There,' he said. 'I went through the war from start to finish.'

We drank. He drank some of the dill-water from the jar of pickled cucumbers, chewed a crust of bread, and added, 'Beginning with the parade in forty-one . . . Then I was everywhere . . . machine-gunner . . . In the Caucasus, for instance . . . We removed those Chechens. They sold out to Hitler! The state prosecutor of their republic was made a general in the German army and fought against us . . .'

He poured out another round, and we all drank.

'It was about the 20th of February, I remember, they took us to a Chechen village, as though we were being sent there on leave – you know, best uniforms and so on . . . And they told the chairman of the village Soviet there was to be a general meeting at six o'clock in the evening, and all the men were to assemble in front of the village hall. We'd make an announcement and then let them go. Well, they all gathered in the square; we had already surrounded the whole village in the darkness – and all of a sudden, before they realized what was happening, we bundled them all into trucks under armed guard! Then we went round all the houses, gave people ten minutes to collect their belongings and get into the trucks. The whole operation was over in three hours . . . But the ones who got away . . . God, did they cause trouble! We chased them into the mountains and shot them down . . . And they fired back at us, of course . . .'

Nikolai Petrovich appeared, looking at the empty bottle and said, 'Time's up! I'm closing.'

We got up. Viktor Ivanovich led the way out and went on with his story.

'I remember one day, our platoon was patrolling the Argun . . . it's a little river in those parts . . . We were mounted on eleven mules, I was second in the file . . . Suddenly we were being sprayed with machine-gun fire from behind a little hill! Two of our lads were killed, and the rest of us took cover behind the embankment alongside the road. We set up the mortar and threw everything we had at the hill where that machine-gunner was sitting . . .'

The next moment I heard something familiar, something I had heard long ago, probably in the Caucasus.

'We should have put them all up against a wall and shot them! We didn't finish them all off then, and now we're paying the price for it.'

After that we went to an outdoor kiosk, which seemed to have been purposely sited at a convenient point on our way home. We changed a rouble into a lot of wet coins, rinsed out the tankards, drew beer from an automatic dispenser, sat down at some dirty tables and began drinking again, nibbling at salted bagels in between swigs.

There was a crowd of people there; as in the bath-house, they all knew each other and kept up a constant flow of greetings and talk. Two men in particular, with wrinkled faces and wearing black overcoats of an old-fashioned cut, attached themselves to Viktor Ivanovich. They were introduced to me as being 'regulars' at this place, two of 'our lads'.

'Now *they* did their bit in the war . . .' Viktor Ivanovich said proudly. 'We were in the same arm of the service, although we never met . . . Yes, there are still a lot of us about!'

He waved his arm, and I involuntarily looked around. It was true: apart from students, who were easy to spot from their clothes and their age, the others were almost all the exact contemporaries of our Viktor Ivanovich . . . They weren't so fit and well-preserved as he was, but there was a certain steady dignity about them. And although

236

they no longer wore uniform or badges of rank, you could sense they had all been through the same school . . . And what a school!

Viktor Ivanovich shouted to his friends as he crunched his bagel, scattering crumbs on the ground, 'I remember those Chechen swine as if it was yesterday . . . I had a personal letter of congratulation from Comrade Stalin! Yes, I did!'

His calm, smiling friends nodded and stretched out their beer-mugs to clink with his.

And I won't conceal the fact – the thought inevitably came to me that the people who had carried out Stalin's will in his name were still alive all around us.

Alive – but what sort of lives were they living?

Were they not racked by nightmares, did the shades of their victims come to haunt them at midnight – to remind those men of what they had done?

No, they did not.

After playing with their grandchildren, they foregather, recognizing each other by signs invisible to most but obvious to them. Clearly the stamp left upon them by their profession is very persistent. And when they get together at the baths or in bars they clink their dirty beer-mugs and drink to their health and their future.

Because they believe they still *have* a future . . .

At dawn, when the thick morning mist over the floor of the valley had barely dispersed and the breeze from the fields carried the reek of burnt grass, the two of us crossed the silent courtyard. The cart and its load of gravestones was still stuck, immobile, alongside the mound of yellow earth that marked the superintendent's grave. Obviously they had been unable to shift it.

We slithered through our hole in the hedge and headed for the cemetery.

The cemetery, however, no longer existed as such. Here and there broken and uprooted headstones were lying around, ready to be taken away, leaving scars of reddish, upturned earth. But when we set off across the fields towards the river, we found more gravestones, laid flat in a long row.

This was a road – a very unusual road – which for some reason did not run towards the village but towards the uninhabited mountains.

My companion appeared to stumble over the first gravestone. He stood there, looking at the ground under his feet, then bent down, first squatting and then kneeling. Turning his head sideways in an awkward movement, he began reading something aloud.

'What is it?' I asked impatiently. 'What's that you're reading?'

Without turning aside from his strange occupation, he said, 'Zuiber lie here.'

'Zuiber? Who's that?'

He shrugged his shoulders. 'Dada . . . Father . . .'

And he crawled on to the next stone . . . 'Here lie Umran . . .'

'And who's he?'

Without looking at me, he repeated as before, 'Dada . . . Father . . .'

And so on, from stone to stone, Hassan . . . Deni . . . Toita . . . Vakhit . . . Ramzan . . . Sotsita . . . Vakha . . .

I looked around. It had now grown so light that we could be seen from a great distance. We had to hasten and get away out of sight.

I urged my companion to hurry. 'Come on, let's go . . . It's time we were going.'

He didn't hear.

Crawling from stone to stone, he read out the names, as though committing the history of his kith and kin to memory.

I don't know how long this would have lasted if the road had not ended abruptly at the high, precipitous bank of a river . . . At the edge of an abyss. Presumably this was to be the site of a bridge, which the army had already started to build.

Avoiding the dangerous precipice, we made our way down to the river, crossed to the other side on stepping-stones, and set out towards the mountains.

My companion kept looking around, trying to imprint the place on his memory.

Neither he nor I, of course, were to know that the time would come when the children and grandchildren of those whose names were engraved on those timeless stones would return to their homeland in the name of justice.

They would find this road, and those returning to this village would remove these memorials to their forebears in order to put them back in their proper place.

They would take them away altogether and the road leading to the abyss would be no more.

'Shall we make a quick dash to the station?' Kolka suggested. 'Then go on up to the farm? It's so good up there! We can cook *chureki* . . . bake pumpkins . . . Well, what about it?'

Alhuzur shook his head and pointed to the mountains. 'Shooting

238

here – up there no shooting,' he muttered obstinately, staring at his feet.

'All right,' Kolka agreed. 'Now that we're brothers we have to go together. My brother and I never went anywhere separately. Understand?'

'Me understand,' Alhuzur nodded. 'One brother two eyes, but two brother – four eyes!'

'That's it – you've got it!' Kolka exclaimed loudly, but immediately looked around and stopped his mouth with his hand. He went on quietly, 'You're just like Sashka . . . He used to say that too!'

'Me Sask . . .' Alhuzur said eagerly. 'Me will be good Sask . . . But there . . .' he pointed to the mountains – 'me good Alhuzur . . . and bread is *bepig* and maize is *kachkash* . . . and water is *khi* . . .'

Kolka frowned. For ever etched into his memory was the sight of a locked, red-brown freight-car at Kuban station, with hands, stretching mouths and imploring eyes calling through the little barred window . . . and the shriek which still assailed his ears: 'Khi! Khi! Khi! Khi!' So *that* was what they had been begging for!

The two boys clambered their way up narrow ravines which became folds in the mountainside. They came across a huge walnut tree; Alhuzur skilfully knocked down the nuts with a stick, and Kolka collected them inside his shirt front. Then they ate sweet wild rosehips and they also found several mushrooms, but these turned out to be bitter.

Heavy swathes of smoke accompanied the fugitives all the way, and Kolka, who was still weak after his illness, often had to sit down and rest. But Alhuzur scrambled over the rocks, his bare legs flickering under his outsize quilted jacket. While Kolka rested, Alhuzur had time to explore the scrub and bring back sour crab-apples and wild pears. 'Good to eat,' he would usually say as he offered the fruit with a smile. 'No smoke in mountains . . . there is good . . .'

Once they came across a party of soldiers, but the soldiers didn't see the boys. They were busy with a truck which had somehow slithered off the road into the ditch and was stuck there. The soldiers were swearing, cursing the mountains, cursing the Chechens, and cursing their truck into the bargain.

Kolka watched from behind some bushes on the hillside above them. He whispered to Alhuzur, 'Shall I go down to them? Ask them for something to eat? What d'you think?'

Alhuzur shivered as violently as he had trembled at the orphanage. 'No! No!' he shouted, causing two of the soldiers to look round.

Hardly had the boys had time to duck when a burst of machine-gun fire rang out. But having fired, the soldiers went back to work on the truck; they had obviously just loosed off a few rounds as an automatic precaution. Echoes of it came rolling back from the mountainsides, making it seem as if they were firing from all sides.

The boys crawled away from the brow of the hill and round to the opposite side.

Towards nightfall they came to an ancient stone hut, known as a *koshara*, usually lived in by shepherds. Alhuzur explained this. Around the *koshara* was a small garden which they found to be completely neglected and overgrown. Even so, the boys did manage to dig up a few carrots, which they wiped clean on the grass and ate. And they finished off the remaining walnuts.

The night was cold; the mountains were making themselves felt. They slept huddled up together on a pile of straw, but even so it was freezing, and they had nothing to cover themselves with. By morning the cold became unbearable; they were both shivering uncontrollably and they could not even talk: their tongues were so stiff with cold.

Alhuzur got up and started running round the hut and singing his strange, gurgling songs.

Kolka ran around, too, yelling his own song at the top of his voice, about the happy Soviet people making up splendid songs about their wise, beloved Stalin ... But the song about Stalin didn't help him to get warm, so he began remembering songs about Budyonny and Klim Voroshilov ... these were all cavalry songs, and it was easier to run in time to the tempo of the gallop. And then he recalled the song which the orphans had sung in the dormitory:

> **My pal and I went out together,**
> **We wandered over mountains wild,**
> **O'er the mountains wild!**

He taught the words of this song to Alhuzur. Together they bawled it out for all they were worth, as they jumped, ran, charged each other with their shoulders ... Then the sun came out and broke through the thick mist, which made it slightly warmer.

They lay down on the grass and went to sleep again, happy because they no longer had to shiver with cold.

Alhuzur dreamed of his home and of his mother scolding him because he hadn't learned his lessons properly. Kolka, though, dreamed of his brother Sashka coming to the *koshara* and asking –

but in the funny way that Alhuzur spoke Russian – 'Why you sleep? Look – all around mountains, and you sleep? Why?' And he kept on shaking Kolka by the shoulder.

Kolka woke up and couldn't understand what was happening. Alhuzur was standing over him, and beside him was a man wearing a reddish-brown sheepskin coat and a shaggy fur hat, and holding a rifle. 'You sleep, yes?' the man shouted in a strange sing-song voice that came straight from his throat. 'You sleep with Russian pig? Yes? And you a Chechen!'

Alhuzur tugged at the man's arm, which was holding the rifle pointed at Kolka.

Only half awake, Kolka still couldn't understand anything. He rubbed his eyes and tried to get up, but the man kicked him and Kolka fell down, hitting his shoulder painfully on the ground.

'Lie down!' the man shouted loudly. 'I shoot!'

Again he aimed his rifle at Kolka and Kolka rolled over and lay face down. As he lay there, he could hear the man shouting and Alhuzur shouting back at him. Alhuzur was talking loudly in Chechen, while the man answered him in Russian, no doubt so that Kolka should hear him. So that he should be quite aware that he was about to be shot dead.

The man roared, 'My land! He come to my land! My house! My garden! For that I shoot him . . . I kill him . . .'

'*Ma tokha tsunna!*' shouted Alhuzur. 'No kill! he save me from soldier . . . He call me brother . . .'

The man looked at Kolka. '*Khan tse khun yu?* Understand? No? What your name?'

Kolka turned over. The man stared at him with a cold, cruel look and the colour of his eyes was as steely as the muzzle of his rifle aimed at Kolka.

Kolka tried to get up again, but the man shouted, 'Lie down! Answer! *Khan tse khun yu? Kho mila vu?*'

'Kolka,' said Kolka, looking up at the man from where he lay. He looked down from the rifle and noticed that the man was wearing galoshes and puttees bound criss-cross with strips of lime-bark. His sheepskin coat was dirty and tattered; it had obviously been through many a thorn-bush. On his head was a shaggy fur hat, equally tattered, and his coat was fastened around his waist with a gleaming silver belt . . . Exactly the kind that Sashka had been wearing. Strangely enough, it was the fur hat and the belt which fascinated Kolka, when these were the last things he should have been thinking about: the man, after all, was intending to kill him . . .

241

'Kolka?' the man repeated, questioningly. 'Why you come? Why you come mountains? Why you follow Chechen?'

'I wasn't following him,' said Kolka. 'I'm *with* him . . .'

'We brothers! We brothers!' cried Alhuzur.

'*So khera khyokh,*' said the man, turning to Alhuzur.

'*Ma kheve so,*' the boy replied.

The man looked at Kolka, at Alhuzur, and then said in Russian, 'Must kill him! He bring soldiers here!'

'*Ma kheve so,*' Alhuzur shouted, and burst into tears.

Thus it was: Kolka lying on the ground and looking up at the man and his rifle, Alhuzur crying piteously alongside him. Kolka thought, without fear, that he would no doubt be killed at any moment. Just as they had killed Sashka. It would probably only hurt when the man aimed the gun at him, and then, when he fired, it wouldn't hurt any more. And he and Sashka would meet again, up there, where people turn into clouds. They would recognize each other. They would both float above the silvery peaks of the Caucasus mountains like little round golden clouds, and Kolka would say, 'Hello, Sashka! Do you like it here?'

And Sashka would reply, 'Yes, of course I do.'

'I've made friends with Alhuzur,' Kolka would say. 'He's our brother too!'

'I think all people are brothers,' Sashka would say, and they would float away, far, far away, to where the mountains come down to the sea and people have never heard of wars in which brother kills brother.

It was quite a long while before Kolka came to; he had no idea how much time had passed since he had been killed.

Or perhaps . . . he hadn't been killed?

Alhuzur was sitting beside Kolka, still crying. But of the man there was no sign; it was twilight, and silent.

Kolka was surprised that Alhuzur was still crying, and asked him, 'Did he hurt you?'

Alhuzur heard Kolka's voice and began crying even harder. He wiped away his tears with his hand and with the hem of his quilted jacket, from which a piece of singed cotton wool was protruding. It smelled of burning. Alhuzur pulled the cotton wool out of the lining and threw it to the wind.

Kolka asked him again, 'Why are you crying? And why did you pull the stuffing out of your jacket?'

Alhuzur wiped his face with his sleeve and looked at Kolka. 'I think – you die.'

242

'What an idea!'

'You shut eyes and go like this: khrr-khrr . . .' Alhuzur imitated a hoarse, rattling sound.

'And I feel bad . . . one brother alone – not brother . . .'

Kolka said, 'If he didn't shoot, then I'm alive. Has he gone?'

Alhuzur pointed up into the mountains.

'He up there . . . guard his land . . . he work here . . . he love his land . . .'

'But what if he had shot me?' Kolka asked. And he suddenly felt cold. And very, very miserable. Even the presence of Alhuzur couldn't prevent the feeling. He realized that the man really had wanted to kill him. And now he would be lying there with his guts spilling out and the crows would be pecking out his eyes, as they had done to Sashka.

Alhuzur looked at Kolka. 'I cry,' he said, and he started crying again.

Then Kolka began to feel better, much better. He did his best to comfort his adopted brother, and explain that now they must really become true brothers. They must each make a cut in their arms and mix their blood.

They found a piece of broken glass, and first Kolka, then Alhuzur cut the skin on their left arms and they rubbed the wounds together.

'There,' said Kolka. 'Now we are real brothers. And we must get out of here. If the Chechens find me again they really will shoot me.'

Alhuzur said nothing.

'Let's go back down to the valley,' Kolka proposed. 'It's warmer down there.'

'Soldiers shoot there,' said Alhuzur fearfully.

'And the Chechens shoot *here* . . .' Kolka exclaimed.

'Everywhere bad!' Alhuzur sighed. 'Why they shoot? You understand?'

'No,' said Kolka. 'I don't think anybody understands.'

'But they more . . . they more clever . . . Is so?'

Kolka did not answer. Evening was coming on. They looked up at the mountains, gleaming high in the distance; neither of them knew how they might go on living.

243

Thirty-one

They were found in some bushes on the lower slopes of the foothills, where they had fallen asleep in each other's arms. A soldier, who had turned aside from the road for a piss, stumbled across them.

When the soldiers tried to pull them apart, the two boys screamed and yelled. Alhuzur started to bite, and Kolka wriggled with all his might, shouting something inarticulate.

First the soldiers tied them up, then released them and fed them. They ate from an army mess-tin, using their hands. They would not look up at anyone, only at each other, communicating in gestures and mumbled remarks, incapable of answering any of the questions put to them.

A woman doctor arrived and diagnosed the boys as being in a dystrophic state; she could not be certain, at that moment, whether they would even survive. Apart from exhaustion and malnutrition, both exhibited signs of mental imbalance. They would not allow themselves to be separated, and raised a terrible wailing if one of them was taken away separately for medical examination.

A month and ten days later they were transferred from No. 16 Paediatric Clinic in the city of Grozny to a Child Reception Unit, where lost or abandoned children were kept before being sent on to orphanages or children's homes.

I remember that place: it was housed in a wooden building that had once been a school, in a quiet suburban back-street.

Although no classes were held, the rooms were still fitted with rows of school desks, and because there were no proper tables we were fed at these desks. They gave us the usual slops: flour and water flavoured with onion, and on rare, fortunate days a black frost-bitten potato or two ... For breakfast we got two dates or a dozen currants, and tea; for supper a piece of rotten salted herring and more tea. Now and again, on Sundays and holidays, there was buckwheat *kasha*.

Children of several different Soviet nationalities lived in our dormitory.

There was a tall, cheerful, clumsy, spotty-faced young Tartar called Musa. He loved playing practical jokes on everyone, but when he lost his temper he would go white in the face and grind his teeth, and he was liable to go for you with a knife. Musa was constantly remembering his native Crimea, his adobe hut on a mountainside near the sea, and his mother and father, who had tended their vineyard.

Balbek was a Nogai. Where his homeland – Nogaya – was, none of us knew, including Balbek himself. He was short and stocky, with prominent cheekbones, and he always played fair with everybody. We tried to talk to Musa, each in his own language, and we achieved a certain success. We could all play knuckle-bones, and Balbek taught us to swear in Nogai . . .

Lida Gross, who was put in the boys' dormitory because she was the only little girl and couldn't have lived all alone in a big, cold dormitory, asked us to call her by the russified form of her surname: Grossova. She knew the name of every medicine by heart. She was also a very tidy girl: she made everyone's bed for him and swept the floor. Of her past she could only remember that she had lived by a big river and that one night some men had come and told them to go away. Her mother had wept with fear. In the train her mother fell ill and was removed from the freight car in which they were travelling. Lida left the train too; she was found, dying, in the railway station of a little town . . .

There were also two brothers – the Kuzmins – who lived in our dormitory; we called them the Kuzmin Twins. Although they were not alike, indeed could not have been more different in looks – one fair-haired and snub-nosed, a typical Russian, the other swarthy, with dark, cropped hair, dark-brown eyes and barely able to speak Russian – nevertheless the Kuzmin Twins insisted (although no one ever asked them) that they were brothers!

In the room adjoining ours there were Armenians, Kazakhs, Jews, Moldavians and two Bulgarians. In the dormitory beyond that one, all the children were blind.

The blind boys had been in the place for a long time; you could tell that, because they knew the way from the dormitory to the classroom that was used as a dining-hall; they all knew their places for meals and could even walk along the street, keeping close to the fence.

We made friends with one of the blind boys called Antosha. He was small, and his face was pock-marked with black spots as though he had been peppered with lead shot. Antosha told us how he had found a hand-grenade and had tried to take it to pieces; describing this, he showed us his hands, from which three fingers were missing from the left hand and two from the right.

Antosha also showed us a book, a strange book with rows of bumps on the pages. Running his fingers along the rows, he read out several lines.

'When I grow up, I'll get a parrot and sell lottery tickets in the market,' Antosha used to say. 'Lots of us tell fortunes there. If you knew how much money they make at it, you'd go green with envy.'

The Kuzmin Twins slept together in one bed. It was December; there was no snow, but it was windy and the dormitory was cold.

Like us, they were waiting to know what their fate would be.

From the Child Reception Unit, our destination might be one of several: some were sent on to a further Reception Unit or to a children's colony: others to orphanages: some to trade and technical schools, depending on their age.

Sometimes, though, miracles happened: parents or relatives might be traced, or a child might be taken in by foster-parents from among people who were in a position to house, feed and clothe them.

The latter possibility in particular gave rise to countless rumours and legends. This was hardly surprising: there you were, displayed like a rabbit in a basket in the market-place – would anyone buy you or not? And suddenly some magician might appear and carry you off. It didn't matter where to – the great thing was to get away from this place. And for ever. Fantasy? But homeless, orphaned children have to believe in fairy tales: unless they have faith in magic, how else can they keep going?

One day a woman came to the CRU and Kolka was called to the superintendent's office. All the others became very excited and crowded as close to the office as possible. Somebody might perhaps call for them, too. No one doubted that the visitor wanted to adopt Kolka.

Alhuzur refused to leave Kolka's side, but he was not allowed into the office. He yelled and made a fuss, but the door was shut and he was left outside, alone.

246

Kolka, though, had managed to whisper to him, 'Don't worry, I won't go away without you!'

The superintendent of the CRU was a fat, elderly woman by the name of Olga Khristoforovna Mueller. From the doorway, Kolka saw sitting beside her . . . Regina Petrovna. Thinner, but still beautiful, she was wearing a headscarf and smoking a cigarette.

Olga Khristoforovna said, 'Kuzmin? Someone has come to see you.'

Kolka stood in the middle of the room, which was furnished with an ink-stained desk and three identical, plain chairs. He stared at the floor.

'I believe you know each other, don't you?' the superintendent asked.

Kolka did not answer.

Olga Khristoforovna glanced at Regina Petrovna and added, 'You may talk in private . . .'

She got up ponderously and went out. Alhuzur tried to push his way in from the hall, but could only shout, 'I'm here! I'm here!'

The door was firmly shut.

'Well, hallo again,' said Regina Petrovna, and smiled. She stubbed out her cigarette, got up and came towards Kolka. But he stood where he was without moving and gave no sign of recognition. His expression was one of dull indifference.

Regina Petrovna stopped half-way towards him, but then, more slowly, she nevertheless came up to Kolka and touched him on the shoulder. He shrank away and took a pace back. He clearly didn't like being touched by a strange hand.

'What's the matter, Kolka? Don't you recognize me?'

'No,' he said, 'I don't.'

'You don't recognize me?' She repeated the question, her features frozen into a fixed smile.

'No.'

She forced a laugh.

'Don't play the fool . . . By the way, "who's who"? . . . Are you really Kolka?'

'No.'

'You're Sashka, then?'

'No.'

'But where . . . where's the other twin?'

Kolka looked at Regina Petrovna's feet and sighed.

'Well, at least sit down,' said Regina Petrovna and sat down

247

herself. Kolka perched on the very edge of a chair, so that if necessary he could jump up and run away.

'I've been looking for you, you know!' Regina Petrovna took out another cigarette and lit it. Her hands were shaking. Kolka looked at her hands, then looked away.

'Demyan Ivanych took me away when it all happened,' Regina Petrovna went on, inhaling deeply. 'He arrived in his cart and said you had both come to grief. He said we must get out of the place, because the Chechens had broken through into the valley. My little boys were both ill after the birthday party. We drove to the station as fast as we could and got on a train . . . Then I came to my senses and wanted to go back, but Demyan wouldn't let me. There's fighting there, he said, all the orphans have gone . . . But it turns out that the army found you . . . By the way, who is that other boy out there?' Regina Petrovna asked, nodding towards the door. 'Is he your new friend? I have a feeling I've seen him before . . .'

'I don't know,' said Kolka.

Regina Petrovna frowned. Her look darkened.

'Are you going to talk to me? Or not?'

At that moment Olga Khristoforovna came back. Breathing heavily, she walked over to her desk and asked, 'Well? Have you had your talk?'

'Yes, thank you,' said Regina Petrovna hastily. 'If you don't mind, I'd like to come and see you again.'

'Don't press your case too hard,' said the superintendent, and looked at Kolka.

'Why? Are there problems?'

The superintendent muttered vaguely, then leaned over and whispered something in Regina Petrovna's ear.

Regina Petrovna asked in amazement, 'Where is he from?'

The superintendent shrugged her shoulders. 'They will come and sort it out. That's why these two are being kept here and not sent away.'

'Very well,' said Regina Petrovna. 'I'll be back in a few days' time . . . Goodbye for now, Kolka.'

Kolka raised his head and looked into her eyes for the first time. He gave her such a look that she could not bear it, and backed away. Slowly he turned around and walked to the door.

Behind his back he heard the superintendent say, 'These are two of the nicest lads . . . You should see some of the others!'

Thirty-two

A few days before New Year's Day 1945, when a new-year tree had been set up in one of the classrooms and an amateur concert was being organized, two men drove up in a car – an army officer and a civilian. An urgent call went out, 'The Kuzmin brothers to the office at once!'

The children were sitting beside Musa's bed; he had suddenly developed a temperature, and they were doing their best to entertain him. Balbek was telling the legends of the *batyrs*, the hero-figures of Nogai folklore. The stories were all alike: a *batyr* would arise and conquer all his people's enemies and the Nogais would be free.

It was then that the summons came for the Kuzmins. It was shouted unnaturally loudly, as though a fire had broken out. Obeying the call, Kolka and Alhuzur were stopped at the office door, and Alhuzur was taken in on his own. Kolka, however, shouted so loudly and banged the door so hard that it was opened and a man's voice said, 'All right, let him in. It may even be better to have the two of them.'

Kolka burst into the office and saw Alhuzur sitting on a chair in the very middle of the room. Facing him was the army officer, while the other, a civilian, was standing by the window. Bald, with glasses, and wearing gleaming knee-boots, the officer was holding a folder of papers and talking, talking, talking. At first Kolka couldn't make out what he was saying, then he realized that he was telling Alhuzur the complete story of his, Kolka's, life. How on earth did he know it . . . ? Because he was bald, like Demyan. Bald men are extra cunning, Sashka always used to say.

The officer asked Alhuzur, 'And where did you two meet, you and Nikolai? Did you meet in Beriozovskaya?'

Alhuzur said nothing.

Turning to Kolka, the man asked in an ingratiating tone, 'You

249

remember where you met him, don't you? I can't get your friend to tell me.'

'He's not my friend. He's my brother.'

'What sort of brother?' The officer showed great interest. 'Adopted?'

'He's my real brother.'

'Your *real* brother?' the officer echoed sarcastically.

'Yes.'

'What is his name?'

'Sashka.'

'He's – *Sashka*? But just take a look!' With two fingers the officer gripped Alhuzur by the temples and forced his head round to face Kolka. 'But he's dark! And you're fair! How can you two be brothers?'

'We're real brothers,' said Kolka.

The officer whispered to Olga Khristoforovna, who went out.

He continued striding up and down the room, his boots creaking, apparently examining Alhuzur from all sides. He paid no more attention to Kolka.

The civilian said nothing. He kept silence all the time, as if he were not there at all.

Suddenly Olga Khristoforovna came in, followed by Regina Petrovna.

'Sit down,' the officer said to her, making it sound like an order. 'Were you one of the supervisory staff at the Beriozovskaya orphanage?'

'Yes,' Regina Petrovna replied quietly, looking at Kolka. This time her glance was somehow sad and imploring.

'Do you remember the Kuzmin brothers, who were inmates there?'

Regina Petrovna nodded.

'Do you remember them *well*?' the officer asked, giving Regina Petrovna an angry look.

'Yes, I do,' she replied.

'Now take a look . . . Do you recognize them?' The officer pointed to Alhuzur; Kolka was standing beside him.

'Yes,' said Regina Petrovna in a barely audible voice.

'And who is this?' The officer then jabbed his finger in Kolka's direction.

Regina Petrovna paused, then said, 'I think . . . that's Kolka.'

'Aha.' The officer nodded with satisfaction. 'And this one?'

Again he pointed to Alhuzur.

250

Regina Petrovna continued to look at Kolka. 'I think . . .' she began – and hesitated.

'You think? Don't you *know*?'

Regina Petrovna was silent.

'I'm waiting! I'm waiting!' barked the officer, and threw the civilian a meaningful look. The latter did not react in any way.

'That's . . . Sashka . . .' said Regina Petrovna in a faint voice.

'Are you certain that is Sashka, his brother?'

Regina Petrovna gave a barely perceptible nod.

'Have you given careful thought to your answer to my question?'

The officer went behind Regina Petrovna's back, and put the question to her as though addressing the back of her neck.

Frightened, Regina Petrovna swivelled sharply round to face him. 'What?' she asked, and immediately replied in a fast gabble, 'Yes, of course I'm certain. There were a lot of children there, so naturally I was a little confused at first.'

'So one might assume that you also could be mistaken *now*?' said the officer insistently, leaning forward over Regina Petrovna's head. Even Kolka was growing weary of the man's hard, undeviating line of questioning, which made all of them feel that this interrogation was like being torn apart with a blunt saw.

Regina Petrovna sighed. No doubt she was longing for a cigarette. 'No, I think I . . .'

'*Thinking* again! Well, don't think!' the officer suddenly advised her, grinning. 'You're an orphanage teacher, aren't you? And no doubt you taught the children not to tell lies, didn't you? So how can you lie now? And in front of them, too!'

'I'm not lying,' said Regina Petrovna, hanging her head like a guilty schoolgirl.

'I'm glad to hear it,' said the officer, taking a few paces up and down the room. 'So you say you are capable of confusing the identity of some of the children, and therefore you are not certain whether these two boys in front of you are brothers or not. Have I understood you correctly?'

Regina Petrovna did not answer.

'Isn't that so?' The officer raised his voice and suddenly touched the back of Regina Petrovna's neck. Her head twitched, but she did not draw away from his touch.

'No,' she said, and looked at Kolka.

'What d'you mean – *no*?' roared the officer, slapping his folder so hard that it made a loud bang and everyone jumped.

251

'No . . . that is, I can remember . . . I meant . . . that they . . . that they are brothers.'

No longer listening to her, the officer was furiously stuffing papers back into the folder. Then without a word of goodbye he left the room and his car could be heard driving away.

The others remained where they were, including the man in civilian clothes. Everyone was waiting for him to speak, but he, too, was silent. A deathly pause settled on the room.

Olga Khristoforovna summoned up the courage to ask, 'Have you . . . excuse me, any questions?'

The man did not move a muscle. He went on staring out of the window, as though the question had not been addressed to him. Then suddenly he turned and said through compressed lips, 'Give me the list, please.'

'The list of children in this Reception Unit?' asked the superintendent.

Making no attempt to explain, he simply stretched out his hand, and Olga Khristoforovna handed him a sheet of paper.

Glancing rapidly through the list, he enquired, 'This Musa – what is he: a Tartar?'

'Yes,' said Olga Khristoforovna. 'At the moment he is seriously ill.'

'Where is he from?' asked the civilian, ignoring the remark about the boy's illness. 'He's not a Crimean Tartar, by any chance?'

'I think he's from Kazan,' the superintendent replied.

'You think . . . And Gross? Is she a German?'

'I don't know,' said the superintendent. 'Anyway, what does it matter? I'm of German origin myself.'

'That's just what I mean.' The civilian's voice was very calm and even: there was something hushed, almost noiseless about him, as though a pair of wings were rustling behind his back. Kolka would have liked him except for his lips, thin and slightly crooked, which seemed to have an independent existence; in the way they twisted when he spoke there was something alien and cold.

'This list is somewhat selective,' said the man, and threw it back on to the table, although Olga Khristoforovna, anticipating his movement, had already held out her hand.

'We do not select them,' she said. 'We simply take them in.'

'You should know who you're taking in!' the man said in a slightly louder voice; again there was neither anger nor threat in his words, but for some reason the two women shuddered.

Although Olga Khristoforovna was clearly a sick woman and found difficulty in continuing the conversation, she said obstinately, 'We take in children. Simply *children* – that is all,' she replied. She took the list and smoothed it with her hand.

Next day all the children in the Reception Unit, including the blind boys, were taken to the theatre. They went in pairs, a sighted boy leading a blind one. The curtain went up, and the magic began, in the form of a play called *The Twelve Months*.

Kolka was sitting beside Antosha, with Alhuzur sitting on the other side of him. They did their best to describe to Antosha everything they were seeing on the stage – but it was so difficult! A wicked stepmother ordered her stepdaughter, in winter, to go and pick wild strawberries; the little girl went out into the ice-cold forest. She was freezing with cold, but suddenly . . . As Kolka was describing all this, all of a sudden, in the midst of a clearing in the forest, it was as if an enormous bonfire burst into flame, and there, sitting around it were the twelve months of the year.

Alhuzur was struck dumb with excitement, while Kolka's mouth dropped open and saliva began to dribble out of it.

Antosha kept tugging at their arms and asking, 'What's happening? What's going on?'

The children had never been in the theatre before, and when they came out they might have been drunk. On the way home Kolka was silent, afraid that words might somehow dispel something of what he had seen.

That evening they were each given a splendid present – Olga Khristoforovna herself handed them out – consisting of a sweet, two biscuits and two bagels apiece. All the sighted children were lined up on one side of the tree, the blind ones opposite them. The blind boys sang a song about the new-year tree, and then Olga Khristoforovna proclaimed in a loud voice, 'Thanks to Comrade Stalin for our happy childhood!'

All the children cried 'Hurrah!' Even Musa, lying sick in bed, heard that shout from his dormitory and joined in.

Then the sighted children each gave a little performance. Kolka recited a poem . . . about the little golden cloud:

> *One night a little golden cloud did rest*
> *Upon a lonely mountain's rugged brow;*
> *Next day, departing for the plains below,*
> *It floated free and sailed towards the west.*

Yet high upon the mountain's summit bare
That cloud left drops of dew where it had lain.
The mountain wept, and flowing to the plain
Its tears of grief brought plenty to the earth.

Kolka stopped and looked at the blind boys: craning their necks forward, they were listening intently, as though afraid to miss even his silence ... But his silence dragged on, because Kolka suddenly found himself breathless, his throat having contracted in an involuntary spasm. He simply could not utter the words: ' ... all alone ...'

He wanted to burst into tears.

Standing in front of his blind companions, it was suddenly brought home to him that his life in the Caucasus had come to an end, and that tomorrow – so they had been told – they would be taken away to a place where they would begin a completely new life.

Alhuzur was standing beside the tree and looking at Kolka. People had already begun to prompt him, whispering the next line of the poem, he could keep it up no longer, however, and ran out into the corridor. But the blind children applauded him as he went.

Next morning they were woken earlier than usual, at six o'clock.

Even Musa was made to get dressed, as he too was being sent away. Only the blind boys were staying behind. When the others were all being lined up to be taken to the station, Antosha appeared and shouted, 'Kuzmin Twins! Are you here? Are you here?'

'Antosha!' cried Kolka, and dashed out of the ranks.

Antosha found Kolka's hand and gave him a piece of paper. It was pierced with the 'bumps' in which the language of the blind is written. 'There – it tells your fortune!' said Antosha, smiling somewhere into space, as only the blind smile.

'But I can't read what's written on it!'

'If you ever come to our town, go to the market!' said Antosha. 'I'll be there! I'll read it to you! You're a good person, Kolka!'

'Line up, children!' Olga Khristoforovna shouted; this was aimed at Kolka. 'Everyone follow me!'

It was cold in the street. A chill wind was blowing. The station was deserted. The children were put on the train, in an empty, dirty, uncleaned carriage. Apart from them, nobody was travelling on that first day of the new year.

Kolka showed Alhuzur the top two bunks and said, 'Those are ours. Sashka and I used to travel up there.'

254

Just then Olga Khristoforovna came into the carriage and shouted, 'Kolka! Someone is asking for you!'

'Who is it?' Kolka grumbled, unwilling to leave Alhuzur.

'Go outside and you'll find out!' said Olga Khristoforovna. With her slow, ponderous gait she moved on down the carriage, checking to see that everyone was properly settled.

'Are you cold, Musa?' she asked the Tartar.

Musa was shivering, but he did not want to complain, being so delighted that he, too, was going away; anything was better than being left behind on his own . . .

Kolka went out on to the open platform at the end of the carriage, and there he saw Regina Petrovna. She was holding two parcels.

She ran towards Kolka, but stumbled. He watched her, looking down from the carriage-platform, as she hastily climbed up the awkward little iron steps, almost dropping the parcels.

'There!' she said, panting breathlessly. 'These are your clothes – the things I gave to you and Sashka on your birthday.' Since Kolka made no response, she ended imploringly, 'Take them! When you're in your new home . . .' And she put the parcels down beside Kolka on the platform floor.

They looked at each other in silence.

'I don't know where they're taking you to . . .' she said. 'For some reason it's being kept secret. What nonsense . . . But please, Kolka, think again – now, while there's still time: why don't you stay with us? Demyan and I have talked it over and he has no objection to adopting you . . .' – she corrected herself – ' . . . adopting you and that other little boy . . .'

Kolka shook his head.

Regina Petrovna sighed. She started to take a cigarette out of a packet, but broke it and threw it away.

'Well, all right,' she said. 'Maybe you'll write though? When you arrive at wherever it is that you're going to?'

Suddenly Regina Petrovna stretched out her hand and stroked his head before he had time to turn away.

'Very well – goodbye, my dear.' She began to go, but suddenly turned round. 'Can you answer me one question?'

Kolka nodded. He knew what she was going to ask, and had been expecting this question.

'Where is your brother? I mean the real Sashka . . . Where is he?'

Kolka stared into the eyes of the most beautiful woman in the world. How he had loved her! How they had both loved her! But now . . . Sashka might have forgiven her for deserting them, but

Kolka could not . . . But nor could he avoid giving her an answer; so he said, 'Sashka went away. By train.'

'A long way away?'

'Yes. A long way.'

'Well, thank God. That means he's alive . . .' she exclaimed with relief.

Regina Petrovna jumped down from the steps; the train had been given the signal to go.

Kolka immediately ran back into the carriage, forgetting all about the parcels. He was afraid that Alhuzur might be upset without him.

But Alhuzur was looking out of the window, deep in thought. Now they both stood looking out of the window at a woman; although it was windy and she was cold, she had not gone away and was looking up at the carriage.

At last the train started. The carriage gave a jerk and began slowly moving. The woman waved.

Kolka put his face near the glass to look at Regina Petrovna once more and for the last time. She seemed to be shouting something; he shook his head, meaning that he couldn't hear her, but she may have understood it differently. Even so she kept on shouting, and quickened her pace. Then she started running . . .

Her headscarf slipped down on to her neck, baring her black hair, and her overcoat came undone. Oblivious to this, she kept running, as though chasing after her happiness . . . And she went on shouting and shouting . . .

Kolka waved to her and nodded, as though he had understood something. Then he lost sight of her. He climbed up on to their bunk, lay down beside Alhuzur and put his arms around him. Suddenly he began to cry, pressing his face to the other boy's shoulder. Alhuzur comforted him, saying, 'Why you cry? Mustn't cry . . . We go and go with train till we get there, yes? We stay together, yes? All our life together, yes?'

Kolka couldn't help himself; he cried all the harder, and only the clicking of the train's wheels seemed to be affirming something: 'Together, yes – together, yes – together, yes – together, yes . . .'